THE LITTLE BLACK BOX

TOP SECRET
PART 1

A SHRAGA MORGENSTERN/PINNY KATZ
MYSTERY TRILOGY

THE LITTLE
BLACK BOX

TOP SECRET
PART 1

Created and written by Libby Lazewnik

TARGUM/FELDHEIM

First published 1995

Copyright © 1995 by Targum Press
ISBN 1-56871-078-X

Phototypeset at Targum Press
Printing plates by Frank, Jerusalem

Published by:
Targum Press Inc.
22700 W. Eleven Mile Rd.
Southfield, Mich. 48034

Distributed by:
Feldheim Publishers
200 Airport Executive Park
Nanuet, N.Y. 10954

Distributed in Israel by:
Targum Press Ltd.
POB 43170
Jerusalem 91430

Chish Printing
TeL: 08-9245749

Contents

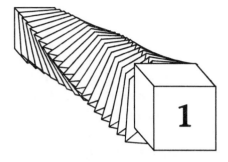

The Problem Next Door

In an unremarkable house on an unremarkable street, lived a very remarkable boy.

It wasn't the way he looked that made you remember him. Shraga Morgenstern was medium-tall (or, depending on how you looked at it, medium-short) and on the chubby side. His hair was brown and the eyes behind the thick glasses were an ordinary, though rather nice, mixture of brown and green. But there the ordinariness ended. From those otherwise unremarkable eyes shone an extraordinary intelligence. Shraga was easily the brightest boy in his sixth-grade class. In fact, some of his teachers thought him possibly the brightest boy in the whole school.

With a reputation like that, you'd think Shraga would have no trouble also winning the title of brightest boy on his own block. But, strangely enough, he did have a problem. The problem's name was Pinny Katz, and he lived right next door.

Pinny Katz didn't wear glasses. He stood several inches taller than Shraga and was skinny as a beanpole — much skinnier than Shraga. Beneath the mop of blond hair his forehead was high.

"That's because of all the brains that have to fit in there," his older brother Ari would chuckle. Ari was fourteen, tall and broad-shouldered and terrific at sports. But he was the first to acknowledge that, when it came to the brains department, his kid brother had him beat with both hands tied behind his back.

Not that Ari and Pinny ever actually fought — or hardly ever, anyway. Ari was proud of his brother's first-class mind, and Pinny was proud (and even a tiny bit envious) of his brother's prowess with bat and ball. Though Pinny had a quick temper, Ari was good-natured and practically unflappable. One of the few things that did bother Ari was when he heard Pinny making one of his caustic comments about the boy next door.

"That Shraga Morgenstern," Pinny would growl, "thinks he's *it*. Well, I've got news for him: he's far from it. As a matter of fact, *it* could wipe the floor with him. Why, he's so far from being *it*, that —"

"You're babbling again, Pinny," Ari would break in, with the frown his brother so seldom saw. "You always do that when you talk about poor old Morgenstern. What'd that kid ever do to you?"

What Shraga Morgenstern had done was not really his fault, but nonetheless it had haunted Pinny all his life. It was all a question of timing. Shraga Morgenstern had made the mistake of coming into the world on the very same day as Pinny Katz.

In Shraga's opinion, the error was all on Pinny's side. However that might be, the outcome was the same. From the very start — and without anyone bothering to ask them what *they* thought about it — the two boys were thrown together.

With fathers who were next-door neighbors, colleagues at work, and best friends besides, it was only natural that the two baby boys who shared a birthday should also share a gala double bris. And it was only natural that they should celebrate their next few birthdays together, too. Side by side, the two toddlers blew out their candles and ripped into their gifts with small grubby fists. Together they crammed home-baked chocolate cupcakes into their mouths and strung together their first sentences. No one who saw them doubted that here was another pair of best friends in the making.

Rebellion set in round about the time they turned five.

Why? Their parents had often tried to figure it out. Maybe it was the fact that everyone *expected* them to be the best of friends that had turned the boys so strongly against the idea. Perhaps, also, it had something to do with the fact that they were so much the same in many ways. Their similar —

and competing — intelligence became more and more apparent as they grew older. They were, to put it in a nutshell, a couple of geniuses. This was the crux of the problem. In fact, it was downright embarrassing! One brilliant boy on the block is a marvel. Two are a joke.

Whatever the reason — and sometimes Shraga and Pinny, in their private hearts, were not even sure themselves what it was — they had long ago decided what to do about it. Though their families were inseparable, the two boys kept their distance from each other. They were determined to remain firm *un*-friends — no easy feat when your families spend most of their free time together.

Pinny's big brother, Ari Katz, might bemoan the decision, and Shraga's younger sister Mindy might shake her head at their foolishness, like a wise old woman instead of a precocious nine-year-old. But there it was. A cold war existed between Shraga Morgenstern and Pinny Katz, much like the one that had raged between the United States and the Soviet Union for so many years. Those two countries had become pretty good friends by now. Shraga and Pinny were not so lucky.

The reason Shraga sat scowling in an upstairs bedroom of his unremarkable house on a warm evening in May was because he had just heard something that thrilled him and cast him down at the same time. His father had just told him some exciting news. There was to be a convention of scientists, and Dr. Morgenstern had been invited

— and his family along with him.

Shraga flopped back on his bed, arms behind his head. He glared at the ceiling, which stared calmly back. It was fun to anticipate a week-long stay in a fancy hotel in the Catskills, together with his physicist father, the rest of his family, and some of the most prestigious scientists the world had to offer.

The only blot on the horizon was the fact that Pinny Katz would be there, too.

"This is the Year of the Brotherhood of Scientists," Dr. Morgenstern had explained as he and Shraga walked home from shul after *ma'ariv* that evening. "I guess someone figured this was a good time to cash in on the warmer atmosphere between East and West."

"Meaning the U.S. and Russia?" Shraga asked.

"Exactly. Groups of scientists from various countries will be getting together in different places all over the world this year, to exchange knowledge and show off their latest finds."

Something in his tone alerted Shraga. "Abba! Including you?"

His father smiled. "Yup. Shmulie Katz and I were invited to join a gathering of prominent physicists in the Lake View Hotel next month. It's quite an honor, actually."

Shraga glanced sideways at his father and lowered his voice. "Will you be telling them about — Little Nicky?"

"Ssh." Placing a finger on his lips, Dr. Morgenstern threw a hasty glance over his shoulder. The reaction was automatic. "Little Nicky" was the code name his firm had given to a very special — and very secret — device they had been working on for several years. Dr. Morgenstern and Dr. Katz headed the Little Nicky research team. Its details were still cloaked in secrecy, but the grand unveiling was drawing closer every day. Soon the whole world would marvel at what "Little Nicky" could do — and at the ingenuity of the scientists who had put it together.

David Morgenstern and Shmulie Katz had met thirteen years earlier as two brand-new employees of M.C.B., a firm that churned out all sorts of exciting new products for Americans to enjoy — and some for the exclusive use of the American Defense Department. From the first, the two mitzvah-observant young men had formed an instant bond, as if the yarmulkas they both wore were magnets drawing them together through a roomful of bare heads. Both, as they quickly discovered, were committed to Torah and to raising their families as good Jews first, and good Americans second. In the years since that first meeting, the two men had made immense strides both in Torah learning — in which they immersed themselves every chance they got — and in their work as research physicists. Their friendship, and that of their growing families, had developed very nicely, too... Except, of course, for the inexplicable coolness between Dr. Morgenstern's oldest son, Shraga, and Dr. Katz's Pinny.

Shraga's father paused at the entrance to their modest two-story brick home and peered at his son. "So that's the story. A whole week at the Lake View." He grinned. "Well? Want to come?"

"Do I want to come?" Shraga repeated incredulously. "What a question! But what about school?"

"That can be arranged. The conference is taking place near the end of June, so you won't be missing much. Any end-of-year exams could probably be taken earlier, and we'll make sure to learn together in the hotel every day. I'll speak to your teachers, Shraga. I'm sure they'll see this convention as an exceptional opportunity for you."

Shraga nodded matter-of-factly. There was little chance that his teachers would stand in the way of their star student. Shraga would certainly not fall dramatically behind his classmates in the last month of the school year. His eyes shone. For a moment he looked less like a prodigy and more like a very excited almost-twelve-year-old. "Wow!"

Then his eyes darkened. "Uh — I guess the Katzes are coming too?"

"That's right."

"All of them?"

Dr. Morgenstern turned the key in the lock of the heavy oak door. "All of them."

"Oh."

The father shook his head as he walked into the house behind Shraga.

The living room was a scene of homey clutter. Ma sat on the sofa working on her latest needlepoint, with baby Aviva playing at her feet. Chaim, ten, was also on the floor, perfecting his "*kugelach*" technique. Gitty, the oldest, was upstairs, studying. Since she'd started high school she'd been spending most of her time that way. Shraga could hear the strains of his sister's favorite Jewish tape floating down the stairs from her room.

Mindy, nine, was almost lost in the huge leather recliner, her nose in a book as usual, while four-year-old Ruchie worked industriously on a giant jigsaw puzzle in the corner. As Dr. Morgenstern stepped into the warm, contented atmosphere, the lingering thought of the thinly-veiled hostility that existed between his son and the Katz boy was the only jarring note. Apart from everything else, it made for some very uncomfortable moments when the two families got together. Dr. Morgenstern frowned. Where would it all end?

Then his natural optimism returned. This convention might be just the thing they needed. Give the boys a whole week in the fresh mountain air and the stimulating company of dozens of brilliant scientists, and who knew what might not happen!

If he'd had an inkling of what was actually waiting to happen to him, to Dr. Katz, and to both of their families, Shraga's father might not have been quite so optimistic as he nimbly sidestepped a roller skate and three giant marbles and greeted his family. The tune he was whistling under his breath might not have been as cheerful, or his smile as broad. But the events waiting to unfold at the Lake View Hotel were something none of the Morgensterns — or, for that matter, the Katzes — could have even remotely predicted.

Which was probably a good thing. For now, at least, they still had something to look forward to.

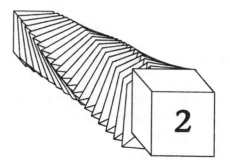

Getting Ready

Whatcha doing, Mindy?"

Mindy Morgenstern spun around. As she did, the long dark pigtails on either side of her head slapped her cheeks and the large, owlish glasses nearly toppled from her nose. She stood poised at the lowest branch of the elm tree at the edge of her backyard, one arm hovering in the air. With a sigh, she abandoned her tiptoe position and sank into a lawn chair.

"Just trying to reach a certain twig," she explained to Daniella Katz. Her young neighbor (Daniella was only seven) had slipped through a gap in the fence that divided the Katz residence from the Morgensterns' and was regarding her now with curious blue eyes. "For my latest collage."

Daniella nodded seriously. Mindy's art was something she knew about, and respected —which was more than Mindy could say for anyone in her own family. Gitty and Shraga were mildly amused by her artistic efforts — when they deigned to notice them at all. Her other brother, Chaim, made sure to notice them. He hooted with laughter whenever he came across one of the strange-looking mishmashes that his sister called her "latest collage," and that Chaim insisted on calling "your newest pile of junk." Even Ruchie wrinkled her little nose as she tried to make sense of her big sister's "art." Baby Aviva, or "Vivi," as she'd been fondly dubbed in the family, was the only one who didn't find Mindy's art funny; but then, she was still too young to have much of an opinion yet.

"This one's going to be a high-tech collage," Mindy continued eagerly, encouraged by Daniella's respectful attention. "I'm going to put together all kinds of stuff having to do with today's most advanced technology. I'm taking it along to the Catskills, to work on during the conference. It's going to be really neat."

Daniella's brow creased in perplexity. She thought she knew what the word "technology" meant. But in that case —

"So what's with the twig?" she demanded.

Mindy smiled. "Good question, Katz. It just hit me a few minutes ago. A brainstorm! You see, we're so proud of the advances *we've* made on the technical front — computers, lasers, rocket ships, all that stuff. But what about all the things *Hashem* made?" She swept an arm around. "Nature is more complicated than anything a mere person could put together, right? So I decided to throw in some leaves and twigs and dried flowers, too. Sort of the other side of the picture. Get it?"

Daniella wasn't sure, but she nodded vigorously. Her respect for Mindy went up another few notches. "Can I help?"

"Well... If you'll hold the chair steady, I'll try for that twig again. I *almost* made it on tippy-toe —"

Daniella obligingly held onto the lawn chair while Mindy strained after the perfect twig. But no matter how she stretched, or how red her face became, it still eluded her.

Daniella looked around for help. She spotted a figure emerging from the Morgensterns' back door.

"Shraga!" she yelled, letting go of the chair and waving wildly. Mindy teetered on her perch. "Hey, come on, Daniella! Hold on!"

Daniella grabbed the chair again, yelling, "Come here, Shragie — we need you!"

Shraga shaded his eyes against the sun to see better. He ambled over. When he was within speaking distance he asked, "What's going on?"

"Mindy needs a branch, only she can't reach high enough," Daniella explained, looking up at the bigger boy trustingly. "*You* could reach it, easy."

"Mindy?" Shraga asked his sister, balancing desperately on the flimsy chair. "What in the world do you need branches for?"

"Not branches," Mindy sighed, climbing cautiously down. "Twigs. Or rather, one twig. For my latest collage." She said it defiantly, as if daring him to laugh.

Shraga didn't laugh. Instead, with a shrug, he reached up one arm. "This one here?"

"No, the one next to it... that's it. You got it! Thanks a lot, Shragie. You made it look so easy."

He shrugged again, blushing slightly. "Don't mention it. Gotta run now. Bye." He trotted up the driveway to the sidewalk, turned the corner, and disappeared. His little sister and littler neighbor watched him go.

Mindy clutched her twig ecstatically. The thick glasses magnified her glowing eyes.

"Perfect!" she said softly. She was thinking not so much of the twig, as of Shraga's reaction to it. He hadn't mocked her efforts at creating something beautiful. He hadn't laughed. Downright respect-ful, that's how he'd behaved. She glanced down at Daniella with a sudden smile. "Know what?"

"No, what?"

"I've just decided what I'm going to do with this collage when it's finished."

"What?"

"Shraga's birthday's coming up soon — his twelfth. I'm going to give him the collage for a present!"

Daniella looked suitably impressed. "I bet he'll love it."

Mindy nodded vaguely. She fell silent, gazing yearningly up at her bedroom window. More than anything, she wanted to run upstairs and find the right place for the twig in the collage that was taking such exciting shape on her cluttered desk.

Only politeness — the good manners her mother had drilled into her, and the good *middos* her teachers insisted on — kept her in the backyard with Daniella now.

She hesitated another long second, and then, with a stifled sigh, sank back into the lawn chair. "So what d'you want to play, Daniella?" Though two years separated the girls, Mindy was nice about playing with her younger neighbor. Daniella's worshipful attitude might have had a little to do with that. Being a great artist is lonely work.

"We could play Parcheesi, if you want," Daniella offered, without much enthusiasm. "Or Monopoly."

"Okay. Whichever. You choose." Mindy sounded equally unenthusiastic.

Daniella glanced at her. "But what I really want to do —"

"Yes?"

"Is see your collage."

"All *right!*" Leaping to her feet, Mindy led the way into the house, with Daniella scampering after her like a pageboy on the heels of his king. As they climbed the stairs together, Mindy turned beaming to the younger girl.

"You know something, kid? You're all right."

Daniella flushed bright pink with pleasure. Mindy continued, "Really, I mean it. You've got good taste, Katz. You respect Art."

As they entered Mindy's room, Daniella could only bob her head and smile until her face ached. Her heart was too full for words.

The half-completed collage was the first thing Mindy placed in her suitcase that evening. Tomorrow afternoon, they were driving up to the Catskills for the beginning of the international physicists' conference.

Ma had said to pack lightly; there would be laundry service in the hotel, so no need to drag half their wardrobes along. Mindy was happy to obey. First she laid the collage tenderly on the bottom of her suitcase, carefully padding it with a few skirts and blouses. Over these she quickly threw a couple of handfuls of socks and underwear. A book or two were inserted at the sides, a pair of pajamas added as an afterthought, and the suitcase was ready to be zipped up. Mindy hauled it off the bed and pushed it against the wall. A few minutes later she was climbing into bed in the place where the suitcase had been.

Her dreams that night were high-tech fantasies, with her beloved collage winning first prize in a worldwide contest: a stunning tribute to the marriage of art and science. She smiled in her sleep, ears ringing to the applause of a thousand admiring fans.

Down the hall, Shraga was packing much more scientifically. There was a list on his desk — prepared after much thought the day before — of all the things he'd need for the week-long stay. The list was ranged alphabetically, from Air Pump (for the tires of the bike his father had agreed to take along, strapped to the top of the station-wagon) all the way to Yo-Yo (Shraga did some of his best thinking while absently whizzing that battered old toy up and down on its string). In between were a few of the more boring items, like Clothes and Soap. Working methodically, he gathered everything he needed into a big pile on his bed and placed them one by one in his suitcase. When he was done, his luggage was a thing of beauty: a testimony to order and neatness.

Not so Pinny Katz's bulging suitcase, next door in the white stucco house with the big upstairs porch his parents had added on last spring. If Shraga's mind was impressively logical, Pinny's was dazzling in a very different way. Pinny was impulsive. His ideas soared, leaped, and some-times crashed — but they never stood still. Where Shraga would slowly arrive at a well-thought-out decision, Pinny often reached his own conclusions in a single flash of intuition.

And the way he thought was the way he packed. He threw things into the case haphazardly, as they occurred to him. Six packages of chewing gum were crammed into a pair of galoshes. A Walkman and eight cassettes were tucked into the pockets of his best Shabbos suit. A woolly hat lay rolled up beside a pair of bright green swimming trunks; after all, you never knew what the weather would be like up in the mountains.

After he'd finished cramming in practically his

entire winter *and* summer wardrobes, Pinny remembered his schoolbooks. He'd promised his teachers and parents to do some studying up in the hotel, and he meant to keep his promise. The only problem was, the suitcase was packed too full to admit another bobby-pin, let alone four or five heavy volumes. After puzzling over the problem for all of ten minutes, Pinny suddenly brightened. He dug up his old camp laundry bag from the back of his closet and put the textbooks and *sefarim* in that. Then, because there was still plenty of room left, he started removing his favorite books from his shelves and added them to the laundry bag. By the time he was through, the bag was twice as heavy as the suitcase, but that didn't bother Pinny a bit. If all else failed, at least he'd have plenty to read up there in the mountains. The thing Pinny hated most was being bored.

He dumped suitcase and laundry bag beside the door. Down the hall, he could hear the thump and bang that were his big brother Ari, packing. His mother had already packed up Daniella and five-year-old Zevy days ago. He pulled a last lone book off the nearly bare shelf, propped himself up in bed, and happily lost himself in a long-familiar adventure story. As far as Pinny Katz was concerned, he was ready for whatever the Lake View Hotel might hand him.

In a small apartment in faraway Tel Aviv, twelve-and-a-half-year-old Shai Gilboa stared glumly at his own suitcase.

Glum was the way he usually looked, and it was hard for him to erase the expression now, even though his heart was pounding wildly at the prospect of his upcoming trip to America. Mr. Drucker — Shai stubbornly refused to call him "Abba" — had been so happy about it, too.

"Excited about our trip tomorrow, son?" he'd asked only that morning at breakfast, before leaving for his research job at the Technion. "You'll get to meet all sorts of scientists, plus lots of other families like us."

But Shai had only scowled. "I'm not your son. And we're not a family!" Rising from his chair like a rocket, he'd dashed out of the room. Watching him leave, Mr. Drucker's face fell. Mrs. Drucker shook her head sympathetically.

They had expected the prospect of the trip to bring a smile, at last, to Shai's face. After the conference week, they planned to take him out to California, and especially to that place so dear to children's hearts: Disneyland. If that wasn't enough to make a kid smile, what was?

But Shai stubbornly refused to oblige them. Smiles were for other kids, kids with regular parents and normal families and homes. What did smiles have to do with a boy like him, who'd lost his own mother and father when he was too small to remember, and who'd been kicked about from one foster home to the next for more years than he liked to count?

The Druckers, it was true, seemed different. For one thing, they were *dati'im* — religious Jews. Not that that meant anything to Shai. All the other foster families had been secular, and that was the way Shai had been raised till now. The Druckers must have been desperate, he thought, to take him in. Probably he'd been the only child they were able to get their hands on. Well, that was their bad luck.

Shai had to admit that they tried. They really did. They wanted him to feel at home — to feel as if he belonged. But the more they tried, the more he resisted. After all, it was surely only a question of time before they, too, booted him out and sent him on to the next place. If he trusted them now, he'd only feel more hurt when they let him down in the end the way all the others had. No, he would not yield. He had to be strong.

And yet, as he regarded his waiting suitcase, it was hard to remain bitter. He'd never travelled out of the country before. He'd never even been on an airplane! At least speaking English wouldn't be a problem, thanks to his American-born next-to-last set of foster parents. He wondered about America. What was the world like outside of Israel? In just a couple of days, he'd find out.

A tentative smile began to show in his eyes. With no one there to see him, it was all right to betray a little of his excitement. Eagerly — the way he had not felt eager about anything for a long, long time — Shai opened his closet door and reached out for a pile of shirts.

Far to the east, in Moscow, another twelve-year-old boy contemplated another suitcase.

Nikolai Gorodnik was making no effort to hide his boundless joy at the prospect of his first trip out of his native country. America! Who hadn't dreamed of the marvels and riches that lay on the other side of the great sparkling ocean? This trip was like a dream come true for him and his mother. For a week, at the Lake View resort in the Catskill Mountains (Nikolai had carefully memorized the strange-sounding names), Dr. Natasha Gorodnik would exchange scientific information with her colleagues from all over the world, while her son discovered what it was like to be an American boy. There would be tennis courts, his mother had told him, and a swimming pool. Maybe he could finally teach himself to swim!

America. The word floated in the air between Nikolai and his suitcase in letters of gold. Just think — in two days from now, he'd be on his way. And two weeks after that (he and his mother would be visiting Boston, where they had relatives, before heading back) he'd be on another plane, homeward-bound. By then, he'd be a seasoned traveler. He'd be able to boast to all his friends at school about the strange new things he'd seen and done.

Taking careful aim, Nikolai tossed a rolled-up ball of socks into his suitcase from across the room. What he really wanted to do was dance and sing with all his might.

America!

America was on the minds of many people that night, as they prepared for their journey to the Lake View Hotel and the International Brotherhood of Scientists physicists' convention. But not all of those people anticipated the trip with Nikolai's simple joy or Shai Gilboa's secret excitement. One person, in particular, could not dismiss a shudder of apprehension as he brooded on the days ahead. It was a shiver of fear — almost of despair. It belonged to a creature locked in the jaws of an implacable trap...

He'd thought and thought, but there seemed to be no way out. He was truly trapped. The only road open to him was fraught with terrible danger. But what choice did he have? It was a heavy price to pay — but pay it he would. He could do nothing else.

He had his instructions. Implicit in every line was the unspoken but ominous message: *You will do as I say — or else.*

He would have to obey. He would travel to the Lake View Hotel in America, and do as he was told.

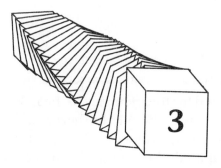

The Lake View Hotel

The car had just made the turn off the narrow country road and into the long, broad drive that swept up to the Lake View Hotel, when it was flagged down.

Two men, dressed in plain dark business suits and ties, waited politely but firmly in the middle of the drive. When it was a couple of yards away from them, Dr. Morgenstern's white station wagon slowed to a stop. Behind him, Dr. Katz's Mitsubishi van did the same.

A head of fine, sandy hair appeared at the driver's window.

"Name, sir?"

"I'm Dr. Morgenstern."

"May I see some I.D., please."

Shraga's father reached into his pocket for his wallet. "Driver's license okay?" he asked, extracting a piece of paper and showing it to the man.

"That'll be fine." The man scrutinized the license, while his partner — slightly shorter, with thick black hair and massive shoulders — strode over to the van to run through the same scenario with Dr. Katz.

The sandy-haired man nodded and handed back the license. Shraga's father accepted it, remarking, "Pretty tight security, I see."

Now that the car and its occupants had been cleared, the man permitted himself an answering smile. "We think it's necessary, sir. There will be some prestigious names staying here this week. And, even more important, some of them are working on things that should not fall into...shall we say, the wrong hands?"

In the back seat, Shraga squirmed excitedly. He tried to catch his father's eye in the rear-view mirror, but Dr. Morgenstern kept his own eyes riveted on the security man. "Hm. I see. When you put it that way, it does seem a good idea. Are you with a private security firm?"

The man shook his head. "No, sir. I'm Ed Wilson; my partner there's Sam Gilbraith. We're Special Agents. F.B.I."

A current of excitement ran through the children, all except for the baby, Vivi, who was yawning on her mother's lap. Shraga's eyes widened. F.B.I.! He studied Wilson, trying to catch a glimpse of a telltale bulge, but he couldn't be sure whether or not the Special Agent was carrying a gun under his jacket. Gilbraith rejoined his partner at the head of the drive. Stepping nimbly to one side, the F.B.I. men waved the car through. A moment later the Katz van, moving very slowly, followed suit.

The two vehicles found neighboring places in the hotel's spacious parking area, and the two families poured out into the pleasant afternoon sun. After nearly three hours' driving, it felt good to be standing on solid ground again. Mindy discovered that one of her feet had fallen asleep and started hopping around in a sort of frantic Indian rain dance in an effort to waken it. Chaim pulled a homemade slingshot out of his pocket and began taking aim at imaginary targets. Shraga took long, deep breaths of clean mountain air. When he took off his glasses to clean them on his shirt, the world turned into a blur of blue and green. He placed the glasses back on his nose and looked around. Apart from their two cars, only a few others filled the big space.

"Are we early, Abba?" he asked.

Dr. Morgenstern was already beginning to untie the cord that held their suitcases and bikes on the roof of the car. "Possibly, though some of the foreigners may already be here. I believe the hotel was to send a car to the airport for them." The organizers of the physicists' convention had sent out written material to each of the invited guests, outlining all the plans for the coming days.

"Foreigners?" Mindy paused in her hopping. "Where from?"

"There'll be scientists from nearly every country

in Europe, Mindy, plus Israel and Russia." Dr. Morgenstern, still busy untying cords above his head, smiled under his arm as his friend, Dr. Katz, strolled over. "It should be an interesting week, eh, Shmulie?"

"Interesting, that's for sure." Shmuel Katz glanced around to make sure they were alone. Then, in a lowered voice, he indicated the attaché case he held firmly gripped in one hand. "Where shall we put Little Nicky? Think the hotel safe is — well, safe enough?"

Dr. Morgenstern frowned. The organizers of the convention had assigned the scientists to small labs to use during their stay. Nothing fancy, only makeshift stuff — it was, after all, a resort hotel and not a real research facility — but the doors would open only to the scientists' personal I.D. cards.

"I think Little Nicky would be secure in our lab," Shraga's father answered finally. "Those electronic locks are fail-safe, I believe. We'll be the only ones with the card that unlocks the door. It should be safe enough there."

"I hope so." Pinny's father rubbed his chin worriedly. "I'll be glad when that thing is out of our hands, David. The boss says there have been rumors of unhealthy interest in the device — from certain not very savory quarters. We'll have to be very careful."

"It won't be long now," Shraga's father said quietly. "We're unveiling the thing tomorrow evening, right after dinner. After that, we lock it away in our lab for just one more night. The firm will be sending an escort for it first thing next morning."

"And after that," said Dr. Katz, patting the attaché case, "Little Nicky will belong to history."

"Under a slightly different name, I hope," Shraga's father grinned. He tugged forcefully at one suitcase which seemed to be jammed. It came loose suddenly into his arms, nearly toppling him. He staggered a few steps. "Oops!"

Shraga ran up to lend a hand. So did Dr. Katz. He put his attaché case down for a moment to help his friend regain his balance. Pinny had followed his father over to the Morgensterns' car and stood behind the others listening, enthralled, to the men's interchange. He was still intrigued by the mysterious thing hidden in the attaché case. "What is it, Dad?" he asked breathlessly. "Can't you tell us now?"

At the sound of Pinny's voice, Shraga stiffened. For the next couple of weeks, he was going to have to get used to the idea of having Pinny Katz around, of seeing him and hearing him wherever he went. He knew it; but that didn't mean he felt comfortable about it. He inched a little further away — and then inched back again. He didn't want to miss a word.

Dr. Katz turned to look down at his son. Both were blond and lanky, but only the father wore glasses. "I can't, Pinny," he said apologetically. "It's still a secret." He brightened. "Tell you what, though. Tomorrow night's unveiling for the scientists — why don't we see if we can finagle an invitation for you boys to sit in, too?" He winked at Shraga. "How does that sound?"

"Great, Dr. Katz!" Shraga's green-brown eyes glowed. For a moment, he forgot himself enough to actually beam at Pinny, who grinned delightedly back. "Little Nicky — unmasked!"

"Yeah!" Pinny crowed softly.

Chaim giggled. "I guess that's about the only way anyone could've gotten you two to sit together."

Immediately, the faces of both boys darkened. There had been so many attempts over the years to throw them together that they had both developed alert antennae for this kind of thing. Had Dr. Katz's suggestion been another skirmish in that old, old campaign? Scowling, Shraga hesitated. So did Pinny. But neither one volunteered to sit out the demonstration. The unmasking of Little Nicky was just too exciting an event to miss.

Wisely, their fathers kept silent. Chaim looked rueful, and Mindy sighed. Their big brother's ongoing feud with Pinny Katz seemed like the stupidest thing on earth. Chaim, helping his father with the suitcases, wished there were something he could do about it. He'd been wishing that for a long time now.

Dr. Katz, followed by Pinny, started back to his van to carry out his family's luggage. Suddenly, he stopped short. "The attaché case!" He'd put it down for a minute, to help his friend... "David, do you have it?"

Dr. Morgenstern's head rose sharply. "Me? But you had it!"

Without taking the time to explain, Dr. Katz began running back towards the station wagon. Pinny and his big brother, Ari, followed him at a gallop. Soon nearly everyone was running in circles around the station wagon.

It was Mindy who bumped into little Ruchie, placidly sitting on the ground sucking her thumb. Only she wasn't sitting on the ground. She had found something to sit on.

"I found it! I found it!" Mindy howled in triumph, her sleeping foot forgotten. Ruchie was not happy about being dislodged from her comfortable seat. Soon she was howling even louder than Mindy had. Her mother came to pick her up and soothe her, while the boys and men went back to their hauling. There was a feeling of relief in the air — but also one of disquiet. Those few moments when Little Nicky had seemed to be lost had given them a taste of fear for the real thing. Dr. Katz held extra-tight to the attaché case as he supervised the unloading.

Ari was already heaving the first of the suitcases out of the van, whistling as he worked, as if the heavy bags weighed no more than the attaché case in his father's hand. Back at the station wagon Shraga helped his own father, ably assisted by his younger brother, Chaim.

Chaim was a solid, down-to-earth ten-year-old, with straight brown hair and no-nonsense brown eyes. He pulled out his mother's wig case, set it down on the ground beside the car, pretended to take a pot shot at it with his slingshot, and suddenly said, "Abba, I just thought of something. Is this place even kosher?" The trip had made him hungry.

Dr. Morgenstern answered from the other side of the station wagon. "Nope. We're getting packaged kosher food — airline style."

Chaim groaned. A trip to Israel two years before had left him with an indelible memory of inedible food. "I hope it's better than that Chicken à la Rubber they gave us on the plane," he muttered.

"C'mon, Chaim," his sister Mindy teased, vigorously rubbing the last pins and needles from her foot. "You know we didn't come here to eat. This next week is going to be an intellectual carnival. Aren't you looking forward to it?"

Chaim was a comfortable *B* student, with no aspirations to rise any higher. Higher physics — or lower physics, for that matter — made about as much sense to him as Chinese poetry. In reply, he turned his back on his precocious kid sister and heaved harder than he had to on the next suitcase. His stomach growled.

"Here, Chaim." Shraga tossed him a Hershey bar. "To stave off starvation for a little while."

"Hey, thanks!" Chaim's face lit up. He tore into the chocolate, ignoring Mindy's longing looks. When he was nearly finished, he smiled sweetly at his sister. "Don't they say chocolate's good for the brain?" Before Mindy could answer, he added,

"Guess I can use it more than you," and popped the last square into his mouth.

"Funny, funny," Mindy muttered.

"Come here, Mindy," her mother called. "Vivi just fell asleep on my shoulder, and I need some help with her things."

"I'll help, Mommy," Rochel piped up.

Mrs. Morgenstern smiled down at the petite four-year-old, the tears still drying on her cheeks. Those little arms seemed scarcely strong enough to hold the rag doll they clutched. "Thanks, Ruchie," she said. "Here, you hold onto Vivi's bottle. She'll want it when she wakes up."

Looking like some sort of modern-day caravan, the long line of Katzes and Morgensterns began dragging themselves and their possessions into the hotel. Stepping out of the bright sunshine and into the air-conditioned lobby with its muted lighting was like entering a different world.

The lobby was lavish, with a decor that consisted mainly of mirrors and marble. Ari Katz whistled through his teeth. "Would you look at that?" he whispered, nudging Pinny in the ribs. "That" was an immense gold-and-crystal chandelier dangling directly above a spouting fountain — like an upside-down chandelier itself — that reigned in the center of the lobby. "Reminds me of home."

"That's big even for Boro Park," Pinny hissed back. Behind them, Daniella stifled a giggle.

"Boy, is Gitty gonna be sorry she missed this," Mindy said softly. Her big sister had chosen to stay with a friend this week, rather than miss the end of her eighth and final year at school. The Morgensterns would be attending her graduation just two days after their return.

The adult Katzes and Morgensterns went up to the front desk to check in. Mrs. Morgenstern still held the sleeping baby over her shoulder, while Mindy bumped the empty stroller along behind and Rochel grasped the baby's bottle carefully in a small and slightly grubby fist.

When the checking-in procedure was finally completed, the two families turned toward the bank of gleaming modern elevators. At that moment, a dark-suited figure loomed up in front of them, blocking their way. He had crinkly brown hair and very blue eyes, startling against his tanned skin. Smiling, he extended a hand to Dr. Katz, then to Dr. Morgenstern.

"Welcome, folks," he said easily. His accent was faintly Southern. "I'm Tom Morrison — senior F.B.I. agent in charge of security for this week. We're going to be working closely with you during the next days." His gaze swept the group, and he nodded in a friendly way at the boys before bringing his eyes back to the two scientists. "I just wanted to welcome you all personally, and to assure you that you, and your work, are in very safe hands."

The physicists returned the Special Agent's smile. Tom's eye fell on the attaché case in Dr. Katz's hand. His voice dropped. "Is there anything you'd like to hand over to me for safekeeping?

That's what we're here for, you know."

Dr. Katz hesitated. "I think we'll hold onto this for now," he answered. "As soon as we're assigned to our lab we'll be locking our stuff up in there."

"Good enough." Tom nodded. "But remember. If there should be any trouble — or even the suspicion of trouble — don't stop to think. You come straight to Papa Tom. That's what I'm here for." Despite the humor in his words, he looked very serious.

Papa Tom? At the moment, Shraga could not think of anything the senior F.B.I. man resembled less than a benevolent old Papa. He looked sober, competent, and very, very tough. Gazing at the Special Agent over his shoulder, he slowly followed his family into the first of the elevators.

"If there should be any trouble — even the suspicion of trouble..." Remembering the words, Shraga's heart pounded in excitement. This vacation looked like it might be even more interesting than he'd hoped.

The Morgensterns and the Katzes found their rooms — third floor, on opposite sides of the broad carpeted hall —and thankfully dumped their luggage inside. Shraga tested the lights. Chaim bounced up and down on one of the big beds. Vivi woke up abruptly and let out a very loud, and very indignant, wail.

The adventure had begun.

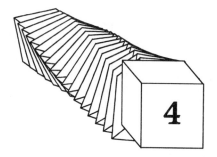

4

First Impressions

Hey, would you look at this?" Pinny waved a piece of paper in the air. "Look, Ari, here's a list of all the services the hotel provides." He ran a finger down the page. "Room service... Laundry... Shoe shines! Hey, Ari, it says if we leave our shoes for the maid at night, they'll be returned to us next morning, all shined up! Let's give it a try!"

Ari looked down at his battered sneakers. "I think these things are beyond help."

"Not those, silly. Our Shabbos shoes. Well? What do you say?"

Ari shrugged. "I'm game."

"Me, too," Zevy called. The five-year-old stuck his curly blond head, so much like Pinny's, through the door of the bathroom — last stop on his personal whirlwind tour of the room the three would be sharing for the next week. "I wanna get my Shabbos shoes shined, too, okay? Okay?"

"Fine," said Pinny. He scrutinized the instruction sheet again. "It says to leave them outside our door last thing at night. Let's not forget."

"I'll be in charge of remembering," Zevy said importantly.

Pinny refrained from pointing out that Zevy would doubtless be sound asleep by the time he and Ari were ready for bed. "Fine, kiddo." He surveyed the room. "A little small for three, but it's okay."

It was a typical hotel room: faded brown wall-to-wall carpeting, beige floor-to-ceiling drapes at the windows, matching bedside lamps and a closet with a sliding door opposite the blue-tiled bathroom. A third bed had been pushed against one wall. Pinny wandered over to the window to drink in the view.

Directly below were the hotel lawns, edged with jewel-like flower beds that added a sprightly touch of color to the scene. A piece of the country road that had brought them here was visible from this window, too, and a patch of the woods that bordered the grounds. In the distance stood layer upon dark green layer of forested mountains. Much closer to where Pinny stood, a smooth sheet of silvery blue lay shining in the sun like a new silver dollar. That must be the lake that had given the hotel its name. Idly, Pinny wondered what the lake was called.

"It is a little squishy," Zevy remarked, digging into his suitcase for his Shabbos shoes. "Chaim and Shraga get their own room, just the two of them."

Pinny turned away from the window in annoyance. The good mood inspired by the lovely view had dissipated in an instant.

"Figures," he muttered. "Why do we need that kid around, anyway?"

Ari glanced up from his unpacking. "Listen, Pinny. I don't know what you have against Morgenstern, except that maybe he almost — I said *almost* — outshines you in the brains department. But for this week, for as long as we're all here together, do me a favor, okay? Just lay off Shraga."

Pinny flushed. "I wasn't planning on starting any trouble, if that's what you mean."

"You already did." Ari turned away from him and continued unpacking his own suitcase with great energy and little regard for neatness. After a moment, Pinny did the same.

It wasn't until later, when they were all three unpacked and ready to leave the room, that Ari thawed.

"C'mon, Pinny. Let's go see what everyone else is doing."

"I'd kind of like to look up that F.B.I. guy — that Tom Morrison," Pinny admitted. "Maybe he can tell us some good stories about chasing crooks and stuff."

Ari's eyes gleamed. Unconsciously, he flexed

his big fists. "Sounds good to me. Let's go."

It turned out that they weren't the only ones with that idea. When they arrived down at the lobby, the scientists — including their father and Dr. Morgenstern — were about to embark on a tour of the lab facilities that had been set up for them to use during their stay. In another, considerably louder, cluster nearby stood children of all ages — mostly boys — avidly drinking in the words of Special Agent Tom Morrison. He welcomed the Katz brothers with his easy smile when they came up to join the crowd.

"How's the room, kids? Up to par?"

"No," said Zevy. "It's up on the third floor."

He listened, puzzled, to the laughter that greeted this comment. Tom stooped down to talk to him, eye-to-eye. "Seriously, kid, how's the room?"

"It's great," Zevy beamed. "The bathroom's got six towels and three soaps!"

"Great," Tom echoed, with a wink at the older kids. Then he quirked an eyebrow at Ari and Pinny. "Well?"

"Oh, it's fine, sir," Ari said.

"Terrific," added Pinny. "Couldn't be better."

The F.B.I. man nodded. "Good enough. Anyway, as I was telling these other kids, this week represents some tough security problems for us Special Agents. We've got the job of protecting not only a couple of dozen top-notch scientists, but their work as well. Some of it," he paused solemnly, "would be worth a fortune in the wrong hands."

Pinny and Ari exchanged a glance. The Special Agent caught the look. He was about to say something when another voice spoke up shyly from the rear. His English was passable, the accent thick and Russian.

"My mother, she is doing the same work as the great Albert Einstein. She says that maybe, someday, she will even continue to go where he left off!"

"And who," Tom asked in a friendly way, though he seemed at the same time to be silently laughing, "might your mother be?"

"Dr. Gorodnik," the boy said, blushing to the roots of his hair at the great man's attention. "Natasha Gorodnik. And I'm Nikolai."

"Well, nice to have you with us, Niki," Tom said. "Welcome to the good old U.S. of A."

"Niki," Zevy giggled softly. "Just like Daddy's Little Nicky!"

Pinny shushed him nervously.

"What was that?" asked Tom.

"Oh, nothing." Pinny sent his little brother a furious glance. "Uh, Little Nicky is just a code word for something our father is working on."

Tom nodded energetically. "That's just the kind of thing I was talking about right now," he said in an undertone. "We were told to keep a special eye on... Little Nicky. From what I understand — and I'm no scientist — it's pretty hot stuff."

Pinny nodded uncomfortably. Then, to give his eyes something else to do, he studied the Russian boy. Nikolai Gorodnik's hair was brown and springy, his eyes brown and alert, his nose snub and freckled. At first glance, he looked younger than Pinny. Then, looking closer, Pinny revised his guess. Niki just might be eleven, too, or even twelve. It was the look of wide-eyed excitement, Pinny decided, that made the Russian look so youthful. He smiled at the other boy. Niki smiled shyly back.

Then they both gave their attention back to Tom.

"...nearly had us stumped for a while. Guns are dangerous things, kids; you're never too young to know that. Well, we put our heads together, me and a couple other Special Agents, and we came up with a few clues that helped us make a mighty shrewd guess about where those bad guys were hanging out..."

As he spoke, Tom strolled along the lobby with a loose, confident stride, the blue eyes constantly in motion. Watching him, so strong and alert, Pinny felt safe. He had the F.B.I. on his side.

Like some modern-day Pied Piper, the Special Agent led his pack of children around the chrome-and-marble lobby for some twenty minutes. Another Russian boy — blond and green-eyed this time — who gave his name as Alexei Pim, was especially interested in the security measures in the hotel.

"My father says it's hard to keep things secure

in such a place," he told the F.B.I. man earnestly. "My father says an important conference like this needs a good — um, planning stra-te-gy." He pronounced the words carefully.

Twinkling, Tom remarked, "Sounds like the words of a military man. Is your dad in the army?"

"No," Alexei said, pulling himself up proudly. "But my grandfather was. He was a big hero in the Second World War."

Tom's lips pursed in a soundless whistle of admiration, but somehow Pinny had the feeling that he wasn't really admiring at all. The feeling grew stronger when, a second later, Tom winked at the others. "A big war hero, eh? Then I guess I'd better tell you all about the security measures we've taken. We don't want Grandpa getting worried, now."

"My grandfather," Alexei said softly, his big eyes bright with sudden tears, "is no longer alive. He died two years ago. He was a very old man."

"Oh. Sorry to hear that. Anyway, kids, you'll be happy to know that we've got those labs under regular surveillance around the clock. Besides, their doors open only to the scientists assigned to them."

He told them about the electronic cards that would lock and unlock the labs instead of keys. Casually, he took a card out of his own pocket to show them.

"This here's the master card." His eyes swept the small crowd. "Now, Alexei, don't you worry.

Just let anyone try anything in our labs this week. With this card, I can get in anywhere!"

The kids hung spellbound on his every word. He was nice about answering questions on how the F.B.I. trained its agents and even opened his jacket for an instant to give them a glimpse of his gun. Then he glanced at his watch.

"I guess that's it for now, kids. Time to wash up for dinner. The dining room's over that way." He gestured to the right, just past the reception desk where the Katzes and the Morgensterns had checked in a couple of hours earlier. "See you inside. I'll be keeping watch by the door."

"When does the F.B.I. get to eat, Tom?" one of the boys called out.

"We eat," Tom told him, suddenly dead sober, "when the job is done."

"He didn't really mean that, did he?" Zevy asked, when he was seated at the big round table beside Pinny.

"Who didn't mean what?" Pinny was abstracted. Shraga and his family had just entered the dining room, and it looked like they were headed this way.

"Tom. When he said that he doesn't get to eat till the job is done. He must be starving!" A new thought struck the little boy. "And doesn't he ever get to sleep?"

"Don't be silly." Pinny frowned as it became clear that Shraga *was* headed their way. Were they sharing a table with the Morgensterns? "The only One who never sleeps is Hashem. The F.B.I. is only human, you know."

They *were* sharing a table with the Morgensterns. And, as it turned out, with a small Israeli family, too: a couple and their son.

"I guess this makes the serving easier for the waiters," Dr. Katz remarked as they took their seats. "We must be the only kosher ones in the place this week."

"I'm Dr. Drucker," the Israeli man said, extending a hand to his fellow physicists. He had a homely, pleasant face and graying hair under his *kippah.* "This is my wife, Bella, and our son, Shai."

At the word "son," Shai scowled furiously but didn't say a word. While the waiters went around filling water glasses and taking orders for the pre-packaged kosher meals — Bella Drucker wanted the vegetarian dinner, and Dr. Katz opted for low-salt — Shai sat hunched in a pool of silence. A small knitted *kippah* kept slipping off his dark hair until his mother offered him a bobby pin. Shai accepted it in sullen silence.

The food arrived.

Shraga gingerly unwrapped the aluminum foil seal and gazed with rapidly fading appetite at a piece of chicken in a murky brown sauce, surrounded by hard little nuggets that looked vaguely like potatoes and carrots. He poked at a potato nugget with his fork. It rolled sluggishly in the gravy until stopped short by a stringy carrot. He sighed and began to eat.

There was not much to be said for the food, so the scientists and their wives said nothing. The children did not follow their parents' example. Just about every Morgenstern child, and the Katz kids, too, had something to say about their dinner. "Ugh" was the kindest word they used.

Dr. Morgenstern put a stop to it.

"That'll be enough of that, kids. It may not be the most appetizing fare, but it's healthy and nutritious, and it's kosher. So eat up nicely."

Obediently, if with no great joy, the kids turned back to their meal.

But Shai let out an exclamation of disgust. "I can't eat this stuff. Why can't I just get the regular food, like everyone else?" He waved a fork at the other diners, happily intent on what looked like a gourmet feast.

"Shai." His mother spoke quietly, with pain in her voice.

"But this stuff tastes like —"

"Enough, Shai," Dr. Drucker said firmly. Embarrassed, he glanced around the table. The younger children were staring at Shai as if he'd fallen from the moon, while the older ones pretended hard not to be interested. The adults gazed from Shai to his parents in sympathy, sensing that all was not right in the Drucker household.

Pinny's mind churned with questions. Why would a religious boy like Shai even think about eating non-kosher food? Or was he just bluffing —

and if so, why? A look from his father told him to keep his eyes firmly fixed on his own dinner. But the curiosity — and the undercurrents all around the table — remained.

Suddenly, Shai snatched off the knitted *kippah.* He stood up and whirled around, coming very close to upsetting his chair. Ignoring his mother's pleading "Shai!" he half-walked, half-ran, toward the door. He passed Tom, standing guard in the doorway, and plowed into the lobby. The others stared at his retreating back until he'd vanished from view.

Into the sticky silence, Shraga murmured, "And I was just about to ask him if he wanted to join us in learning Gemara tomorrow."

The Druckers exchanged a pained glance.

Then Mr. Drucker sighed. "I wouldn't bother if I were you," he said sadly.

Neither he nor his wife said much during the rest of the meal. Shai did not return.

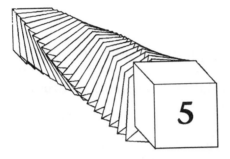

Two Plots

The rest of the meal was strained. Everyone concentrated on the food, bad as it was, and on avoiding everybody else's eyes. Pinny wasn't sorry to *bentch* and escape the dining room.

"Hey, wait up," Ari commanded, running along a few feet behind him. "Where are you headed?"

Pinny strode on, away from the dining room. "Tom said there's a game room we can use, remember?" Pinny pointed in the direction the Special Agent had shown them earlier. "Let's check it out."

"Okay by me."

They talked in undertones as they walked. "No sign of Shai Drucker," Pinny said, looking around. "Did you see his mother's face when he ran out like that?"

"Yeah." Ari's nod was somber. "What's with that kid, anyhow? He sure acted weird."

"I don't know," Pinny said unhappily. "Maybe we can talk to him tomorrow. You know, make friends."

Ari was about to agree, when he abruptly changed his mind. With a sideways look at his brother, he said, "Uh-uh. Not me. He's *your* age — yours and Shraga Morgenstern's. It's up to you guys to pal around with him."

Pinny fell silent. He looked even unhappier.

With the Morgenstern kids not far behind, and Niki Gorodnik and Alexei Pim and some half-dozen other kids just behind them, Pinny and Ari led the procession into the Lake View Hotel game room.

In the doorway, they stopped short.

"Wow," Pinny breathed.

"You said it," said Ari. He waved a jubilant arm above his head "Let's go!" he crowed, leading the pack in a wild, happy surge inside.

The game room of the Lake View Hotel was calculated to keep a large number of kids busy for hours on end. There were video games, pinball machines, skee-ball, shoot-the-basket, and three full-color computers with a full array of computer games on diskette. Ari Katz made directly for the nearest skee-ball rig. Chaim Morgenstern reached for a basketball to shoot some miniature hoops, while Shraga and Pinny bumped into each other by the video games.

Shraga stepped back quickly. "Excuse me," he said, icily correct. "Did you want to use this game?"

"No, I'll start with this one." Pinny's tone was

equally cool, and equally polite. For a few moments the two played side by side in a silence that was like a cold empty space in the happy, noise-filled room. As more children came in to test the delights of the game room, lines began forming for the different games. Shraga soon made way for Nikolai Gorodnik at his game.

The Russian boy studied the controls. "I'm not sure how you do this," he muttered.

"Here, I'll show you," Shraga offered. Pinny stepped aside as Alexei Pim came up to peer over Nikolai's shoulder. Alexei threw out a question in Russian. Nikolai answered distractedly, his fingers moving over the controls. "I think I'm getting it," he said in his slow, careful English. Triumphantly, he scored a few more points. "Yes! I have it!"

"Would you like to try this one?" Pinny asked Alexei. The other boy answered him in rapid Russian, then blushed and switched to English. "I am sorry. Yes, I would like to play. My father says it is good to keep up with the latest — how you say? — the latest tech-no-logy."

Pinny eyed Alexei curiously. Every other word he said seemed to revolve around his father. He wondered why. "Is your mother here, too?" he asked, partly out of curiosity and partly just to make conversation.

"No." Alexei looked suddenly downcast. "My mother, she died when I was a little boy. My father and I, we lived with my grandparents."

"The war hero?"

"Yes."

Shraga's ears perked up. He'd missed the session with Tom Morrison, though he'd heard a little of the highlights from Ari Katz at dinner. "Which war?" he asked, interested.

Alexei turned to Shraga, the video game forgotten in his pleasure at the question. Apparently, his love for his father was only matched by his pride in his famous grandfather.

"World War Two," he said eagerly. "My grandfather, he led a whole division of soldiers into a difficult mountain pass, and held it against the enemy for a long time. My grandfather," he ended, beaming with bashful pride, "helped Mother Russia win the war!"

It seemed a large claim for one man, but Pinny and Shraga nodded respectfully. "Did he get a medal?" Pinny asked.

"Yes — several of them. I have them in a box at home."

The whoops and cheers from the skee-ball corner were growing louder. Ari was matching skills with a big teenager with red hair and a determined glint in his eye. With a quick "Hey, that's my brother!" Pinny hurried over there. Niki and Alexei were hard on his heels. After a moment's hesitation, Shraga followed.

"What's the score?" Pinny asked Chaim, who was watching at Ari's elbow.

"Two hundred for Ari, and one-eighty for the other guy. Let 'er go, Ari!" Chaim yelled.

Ari let 'er go. The ball swept gracefully into the air and landed with a soft thud in the "50" slot. A ragged cheer rose from the crowd.

"Last round," cried another boy. "C'mon, Bill. Win this one!"

But Bill's ball fell with a dejected little *plop* into the twenty-point slot.

"Ari wins! Ari wins!" Chaim shrieked, dancing hysterically around the victor. To anyone who would listen, he added, "That's my neighbor. Did you know that we're neighbors? I've known him all my life. Way to go, neighbor!"

Ari shrugged modestly. Pinny shook his brother's hand. "Good going, Ari!"

Then another hand was extended. Pinny stiffened.

"Nice game, Ari," said Shraga.

"Thanks, kid." Ari shook hands with Shraga, then smiled at Pinny. Seeing the stony look in his brother's eyes, his own hardened. He walked away, head lowered in thought. Redheaded Bill challenged another boy to a game. Ari slipped out of the game room unnoticed.

Outside, he was surprised to find the carpeted corridor already occupied by a small, pacing figure. It was Chaim Morgenstern.

At this intrusion on his privacy, Chaim looked up. "Oh, hi, Ari." He resumed his pacing, sunk in thought.

He looked at the ten-year-old curiously. "Whatcha thinking about so hard, Chaim?"

Chaim hesitated, then decided to confide in the bigger boy. "It's Shraga — and Pinny."

The frown settled again between Ari's eyes. "I know," he said glumly. "I know."

"It's all my fault," he said. "Remember when we were in the parking lot before? The two of them were almost at the point of talking to each other — about Little Nicky, it was — when I opened my big mouth and put my foot right in it."

"What'd you say?"

"Oh, I just made some sort of dumb comment about Little Nicky being the only thing that could get the two of them together. They clammed up right away and haven't gotten much better since."

"I know," Ari said again. He remembered the coldness between the two in the game room. "It's the stupidest thing I ever saw! Those two are the smartest kids I know. You'd think they'd have everything in common."

"*Too* much, my mother says," Chaim sighed. "They see each other as competition. They don't trust each other."

"Maybe," Ari conceded. The psychology of his brother and his neighbor didn't interest him much. Action did. "So what can we do about it?"

"Do?" Chaim looked up in sudden interest. "Hey, you know something, you're right! Maybe the two of us can hatch a plot to bring them together — finally!"

"Yeah, but what?"

The big boy and his young neighbor each lapsed

into their own thoughts. Up and down the corridor they paced, crossing and recrossing each other, their steps muffled by the thick carpet. From the game room came the sounds of light chatter and the occasional cheer as a ball found its mark.

"I know!" Ari's exclamation was as gleeful as it was abrupt. He'd just remembered something. A sheet of paper in a hotel room...and a special service offered by the hotel. "Shoe shines!"

Chaim gaped at him. "Did I hear you right? Did you just say '*shoe shines*'?"

"Yup. Listen to this. You know that if you leave your shoes outside the room last thing at night, they bring them back all shined up in the morning? Well, how about if we..."

In another corridor, this one deserted, another figure was pacing up and down.

He paced nervously, stopping in front of the hotel phone that hung on the wall at one end of the hall as if willing it to ring. It remained stubbornly silent. The man waited, and paced and paced.

At last, just when it seemed his nerves would come completely unraveled from the tension, the phone let out a shrill ring. The man happened to be at the opposite end of the corridor when the noise erupted. He ran the length of the hall and snatched up the receiver.

"Yes?" he gasped.

"It's me. Listen carefully. I'm only going to say this once."

"Yes?" the man said again. His knees were trembling. Casting an anxious look down the empty corridor, he leaned against the wall for support, clutching the receiver in one perspiring, white-knuckled hand.

"Tomorrow night's the night," said the voice at the other end. The voice was muffled, as if the speaker were trying — successfully — to disguise it.

"T-tomorrow?" The man closed his eyes.

"Tomorrow. You just do the job right, and all your troubles will be over. Now, pay attention. From here on in, we're going to communicate by e-mail. Do you know what that is?"

The man in the corridor nodded. Then, as if realizing the absurdity of the gesture, he said aloud, "Yes. It's mail that's sent through the computer."

"Exactly. I'm going to be sending you a letter with very precise instructions at exactly 9 A.M. tomorrow. Be at your computer to receive it. Memorize the instructions, then erase the message immediately. Understand?"

"Yes." The word was whispered.

"Any questions?"

The man thought. "Just one," he said slowly. "How will I know which is your message? How will you sign yourself?"

There was a low chuckle at the other end. "I'll just sign myself...Mr. Big." The chuckling continued, horrible in the trembling listener's ears. At last it stopped. The voice said sharply, "You still there?"

"I'm...here."

"Well, don't sound so terrified. It'll be a piece of cake. And once the job's done, your troubles will be over."

"Yes." The man didn't sound convinced. He heard the definite click of the receiver being replaced at the other end. Very slowly, he hung up his own phone.

Then, more quickly, he started down the corridor with quick, apprehensive steps. He didn't dare breathe again until he'd reached the service stairs and was climbing.

Tomorrow night, the voice had said. After that, his troubles would be over.

Somehow, he found that hard to believe.

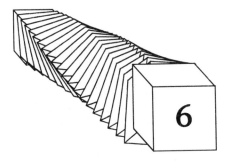

6

The Great Shoe
Mix-Up

That's funny," Shraga said as he stood in the doorway next morning, gazing down at something he held in his hands. "I think the maid must've made a mistake. These aren't my shoes."

Chaim, still in his pajamas, trotted over to have a look. "Are you sure? They look a lot like yours."

"All Shabbos shoes look more or less alike," Shraga replied impatiently. "Sure I'm sure." He stood looking uncertainly at the strange pair of shoes. Who did they belong to? And how did one go about retrieving one's own shoes in a big hotel like this? Should he hang around the room until the chambermaid showed up — or was there a lost and found office for missing shoes?

While the boys stood in the doorway of their hotel room, debating the solution to the mystery, the door next to theirs opened, just the tiniest crack. A cautious eye appeared in the crack. Observing the great shoe mix-up, a smile crept into that eye. Gently, the door closed again.

A few doors opposite and a little further along the hall, Pinny Katz yawned mightily and rolled over in bed. A second later, his eyes flew open. This was no ordinary school morning. He was at the Lake View Hotel, where you were liable to bump into brilliant scientists and secret inventions and tough F.B.I. agents wherever you turned. In a twinkling, he had washed his hands and thrown on his clothes.

"Rise and shine, Ari," he sang out. His big brother still lay inert under the covers. "Abba said last night that he wants to drive over to a kosher hotel not far away, to see if we can rustle up a minyan."

The lump under the covers heaved and rumbled like a volcano readying itself for action. Slowly, a hand emerged and pulled the blanket away from the smaller lump that was Ari's head. He gazed at Pinny, bleary-eyed. "Oh, yeah, right. Make sure he doesn't leave without me." Yawning, he closed his eyes again.

Pinny went to the window and drew the long beige curtains. A sparkling day waited on the other side. Yellow sun poured over everything the eye could see, making the lawn greener and the roses in the rose bed pinker and every tree on the distant mountains stand out in bold relief. Pinny took a deep breath and smiled happily. It was a day made for adventure. Something wonderful was going to happen today. He just knew it.

The door opened and Zevy came scampering in. Pinny hadn't even noticed that his little brother's bed was empty.

"Hey, guys, you finally up? Abba says to hurry. He wants to leave soon."

"We're on our way," Pinny told him, going back to sit on his bed and put on his sneakers. "Keep our places warm for us."

"It's gonna be some squeeze," Zevy remarked. "That Israeli man who sat at our table —"

"Mr. Drucker?"

"That's the one. He's coming with us."

On the other side of the room Ari opened his eyes, interested. "His son, too?"

"Nah," said Zevy. "Mr. Drucker said Shai isn't coming. Abba didn't want to ask why." He paused. "The Morgensterns are coming along, too."

Pinny started to groan; then, with an uneasy glance at Ari, he suppressed it. Silently, he bent to lace up his sneakers. He wouldn't let the thought of Shraga Morgenstern ruin his good mood. It should be easy enough to avoid each other in the crowd.

"Well, I guess there's no putting it off anymore," Ari said resignedly. He heaved himself into an upright position, his hair standing up like a rooster's comb.

Zevy giggled, pointing. "You need a comb, Ari. Which reminds me..." He went to rummage among the jumble of clothes, books, and odds and ends on the long hotel dresser until he found what he wanted. "Ima said I should come back and comb my hair." He ran the comb quickly through his dark blond curls, still chattering on. "I was the first one up, you sleepyheads. I even got dressed, the first one in the whole family." He gave a final vigorous swipe with the comb and replaced his yarmulka. "There. All ready." He sounded smug and very satisfied.

"The first one up," Pinny announced, "gets a special reward."

"Really? What?" Zevy's face lit up.

"Well, you know what they say — the early bird gets the worm."

Ari chortled. "I'll help you dig later, if you want, kid," he offered.

"Ha, ha." Zevy drew himself up. "You guys sure think you're a riot." He stalked to the door. "I'm going back down. Abba said to meet in the lobby, pronto. If you're not down soon, we're leaving without you."

"We'll be there," Pinny said, grinning. He knew he shouldn't tease his little brother, but the urge was sometimes too strong for him. "Right, Ari?"

Ari was more or less vertical by this time. "Yeah, right." He searched drowsily along the floor by his bed. "Anyone see my slippers?"

"Oh! Speaking of that —" Zevy, at the door,

turned "—here are your shoes, guys, all shined up. I brought mine in already. *Before*," he added pointedly. "While you were still sleeping."

"Any worms inside?" Pinny murmured. Zevy, leaving, either didn't hear him or else pretended not to.

Ari moved into high gear. "If you're bringing your shoes in," he called as he trotted into the bathroom, "get mine too, will you?"

"Sure." Pinny opened the door through which Zevy had just left, and stooped for the two pairs of shoes lined neatly against the wall outside. He took a closer look and frowned.

"Hey, these aren't my Shabbos shoes!"

Ari, running water in the bathroom sink, didn't hear him. Still frowning, Pinny brought the shoes inside. "Ari!" he yelled.

The water stopped running. "What?"

"They brought back the wrong shoes. These aren't mine."

Ari came out, toweling his face. "They mix up mine, too?"

"I don't think so. Take a look."

Ari gave a cursory glance at the shoes Pinny proffered with his left hand. "Yep, those're mine, all right." His glance traveled to Pinny's right hand. "You're sure those aren't yours?"

"Positive. What d'you think I should do, Ari? I'd feel kind of silly, knocking on doors to ask people if they have my shoes."

Ari wiped some more water out of his eyes and

looked again, more closely, at the shoes. "Those look like your size, though," he said thoughtfully. "Hey, maybe they're Shraga's."

"Hm. Maybe." Pinny didn't sound too excited at the notion. "Maybe he'll come in here soon, looking for his shoes. If he does, you give them to him, okay?"

"Not me," Ari said cheerfully, grabbing a handful of clothes from a drawer and retreating rapidly into the bathroom. "I've gotta get dressed, remember?" An instant later, the shower was turned on full blast, and Ari began merrily singing at the top of his lungs.

Pinny put the shoes beside his bed and sat down to gaze at them. He put his brain to work. Of all the boys his age in the hotel this week, he and Shraga — with the exception of the difficult Shai, who was a head shorter and presumably wore a smaller shoe size than either of them — were the only ones who were frum. They were possibly the only ones who'd brought along a pair of dressy shoes especially for Shabbos. The Morgensterns had their rooms just across the corridor and down a bit from the Katzes. It wouldn't be hard for a chambermaid to make the simple mistake of mixing up their Shabbos shoes. Ergo, the shiny black leather footwear he was looking at now probably did belong to Shraga, as Ari had guessed. The probability, he figured, was at least eighty percent.

What to do?

He considered waiting for Shraga to knock at his door. Without actually thinking about it, he assumed that Shraga would come to the same conclusion as he had. Or he could wait until they were riding to *shacharis* in the mini-van and ask him then...

Suddenly he straightened his shoulders and stood up. This was ridiculous. He wasn't scared of talking to Shraga. Just because he didn't care for the kid didn't mean he couldn't behave politely to him. Ari's chilly comments still rankled in his memory. He walked resolutely to the door, shoes in hand, and flung it open.

Standing on the other side, hand upraised to knock, was Shraga.

Both boys gaped and then smiled sheepishly. Shraga had a pair of shoes in his hand, too. He held them out.

"Yours, I presume?"

"You presume right. The maid must've gotten them mixed up." The exchange was made. With a mumbled "Thanks," Shraga half-turned to go. Pinny glanced over his shoulder at the still-closed bathroom door, listening to the bellow of song coming through it. He said awkwardly, "Uh, Shraga?"

Shraga faced him again. His round cheeks were very pink. "Yes?"

"Sometime... When you get the chance... I thought we might talk about that Drucker kid. You know — Shai. Ari thinks that since he's about our age, we should do something about him. You know, make friends or something."

Shraga nodded slowly. "He sure could use some help. Wonder what's eating him?"

Pinny shook his head, perplexed. "He took off his yarmulka yesterday evening. He talked about eating non-kosher food. He's old enough to know better! And even if he was just talking, why would a kid do that?"

"And did you see how his parents looked when he ran out like that?" Shraga asked. "I guess you're right. We should do something."

"But what?"

They thought a moment. Presently, Shraga consulted his wristwatch. "Listen, they're waiting for us in the lobby —"

"To find a minyan for shacharis. I know. Maybe we can talk about it on the way, in the van."

"Okay. Or better yet, later, when the others won't hear. We have to be careful about lashon hara."

"Right."

Shraga shifted awkwardly from one foot to the other and finally bobbed his head. "Well, see you."

"See you." Pinny closed the door, waited until he was sure Shraga must have started down in the elevator, and then opened it again. Before he left he shouted at the bathroom door, "Meet you downstairs, Ari!"

The song stopped for a second, and a distant "Okay!" floated back at Pinny. Then the singing started up again, louder than ever. Pinny went out and closed the door behind him.

As soon as Pinny had disappeared down the hall, first Ari's head, and then the rest of him, emerged from the bathroom. He was dressed, with his springy red hair smoothly plastered to his head for once. He tiptoed to the door and pulled it open. Poking his head out, he whistled softly.

The door of the boys' room across the hall opened. Chaim Morgenstern stuck his own head out. A little further down the hall, another door opened a crack, and Mindy and Daniella peeked out.

"It worked!" Chaim whooped softly. "We did it!"

"We sure did," Ari said, grinning broadly. He quickly sobered, however. "Remember, it's only a beginning. But at least we got them talking."

"I was sure they'd go downstairs together," Chaim complained. "Why're those two so — so standoffish?"

"What's stoffish?" Daniella whispered to Mindy.

Mindy glanced down. "Oh, were you listening too? Well, make sure you don't tell Shraga or Pinny what Chaim and Ari just did. Chaim told me last night, but made me promise not to tell anyone. Promise?"

"I promise," Daniella said solemnly. She looked up at Mindy. "What'd they do?"

Mindy giggled. "Never mind."

Down the hall, Ari began to close his door. "I've

gotta finish getting ready. Time for minyan."

"Wait!" Chaim called urgently. What's our next step?"

"The next step, I think," Ari said thoughtfully, "is going to belong to someone else. Someone named... Shai Drucker."

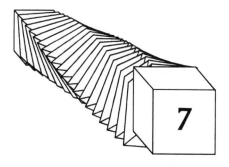

All Wrong

The name," the Israeli boy said stiffly, "is Gilboa. Shai Gilboa. *Not* Drucker."

"Oops." Shraga smiled uncertainly and pushed his glasses up with one finger, trying not to show the confusion he felt. "Uh, we just thought, since your father's name is Drucker —"

"He's not my father." The statement came out flat and sharp as a pistol shot. Shai quickened his pace across the emerald hotel lawn. Behind him, Shraga and Pinny exchanged a quizzical glance and trotted faster to keep up. The boys' sneakers hardly left an imprint on the grass as they flew over it.

"How old are you?" Shraga panted. Not very original, but as an opener it would do as well as anything else.

"Twelve," Shai shot back. Shraga was glad the other boy was in front of him and couldn't see the look of surprise that crossed his own face. That meant Shai was a little older than he was, though the Israeli was so slight he might have been mistaken for a much younger boy. Shai galloped on through the warm, fragrant air, past rolling lawn and sparkling flower beds, with his two attendants running for all they were worth to keep up. It was the strangest conversation Shraga had ever had.

Still, it *was* a conversation of sorts. "Where do you live?" Shraga gasped. His sides were beginning to ache.

"Tel Aviv." Shai glanced back over his shoulder. "What's this, an interrogation?"

Shraga shot Pinny an imploring look. He had just about enough air left in his lungs to continue breathing — barely — as he pounded on behind Shai. Pinny took up the conversational ball.

"We wanted — to — invite you," he said jerkily, between gulps of air, "to learn with us — this morning. We promised — our rebbes we'd keep up — while we're here."

Shai spoke without looking back. "Learn what?"

"Er — Gemara, of course."

In Pinny's world, "to learn" meant to learn Torah. But Shai, apparently, did not take this for granted. He shrugged and broke into a lightning sprint. "No thanks!" he hurled back over his shoulder. The tone was not very polite.

"Hey, wait up!" Shraga called desperately. He was no athlete. His full cheeks were puffed with the effort of trying to run and breathe at the same time, and the dark straight hair clung damply to his forehead. "What's — the — big rush?"

Shai's voice came floating back. "I've got things to do."

What there was for him to do at the far edge of the hotel grounds, Shraga hadn't a clue, and neither, when he silently consulted Pinny with a lift of his eyebrow, did his neighbor. There was nothing there but trees, trees, and more trees, waving greenly in the sun that was quickly warming up the cool morning.

With a determined surge of speed, Pinny gained on Shai, swerved to the right and around, and planted himself in front of the running boy. Shai was forced to stop. He fixed his hands on his hips, glaring — and waiting.

It took Pinny a few seconds to catch his breath. Shraga, loping up behind him, was wheezing painfully and clutching his sides.

"Shai," Pinny said nervously, when he could talk, "we just wanted to say that we — er — we missed you at minyan this morning. It was really neat. There's a big kosher hotel only twenty minutes away from here, and after davening they served cake and coffee and —"

With a quick sideways movement, Shai darted around Pinny and started running again. Pinny, caught by surprise, was not fast enough to catch up. Shai was flying now, as if some secret, terrifying enemy were after him. Suddenly, he stopped short, almost causing a pileup behind him. Whooping in his effort to get a little air into his outraged lungs, Shraga skidded to a grateful halt. Pinny stopped last of all. He stood very still, breathing hard, a question in the eyes he fixed on the Israeli boy.

Shai answered the unspoken question very, very clearly. "In case you haven't noticed," he growled, "*I'm not interested.* Not in your 'learning,' or in your 'davening.' So why don't you just *leave me alone*?" The last words were shouted. Pinny flinched.

But Shraga wouldn't back down. There was something here — something about this boy, with his dark, pain-filled eyes and angry words, that seemed to call out to him to help. He'd never met anyone like Shai Gilboa before. He wanted to understand what made Shai tick.

Ignoring the last part of Shai's remark, Shraga gulped down a final swallow of air into his starved lungs and said quickly, "Why not? *Why* aren't you interested?"

Shai hesitated only an instant, before flinging out his arms in a gesture of contempt. "Why? Because all that stuff belongs to the past, that's why. Modern people don't do those things. At least not in *my* world. They don't wear *kippahs* or make Kiddush or do any of that stuff. And I'm not interested in anyone who does." His black eyes smoldered. "Satisfied?"

Pinny stared at Shai in amazement. "But your parents —"

"For the last time: *They're not my parents!* "

And with that, Shai wheeled around and set off again, not running this time, but walking with a slow, sure dignity that said, more clearly than any words: *Stay away*.

Neither Pinny nor Shraga said much as they walked dejectedly back to the hotel. After the bright warmth outside, the air-conditioned lobby made them shiver. The lobby was less crowded this morning than it had been last night. The guests were no doubt outside, enjoying the sun, and the scientists were puttering away in their labs at the back. Pinny and Shraga, allied for a while in a temporary truce, hovered undecided by the elevators. With Shai out of the picture, there seemed to be no reason for them to stay together.

"Well, I guess we tried our best," Shraga said finally.

"Yeah, I guess so. Well, see you."

"See you."

Shraga punched the button for the elevator. Pinny turned away. He'd go find Ari and something to do... At that moment, a second pair of boys came hurrying across the lobby, hailing them and waving for them to wait.

"Hello," said the first, when they'd reached the elevators. Pinny recognized the speaker as Nikolai, the Russian who'd accompanied his mother to the conference. He must have spent some time in the sun this morning; the sprinkling of freckles seemed to have multiplied to cover most of his round, engaging face. With him was Alexei, blond and serious. Shraga and Pinny joined the Russian kids at one side of the elevator bank, well out of the way of the milling crowd.

"Hi," Pinny answered, smiling. "What's up?"

The Russians looked at each other. "Up?" asked Alexei.

"You know. How are you? What's happening?"

"Oh!" Nikolai smiled. "I understand. Well," he said, as the four began strolling together through the vast lobby, "we were just wondering."

A small silence ensued. Shraga prompted, "Wondering what?"

This time, Alexei answered. "About — Little Nicky."

Shraga and Pinny exchanged a careful glance.

"Yes," said Nikolai eagerly. "You know — the secret weapon."

"So much for security," muttered Pinny. To the Russian boys, he asked, "Why do you think Little Nicky has anything to do with secret weapons?"

Alexei opened his green eyes very wide. "We heard you talking about it with that F.B.I. man yesterday. Remember?"

Pinny remembered. Shraga gave him a quick look. "What F.B.I. guy?"

"Tom Morrison," Pinny told him, trying to sound offhand. "He already knew about — about it. We talked a little, that's all."

"In front of everyone?"

Pinny flushed. "It wasn't the way it sounds."

Shraga looked unconvinced. He cleared his throat. "Well, sorry, guys, but we're not allowed to talk about it."

Nikolai's and Alexei's faces fell. Oblivious to the people passing them on both sides, Nikolai blurted, "Oh, please! We can keep a secret."

"*You* know all about it, I'm sure," Alexei put in, turning to Pinny again. "My father told me that you are a genius."

"Oh, not really." Pinny glowed. Shraga scowled.

Nikolai said coaxingly, "We really want to know."

It was on the tip of Shraga's tongue to say, "So do we." He had long wished he knew more about the secret and oh-so-mysterious Little Nicky. But Pinny spoke instead. The glow of the "genius" remark was still with him.

"You see, Niki, Alexei, it's like this. It's about alternating currents — you know, as in electricity. The device is based on some work that a man named Tesla did, a long time ago — back at the turn of the century." He brought a finger to his lips and winked. "The rest, I'm afraid, is classified. Sorry, guys."

The Russian boys looked impressed — and agog to hear more. Shraga turned on Pinny furiously. "You and your big mouth! You know you aren't supposed to say anything about it!"

Pinny was startled. Then he felt the red anger gathering. "You're just jealous because you didn't know that. My father trusts me." He folded his arms smugly across his chest.

"Trusts you to do what — not to tell? Ha! How's he going to feel when he finds out you've already spilled the beans?"

"Only some of them," Pinny retorted hotly. "And our fathers are planning to unveil the thing tonight anyway. My dad won't mind. Besides," he added cautiously, as an afterthought, "who's going to tell him?"

Furious as he was, Shraga wouldn't say, "I will." He just glared at Pinny. Pinny glared back. Inside, though, he was sorry he'd spoken out the way he had. It was true, he wasn't supposed to say a word. But the eager, admiring looks in the Russian boys' faces had drawn the words from him as if with a magnet. He felt ashamed of himself — and angry with Shraga. What right did that Morgenstern kid have to rank him out in front of everyone?

"You're just jealous," he repeated defiantly.

Shraga clenched his fists. It was true — he *was* jealous. Jealous that Dr. Katz had confided some of the long-kept secret to Pinny, while his own father, Dr. Morgenstern, had said nothing to him. Jealous, too, that Nikolai and Alexei had spoken of Pinny as a "genius," while Shraga, the wonder boy of his own circle back home, stood beside them on one foot, feeling like a fool. Some of his irritation spilled over onto the Russian kids. Ignoring Pinny, he fixed them with a cold eye.

"If you're smart, you'll leave off asking about our fathers' work. It's top secret. The F.B.I. wants it kept that way."

The words came out harsher than he'd intended. Nikolai flushed a dull red.

"Oh, sure," he said, clenching his fists. "You can just keep your precious secrets, you *and* the F.B.I. Who needs you — a couple of stupid Jews?"

Shraga gasped. Alexei touched Nikolai's arm and whispered something to him. Nikolai glanced at Shraga and Pinny from under lowered lids and muttered, "Sorry."

Pinny took a long, deep breath. What had begun as a friendly conversation had quickly degenerated into something cold and ugly. "That's okay," he said softly. "We'll just forget you ever said that, Niki."

The color shot up into the freckled face again. "My name is not Niki!" he shouted. Paying no heed to the startled passers-by, the boy darted away and was soon lost in the crowd.

With a sad little shrug, Alexei followed him. Pinny and Shraga were left alone, standing in the middle of a quivering circle of ill feeling. With a short, stiff nod, Shraga turned his back on Pinny and made for the elevators. Pinny watched him go with a strange feeling of desolation.

My name is not Shai Drucker!

My name is not Niki!

He seemed to be getting all the names wrong.

Pinny sighed — a deep, deep sigh. He seemed to be getting everything wrong today.

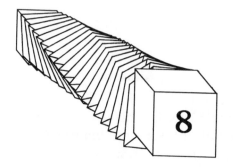

8

A Secret Note

His heated exchange with Shraga was still echoing in his mind as Pinny stomped into the room he shared with his brothers. It was empty. He splashed some water over his face, which helped cool him down a little, and then slumped onto his bed.

The door opened, and Ari came in. Pinny tried to rearrange his face into a semblance of good cheer. "Hi, Ari. What's up?"

"You," his brother said, coming over to the bed. "You're up — and you're supposed to be downstairs, remember? Abba's waiting for you."

"Yikes!" Pinny struggled to his feet. "Is it that late already? I thought you were learning with Abba first."

"I'm finished. It's your turn — yours and Shraga's."

"Yippee." There was no mistaking the way Pinny

regarded the prospect.

Ari frowned. Just that morning, he and Chaim had witnessed a thawing of the ice between the two boys. And after breakfast, he'd seen with his own eyes the way Shraga and Pinny had followed Shai out of the hotel together. His eyes narrowed. "What's the matter, Pinny?"

Pinny shrugged. "Nothing." His tone said, "Everything." But before Ari could question him further, he was out the door and halfway to the elevator bank.

Pinny found his father and Shraga's waiting in a corner of the lounge. Shraga was there already, looking just as miserable as Pinny felt. Pinny nodded stiffly and sat down.

"It's a good thing you boys are learning the same Gemara this year," Dr. Katz said heartily. "Saves us all a lot of time."

"And it's fun learning together," Dr. Morgenstern added, opening the small travelling Gemara he'd brought along to the conference.

"Yeah, right," Shraga muttered. "Fun."

Pinny didn't say anything, but the expression on his face said that he agreed fully with the other boy's sentiments.

Their fathers exchanged a glance. Quietly, Dr. Katz said, "Let's begin."

For a while, as they enjoyed the cut-and-thrust of learning, the boys almost forgot their antagonism. For each, it was a pleasure to match minds with a worthy opponent. This, thought Dr. Mor-

genstern, listening to them, was the only battle-
ground the two boys should ever meet on: the field
of Torah learning, where everyone emerged a win-
ner. How alike they are, Dr. Katz thought fondly,
watching the boys. What a pity they've never gotten
along. Like the Morgensterns, he had high hopes
for this convention. Spending a week in the same
place, eating and playing and learning together,
their sons just might become real friends again,
after all this time.

But the minute the session was over and Dr.
Morgenstern had closed the Gemara, the shuttered
look fell back over both boys' features. It was as if
a door had been slammed somewhere inside.

"Well," said Shraga's father, "time to get to work
now, eh, Shmulie?"

Dr. Morgenstern nodded. "Want to come along
and take a look at our lab, boys?"

"Maybe later," Pinny said. He didn't want to do
anything just now that included Shraga. He carefully avoided seeing the surprise on his father's
face. Just last night, he'd been begging for a lab
tour.

"Shraga?" asked Dr. Morgenstern. "Want to
come?"

"Sure, Daddy."

"So," said Pinny's father, turning to him. "What
are your plans for the rest of the morning, Pinny?"

"I dunno," Pinny answered, getting up. "I guess
I'll go find something to do with Ari. See you later,
Abba." With a halfhearted smile, he started away

at a rapid clip. When he judged himself at a safe distance, he peeked back over his shoulder. There were the two scientists, with Shraga walking between them. Shraga would get to see the lab before him. Chagrined, Pinny watched the trio move away until they were out of sight. Then he went in search of Ari, in the hopes of salvaging the rest of what was proving to be — except for the brief exhilaration of the learning session — a perfectly miserable morning.

Shraga didn't enjoy the tour of his father's lab as much as he'd expected. Pinny's face kept rising up in front of him, wrecking his concentration. That kid had no right to go spilling the beans about Little Nicky — and to Russians, at that! All right, the Russians weren't exactly their enemies anymore. And okay, their fathers were planning to tell all the other scientists about the invention this very evening. That didn't make Pinny's blooper any better.

His thoughts reminded him of something he'd been meaning to ask his father. "Daddy," he said, unaware that he was interrupting a fascinating demonstration of the sophisticated centrifuge in one corner of the lab. "Did you get permission for Pinny and me to sit in on the Little Nicky demonstration tonight?"

His father looked rueful. "We tried, Shraga. Unfortunately, the planning committee ruled out kids. If they allowed the two of you in, they'd have to let other kids in, and they don't want that to happen. We'll be discussing sensitive material, in a great deal of technical detail which will be way over most kids' heads anyway."

"But not yours or Pinny's," Dr. Katz added. He paused thoughtfully. "David, why don't you and I give the boys a private unveiling?"

"Today, you mean?"

"Why not? This afternoon, just a couple of hours before the real demonstration, in the privacy of one of our rooms, we can tell them about the device and explain what it's all about. I don't think the boss would mind that, do you?"

Dr. Morgenstern thought it over. "I suppose not. Well, how does that sound to you, Shraga?"

Shraga's shining face was all the answer he needed. His father nodded, satisfied. "Will you go find Pinny and tell him, then?"

"You can tell him at lunch, can't you?" Shraga asked, suddenly uncomfortable again.

"I'd rather he knew now," Dr. Katz said smoothly. "So that he doesn't make any other plans."

Shraga was nonplussed. "All right, I'll tell him." Actually, the news was so exciting that he didn't mind sharing it with Pinny. That kid might have a lot of nerve and a swelled head and be a royal pain in the neck, but Pinny would be as excited as he was to know that later that day, for the first time, he'd be learning the super-secret details of the mysterious Little Nicky.

Shraga left the lab and started down the corridor for a side door he'd noticed earlier that led out of the hotel. He passed several other labs and absently noted the names on their doors.

Dr. Ilya Pim — that must be Alexei's father. Dr. Natasha Gorodnik, Niki's mother — her lab was a couple of doors further on. A white-coated scientist emerged from his lab and passed Shraga with a brief nod. He was very tall and very thin, with loose arms and legs that reminded Shraga of a scarecrow's. There was nothing comical about that physicist though. He looked...well, the closest word would be aristocratic. Curious, Shraga glanced at the sign on the door he'd just stepped through. "Manfred Isingard." What a strange name, he thought. Wonder what country he's from?

He passed the name Magda Brenner — sounded Hungarian — and then the last name in that row of labs, Marcus Fowley. Shraga reached the end of the corridor and the side door leading outside. He stood in the doorway, squinting into the bright sun. Where was Pinny?

Pinny was tossing a ball to Ari on the back lawn at that moment — and not very well, either.

"Harder, I told you," his big brother called, exasperated, as the ball fell to the ground a full six feet from his toes. "Didn't anyone ever teach you the right way to throw a ball?"

"No. Didn't anyone ever teach *you* calculus?" Pinny retorted. It was old news in the Katz household that Pinny had taught himself the basics of high-school calculus at the age of ten, while Ari struggled for passing grades in math each year.

Unoffended, Ari grinned. "Oh, I'm not competing with you in schoolwork, buddy. Or on the ball field, for that matter. I just want to be able to enjoy a simple catch with my kid brother, that's all. Here." He scooped up the ball and looped a neat curve back to Pinny. "Try again."

Biting his lip, Pinny wound up for a hard one. He pulled his arm back, and was just about to let 'er rip, when someone cleared his throat at Pinny's back. Startled, Pinny dropped the ball. He turned, to find Dr. Drucker, Shai's father, smiling at him apologetically.

"I'm sorry to disturb you — Pinny Katz, isn't it? I just wanted to ask you something."

"Oh, that's all right." Pinny bent to retrieve the ball, while Ari trotted over to where they stood. "What can I do for you?"

"Have you seen Shai?"

"Uh, not lately."

Dr. Drucker looked at Ari.

"Not since breakfast," Ari said.

"I noticed you and the Morgenstern boy walking with Shai after breakfast," Shai's father told Pinny, though "zooming" would have been a better description of their progress across the grounds. "I thought maybe you knew where he went. It's nearly lunchtime, and I haven't seen a sign of him all morning." He didn't add that he and his wife had hoped to spend some quiet, relaxed time with their foster son today. He had a niggling suspicion that Shai was avoiding them.

"He was headed that way." Pinny gestured toward the copse of trees at the edge of the hotel grounds. "I'll go look for him, if you want."

"I'd appreciate that." With a nod, Dr. Drucker started back for the hotel, and the lab he'd abandoned because he couldn't concentrate this morning. He'd try to get a little work done before lunch. It was too late now to do anything with Shai anyway, even if the Katz boy managed to unearth him from wherever he was hiding.

Shai was feeling the closest thing to peace that he had felt in a long time. He was alone at the top of the world, high up in the branches of an elm tree, one of many at the edge of the hotel grounds. From his perch he could see the hotel, sprawling elegantly in its envelope of green, green lawn. He could see some of the colorful flower beds that lined the lawn, and the two boys playing ball near the flowers.

He recognized the boys as Pinny and Ari Katz. Part of him longed to jump down from his solitude and throw a ball with them, but another, stronger part, wanted to hide away from all of them. Even his foster parents. Especially his foster parents. He stayed where he was.

If he turned his head to the right, he could just catch a glimpse of the drive leading up to the hotel from the country road. The two F.B.I. agents, the sandy-haired one and the dark one with the big shoulders, strolled in a bored way along the drive. There weren't many cars coming up the drive today. The scientists and their families had already arrived, and there was no room for new guests this week.

Shai thought about the differences between Israel and America — or at least the tiny part of America he'd managed to see so far. Everything was bigger, for one thing. Much bigger. The airport and the cars and the buildings seemed to swallow up the ones he remembered from home. The Druckers had taken him on a whirlwind tour of New York City on the way up here. Talk about big! In the face of that vastness, Shai felt even more lost than usual. New York was no place for a scared and lonely boy to be. Up here in the country it was a little better. He was still lonely, but not so scared.

A sound came to his ears: a soft shuffle. Someone was walking below his tree, his footsteps muffled by the cushion of pine needles that covered every inch of the ground. Through the leaves, Shai saw a dark head, bent as if to read something. After a moment, the man crumpled something in his fist. He dug a small hole in the ground with the toe of his shoe and tossed a piece of paper in, then kicked some pine needles over it. He passed along beneath the shadowy trees and vanished from Shai's sight.

Who was he? And what had he tossed away? Grateful for something to alleviate the morning's tedium — he'd been sitting still for what seemed like hours — Shai climbed down the tree until he stood on solid ground again. There was no sight of the man. The woods were very quiet. He peered at the place where the man had thrown the crumpled paper. A tiny edge of white stuck out from beneath the carpet of needles. Shai crouched down and caught it between his finger and thumb.

It was a plain scrap of white notepaper, the kind the hotel offered in each of its rooms. Printed in tiny letters on the paper were a few words. Shai's English reading skills were not especially good, but even if they had been, the message was too cryptic for him to fully understand.

Meet south entrance midnight. Bring our little friend.

It was signed, *Mr. B.*

He wasn't sure what "entrance" meant, though he was pretty sure "midnight" was the same as *chatzot*, the middle of the night. Shai studied the note for another moment and then, shrugging, made to toss it away. At the last minute, remembering how littering was frowned upon in his tiny Israel, he put the crumpled note in his pocket. He'd throw it into a wastebasket later.

"Shai! There you are!" Pinny Katz burst into view, breathing hard from his run across the grounds. "Your father's looking all over for you."

Shai refrained from repeating that Dr. Drucker was not his father. Suddenly, he was sick and tired of explaining his life, and even more sick and tired of being alone in the great, echoing woods.

"Okay, I'm coming," he said. Thrusting his hands into his pants pockets, he started walking as if he didn't care whether Pinny came with him or not. Pinny was encouraged. At least Shai wasn't running away from him this time. For a fleeting second, he wished Shraga were there. What to say?

He debated on several approaches, until sheer curiosity conquered him.

"If the Druckers are not your father and mother," Pinny asked carefully, "then who are they?"

Shai glanced at him coolly, though his dark eyes smoldered. "That," he said, "is none of your business."

And then he did start running.

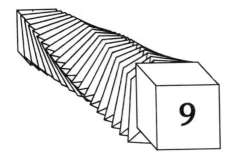

The Great Tesla

Lunchtime would have been a very strained affair, with Shraga and Pinny avoiding each other's eyes and Mindy and Ari glancing from one to the other in puzzled exasperation, if not for the anticipation that ran like an undercurrent throughout the meal. Pinny and Shraga were counting the hours until their fathers' promised revelation: the true story of Little Nicky. What was the device the two scientists had been working on so assiduously — and so secretly — for such a long time?

Thinking of the F.B.I. man, Tom Morrison, and the way he'd dropped his voice to say, "I hear it's pretty hot stuff," Pinny had to repress a shiver of excitement. As for Shraga, he picked at the unappetizing airline-style food without really seeing it. He was recalling what Pinny had told the Russian kids that morning. Tesla. It had something to do with alternating-current electricity, Pinny had said — and someone named Tesla. It didn't sound like much to Shraga, not yet. He was agog to hear more about the mysterious device that had piqued his curiosity for so long. His father had been working on this project just about forever, it seemed. Well, tonight, Little Nicky would go public... But not before he, Shraga, got to hear all the juicy details!

Mindy Morgenstern had abandoned any pretext of eating her packaged lunch and was chattering to anyone who would listen about the collage she was working on. The only one who was paying any attention at all was young Daniella Katz. Ari, catching a sentence or two as he reached for the water pitcher, rolled his eyes.

"Help — I'm surrounded by geniuses! Even these pipsqueaks are into 'high tech.' " He heaved a long, humorous sigh. "You know, I'm beginning to get the feeling I'm in the wrong place."

Mindy giggled. "Oh, I'm no genius. Not like Shragie anyway. Or," she added judiciously, "like your brother Pinny. I'm just working on a very interesting art project that combines the best elements of 'high tech' with the —"

But Ari wasn't even listening. He seemed to be gazing into the distance. With a good-natured shrug, Mindy resumed her monologue to the ever-admiring Daniella.

Ari's glance roved over the neighboring tables. At one of them, not far away, he saw the Russian boys who had spoken to Tom Morrison yesterday. Nikolai's mother, Dr. Natasha Gorodnik, was conversing pleasantly with Alexei's father, Ilya Pim, and another scientist. They were drawing something — probably some sort of physics formula — on a napkin. Geniuses to the right of me, Ari thought with an inward grin; geniuses to the left...

All at once, he had the strange feeling that someone was watching him.

Sure enough, he quickly found the pair of round brown eyes that were fixed so earnestly on him. The instant he met those eyes, they shifted to someone else, someone at his own table. It was one of the Russian boys who was doing the staring. Who was he gaping at like that, and why?

Pinny noticed his big brother's absorption in the next table. Glad for the distraction — he had no more liking for the food than anyone else at his table — he followed the direction of Ari's gaze. Before long he found himself looking into the face of Niki (sorry, *Nikolai*) Gorodnik. Before he could think how to react, Nikolai gave him a small, tentative smile. Startled, Pinny managed a lopsided grin in return. Nikolai transferred his gaze to Shraga, who was busy erecting a pyramid of slippery green peas on his fork. Pinny motioned surreptitiously across the table, until he caught Shraga's attention and got him to look where he wanted him to. The Russian boy, seeing that he had Shraga's attention at last, gave him a smile, too, and then a small, shy nod to both boys.

Shraga nodded back, uncertain. Nikolai's gesture was a peace offering, he knew, for the horrible words the Russian had blurted earlier, in his disappointment at not hearing the inside story of Little Nicky. *Who needs you — a couple of stupid Jews...* Without seeming to, he studied the other boy's round, freckled, and perfectly pleasant face. How could such a nice kid spout such garbage? It was more than Shraga could understand.

For the rest of the meal, he was lost in his own thoughts. And, by the look of them, those thoughts were not very pleasant ones.

"What's wrong?" his father asked softly as they left the dining room a little later. "You're awfully quiet suddenly."

Shraga hesitated. "Daddy —"

"Yes?"

"One of the Russian kids said something...not so nice, to me and Pinny before. About...about being Jews. You know."

"Yes," Dr. Morgenstern said grimly. "I know. Or rather, I can imagine." He stopped to let an elderly female scientist with a regal gait pass him. "Good afternoon, Dr. Brenner," he said courteously.

The white head was graciously inclined. "Good afterrrnoon, Dr. Morgensterrrn." She swept on her way. Shraga's father turned back to him. "Why did he say it, Shraga?"

"Oh, he was just mad." Shraga's face was hurt and bewildered and somehow very young. "Why,

Daddy? We didn't do anything to him. Why should the first thing he says when he's angry be something like — that?"

His father sighed. "It's always been that way, Shraga. Ever since Yaakov and Eisav, there's been hatred between gentile and Jew." He paused. "I was hoping to avoid this sort of thing at this conference. You'd think the field of science would be one place where Jew and non-Jew might meet in peace, at least. Who was it, may I ask?"

"A nice kid, otherwise. Niki — uh, Nikolai — Gorodnik."

"What?" Dr. Morgenstern stopped short.

Shraga stopped, too, staring up at him. "What's wrong, Daddy?"

"The *Gorodnik* boy said that to you?"

"Yes. Why are you so surprised?"

Dr. Morgenstern resumed his walk, his steps slow, steady, and a little heavier than before.

"I'm surprised, Shraga," he said, shaking his head sadly, "because I happen to know that Dr. Gorodnik, his mother, *is* Jewish." He turned to look his son in the eye. "I don't know if he's aware of it, but your Niki is a Jew."

For the next hour, the Morgenstern and Katz parents and babies enjoyed brief naps, and the children — particularly Shraga and Pinny — endured agonies of impatience. Then at last the scientists and their families convened for their long-awaited meeting.

The fathers had decided to include everyone in their talk. The younger children were adjured to keep quiet, even if they understood little or nothing of what was being said. Daniella and Zevy Katz and Rochel Morgenstern all declared loudly that they would understand every single word. Little Vivi was the only one who was content to entertain herself with some blocks on a corner of the rug. The rest perched on every available sitting place in the Katz bedroom — chairs, beds, even the dresser — and waited with bated breath for the men to begin.

"Where's Little Nicky, Abba?" Pinny asked eagerly. He'd expected the device to star in this afternoon's performance.

"Locked away in our lab, where it belongs," Dr. Katz answered. "When you hear what our good friend, Little Nicky, can actually do, you'll be glad it's under lock and key — or rather," he grinned, "under electronic lock." He patted his pocket. "The card I have here, and a similar card your father carries, are the only things that can unlock the door of our lab."

"We know," Chaim offered. "Tom showed us — the head F.B.I. guy."

Dr. Katz nodded. "Yes, Little Nicky is secure. Tonight, as we told you, we present the device, and the relevant scientific background, to the conference. Tomorrow morning the boss of our firm is sending an armored car to pick it up and take it back into the city. It will move out of our responsibility then — and, for me at least, none too soon."

"Me, too," Dr. Morgenstern added fervently. "As far as I'm concerned, the sooner it's out of our hands, the better. That thing makes me nervous!"

Dr. Katz nodded and resumed his talk. "So, as of tomorrow, phase one of the project — and our part in it — will be over. Others will take over from here."

"Are you sorry, Daddy?" Shraga asked. "Won't you miss it, after all this time?"

Dr. Morgenstern looked thoughtful. "The answer to that has to be yes — and no. It's been a fascinating project, one that's taken all our intelligence and creativity to unravel. But it's also a dangerous one, with terrifying possibilities should it fall into the wrong hands."

"That's what Tom said," Chaim volunteered.

The two men nodded. Dr. Morgenstern smiled at his wife and at the children scattered eagerly around the room, trying to disguise their impatience. "Well, you've waited long enough, folks." His voice grew soft and dramatic. "Let me tell you about a brilliant and eccentric inventor, named Nikola Tesla."

"Tesla," began Dr. Morgenstern, "was born in 1856, in a country called Yugoslavia. That country doesn't exist anymore — it was recently divided into two parts — but Nikola Tesla's discoveries have held scientists' interest for over a century now. He came to America in 1884 with four cents in his pocket, a few poems he'd written, and his own calculations for making a flying machine."

"Four cents!" exclaimed Zevy. "What could he do with that?"

"Not much," his father admitted, taking up the thread. "So he got a job — with Thomas Edison. Who knows who that is?" He addressed the question to the younger kids.

It was Daniella who answered. "He discovered electricity, right?"

"Right. But, believe it or not, there are actually two kinds of electricity. I won't go into detail, but suffice it to say that one kind is called AC, or 'alternating current,' and the other is called 'direct current,' DC." He waited a few seconds to let the kids absorb his words. "Edison worked with direct current electricity. Tesla, who soon fell out with Edison and got another job working for the rival Westinghouse Company, was interested in the alternating current kind. All clear so far?"

Heads nodded all around the room. Zevy's eyes were beginning to look glazed, and little Ruchie Morgenstern was frankly bored. Her father forged ahead.

"Eventually, Nikola Tesla opened his own lab, where he experimented with shadowgraphs, which led eventually to the X-rays we have today. He also invented different kinds of lighting. Sometimes he gave exhibitions in his lab, where he would light lamps without wires by letting electricity flow through his body. That was to allay people's fears of electricity."

"Why would they be afraid to turn on a lamp?" Mindy wondered.

Dr. Morgenstern smiled. "People are often afraid of something new — especially if it can do things they've never seen before. Anyway," he continued, "at the turn of the century, around the year 1900, Tesla made what he considered his most remarkable discovery. He called them terrestrial stationary waves. This is a little complicated; I'll just say that he discovered that the earth itself could be used as a giant conductor of electricity. By creating electrical vibrations of a certain pitch, he was able to light two hundred lamps without wires — from a distance of twenty-five miles!"

As gasps of astonishment met his words, he held up his hand with a smile. "That's not all. Tesla created man-made lightning, producing flashes that measured 135 feet across."

"Incredible," breathed Pinny.

"It was," agreed his father. "It still is. The potential in his work is enormous. In fact, it's still being plumbed to this very day. Which brings us to..."

"Little Nicky!" Shraga exploded. He squirmed in his seat. "Where does that come in?"

"I'll tell you." His father reached up absently to adjust his yarmulka while he marshalled his thoughts. "Because of a lack of funds, most of Tesla's ideas remained in his notebooks, which scientists today are still examining for clues. After he died, in 1943, the American government impounded his papers. Some of them disappeared under mysterious circumstances, and others found their way into the Nikola Tesla Museum in Belgrade, Yugoslavia." He paused for effect. "It's those stolen papers that have interested physicists for many years. Some of them were unearthed eventually and formed the basis for our work. The result: our good friend, Little Nicky."

"Which is what, exactly?" Shraga couldn't help prompting.

His father looked at him. "Remember when I said that Tesla could light lamps without wires, from a distance of twenty-five miles? Well, from his notes and equations, we've been able to figure out how to cause other kinds of remote-control effects."

Zevy's wristwatch beeped. "Five o'clock," he remarked to the room at large.

"Sssh," scolded Mindy.

"Remote control?" Pinny prompted.

"For instance," Dr. Katz said, "using the device, we would be able to blow up a building a hundred miles away — without any wires. We'd only have to use one small, black box. The magnetic waves of the earth itself would do the rest."

"A hundred miles away!" Shraga exclaimed softly. His face was serious as he considered the implications of the scientist's words. Somebody sitting in his own house could, with the press of a button or the twist of a knob, cause another building, a hundred whole miles away, to blow up! It was a frightening prospect. Suddenly, the chilling words came back to him: *In the wrong hands...*

He looked up and met his father's eye. As if reading his thoughts, Dr. Morgenstern nodded.

"Exactly. Other countries and private groups have been examining Tesla's work, too — some of them with less honorable intentions than ours. Just imagine if a terrorist organization got hold of one of these devices. No longer would they have to create bombs or take the trouble to plant them. All they would need is our friend Little Nicky — and no building would be safe from them anywhere within a very, very large radius." He held the eyes of his audience, who were listening raptly. "Why, with this device, someone sitting in a motel room a hundred miles away from here could conceivably, with the pressing of a button, blow up this entire hotel!"

"*Chas v'shalom!*" gasped his wife.

"*Chas v'shalom,*" he agreed gravely. He gave a little shiver.

"So what's the American government planning to blow up, Daddy?" Mindy asked.

Her father shook his head quickly. "Nothing! Our government will be using our device for energy-generating and defensive purposes. But people with evil on their minds could wreak havoc with our little friend Nicky."

Pinny's mother shivered. "Horrible," she murmured.

"Horrible," echoed Zevy. His eyes looked enormous in his small face. "Are you sure that thing's locked up okay, Abba?"

Dr. Katz laughed, dissipating some of the tension that had suddenly sprung up in the hotel room.

"I told you, it's locked in the lab, and only one of these electronic cards can open the door. And, apart from that, there's a computer diskette that goes with the device. It's bright red, so we can spot in an instant whether it's missing. The red diskette carries the passwords needed to make the final linkages that will make Little Nicky work. Without that diskette and the passwords, the device is virtually useless. So don't worry, Zevy. Little Nicky is safe from men of evil purpose."

"That's right," confirmed Dr. Morgenstern. "In fact, we have something called a super-user password that only your father and I know, Zevy. That special password is like — like the master key of this hotel that can open any door. Without it, even if someone, somehow, did manage to get into our lab and steal the device, he would still be denied access to some of the most crucial bits. He'd have to work hard to try and reconstruct them — and that takes time."

"Time for the good guys to track him down," Dr. Katz said lightly, with a smile.

But even as he spoke the words, Dr. Katz looked worried. So did Dr. Morgenstern, who got up and began pacing the room restlessly. Putting into words the ominous possibilities of the secret they'd harbored for so long made the danger seem more real. Anyone with a good knowledge of how computers work — and, of course, with the passwords to be found in the red diskette — would have a good chance of "breaking into" their program, just like a skilful burglar might use his bag of tools to break into a securely locked house. The sooner the diskette, and the prototype of the device, were out of his hands, the happier he'd feel.

Dr. Morgenstern stopped abruptly in his pacing and turned to the children, who were watching him anxiously.

"Now, remember, kids — mum's the word. We'll be telling all this to the other physicists in a few hours. But till then —" He put a finger to his lips in a gesture even the youngest of them understood.

Everyone nodded. Shraga's father smiled. "And kids?"

"Yes, Daddy?" Mindy asked.

"Don't be afraid. This thing's the property of the United States government now. Good old Uncle Sam'll make sure it stays in the right hands — to serve our citizens and to combat evil. So don't worry."

The children nodded again. They were quiet, each one submerged in his own thoughts. Slowly, they struggled to their feet and made for the door.

Ari flexed his arms; all at once, he wanted nothing more than to get out into the clear, fresh air and play ball. He looked around for Pinny. "Wanna have a catch?"

"Fine with me."

"You too, Shraga," Ari offered generously.

"Me, too!" Chaim said immediately.

"And me!" piped up Zevy.

Ari grinned. "Looks like we've got us a game going. C'mon, gang." Whistling a merry tune, as if to dispel the dark shadow that had seemed to fall over the gathering at the prospect of Little Nicky's awesome powers, he led the other kids out into the sunshine.

"Mommy," said Ruchie, when the big kids had gone. "Where *is* Little Nicky, Mommy? I don't see him."

Her mother stooped and gathered the little girl into her arms. "Believe me," she said quietly, "it's no one you'd want to know."

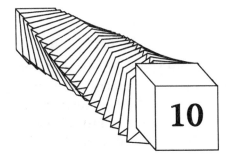

10

Pointless Plans

Many of the guests staying at the Lake View Hotel for the physicists' conference were making plans for that evening.

"I think I'll call Gitty after dinner," Mrs. Morgenstern said to Mrs. Katz as they descended to the dining room. "I'm sure she's fine and having a great time at her friend's house this week, but..."

"...but you miss her," Mrs. Katz finished with a twinkle.

Mrs. Morgenstern laughed. "You know something? I do."

Still smiling, she followed her friend past Special Agent Tom Morrison, standing ever-alert just inside the doors, and into the dining room. The place smelled of all kinds of good things to eat. She thought with a tiny sigh of the packaged food she and the other religious Jews at the conference had waiting for them to eat. Already her mind was turning over fantastic menus for when she and her family returned home next week.

Just as she took her place beside her husband, a waiter set down a scrumptious-looking steak in front of someone at the next table. Mrs. Morgenstern decided it was easier not to look. To distract herself, she shook out her napkin and placed it in her lap, thinking of her daughter and of the things she would say to Gitty when they spoke on the phone later.

But the call she was planning with such pleasure was not to be. Not that night, anyway. Other events were shaping up — events that would wipe every thought of home from her mind, and every feeling except fear and dread from her heart.

Dr. Katz lingered for a while in the lab after Dr. Morgenstern went back to his room to wash up for dinner. He punched in some words on the keyboard of his computer and studied the results carefully on the glowing, multi-colored monitor. Of the two scientists, he knew more about using computers, so he'd been put in charge of the computer portion of their demonstration on the Tesla coil later in the evening.

Of course, he wouldn't give away any of the actual passwords that would to make the device work. That was a secret known only to himself and his partner — and his computer. Still, to describe the way the device worked, he had to show at least a little bit — the unclassified part — of the computer program he'd created for this new, potentially lethal, and terrifying secret. Dr. Morgenstern would explain the ins and outs of Nikola Tesla's exciting theory and how they had managed to unlock the secrets of Tesla's notebooks to put his ideas to work for them today.

Dr. Katz stared at his monitor, hypnotized by the many-colored circuitry diagrams and by his own thoughts. It felt strange to think that, after tonight, the long-kept secret would be a secret no longer. The United States Defense Department had granted his firm, M.C.B., permission to reveal to the physicists at this week's conference what the Katz-Morgenstern team had been working on for the past few years. The main outlines of the theory were known to several countries by now anyway — and most likely to more than one outlaw terrorist group, too. Dr. Katz suddenly shivered. What a weapon it would be in the hands of a ruthless band of murderers!

But the invention — or at least the only prototype in existence, the one sitting right here in this lab —was safe. Its secrets, too, were safe inside the little red diskette. Telling the world about the breakthrough — though not how it worked — might just be a good thing. It would raise the stature of the "good guys" a notch higher and hopefully make the "bad guys" hold the U.S. in a bit more respect.

And so, in just an hour or two, after dinner, he

and his old friend David Morgenstern would be standing up in front of the assembled physicists, gathered together from many different countries of the world, and telling them all about it. The result, for the two of them, would be something they'd looked forward to for a long time. Their bosses at M.C.B. had promised them a reward upon the successful completion of this project. Not fortune, not fame (though some of that would come anyway, he knew). No, their reward would be something the two had long craved. A chance to work more independently, making their own hours for research and increasing the amount of time they could devote to their real passion: Torah. Dr. Katz smiled as he made a last check of the lab, making sure that everything was shipshape and secure.

The red diskette lay in its special holder, beside the prototype of the invention. "Little Nicky" lay on the lab counter, looking just like an ordinary black box, with a few interesting knobs and digital displays built into one smooth side. He saluted his old friend in farewell, pulled out his electronic card, and locked the lab.

Whistling softly under his breath, Dr. Katz went along to the dining room to find his family and the silver-wrapped, airline-style package he must call "dinner." He wasn't much looking forward to the food, but the after-dinner presentation was something else again. He felt a pleasant tingle of anticipation, and more than a touch of relief. Tonight would be their moment of glory, when their long, hard work would be recognized at last. After tonight, he and his friend David would be turning their minds to new projects. Little Nicky would be delivered to other, safer hands. His worries would be over.

But Dr. Katz was wrong. After tonight, his worries would only be starting.

Another Niki — short for Nikolai, this time — was taking his seat in the dining room in a state of uneasiness. His stomach fluttered as if a dozen dancing butterflies had mistaken it for a ballroom. He kept wiping the palms of his hands on his pants. Tonight, he was going to do something very hard. He was going to apologize to Shraga and Pinny for the horrible thing he'd said to them this morning.

He hadn't wanted to. He'd wanted to push the whole thing out of his mind as if it had never happened. But Shraga's father, it seemed, had gone over to Nikolai's mother this afternoon to tell her about it.

Natasha Gorodnik had been very angry.

"That is no way for a scientist to talk," she'd scolded her son. "That is no way for a human being to talk!"

"I'm not a scientist," he retorted lamely.

"And human? Are you a human being? Do you possess a heart? Then you should never say such things to another. American, Christian, Russian, Jew — they are all human beings. You must treat them all with respect!"

Miserably, Nikolai had nodded. Mother was right, of course. He'd regretted the words as soon as they'd burst from his mouth. He actually liked those American boys. It would have been fun to do things together with them this week — with them, and his newfound Russian friend, Alexei Pim. He'd tried, at lunch, to smile his apologies at the boys, but that was not enough for Natasha Gorodnik. "Apologize!" his mother had ordered. "This very evening — right after dinner — do it!"

And he'd agreed. He would do it.

He remembered something else his mother had said, right before they ended their little talk and she returned to her lab. "Nikolai...it is interesting that you chose to call those boys, of all things, 'stupid Jews.' Don't you know that I, too, am Jewish?"

He flushed. "I know. I honestly don't have anything against Jews, though some of the boys at school do — a lot. They only let me play with them because they know that Father wasn't Jewish, and so neither am I."

There was a glint in Natasha's eye as she answered, "No? Well, do you know something? That man — Dr. Morgenstern — he just told me something very interesting. Did you know that according to Jewish law, the faith of the child depends not on the father, but on the mother? Did you know, my Nikolai, that not only I, but you, too, are a Jew?"

Nikolai thought about that now, as he stared

down at the delicious-smelling steak in front of him. He felt absolutely no appetite at all.

Shai Gilboa had agreed to put on his *kippah* for dinner — and to keep it on. He'd acted like a silly child last night; he knew that. He didn't know; where all that anger came from, the rage that made him lash out at the Druckers the way he did and feed his hatred of them, of himself, of the whole world. It was a heavy thing to carry, that anger. Sometimes he felt as if he weighed a thousand kilos!

To the right of him sat Shraga Morgenstern. Pinny Katz was to the left. Both boys tried from time to time to engage him in conversation, but his answers were so short that they soon grew discouraged. But, though he didn't show it, he *was* interested in them. If they would just steer clear of all that talk about learning and davening, he might even consider hanging around with them this week. Oh, nothing serious like real friendship — that was something he couldn't even imagine. He'd never stayed in one place long enough to make real friends, and he'd long ago given up trying. But as companions for the remaining days of the convention — why not?

Tonight, he decided. Maybe we'll all go to the game room again, and I'll play skee-ball or something with them. Thinking of it, his heart lifted. A bit of lighthearted fun seemed a very attractive thing just then.

But Shai was to be disappointed. He *would* be spending some time with the Katz and Morgenstern boys that night, but there would be nothing light-hearted about it. Nothing at all.

Mindy Morgenstern was thinking about her collage as she went down to dinner, with Daniella Katz, as usual, trailing her like a faithful shadow.

Mindy was growing a little tired of that shadow, but she hadn't figured out what to do about it. Sometimes she actually enjoyed having that admiring little face looking up at her with such devotion. Most of the time, though, it was kind of tiring. After all, a girl can't be perfect all the time! And yet, that was just what young Daniella seemed to expect from her: perfection. Mindy was smart. Mindy was artistic. Mindy could do no wrong. How do you brush off a kid who thinks that about you?

So Mindy had found the easiest path: to behave most of the time as if Daniella just weren't there. When she felt like talking to the younger girl, she did. The rest of the time, as she read or put together her birthday collage for Shraga or rambled around the hotel looking for objects to add to it, she simply, and not unkindly, ignored her. Daniella didn't seem to mind at all.

Mindy was planning to put a few more touches on the collage tonight, after dinner. She had to do it secretly, in the room she shared with Daniella, so that Shraga wouldn't stumble across his birthday present before it was ready.

She was an orderly girl who liked to make schedules for herself. She was pleased with her schedule for this evening. After dinner, maybe she'd visit the game room again with the others — that had been fun last night. Then to her room, to work on the collage. And after *that* (her face lit up as she remembered) there was the brand-new book she'd taken out of the library just before they'd come, and packed into her suitcase. She couldn't imagine a better way to wind up her first full day at the Lake View Hotel than to curl up in one of the big hotel beds with a good book.

The schedule was a good one. Unfortunately, it would not be of much use to her that night. Out of all the things Mindy was planning for that evening, only one of them — the visit to the game room — would actually take place. The peaceful read by the light of her bedside lamp was not to be. A peaceful *anything* was not to be that night — for any of them.

There was one person sitting down to dinner with the others who held the key to that evening's events. *He* knew what the next step would be — or at least, what he was planning for it to be. Part of him was hoping it would come off successfully, while another part was praying just as hard that somehow, some way, he would fail. It's a strange feeling to wish for your own efforts to fail. But then, he'd been living in a strange sort of half-dream ever since he'd received that first message, weeks ago, from the sinister "Mr. Big."

The small, handwritten note he'd found waiting for him first thing that morning he'd thrown away in the woods, hoping it was the last he would hear until the deed was actually done. But just half an hour ago, when he'd checked his computer for electronic mail before locking up, the message had shown up on the screen.

This last message came at five o'clock — at the precise time, if he could have but known it, that little Zevy's wristwatch was beeping the hour in the hotel room, as the Morgenstern and Katz families were introduced for the first time to the awesome potential of "Little Nicky." He'd been thinking vaguely about going in to dinner (though he was so nervous he was sure he wouldn't be able to force down a single bite), when the words had flashed onto his e-mail board. He read them, and then read them again, his eyes widening in an apprehension that only seemed to grow stronger with each passing second.

The message had read simply: *Don't fail me.*

It was signed, *Mr. Big.*

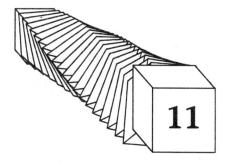

What Dr. Katz Found

Dinner proceeded as it had the night before, except that the packaged food was, if possible, even worse. And the complaints even louder.

"Are these supposed to be potatoes?" Ari asked, prodding something round and lumpy with his fork. "Looks more like an old tennis ball to me."

"This cutlet looks exactly like a sole," Mindy announced.

"As in fish?" asked Shraga.

"No," sighed Mindy. "As in shoe."

Zevy giggled. "And these peas," he said, "taste like —"

"That'll be enough of that, kids," Mrs. Katz said, a trifle wearily. She gazed without enthusiasm at her own dinner. "We have to speak respectfully of the food we eat."

"What about the food we *don't* eat?" Pinny

grumbled. But he said it under his breath.

Shai, sitting next to Pinny, was the only one who caught the remark. He stifled a laugh. These American kids were so funny. He looked at his plate. The gravy looked like...mud? Not so hilarious, but maybe worth a try. He glanced shyly at the Americans beside him, but the topic had already changed.

"Boys, an interesting point occurred to me about the *gemara* we learned this morning," Dr. Morgenstern said. He launched into a discussion that — whether by accident or design — served to distract Shraga and Pinny, at least, from the disappointing meal. Ari listened in. Dr. Katz, still struggling valiantly to dissect his cutlet (he was hungry!) put in a word now and then. The discussion grew very lively. Pretty soon, Pinny and Shraga were matching wits, while their fathers and mothers listened with pleasure, *shepping nachas*. True, the boys were behaving more like a couple of people fighting a duel than a pair of *chevrusos*, but it was a step in the right direction. If they were talking together in Torah, could friendship be too far behind?

At the next table, Niki Gorodnik was watching. He watched the way Shraga and Pinny and their fathers waved their arms and raised their voices as they tried to pin down a point. His own father was only a distant memory to him, having died when Nikolai was just a baby. There was a picture of him on his mother's dresser at home, but it might as well have been the picture of a stranger. What were those four talking about so eagerly? He strained to catch a word or two, but what he did manage to overhear made no sense to him. Either his English was not as good as he'd thought, or else they were speaking another language. It was a mixture of the two, he decided finally.

His mother, Natasha, followed the direction of his gaze. "Nervous?" she murmured. She was thinking, he knew, about he apology he'd promised to make right after dinner. He nodded briefly. He still wasn't feeling very comfortable with his mother, after her stunning news. In fact, he wasn't feeling very comfortable with himself! His classmates back in Russia often taunted Jews — what would they say if they knew that he was one? Dared he tell them?

"If you're not having any dessert," a voice said in his ear, "I'll be glad to take it off your hands." The voice spoke Russian. It was Alexei Pim.

"Oh, sure," Nikolai said, sitting back and giving up any pretence of eating. "Take it, if you want."

"I already had my father's, too," Alexei said happily. "He got some mousse on his tie and had to go wash it off." Sure enough, Dr. Pim's seat was empty.

"Everything all right, ladies and gentlemen?" The smooth tones of the hotel manager interrupted the table talk. Mr. Manicotti, a dapper man with slim white hands that waved graciously in the air whenever he spoke, was making his rounds.

"Oh, just lovely," Natasha said, with a smile.

"Especially the steak." She inclined her head to include her fellow diners. "I speak for all of us — no?"

Murmurs of agreement were heard around the table. "In the name of my father and I," Alexei said, with mock-solemnity, "I thank you for a wonderful meal."

"*And* three desserts," Nikolai added in a stage whisper. The words came out louder than he'd intended them to. He was startled to hear the hearty laughter. The success of his little joke made him feel better than he had since he'd sat down to dinner. He glanced again at the next table, where Mr. Manicotti had glided over to say his piece. Maybe the evening would turn out to be a good one after all...

A sudden flash made the lights in the big dining room flicker momentarily and then come on again. Immediately afterward came a deep and ominous rumble of thunder. Rain began to fall past the big windows in a hard steady stream. Drops spattered sharply against the window sills, like bullets. A real summer storm had sprung up, seemingly out of nowhere. The falling dusk had masked the buildup of clouds coming in from the north.

"Boy, that was sudden, wasn't it?" Pinny blinked, drawn abruptly out of his world of Gemara and back into the here-and-now.

"I'll say," Ari said fervently. "My heart nearly jumped out of my skin!" He pressed a dramatic hand to the regions of his shirt where that organ presumably lay. "Honest, I can still feel it beating."

"I should hope so," his mother said briskly. "Finish up, kids, and *bentch*. We don't want to be stuck here if there's a power blackout."

"Where *do* we want to be stuck, Ima?" little Zevy asked. But his mother had started *bentching* and didn't answer.

Dr. Katz had been the only one to notice the faint rumble of thunder that had preceded the onset of the storm. He had quickly *bentched* before the others. Now he rose to his feet, with a smile for his wife and a quick word to Dr. Morgenstern.

"Well, this is not exactly a dinner worth lingering over. I think I'll go back to the lab."

"What for, Abba?" asked Daniella. "And can I have your dessert?"

Dr. Katz eyed with distaste the canned pineapple rings in their thick syrup. "By all means, Daniella. And hearty appetite."

"Why are you going to the lab, Abba?" Ari asked, as his sister dug into the pineapple with every appearance of pleasure.

"To unplug the computer. You know what can happen in these thunderstorms."

"What?" Pinny asked, interested. But he was speaking to his father's back. Dr. Katz was already hurrying through the dining room to the big doors still guarded by Tom, the F.B.I. man.

"Power surges," explained Shraga's father. "If the electricity goes off and then on again, it can cause a big surge of power to the computer. That's not a very healthy thing to happen to it. Your father's gone to unplug the computer before that can happen."

"Why doesn't he do that at home?" Ari wondered. "At least, I don't think I've ever seen him do it."

"At home you probably have something called a surge protector," Dr. Morgenstern told him. "It's a little gadget you can plug into the wall to keep your computer from being damaged."

The air seemed chillier, maybe because of the rain pounding noisily to the ground all around the hotel. People were beginning to think about sweaters and warm socks. Mrs. Katz and Mrs. Morgenstern, eyeing their combined broods, had thoughts along the same line. Only Vivi, the Morgenstern baby, had come equipped with a light jacket in pale pink.

"Hurry up and *bentch* already, kids," Shraga's mother urged. She passed out small pocket *bentchers* to those who could read and bent to recite the grace after meals with Ruchie. Mrs. Katz did the same with Zevy. Vivi was busily plucking tiny green peas out of the unidentifiable mush on her plate. Outside, the lightning flashed and the thunder thudded on with a heavy, dread beat.

Dr. Katz hurried down the corridor toward the labs. He didn't know why he felt so nervous tonight. Maybe it was the presentation he was due to be giving shortly. He always got a little jittery before a speech.

"Face it," he thought with a laugh. "A public speaker I'm not!"

He just wanted to reassure himself that all his equipment was in order. He'd unplug the computer and then go upstairs to rest for a half-hour or so, before it was time to begin setting up for their presentation. The scientists were going to assemble in the dining room — cleared of the remains of dinner, of course — at seven o'clock sharp.

He passed the doors of his fellow physicists' labs. Marcus Fowley... Manfred Isingard... Magda Brenner. Through the window at the end of the corridor he caught a glimpse of the drive sweeping up to the hotel. There was no sign of either Wilson or Gilbraith, the agents in charge out there. They must be sheltering from the rain, he thought vaguely.

Natasha Gorodnik... Ilya Pim... Here he was — his and Dr. Morgenstern's lab. He pulled out his electronic card and let himself in, blinking in the bright light. He frowned. Something was wrong — not as it should be. Then he had it. The light! He was sure he'd switched it off before he'd left earlier. Or at least, he was almost sure...

With an uneasy shrug, Dr. Katz went over to his computer and pulled the plug. As he did, his eye fell on the counter close by, where he'd left Little Nicky.

The counter was empty.

His heart stood still. Gone! Little Nicky had disappeared — vanished into thin air!

For a long, long moment, Dr. Katz remained frozen in place. It was as if his mind, his body, his entire being, had turned into a lump of wood or stone. He couldn't think or feel. Then, slowly, the thoughts came. Unbelievable as it seemed, someone had actually made away with the prototype of the secret device he and his partner had guarded so carefully and so long.

Frantically, he began to claw through the equipment on the counter, hoping against hope that the device was there, shoved back against the other things — though he clearly recalled placing it exactly where it should have been. There was a blank space there now, and no Little Nicky to be seen anywhere else on the counter.

When he was absolutely sure that Little Nicky was gone, he wheeled around, eyes wild. He must find his partner, David Morgenstern. Then the F.B.I. people...must tell them at once — institute a hotel-wide search! Maybe the culprit hadn't gotten away yet. It might still be possible to catch him red-handed, with the device in his possession.

There was no time to speculate on just who that mysterious somebody might be. There'd be time for that later. Dr. Katz was at the door of the lab and fumbling in his pocket for the electronic card to lock it, when another thought struck him. The diskette! Without the red diskette, the black box would not be of much use to its robbers. With shaking fingers he flipped through his box of diskettes. But long before he'd gone through the whole pile, his eye had already seen what his heart refused to believe: there was no bright red diskette among them. The passwords and the rest of the crucial information, like the device, were in the hands of the enemy.

Dr. Katz squeezed his eyes tightly shut. This was like a nightmare — his worst dreams come horribly true. He murmured a snatch of prayer to Hashem: "Help me, please! Help me find the person who did this. And let the device be safe. Don't let it fall into the wrong hands..."

But he was all too afraid that his prayer had come too late. It looked like the deadly black box had already fallen into evil hands. Pale as a sheet, Dr. Katz rushed back out of the lab and straight back to the dining room to raise the alarm.

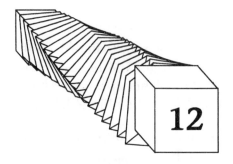

The Search

The box was heavier than he'd expected.

Except for the tiny flashing lights and digital displays cunningly worked into one side, it looked like a lightweight child's toy. But the instant he hefted it and felt the solid metal beneath his fingers, he knew it was clearly no plastic plaything. Far from it! He shuddered to think of all the devastation he could wreak with a twist of one of those knobs, or a push of a button. Not for me, he thought. I'll just hand it over, as ordered — and I'll be out of it. Free and clear...

Tucking the weapon under one arm, he seized the precious red diskette with the other. For another moment he stood riveted to the spot, staring in a kind of wonder at the two objects he held. He'd done it! After all the sleepless nights, the agonizing, and the deciding, it was hard to believe that the deed was actually done. He wasn't sure how he felt about it, but there was no time now to figure it out. The first thing to do was to get the box and the diskette up to his room. Only when it was well-hidden from prying eyes would he be able to breathe easily again.

Because it was the dinner hour, the big lobby was all but deserted. Outside, it began to rain — a hard, steady summer rain, punctuated by startling booms of thunder and vivid streaks of lightning. With one ear he listened to the music of the thunderstorm, while the other was alert for sounds of pursuit. So far, there were none. And how could there be? Everyone was in the dining room, little suspecting that underneath their very noses the theft of the century had just taken place!

He was nearing the elevator bank when a particularly bright flash of lightning stopped him in his tracks. The lobby lights flickered a little, and then held steady. He halted at the elevator, uncertain. Dared he risk it? His room was on the seventh floor — a long, tiring walk up, especially with the black box weighing him down. On the other hand, what if there was a power failure while he was riding up? The elevator would be stuck between floors, with him and his secret burden trapped inside. Horrified, he pictured the rescue mission. That's what they'd find when they managed to get him out — him, *and* his burden...

It was a risk he was not prepared to take.

Turning away from the elevators, he began retracing his steps to the staircase. He tried to walk casually, but his heart was beating so loudly in his own ears that it seemed incredible the whole hotel could not hear it. His eyes darted nervously toward the reception desk, where a couple of bored girls manned the phones. No one was looking in his direction. Heartened, he quickened his pace. Then — realizing that he was practically running, and that was certainly *not* very inconspicuous — slowed down again. Very soon now, he'd be safe in the haven of his own room. The stairs were ahead, just past the big doors leading to the dining room...

Suddenly, a figure shot out of the back corridor, where the labs were. It was the very same corridor the man with the black box had emerged from just minutes ago. Frightened, he pressed himself against one of the ornate pillars that decorated the lobby. The figure shot right past without seeing him, intent on reaching the dining room with all possible speed. With his ginger hair and yarmulka, he was easily recognizable. It was Dr. Katz.

The man with the box hesitated. He knew he should get out of the area as fast as humanly possible, but curiosity overcame him. Cautiously, he inched a little closer to the dining room doors. He could see Dr. Katz, just inside the door, waving his arms in great excitement as he spoke to Tom Morrison, F.B.I.

"It's gone, I tell you!" Every trace of Dr. Katz's calm good humor had vanished like the black box. "The box — the device! The secret invention — gone!"

Tom blinked at him as if this were too shocking to take in all at once. "Y-you mean, Little Nicky?"

"That's exactly what I mean! You've got to call your men and institute a search immediately. Find out if anyone drove away from the hotel in the past hour. The person who took it could not have gone very far. For all we know, he could even still be here, in the hotel." Then as Tom Morrison still stood unmoving, Dr. Katz raised his voice. "Hurry, man! It may not be too late!"

The shout seemed to snap the Special Agent out of his trance. Whipping his radio out of its holder on his belt, he spoke softly and urgently.

"Sandy — Sam! Do you read me?"

The man with the box did not wait to hear more. While Dr. Katz and the F.B.I. man were intent on the radio, he slipped away from the pillar and walked, very quickly, away from the dining room.

He had only seconds in which to decide his next step. Too late now to try for his room. Already the agents in front of the hotel would be dashing through the rain, making straight for the front doors. He would be in full sight the instant they set foot inside the lobby.

The elevator? Still too risky. The stairs? Risky, too. Imagine if he met even a single chambermaid or bellboy on his way. Later questioning — and there would be questioning, and a lot of it, he knew that — would bring to light the fact that, instead of eating his dinner like his fellow scientists and their families, he'd been roaming the hotel this evening, a strange lumpy bundle under his arm. No, not the stairs.

His throat felt tight and a cold sweat stood out on his forehead. Where? Where? His whole being clamored with the question. Then, just as the sandy-haired Special Agent and his partner with the broad shoulders came dripping through the front hotel door at a furious pace, the man with the box spied an open door to the right of the dining room. A sign on the door read GAME ROOM.

He didn't stop to think. There was no time for thought any more, no time for anything except a breakneck dash into the empty room, past the silent video monitors and computers and games and...

Wait! The computers — that was it! With trembling fingers he took the red diskette and slipped it into a stack of computer game diskettes lying beside the monitors. It would be safe there, anonymous in its pile. He'd return for it later.

He turned his attention to the bigger problem: the box. He couldn't just leave it here like the diskette. It was too big. It would be noticed instantly, and he couldn't risk having one of the kids pick it up and start experimenting. Not with that deadly device!

He stepped back to the game room door and peeked out. A crowd had gathered just inside the doors of the dining room. Some of the guests had been attracted by the noise of Dr. Katz's entrance, and had watched him speaking agitatedly to the F.B.I. man they were used to seeing guarding the doors as they ate. Then, to make matters even more dramatic, the other two Special Agents had burst in, flushed and breathing hard. With all four of them conferring in low, urgent voices, the sight was too much for the diners' curiosity. First in ones and twos and then in droves they left their tables to find out what was going on. A babble of questions rose into the air.

The man with the box watched them, heart thudding. He tried to calm his panic long enough to formulate a plan. His crime had been discovered much earlier than he'd ever expected. How could he have known Dr. Katz would take it into his head to visit his lab before dinner was over? There was no time to hide the thing properly. He must dispose of the weapon before it could be traced back to him — and quickly. There was no other choice.

With an expression of casual unconcern, the man slipped into the crowd, the black box making a big clumsy lump under his jacket. No matter — no one was paying any attention to him. They were riveted to the group at the door, and the appalling news Dr. Katz had brought.

The man took a deep breath and began to slip past the edges of the crowd. He made for the first empty table he saw. A small pink windbreaker lay abandoned on a chair. In less time than it takes to write the words, the windbreaker was no longer alone. It had company — black, sinister company.

"Okay, everybody, step back now! Step back!"
Tom Morrison had recovered his air of authority
and was gesturing forcefully at the crowd. One of
his hands still held the radio he'd used to summon
his fellow agents. "You'll hear everything in a minute. In fact, we'd like to request that everyone stay
right here in this room until we complete our
investigation. If you'll just step back a little..."

Reluctantly, the crowd of physicists, wives,
children, and assorted other guests fell back.

"Abba! What's going on?" Pinny Katz exclaimed.
He'd pushed forward with the others to see what
all the excitement was about. Now, for the first
time, he saw with surprise that his own father was
in the thick of it. He wished his mother hadn't left
the dining room with Mrs. Morgenstern and the
little ones just before all this had happened. "What
happened?"

"Sssh. Later, Pinny." Dr. Katz could hardly concentrate on anything except the vision of the black
box and what an unscrupulous man or group had
the power to do with it. Where was the device right
now, this very minute?

"We have to find him — the man who took it!"
he said to Tom for perhaps the dozenth time. "You
have no idea what it could mean for all of us — for
the world — if we don't recover that thing, and
quickly."

"I have a pretty good idea, Doctor," Tom Morrison replied grimly. "But running wild after some

unknown person or persons won't do any of us any good. We have to hear the whole story first. And the hotel must be searched for clues." He frowned, considering. "I may have to radio for reinforcements."

Dr. Katz nodded, but he was seething with impatience. There was a time for careful, plodding detective work — and time for action! In his opinion, this was the time for the latter.

Dr. Morgenstern, pushing his way to his partner's side, agreed.

"There's not a second to waste! Why, a child could operate that device! If the wrong —"

"They took the diskette, too, David," Dr. Katz told him in an undertone.

Dr. Morgenstern paled. "Then — they have the passwords, too. They have everything... Oh, no — it's worse than I thought." He turned anguished eyes on Dr. Katz. "What do we do now?"

"The first thing to do," Tom stated, "is to instigate a hotel-wide search for the thing. We —"

"Two things," Dr. Katz interrupted. "Two things were taken. The device itself, and a diskette containing the passwords to make it work."

Tom looked thoughtful. "That makes our job harder. The places where a bulky box might be hidden are limited. The diskette, on the other hand, could easily be carried away on someone's person." He turned back to the tense, restless crowd. "Calm down, please, folks. We've got the situation under control."

"But what *is* the situation?" The white-haired Hungarian professor, Magda Brenner, spoke in a low but resonant voice. "What exactly has happened, officer?"

In a few clear, succinct sentences, Tom outlined the crisis. There was a stir of excitement at his words, tinged with panic. He commanded them again to stay calm.

"I'm afraid we're going have to ask you to turn out your pockets for us. A valuable diskette has been stolen, along with the prototype of a new invention that Drs. Katz and Morgenstern were to talk about to you this evening." He gave a wry smile. "Lecture's postponed, I'm afraid."

There was a nervous titter at this sally. Shraga, at the edge of the crowd, clenched his fists. How could anyone laugh at a moment like this?

Then again, the others didn't know what he knew about Little Nicky. They couldn't see in their minds' eye, the way he could, buildings blowing sky-high at the press of a button a hundred miles away... He closed his eyes.

"Everyone back to your own places, please," Tom Morrison ordered. "We'll do a table-to-table search."

Obediently, like a flock of bewildered sheep, the physicists and their families shuffled back to their tables. As if in a dream, Shraga watched them. He'd begun to put some of the scientists' faces together with the names he'd read on various lab doors. The wiry, redheaded Englishman was Dr. Richard

Fowley. Beside him, tall and very patrician-looking with his long jaw and brushed-back, gray hair was the Norwegian, Dr. Manfred Isingard. Magda Brenner — the diminutive, white-haired Hungarian physicist, glared at the Special Agents with snapping black eyes.

"Shragie, what's going to happen?" It was Mindy, looking very young and scared. "Who took Little Nicky?"

Shraga shook his head. Nearby, Ari and Pinny had their heads together and were talking very quietly. Slowly, Mindy took her seat. Zevy climbed back into his own chair, beside his mother's empty one. On his other side was the empty chair where Vivi Morgenstern had sat just a short time ago.

Only it wasn't empty. She'd left something behind. A pink windbreaker. With his mind on all the excitement, the little boy reached absently for the jacket. He'd bring it upstairs later; his mother would be proud of him for returning it.

The Special Agents began their search. They were polite but thorough. The sandy-haired agent, Ed ("Sandy") Wilson, started at the table nearest the door. Sam Gilbraith, began near the kitchen entrance. Tom Morrison started in the center, at the table occupied by Nikolai and Alexei. He looked very grim. Not far away, at the next table, Dr. Katz and Dr. Morgenstern conferred together in low, worried voices. Ari, Pinny, Shraga, Chaim, Mindy, and Daniella gazed at their fathers with big eyes. Who, they each wondered, had stolen the invention? And — even more important — what would they do with it now that they'd got it?

Dr. and Mrs. Drucker offer a word of quiet sympathy, and then, like the children, lapsed into silence. As for Shai, he was afire with curiosity. All the rapid talk in English had passed over him without giving him a true picture of the problem. Something was missing — that much was clear. But what was "it" exactly? And why did it cause everyone to sit there with such long faces? He longed to ask, but sensed that this was not the right moment.

Gradually, as one scientist after another submitted to having pockets and purses checked for the missing red diskette, the talk subsided all through the big dining room. Every pair of eyes followed the progress of the search.

It was into this near-silence that, without warning, Zevy Katz's young voice rang out, over-loud in the stillness. Heads turned sharply.

"Look at this, Abba. Look what I found, right under Vivi's jacket. Is this the box they're all looking for?"

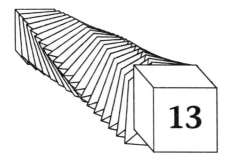

13

The Name of the Game

Sandy and Sam, the F.B.I. men, came toward Zevy at a run, weaving among the tables and chairs and elbows and feet in their way. They were followed — at a more leisurely, but no less determined, pace — by their superior, Tom Morrison. In a very short time they were skidding to a halt in front of Zevy, who was still clutching the black box and gazing up at the Special Agents with big, bewildered eyes.

"Can I see that?" Tom Morrison held out a hand for the device. As Zevy hesitated, he snapped, "Now!"

The little boy glanced questioningly at his father. He looked scared.

"Just a minute, Mr. Morrison," Dr. Katz said

sharply. "No need to frighten him." He nodded at Zevy and said, gently, "Give it to the F.B.I. man, Zevy. You're a good boy for finding it."

"Is it really Little Nicky?" Mindy Morgenstern asked in an awed whisper.

"It is," her father answered calmly. He watched as Tom gingerly inspected the box. "Well, Mr. Morrison?" he said. "All's well that end's well, eh?"

"I wouldn't say it's ended yet, David," his partner said strongly. "The diskette's still missing. And don't we want to find out who took them in the first place?"

"Exactly," Tom agreed. "The culprit must be tracked down and made to pay for his crime." He sounded pleased at the prospect. The long, tedious hours he'd spent guarding a group of international scientists as they worked, slept, ate, and played, had clearly whet his appetite for some real action. He finished his inspection of the dangerous box, handling it as if it might explode in his face at any moment. It was more likely, Pinny thought grimly, to explode in someone else's face — miles and miles from here. But, on the other hand, hadn't his father said that without the passwords the device was unusable?

Tom Morrison seemed almost to read his thoughts. "Is that diskette really necessary?" he asked the two men who had put Little Nicky together. "What, for instance, would happen if I were to turn this little knob?" He indicated one of the black buttons protruding from the box's sleek side.

"Nothing," Dr. Morgenstern answered promptly, "without inputting the passwords first. The passwords act as a sort of safety catch — like the kind guns have. Without them, the computer chip inside the box won't be activated, and neither will the Tesla coil... It's hard to give all the technical details on one foot like this." It was also impossible for him to tell Tom everything he knew about that valuable diskette. He spread his hands in a rueful gesture. "We were supposed to do that this evening."

"Then our job," said Tom, "is to find that diskette — pronto!" To his men he said, "Sandy, Sam, carry on with the search. I'll continue the questioning here."

But Pinny had a question of his own. "Daddy," he said urgently to his father, "how do you suppose Little Nicky got here, to our table?"

"Exactly," said Tom, "what I was about to ask." He eyed Dr. Katz, then Dr. Morgenstern. "Well?" His voice held a new, speculative note.

The scientists sat up straighter. Dr. Katz asked incredulously, "Are you implying that *we* had anything to do with the theft?"

"Shmulie — Mr. Morrison," Dr. Morgenstern broke in quickly. "I don't think the children need to be here now. Do you?" His eyes appealed to the Special Agent.

Tom hesitated. "I suppose it would be all right for them to leave the dining room. They can stay somewhere close at hand — say, the game room —

in case we need them. But first, please turn out your pockets, kids."

"Them, too?" Dr. Katz asked.

"Afraid so. We've got to make sure that diskette doesn't leave the hotel. That means searching everyone who had access to it — including the kids."

Shraga felt vaguely ashamed as he showed the F.B.I. man the insides of his pockets, as though he were some small-time pickpocket under suspicion. At the sight of his long face, Tom winked. "Just a formality," he explained. The cold, almost suspicious note a moment earlier might never have been there. It was the old, genial Tom again — only now, with a purpose. He had a job to do.

The Special Agent turned to Ari. "Next?"

Soon, the search completed, Tom waved the kids off. "Out you go, then. Don't wander too far away now."

"We won't," Daniella assured him. The older kids were silent as they trooped away from their table, past the pair of Special Agents continuing their search for the red diskette, and out through the dining room doors. Pinny walked with his head down, looking thoughtful.

Shraga looked worried.

As for Ari, he looked good and mad.

"What kind of nerve does that Tom have, accusing Abba and Dr. Morgenstern of stealing their own invention!" Ari's face was dangerously red.

"He didn't do that, exactly," Pinny said. "He was

just wondering how the thing ended up at our table."

"How *did* it end up there?" Shraga wondered aloud, as the boys, trailed by their younger sisters, approached the game room.

"Please," said Shai Gilboa. "What is in that box?"

Shraga turned around, surprised. He'd nearly forgotten the Israeli boy was with them. Was it only this morning that his biggest problem had been figuring out a way to strike up a friendship with Shai?

"It's a secret invention," Shraga explained. "Well, not so secret anymore, I guess. It was stolen today."

"Stolen? Then why was it at our table?"

Shraga sighed. "The sixty-four-thousand dollar question."

At the other boy's look of incomprehension, he added, "We don't know either, Shai. It's a mystery."

"It's simple!" Pinny declared. "Whoever stole it left it there. Obviously."

"It's not that obvious to me," Ari said in exasperation. "Why in the world would a guy go to the trouble to steal something — only to leave it back with the people he stole it from!"

Looked at that way, the thing didn't seem to make much sense. They'd reached the game room by now. It was empty, its garish colorful playthings waiting patiently for the children. Dispiritedly, they entered the room. They had never felt less like playing in their lives.

As the search in the dining room progressed from table to table, more children were freed to leave. Soon, table by table, the adults were permitted to follow them out. Alexei's father, Ilya Pim, told his son briefly, in Russian, to go play. He also told him not to worry; something had been lost but would soon, he was sure, be found by the efficient American F.B.I. Nikolai's mother, Natasha Gorodnik, also waved her son off.

"Go enjoy yourself, my son. This is no business for children." There was a worried look in her fine gray eyes as they met Ilya Pim's. This sinister event could well set off an international incident. After all, it hadn't been so long ago that Russia and the United States were mortal enemies. Even now, they were like a pair of cautious dancers, circling each other warily but not quite clasping each other's hands in friendship. This international conference was supposed to be another small step in cementing the relationship between East and West. Would it all backfire now — all because of a little black box and a red computer diskette?

Alexei and Nikolai discussed the theft as they walked slowly in the direction of the game room. Neither one was exactly sure what had been stolen, except that it had something to do with the innocent-looking box the F.B.I. man, Tom, had held under his arm. "Well, they have it back now," Alexei shrugged. "So what's all the fuss about?"

Nikolai shrugged, too. He didn't know any more

than Alexei. But as he approached the game room, he realized that he had a difficult moment coming up. It was impossible to put it off any longer. He still had his apology to make. He would do it — now.

He stood in the doorway and surveyed the room. Ari, Pinny, and Shraga were discussing something heatedly in one corner, with Shai Gilboa hovering at the edges of their little group, trying hard to follow what they were saying. At the miniature basketball game, Chaim was halfheartedly tossing small orange balls at a plastic hoop. Mindy and Daniella were trying their hands — not very successfully — at a difficult video game. Alexei Pim made a beeline for a computer and reached for the box of diskettes to find a game he could play.

Nikolai took a deep breath and went straight over to where Shraga and Pinny stood. "Excuse me?"

They were so deep in talk that they didn't hear him. He raised his voice slightly. "Excuse me!"

This time, Shraga did hear. He turned. "Oh. Hi there, Niki. I mean, Nikolai."

The other boy included Pinny in his shy smile. "Niki is okay. I like it. It sounds — American."

"That's okay, then," Pinny said lamely.

There was an awkward silence. Then, in a rush, Niki said, "I wanted to tell you that I am sorry for — for what I said before."

"Don't mention it," Shraga said quickly.

"It's okay," Pinny said, just as fast.

"No, it was wrong," Niki insisted. "And I apologize." He glanced uneasily over his shoulder to where Alexei was fiddling with the computer. "I didn't know it this morning, but...but... Well, it seems I am Jewish also. So it was doubly stupid of me to say what I did."

"Forget it," Shraga said warmly. "We already have."

"That's right," agreed Pinny.

Niki heaved a sigh of relief. "Thank you." He hesitated. "Do you mind telling me what happened just now, with that black box?"

"It was stolen," Shraga said. He looked worried again.

"And then found again," Ari put in, scowling mightily.

"Except the diskette," added Pinny.

"And we don't know who did it, or why they returned it," Shraga ended on a sigh. "That's the story, in a nutshell. Doesn't seem to make much sense, but there it is."

"The real question now," Ari said, "is — *where is that red diskette?*"

There were many other people in the Lake View Hotel who were wondering that very same thing. The physicists wondered. Dr. Katz and Dr. Morgenstern wondered. The F.B.I. men wondered. In the whole place, only one person knew where the diskette was — but he could not get close enough to take it.

Passing the entrance to the game room, he paused to look in for an instant — but only for an instant. It would be fatal to risk attracting any untoward attention now. To the casual eye, he was merely loitering for an idle moment, watching some children at play. In reality, however, his intent was anything but idle. He had a mission to carry out.

The box itself — the weapon he'd been instructed to steal — was out of his hands now. Because Dr. Katz had raised the alarm earlier than expected, he'd been forced to abandon the prototype in the dining room. The F.B.I. man, Tom Morrison, had it now. It had been a stroke of genius —well, to be honest, more a matter of luck, actually — that the box had been left at that particular table. It had diverted suspicion towards the Jewish scientists themselves. Let the lawmen try and sort that one out! Meanwhile, he'd do his best to get hold of the diskette again, and the invaluable passwords that were the key to a weapon of more deadly significance than the world had seen for a long time... The man closed his eyes. For an instant, he fought back an urge to run away — to escape this horror.

Then he opened his eyes again. It had to be done. He'd thrashed it all out over and over, back home, and here at the hotel. He'd made his decision, and he would stick to it. The job was only half-finished now. It was up to him to see it through to the bitter end.

Elaborately casual, he glanced back into the

room. What he saw made his heart drop, with a thud he could almost hear. Someone — from the back it looked like one of the Russian boys — was sitting at the computer and rifling through the very box where he'd stashed the red diskette!

It took every ounce of willpower he had to force himself away from the door. Molding his steps into a leisurely saunter, the man walked back into the thickening crowd in the lobby. A few minutes passed — agonizing minutes of seemingly aimless wandering, through the glass-and-marble lobby and along past the dining room, until he returned once more to the game room door. He came just in time to see an interesting drama taking place at the computer.

Alexei, having discovered an unusual-looking red diskette in the box, had inserted it into the computer to see what games it might hold. He waited and waited, but nothing appeared on his monitor except a long, boring line of letters and numbers. He tried pressing different buttons on the keyboard — to no avail. The computer screen refused to produce a game to entertain and amuse him. He pulled it out.

"What game is this?" he asked aloud, to no one in particular. Chaim, standing nearby with his basketball, heard the question but as it was in Russian it meant nothing to him. Alexei turned it over. "There's no name."

With a shrug, he tossed the red diskette into a

wastepaper basket nearby.

A little girl with round blue eyes saw him do it. She came over, hands tucked in the oversized pockets of her small flared skirt.

"Why'd you throw that away?" Daniella Katz asked. "That's a good diskette — and it's a pretty color, too."

"No, it's not," Alexei told her over his shoulder, as he reached for another computer game. "There's something wrong with it. When you put it in, nothing happens. Must be defective." He turned back to his monitor.

The man positioned just outside the game room door was as rigid as the wooden frame of the doorway he stood in. For a moment frozen in time, he stared at the wastepaper basket that now housed the precious diskette. Then, coming alert again, he took careful note of the position of the basket and passed on his way.

The diskette was safe now. Later, when all of those kids had wandered sleepily up to their beds — that was when he would return for the treasure, the red diskette. That was when this whole nightmare would finally end.

This time, as he strolled away, his steps were genuinely casual. For now, he was in no rush at all.

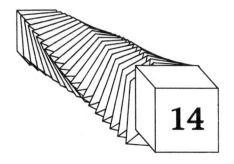

Suspicion

In the dining room, Tom Morrison tilted his chair back. After the search for the missing diskette failed to produce results, he'd dismissed all the wives and children and kept back only some of the scientists — specifically, those whose labs shared the corridor with the lab from which the weapon prototype had been stolen.

The Hungarian physicist Magda Brenner of the white hair and snapping black eyes was there, and restless, redheaded Richard Fowley from England, and the patrician, silver-haired Norwegian, Manfred Isingard, tight-lipped now and unsmiling. Ilya Pim and Natasha Gorodnik, the Russians, were asked to stay, as well as Dr. Drucker from Israel and, of course, the two Jewish physicists from New York.

It was a somber group.

"Let's go over it one more time," Tom said patiently. A rumble of thunder from the receding storm punctuated his words. The rest of the dining room was vast and quiet. Even the waiters had been asked to go. "What time did you leave your lab for dinner, Dr. Katz?"

"At six. My lab partner, Dr. Morgenstern, had already gone upstairs to wash up. I stayed behind to prepare for the presentation that was scheduled for this evening." He anticipated the Special Agent's next question. "I must have entered the dining room at — oh, six-fifteen or so."

"What made you leave again so soon?"

Dr. Katz grimaced wryly. "The food, for one thing. It was, to put it mildly, not very appetizing. Also, the thunderstorm was making me uneasy. I was worried about a power outage and what it might do to my computer. I decided to skip dessert and go back to the lab to unplug it."

Tom nodded and made a note in his pad. "Okay, we know the rest. The question is —" his glance swept the group "— who, besides you ladies and gentlemen, has access to that particular corridor?"

"Everyone!" Dr. Morgenstern burst out. "There's a side door at the end of the hall, leading out onto the grounds. Anyone could have slipped inside while we were at dinner, without being seen."

Magda shook her head. "It is not likely," she declared. "How would an outsider know that the labs were unoccupied at that hour? Everyone knows that a scientist does not live on his stomach alone. Any one of us might have been working through dinner."

"Besides," added Manfred Isingard, addressing Tom Morrison, "you had your two men patrolling the grounds, didn't you? Surely it would be too risky for an outsider to try to get past them."

"There are some risks a determined man would consider acceptable," the F.B.I. man returned acidly. "Now —"

"What I want to know," Richard Fowley interrupted, in his clipped British accent, "is how the culprit entered the lab? We're the only ones who were issued those electronic cards." He ran a hand through his rumpled red curls, mussing them even further.

"Give me an old-fashioned key anytime," muttered Magda.

Tom turned slowly to the Jewish scientists. "We always come back to that, don't we? Who had access to the lab? Who had the card that would allow him in? Who knew exactly what to look for — and what to take?"

"Mr. Morrison." Dr. Morgenstern sat up straight and spoke very clearly. "You seem to find that the evidence, such as it is, implicates Dr. Katz and me. But does that make any sense? We've certainly had ample opportunity to take Little Nicky — er, the device — at any time these past two years. Why pick this time, this conference, to make away with it?"

"And why should we do it in the first place?" Dr.

Katz exploded angrily.

Tom gave them a considering look. "People can be tempted," he said softly. "Offered enough money, anyone can break."

"Not us!" Now Dr. Morgenstern was as furious now as his friend. "We worked on that thing for two years and more! We're absolutely loyal to our firm —"

"And to the United States?" Tom broke in to ask.

"Eh? What do you mean by that?"

"No offence, Doctor. But we all know that a man might have — shall we say, divided loyalties? And who more so than, pardon me, a Jew?" He turned from the New Yorkers to fix Dr. Drucker with a hard stare. "There are three of you here, in fact, who count Israel as your own. Who's to say what a man might not do for his homeland?"

"Each of us," Magda Brenner stated, her black eyes glinting with proud fire, "is loyal to our own country. Does that mean we bear any malice towards the United States?"

"That's right!" The Englishman, Fowley, nodded in vigorous assent.

"Come now, Mr. Morrison," Dr. Isingard said in a calm, almost bored voice. "Don't you think you're looking for bogeymen in the closet? There's no evidence to implicate any of these men."

Dr. Katz inclined his head in gratitude to Dr. Isingard. For the first time since the proceedings had begun, Dr. Morgenstern relaxed a little. But Tom Morrison remained unmoved.

He spread his hands in a don't-blame-me gesture. "Don't think for a minute that I enjoy throwing suspicion on anyone, ladies and gents. You're a fine bunch of scientists — the last people in the world I'd have said would ever be under the shadow. But the fact remains —" he ticked off on his fingers "— the invention was stolen. The ones who had easiest access to that corridor were you people. All of you. More specifically, Drs. Katz and Morgenstern. They also had the means and the knowledge. I don't like to even think it, but men — good men — have been subverted before this. Unfortunately, too many of them."

"It's not right," Dr. Ilya Pim muttered. "It's just not right." His compatriot, Dr. Natasha Gorodnik, nodded her head, though just what it was that was "not right" wasn't made clear to the others.

Tom got to his feet.

"Ladies, gentlemen, thank you for your time. Until that diskette is found, I'm afraid I'm going to have to confine all of you to this hotel and its grounds. As for you," he turned to Dr. Morgenstern and Dr. Katz, "I'm going to radio in a report of this night's events to headquarters in Washington, stating the facts of the case as I see it. In my opinion — and I speak personally now — you two are innocent. Clean as the driven snow." He looked suddenly very serious. "Let's just hope my superiors feel the same way."

Slowly, the game room began to empty. Shai

Gilboa wandered over to one of the computers where he stood for a while, listlessly watching Alexei Pim play a game. After a while, Niki Gorodnik began a half-hearted game of skee-ball against himself. The Katz and Morgenstern children decided to go back to the dining room to see what, if anything, the F.B.I. search had accomplished while they were absent.

Special Agent Ed Wilson — the one the others called "Sandy" because of the color of his hair — stood outside. Firmly, he prevented the group from bursting through the dining room doors.

"Sorry, kids. Dining room's off-limits for now."

"Did they find the diskette?" Pinny asked breathlessly.

Sandy shook his head. "No. Mr. Morrison's in there now, talking to your fathers and to some of the other scientists, trying to reconstruct the crime." As the kids showed signs of lingering by the doors, he added, "No use waiting around here — no telling how long they'll be. Might as well get some shut-eye."

Sleep didn't seem a very appealing prospect. Shraga, for one, was sure he wouldn't close his eyes all night — not with this mystery hanging over their heads.

Suddenly, Pinny spun around to face Ari. "Ima!" he exclaimed.

"Huh? What about —" Ari's face cleared. "That's right. She doesn't know yet."

"Neither does my mother," Shraga said. "C'mon, let's go up!"

"Wait a second," Ari advised. "We'd better tell the girls where we're going. They might look for us and get scared."

The boys ran back to the game room. "We're going upstairs," Ari beckoned. "Come on."

"We'll follow you soon," Mindy called. She was busily engrossed in a video game, with Daniella watching over her shoulder. Ari, Pinny, Shraga, and Chaim turned away and in a moment were thundering towards the elevators.

It seemed to take twice as long as usual to rise the four flights to their rooms. Once there, they found their mothers in the process of putting the little ones to sleep, so there was another wait to be endured. At last, Mrs. Morgenstern stepped out into the corridor, gently closing the door of her room behind her.

"There. Vivi's finally asleep. I'll just check on Ruchie..."

"I already did, Mom," Shraga said quickly. "She's out like a light."

Mrs. Katz came out of her room to announce softly that Zevy had finally dropped off. "I didn't like to leave him till he was sound asleep," she told Mrs. Morgenstern. "He seemed upset about something." She stopped and gazed in some surprise at the small gathering in the corridor. "What is this, a convention? Why aren't you kids downstairs?"

"That's just what I was going to ask them," Mrs. Morgenstern said. Her eyes searched the group and found her older son. "Shraga? Is everything all right?"

Now that the moment had come, Shraga suddenly wished it had fallen to someone else to give the bad news. He took a tiny step forward. "It's Little Nicky, Mom. It was stolen —"

His mother emitted a small shriek. "*Stolen?*"

Mrs. Katz began, "Who —?"

"They found it again, though," Pinny said hurriedly. "Zevy was the one who found it. In the dining room. At our table, in fact." He tried to keep the worry from his voice.

"So that's what Zevy was talking about!" Mrs. Katz exclaimed. "He kept talking about a 'black box...' " She paled. "Did he really mean the prototype?"

Ari nodded soberly. "He sure did, Ima. The F.B.I. searched everyone — even us — for the diskette with the passwords, but as far as we know, it's still missing."

"Oh, no!" Mrs. Morgenstern went very white. She looked as if she might faint.

"Mom?" Shraga said, coming closer. "Are you okay?"

With an effort, she nodded. "This is just so — shocking. With that diskette in some crazy person's hands, who knows what might not happen, *chas v'shalom?*"

Beside her, Mrs. Katz nodded solemnly.

"I don't get it," Chaim complained. "If all that diskette has is some passwords, what's the problem? Without the black box, those passwords are no use to anyone!" The other kids nodded their heads. He might be no more than ten years old, and no genius like his brother, but Chaim's logic seemed impeccable.

The mothers exchanged a long look.

"What is it, Ima?" Pinny asked urgently. Something was far wrong — even wronger than he'd already thought it was. His mother took a long time answering, and when she did it was in a very low voice.

"I don't think Abba and Dr. Morgenstern told you kids the whole story. That diskette —"

"Yes?" four young voices clamored at once.

"— contains more than just the passwords." Mrs. Katz bit her lip and fell silent.

"The diskette," Mrs. Morgenstern finished for her friend, very quietly, "contains the blueprints for building the real thing."

Shraga stared at her, aghast. "You mean —"

"Yes." She smiled bitterly. "Everything there is to know about making another Little Nicky is right there, spelled out in clear little computer bytes, for anyone who might care to read it!"

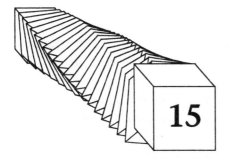

15

Teaming Up

Shai, Niki, and Alexei were strolling slowly across the sparkling, dew-drenched lawn. It was early the next morning, right after breakfast. The boys took big breaths of clean, cool air, especially refreshing after last night's thunderstorm. The whole world — or at least the part of it that they could see — seemed new-washed and happy.

The boys, it was obvious, felt rather differently.

"You should have seen the long faces at my table this morning," Niki sighed. "My mother would hardly even talk to me. And all because that black box was stolen."

"I don't understand," Alexei complained. "It was found again, wasn't it? So what's the problem?"

"I'm not sure I understand all of it, either," Shai said slowly. His Israeli-accented English sounded different, in some undefinable way, from the others' Russian-accented one. "But I think the problem is that it was stolen in the first place. That means that someone was able to get into the hotel and into the lab, even though the place was guarded by the F.B.I." ·

"There was also something about a computer diskette?" Niki asked tentatively.

Shai nodded. "Yes. It has some important information, too, I think." He sighed. "I wish I knew more about it."

So did Niki. His mind was still befogged and benumbed by yesterday's revelation — that he was a Jew! He welcomed the opportunity to think about something else. This mystery had come along just in time to distract him from his own worries.

"Who does the F.B.I. suspect?" he asked, eager to play detective.

Shai shrugged. The Druckers had talked together in low voices through most of the previous night, but they hadn't invited him to join their conference.

"If my grandfather was still alive," Alexei declared suddenly, "I'll bet he'd solve the mystery in no time! He was so smart — *and* very brave."

"Your grandfather?" Shai looked at him curiously. "You're always talking about him. What'd he do that was so brave?"

It was a story Alexei never got tired of repeating. His eyes shone as he related it now, just as he'd heard it time and time again from his own father, back home in Moscow.

"He was a captain in the Russian army, during the Second World War. The German Nazis were coming up fast. Soon they would surround our men, and that would be the end! But no —" a grin of sheer delight lit up the green eyes "— not with my grandfather there! He thought of a plan — a strategy — to ambush the Nazis and save the day."

The others were suitably impressed. They'd reached the edge of the woods by now, and Niki dropped onto an old tree stump. "Did he lose many men?"

"Well, sure, he lost some. What do you expect, when you're dealing with a ruthless enemy? But he got a medal. He was a big hero..."

Shai listened with half an ear as Alexei raved on about his hero grandfather. Something was bothering him. He looked up at the trees that had sheltered him from the eyes of the world for hours yesterday. How comfortable he'd felt, hidden way up high, where no one could find him or hurt him... Alexei stepped noisily into a withered pile of last year's leaves. Shai jumped. That sound — the crunch of feet in the leaves —

"Hey, I just remembered something!" As the other two watched him in surprise, he dug down into his pants pocket. They were the same pants he'd worn yesterday. Where *was* that note? Could he have thrown it away?

At long last, his searching fingers located the scrap of paper he'd seen someone toss away yesterday, with its mysterious message. He showed it to the Russian boys.

"*Meet south entrance midnight,*" Niki read haltingly out loud. "*Bring our little friend.*" He looked up. "Who sent it? What does it mean?"

"What little friend?" asked Alexei, bewildered.

"Don't you get it?" Shai asked in mounting excitement. "It was him — the one who stole the black box! It has to be!"

Niki was more cautious. "It could be," he admitted. "But who sent him that note? And why did he throw it away?"

"And who is the little friend?" Alexei asked again.

"There are a lot of questions," Shai said, jumping to his feet as if he couldn't bear to sit still a minute longer. "And I think we should try to find the answers."

Niki frowned. "Shouldn't we just bring it to the F.B.I.?"

"I say no!" Shai said energetically. "Who needs the F.B.I. — or any of them? Let's solve the mystery ourselves!"

Alexei remained silent, unconvinced. But Niki responded with an eager glow: "Yes! We'll be — how do you say it? — detectives. It will be fun!"

"Sure it will," Shai said. Niki beamed. The two boys, each unhappy in his own way, felt their spirits rise as they walked together, slightly ahead of Alexei, each immersed in thoughts of the black box and the mystery they had undertaken to solve.

Wouldn't it be fun to present Shraga and Pinny and their fathers with the solution to the mystery!

As for their own troubles — well, those could wait. The problems weren't going to run away, that much was certain.

As they climbed up the last curve of the path to the front of the hotel, they just missed seeing Shraga, Pinny, and Ari emerging into the sunlight from the side door that led from the labs.

A few minutes later, the three boys stood in a heavy silence, facing each other. Without discussing it, they had chosen to walk away from the hotel, past the tennis courts and up a gently sloping hill that lay peaceful in the sun. They were like a trio of identical photographs in black-and-white: pale white faces and dark shadowed eyes.

Ari threw himself down on the grass, where he lay picking at the long stems. Pinny sat beside his brother, gazing unseeingly down at the tennis court, glistening under the sun. Shraga spoke first.

"It's crazy, that's what. Just — plain — crazy!"

The Katz boys nodded dully, as if that about summed it up. Pinny said in a dazed voice, "Do you think they'll put our fathers in jail?"

Ari sat up with a jerk. "What? Are you nuts, Pinny? Abba and Dr. Morgenstern didn't do anything! It was their work that was stolen from them."

"Tom said," Pinny continued in the same stunned way, as if he hadn't heard his brother speak, "that his bosses at the F.B.I. are 'taking a very serious view of the matter.' He says they definitely suspect Abba and Dr. Morgenstern, because they're the only ones who knew how it could be used as a weapon, and who had the means and the opportunity to take it."

"Why should your father announce that it was missing?" Shraga objected. "If he'd stolen it, that wouldn't make sense."

Pinny shrugged. "To divert suspicion, I guess. That's what they'd say anyway."

"And motive?" Ari was furious, but not at Pinny. He was raging at the injustice of it all — that the two men who'd labored over that device for two years should be accused now of being its robbers! "Well? What about that?"

"They think our fathers are spies," Shraga answered for Pinny in a voice brimming with misery. "For Israel, maybe. Or else that they did it for money." He attempted the ghost of a grin. "We'd all better make sure not to start spending big suddenly. That'd confirm their suspicions."

"There were lots of other people with 'means and opportunity,' " Ari insisted, returning stubbornly to the original point. "Any one of the scientists who works near our fathers' lab could have slipped in —"

"Through a locked door?" Pinny snorted, roused finally out of his stupor.

"There are ways," Ari said darkly.

"At least," said Shraga, trying to find a sliver of light in all the gloom, "the bad guys haven't got the box. And if they were forced to abandon that, maybe they lost the diskette, too."

"That's right," Pinny said, slightly heartened. "At least Little Nicky is safe."

"Safe in the hands of the F.B.I.," retorted Ari, "who are the ones accusing our fathers of stealing it!"

"Not accusing, exactly —" Pinny began.

"No." His brother's shoulders slumped. "No, not out loud. They're just 'investigating possibilities.' And while they do, Abba and Shraga's father are confined to the hotel grounds."

"So are some of the other scientists," Shraga pointed out. "Let's be fair."

"Fair!" Ari exploded. His face was scarlet. He ran a distracted hand through his light brown hair, so that it looked as if a violent wind had rifled through it. "Tell me one thing that's fair about this whole mess? Little Nicky disappears and then shows up again — at *our* table! The diskette containing plans for building the ultimate death-ray is floating around somewhere, maybe in the thief's pocket, maybe who-knows-where else." He threw out his arms. "Fair? It's not fair. It's crazy! It's simply the craziest thing I ever heard of!"

"Which brings us," Shraga sighed, "right back to where we started."

The three fell into another silence, this one more profound and even more hopeless than the earlier one had been. Through the silence came the sounds of some guests down at the pool, their laughter echoing off the water. Gradually, Shraga became aware of another noise. Someone was climbing up the hill toward them. Turning his head, he saw his younger brother, Chaim.

"There you are!" A yarmulka bobbed up and down as the boy started to run up the last few yards. "Why'd you guys go off without even telling me?"

"We've got troubles, Chaim," Shraga said heavily. "Go away and play."

"Play?" His whole being quivered in outrage. "Play! In case you've forgotten, it's *my* father who's in trouble, as much as yours!" He plopped down onto the grass beside the others. "I want to help, too."

"Oh, what's the use?" Shraga said, palms turned upward in a gesture of futility. "There's nothing anyone can do. We just have to wait till something turns up — and hope for the best."

Chaim snorted. "Well, of all the dumb things I've ever heard, this one takes the cake. Wait? Hope for the best?" He leaned forward on his hands. "What's the matter with you guys?"

"Nothing's the matter with us," Pinny said, stung. "You're just too young to understand, that's all."

Chaim sprang to his feet. "I may be too young to understand everything that's been going on," he blazed, "but there's one thing I do know. Here you sit, a couple of so-called geniuses, and one more who's no genius but pretty smart anyway, and pretty strong, too — and all you can talk about is 'waiting' and 'hoping.'" He planted his hands on his hips. "You guys are *the limit!*"

"What do you mean, Chaim?" Shraga had finally abandoned his listless posture and was really listening. "What can we do?"

"How do I know?" he replied impatiently. "That's your department. All I know is, it's time somebody spoke up around here. It's time someone finally told you, Shraga, and you too, Pinny, how totally dumb you've been acting. It's time to team up! You should be putting your two thick heads together and figuring out something — anything — to help Daddy!"

With that, he spun away and pounded back down the hill.

The three shifted uncomfortably on the grass. Shraga and Pinny avoided each other's eyes. Suddenly, Ari let out a soft exclamation.

"You know something? He's one hundred percent right!"

Shraga and Pinny faced him questioningly.

"Yes! Why shouldn't the two of you think up some plan to help? At the least, even if you don't catch the actual thief, you could figure out a way to find some clues about him so that our fathers'll be let off the hook. I may not be much help in the brains department, but —" he flexed a muscle "— if there should be any need to tackle a bad guy or two, count me in!"

Slowly, Pinny straightened his back. So did

Shraga. Pinny took a deep breath. "I guess they're right," he said. "What do you think?"

"What do I think?" Shraga repeated the question slowly, a trick he had to stall for time when trying to formulate an answer. "What do I think? I think — I think it's time we stopped this stupid feud we've been living all our lives. I think it's time we behaved like a couple of big kids instead of babies. And I think —" his eyes glittered with a new purpose "— that we should use every bit of brain power Hashem gave us, to find out the truth!"

"Atta boy!" applauded Ari. "Well, Pinny?"

"Sure thing!" Pinny thrust out a hand. So did Shraga. They shook. "I'm with you one hundred percent."

"Now you're talking," Ari said approvingly. "So —" he glanced eagerly from one to the other "— where do we start?"

"Whoa," laughed Shraga. "Give us a little time to think, will you?"

"Like a few seconds or so." Pinny was laughing, too.

Ari remembered what Chaim had said in the parking lot the day they'd arrived. "Little Nicky is probably the only thing that could get you two together." He hadn't known it then, but how right — how sadly right — he'd been.

But there was no time for dwelling on the past now. They had to act. Their fathers needed them.

The hopelessness of a few minutes earlier was forgotten. The two bright boys put their heads together on the sunny hilltop, while Ari listened attentively and inserted his own two cents here and there. Shraga talked quickly, setting forth ideas only for Pinny to knock them down. Pinny made one suggestion after another, which Shraga vetoed. Still, there was a sense that they were moving forward. Soon, very soon, they'd have the best plan that two first-rate minds could come up with. That, plus their fervent belief that Hashem would help them, was enough to set them on fire.

Gone was the attitude of "Wait and see what will happen." They would *make* something happen!

He tested the door to the game room, then breathed a sigh of relief. It was unlocked. At this time of the morning, he hadn't been sure whether it would be. He was about to swing the door open and enter, when a new worry assailed him. Suppose there were someone inside — a couple of children, perhaps, intent on perfecting their skill in some game or other?

Unlikely, he decided at last. And, in any case, he had no choice. He *must* retrieve that diskette at once!

He remembered his chagrin when, late on the previous night, he had sauntered confidently to this door for the very same purpose. To his horror, it had refused to open. Some hotel official had, seemingly, locked up at whatever hour he was accustomed to doing so. The diskette had lain in its wastepaper basket all night long.

"Mr. Big" hadn't been very pleased about that. His message on the computer's e-mail screen had been very clear on that point. Carefully, he turned the knob and pushed the door open a crack.

There was no noise from inside, no young voices raised in the throes of playing. Good.

He refused to wonder if the basket had been emptied since last night. There was only so much one could be anxious about at one time. It was now immediately after breakfast; for one reason or another, it hadn't been possible for him to come a moment earlier. Not without raising suspicions. But suppose — the worry kept returning, though he tried to push it away — suppose the game room *had* been cleaned? He shook his head. There was only one way to find out... Hardly aware that he was holding his breath, he pushed open the door.

The room was empty. The wastepaper basket was in its place, as full as it had been last night. Smiling broadly in sudden sharp relief, he hurried forward. One second to snatch the red diskette, another to recross the room and close the door behind him, and his troubles would be over. He wouldn't think about the sleepless nights to come, when his conscience would torment him and not leave him in peace. That was the price he had agreed to pay. He would do what he had to do. With long, eager strides, he went to the wastepaper basket.

The diskette wasn't there.

Frantically, his fingers scrabbled through the

crumpled candy and bubble-gum wrappers, a discarded diskette envelope or two, some scribbled scorecards. No diskette! It should have been lying right on top, in plain view. Straightening up, he riffled through the diskette box with shaking hands, hoping against hope that someone had returned the diskette there. But the box held only sober black diskettes, without a single red one to enliven the color scheme.

With a groan, he sank into the computer chair and buried his head in his hands. Last night's ominous message from Mr. Big echoed through his mind. *Find that diskette...or else.*

What in the world was he going to do now?

Coming Soon!

THE LITTLE BLACK BOX

Part 2:

The Second Secret

It's the morning after the mysterious break-in that led to the theft of the super-secret new device, code-named "Little Nicky." A cloud of suspicion hangs over the heads of its inventors, Shraga and Pinny's fathers.

Never had Shraga recited the familiar words of shacharis with so much fervor. If ever a family — two families — needed Hashem's help, this was the time. What if the scientists were put on trial, or worse, in jail? And where was that diskette with the missing blueprints for the weapon? He wished he'd never heard of Nikola Tesla, or of secret weapons, or of the Lake View Hotel. Had it only been two days ago that life was still simple and uncomplicated? It felt like a million years ago.

Others are feeling the strain, too.

Shai, the Druckers' foster son, moodily bit into a muffin. That wasn't so unusual, as Shai's normal expression was moody. But there was a certain extra tension in his face this morning. He was trying to make up his mind about something, and the process was making him feel edgy.
Should he show the note to Shraga and Pinny or keep it to himself? To tell or not to tell?

And what does Niki Gorodnik have on his mind?

Niki was in an agony of indecision. Should he blurt out the other tiny little fact that had been weighing so heavily on his mind all day? Or did his loyalty lie in another direction?
One part of him urged him to speak, while another, equally strong, bade him to remain silent. Which to choose?
In the end, the elevator doors closed upon his new friends without his having said a word except "Good night." He rode the rest of the way up alone. Silence had won.

The plans for the device are still at large. The

elusive and sinister "Mr. Big" is sending threatening messages. A series of frightening "accidents" terrorize the families. It promises to be a busy — and difficult — next few days. Unless our boys can do something about it.

Dr. Katz opened his eyes again and smiled at his son. The old merry look was back. "Cheer up, Pinny," he said. "All is not yet lost."

"I'm okay," Pinny said, not very convincingly.

His father either believed him or pretended to. "Good. Could you ask Ari if he minds postponing our learning session till after lunch? I think Dr. Morgenstern is right. With our bosses coming up, and more Special Agents, and everything up in the air like this, it's a little hard to concentrate this morning."

Pinny sat up straighter, proud at the way his father was talking to him — just like one adult to another. "Sure, Abba. And don't you worry. Me 'n Shraga will come up with a plan to solve all this, once and for all."

Hopeful words — but will they really succeed? Hang on to your seats as our band of young detectives leaves no stone unturned to find the culprit! Catch the action — and there's lots of it — in *The Second Secret*, part two in the riveting three-part mini-series: *The Little Black Box*.

A SHRAGA MORGENSTERN/PINNY KATZ
MYSTERY TRILOGY

THE LITTLE BLACK BOX
PART 2

———

THE SECOND SECRET

Created and written by Libby Lazewnik

TARGUM/FELDHEIM

First published 1995

Phototypeset at Targum Press

Printing plates by Frank, Jerusalem

Published by:
Targum Press Inc.
22700 W. Eleven Mile Rd.
Southfield, Mich. 48034

Distributed by:
Feldheim Publishers
200 Airport Executive Park
Nanuet, N.Y. 10954

Distributed in Israel by:
Targum Press Ltd.
POB 43170
Jerusalem 91430

Printed in Israel

Contents

The Little Black Box:
Our story so far...

Shraga Morgenstern and Pinny Katz have a lot in common. They live right next door to each other. Each is the smartest boy in his class, and possibly in his whole yeshiva. They're both almost twelve years old. (In fact, they even share a birthday!) Their fathers work together as research scientists at M.C.B., a firm that produces many interesting new high-tech devices...including a secret one that, in the wrong hands, could be a potentially lethal weapon. Drs. Katz and Morgenstern have been working on this device — code-named "Little Nicky" — for two whole years, and it is about to be unveiled at last.

One sunny day in June, the two Jewish scientists bring their families, plus the only existing prototype of the device, up to the Catskills for a week-long convention of physicists from all over the world. Shraga and Pinny are excited to be included in this event. The only cloud on the horizon is that the boys dislike each other. Pinny's big brother, Ari, is always after Pinny to be nice to his neighbor, as is Shraga's younger brother, Chaim. Unfortunately, both boys turn a deaf ear to their pleas. They are determined to remain unfriends.

At the hotel, they meet Tom Morrison and his team of F.B.I. Special Agents, whose job it is to guard the scientists and their work during their week-long stay. They also meet Alexei, son of Russian scientist Ilya Pim and grandson of a famous war hero. They have a run-in with Nikolai ("Niki") Gorodnik, another Russian kid who spouts some unpleasantly anti-Semitic remarks until he discovers, to his surprise and dismay, that he himself is a Jew. Shai Gilboa, an Israeli foster child, is another problem for the American kids to tackle. But all other troubles fall into the background when the unthinkable occurs: the prototype of the dangerous device is stolen from the lab that Dr. Katz and Dr. Morgenstern share, along with the red diskette containing the secret computer passwords and detailed blueprints for building the original!

The prototype is soon found, but not the diskette. The F.B.I., in charge of investigating the theft, accuse Shraga's and Pinny's fathers of stealing the invention themselves! Faced with this horrifying situation, Shraga and Pinny decide to bury the hatchet. Together with Ari Katz, they determine to find the real culprit, clear their fathers of suspicion, and — most crucial of all — recover the plans for the weapon...before they can fall into the wrong hands.

Little do the boys know that they are about to become embroiled in a game with higher stakes than they'd ever imagined possible!

1

The Clouds Thicken

It was Friday morning. A bluebird sang with all its might on a limb of the elm tree outside Shraga's hotel room, but he wasn't listening. Who had time or energy for enjoying birdsong, however pretty, when gloom and doom surrounded them on all sides? Shraga turned over in bed, piled the pillow on his head, and tried to avoid facing the day — his third at the Lake View Hotel — for a few more minutes.

"Rise and shine, Shragie!" The familiar voice of Mindy, his nine-year-old sister, sang out from the doorway. "Time for minyan!"

He groaned. "Don't you believe in knocking first?"

"I did — you didn't hear me. And how could you, with that pillow over your head?" Mindy asked reasonably, coming in. "How come you're in bed so late, anyhow?"

Her brother propped open one eye and regarded her glumly. She looked bright and perky as ever, with her hair parted neatly into two pigtails and a sprinkling of freckles on her nose over her new country sunburn. He twisted his neck to take in the empty room. "Where's Chaim?"

"Downstairs already. C'mon, don't be a lazy-bones. Abba and Dr. Katz and the boys have been waiting for ages."

That brought Shraga up to a sitting position. "Hey, wait a sec! Didn't that F.B.I. guy — Tom what's-his-name — say that Daddy and Dr. Katz are confined to the hotel till the mystery's solved? How can they go out to minyan now?" Since the Lake View was not a kosher hotel, they'd been travelling to another hotel for davening.

"It's not just Daddy and Dr. Katz," Mindy replied crisply. "None of the scientists are being allowed out today. You'll be davening here in this hotel, instead of in the one you went to yesterday."

Shraga frowned. "Without a minyan?"

"What choice do you have?"

Shraga made no reply. A perfect beginning to a perfect day, he thought sourly. He was normally a sunny-tempered kid, but it's not every day that your father and his best friend fall under suspicion of espionage. Because that was what it amounted to. Tom Morrison and the rest of those F.B.I. bigwigs suspected Shraga's father, and Pinny's, too, of being spies in the pay of some other country — possibly Israel — and of stealing the secret weapon that they themselves had worked for two whole years to create! If it hadn't been so serious, it would have been laughable.

Flinging aside the blankets, Shraga heaved himself out of his rumpled bed. The bedclothes looked the way he felt: tired, messy, and hopeless. He forced a smile to his face; after all, there was no use in taking his low spirits out on Mindy. "Give me a minute to shower, okay? I'll be down real soon."

"Okay." Mindy grinned back. "While you men daven, the rest of us will be in the dining room enjoying a deluxe breakfast..." She made a face and her voice drooped as she added, "...airline style." The packaged kosher food the Jewish families were served during this convention week was not high on Mindy's list of favorite things. In fact, none of them — with the possible exception of young Daniella Katz — liked it much.

"Enjoy it. We'll be the ones suffering the second shift."

Mindy seemed disposed to linger. As Shraga trailed around the room, collecting his things, she said chattily, "How anyone can come up with such horrible-tasting stuff and call it 'food' is beyond me. D'you think that's the kind of thing Daddy would have to eat if he went to jail?"

"How can you joke about a thing like that?" Shraga exploded.

"Like what?"

"Jail," he said bitterly. "You think that's funny? Don't you know what's at stake here?" He turned away, gathering his robe and some clothes as he went. Then he faced her again, a look of pain on his face. "How can you joke about it?"

Mindy sighed and rose to her feet. Softly, she asked, "What else is there to do?"

Mindy might not have known what else to do, but her father and brothers sure did. Together with the male contingent of the Katz clan, they davened that morning as never before. Never had Shraga recited the familiar words of *shacharis* with so much fervor. If ever a family — two families — needed Hashem's help, this was the time. What if the scientists were put on trial, or worse, in jail? And where was that diskette with the missing blueprints? For two years, Shraga had kidded around about the mysterious "Little Nicky," code name for the deadly device that was taking up so much of his father's time and concentration. Now he wished he'd never heard of Nikolai Tesla, or of secret weapons, or of the Lake View Hotel. Had it only been two days ago that life was still simple and uncomplicated? It felt like a million years ago.

"Psst, Shraga," whispered Pinny, as the men folded their prayer shawls and put away their tefillin. "Let's meet after breakfast to plan our strategy."

"Mmm." Shraga nodded noncommittally. A fat lot of good their planning seemed to be doing.

Yesterday, when he and Pinny and Ari had pledged to do their best to help their fathers in this sticky situation, he'd been full of optimism. But all their thinking had turned up not even a shadow of a workable plan. Shraga felt depressed. What could a handful of kids do against a band of terrorists? If, that was, it was terrorists who had stolen the weapon, and not an enemy government. That was the crazy part, he thought as he entered the busy dining room behind the others: not knowing exactly who it was they were up against. It was like stumbling through a dark room, blindfolded.

Mrs. Morgenstern and Mrs. Katz greeted their husbands and sons with a semblance of cheerfulness, though Shraga could see the lines of strain around his mother's eyes. Little Ruchie Morgenstern was working through a pile of scrambled eggs, while her baby sister, Vivi, gleefully tore a piece of toast into shreds in her high chair. The menfolk took their seats.

"Abba," Zevy Katz's clear voice piped up, "I davened real hard for you today."

Dr. Katz looked startled. "You did?"

"Uh-huh. Ima said you're in some kind of trouble 'cause of the black box I found yesterday. But I told Hashem all about it, and I know He's gonna make everything okay."

Dr. Katz exchanged a strange sort of sad-happy glance with Dr. Morgenstern. But his voice, when he answered, was only happy.

"That's the spirit, son. You just keep on davening. We all will. And I'm sure everything *will* turn out all right."

As the waiter came to deposit the inevitable foil-wrapped package in front of him, Shraga felt his spirits rising. Though he was only a little kid, that Zevy had his head on straight. Instead of wallowing in depression, he'd tried to do something to help. Shraga turned to Pinny, beside him, and said low-voiced, "After breakfast we learn, right? Let's get together to make a plan after that."

"Sure thing." Pinny looked excited. A summer breeze came through the nearby window to ruffle his blond curls, making them stand up like a rooster's comb. He nudged his big brother Ari in the ribs. "Hey, Ari, plotting session right after learning this morning. Okay?"

"*Plotzing?*" asked Zevy, overhearing. "Who's *plotzing?*"

He didn't understand why the three bigger boys dissolved in laughter at his question. But for all of them, some of the tension had flown out onto the summer breeze, to be carried away from them for a little while.

The tension didn't stay away for long. Before breakfast was over, the sight of the other scientists' grim faces reminded Shraga and Pinny of last night's horror.

At the next table sat some of the prestigious physicists whom the F.B.I. man, Tom Morrison, had interrogated after the black box had been discovered stolen last night. A pale Dr. Ilya Pim, one of the Russians, toyed with his food. So did Dr. Natasha Gorodnik, Niki's Jewish mother. At the table beyond, Dr. Magda Brenner, a tiny Hungarian woman with a mane of white hair and snapping black eyes, conferred quietly with Dr. Richard Fowley, the wiry redheaded Englishman. Dr. Fowley was stabbing his food with his fork as they talked, as if he wished it were something — or someone — else. On Fowley's other side sat tall, silver-haired Dr. Manfred Isingard, from Norway, occasionally putting in a word but otherwise eating in a brooding silence. All in all, it was not exactly what Shraga would have called a festive breakfast.

The mood was not much lighter at his own table. And the food wasn't helping any.

"This bagel tastes stale," Ari Katz complained, pushing his away.

"Try this trick," his brother Pinny offered. "See?" He'd smothered his own bagel with so much marmalade that whatever flavor it might have possessed was completely masked.

Ari grimaced. "No, thanks."

"Shraga, would you please pass the coffee?" Dr. Drucker, the Israeli, requested. As Shraga reached for the coffee pot, he studied the Israeli scientist curiously. Dr. Drucker had come under nearly as much suspicion as his own father and Pinny's. Being an Israeli — as Tom Morrison had broadly hinted — gave Drucker a motive for wanting to lay his hands on the super-secret new weapon before his enemies, the Arab terrorists, could.

Dr. Drucker poured some coffee into his wife's cup, then into his own. Shai, the Druckers' foster son, moodily bit into a muffin. That wasn't so unusual, as Shai's normal expression was moody. But there was a certain extra tension in his face this morning. He was trying to make up his mind about something, and the process was making him feel edgy.

Should he show the note to Shraga and Pinny, or keep it to himself?

Niki and Alexei, the Russian kids, had agreed to play detective with him yesterday, when he'd told them about finding the mysterious note in the woods. Since then, however, some of their enthusiasm had drifted away. The trail seemed cold. The F.B.I. appeared to have matters well in hand and had called in reinforcements, who were expected momentarily. What could Shai, or any other kid, do that the F.B.I. could not?

Shai cast a doubtful look at Shraga and Pinny, at his own table. If anyone had a stake in finding out the truth, it was these two. After all, their own fathers had invented the stolen weapon, and, from what he'd managed to pick up from his parents' worried conversation, those same fathers were under a cloud of suspicion now. Shraga and Pinny would not "play detective" — they would try earnestly and with all their might to discover what lay behind the theft of that black box. Shouldn't he help them if he could?

On the other hand, that note was the only clue he had. If he gave that up, he'd have nothing. Shai stared unseeingly into his glass of orange juice. To tell or not to tell?

"Shai?" his foster mother asked, breaking into his thoughts. "The boys will be learning with their fathers in the lobby in a little while. Abba and I thought... Well, it might be nice if you joined them."

He's not my abba. Mrs. Drucker's hopeful face swam before him. He'd been about to retort, "Nice for who?" Instead, with an effort, he changed it to, "No, thanks. I'm not interested in that stuff."

His self-control encouraged Mrs. Drucker to try again. "But it's really very interesting. I mean, I myself have never learned Gemara, but Abba would be quite happy to teach you..." The words trailed away as she saw the implacable look returning to Shai's eyes. She sighed. It was no use. Nothing that she or her husband tried seemed to be able to reach this boy whom they'd taken in, and whom they were so prepared to love. Not even this trip to America.

The theft of the weapon and diskette had shaken the entire hotel, and her own husband was not clear of suspicion. Yet now, at this moment, Mrs. Drucker's heart had room for nothing but love and anxiety for the boy seated beside her, deliberately not meeting her eyes.

The learning was a hurried affair that morning. Everyone had difficulty concentrating. Dr. Morgenstern and Dr. Katz thought about their bosses from M.C.B., who were on their way up to the hotel this very minute. They'd already received the bad news about "Little Nicky." How would they react when they met face to face? Would the two scientists still have jobs when the meeting was over?

Never had their careers looked so shaky... And never had there been a greater need to be strong and have faith in Hashem. Still, they were only human. With all their worries preying on them, it was hard to follow the logic of the *gemara* they were learning with their sons.

Shraga and Pinny were faring little better. It was fun learning with a partner as smart as you were, to match wits with a mind that equalled your own — as each of them had begun to discover yesterday. Or rather, it *would* be fun, once this nightmare was over. Right now, their minds were spinning with plots and stratagems, like wheels stuck in a sand dune and getting exactly nowhere.

Finally, Dr. Morgenstern sat back with a sigh.

"I think we'd better stop here. Maybe when all this clears up we can enjoy some really good learning. But I'm finding it hard going this morning." He glanced at Dr. Katz. "I'm sorry, Shmulie."

"I know just how you feel, David." Dr. Katz leaned his head against the cushions of his armchair and closed his eyes. Pinny watched his father anxiously. Abba looked so pale suddenly, so tired, so...old.

Then Dr. Katz opened his eyes again and smiled at his son. The old merry look was back. "Cheer up, Pinny," he said. "All is not yet lost."

"I'm okay," Pinny said, not very convincingly.

His father either believed him, or pretended to. "Good. Could you ask Ari if he minds postponing our learning session till after lunch? I think Dr. Morgenstern is right. With our bosses coming up, and more Special Agents, and everything up in the air like this, it's a little hard to concentrate this morning."

Pinny sat up straighter, proud at the way his father was talking to him — just like one adult to another. "Sure, Abba. And don't you worry. Me 'n Shraga will come up with a plan to solve all of this, once and for all."

The scientists watched their sons walk out of the lobby together. "Will wonders never cease?" murmured Dr. Morgenstern. Why, until just yesterday, it had been his dearest wish to witness what he had just seen: friendship between his son and David Katz's son. After so many years of enduring the silent hostility between the two boys, the change warmed his heart. "Who would have believed it?"

"You know what they say," Dr. Katz said, rising to his feet. "Every cloud has its silver lining."

"Our 'lining' is giving me a lot of *nachas*," Dr. Morgenstern admitted. He stood up too. Both men began walking towards the small lab they'd been assigned at the back of the hotel. "But the cloud's not getting any smaller, Shmulie."

"I know," said Dr. Katz. "I know."

Under a tree on the hotel lawn, Shraga and Pinny knew it, too.

They waited until Ari came running out to join them, comfortingly strong and solid. Ari gazed with approval at his two partners in detection.

"Two giant brains and a set of superior muscles," he said. "Now that's what I call some team. Well, come on. Let's start hatching those plans, guys."

And the three put their heads together to do just that.

2
Lists, Lists, Lists

Okay," began Pinny, trying to sound like a businesslike detective instead of a very scared almost-twelve-year-old. "First thing to do is try and reconstruct the crime."

"That's easy," said Shraga impatiently. "While we are all at dinner, someone strolls over to our fathers' lab, somehow manages to pick the lock — an *electronic* lock, mind you — and walks away with the black box under one arm and the diskette in his pocket. Then, for some reason I can't fathom, he decides to dump the prototype but hold onto the diskette. At least —" he stopped suddenly as a new idea struck him "— I *think* he kept the diskette..."

"What makes you think he doesn't have it?" Ari asked.

"I don't really think it," Shraga answered slowly. "At least, I don't *think* I think it... It's just an impression I get from Tom Morrison and those other F.B.I. guys. They've been searching the hotel pretty thoroughly, you know. And some more men have been called in, I've heard, to help with that. They must be on their way up right now."

"It's a big place," remarked Ari, casting an eye over the spacious lawns and flower beds, and the thick fringe of woods where the grounds ended. "Anyone could have dumped the diskette in there, for safekeeping —" he pointed at the woods "— and no one would ever find it. Later, when interest dies down, he can quietly go and dig it up."

Pinny shook his head. "Not likely. Sandy and Sam, the Special Agents guarding the entrance, are positive no one left the hotel during dinner last night."

"Maybe through a back door?" Ari asked doubtfully. "The one near the labs would be closest."

"Not likely," Pinny said again. "Once he'd passed through the door, he'd be in sight of the driveway — and the F.B.I. No, I agree with Shraga: the diskette's still in the hotel. But not necessarily abandoned, like the prototype. The crook may still have it. After all, no one's been allowed to leave."

Indeed, gazing around the grounds from their vantage point on a slight elevation, all three boys could see that the place was unusually full on this Friday morning. Normally, the scientists would be in their labs or attending the many small seminars that had been planned for this conference week. The few non-scientific guests would be frolicking at the pool or driving away in their cars down the shady country roads, bent on some pleasure outing.

But today, no one seemed to have the heart for fun in the sun. The pool was nearly empty, and only one couple swatted a ball lackadaisically across the deserted tennis courts. Even the scientists seemed unable, on this day, to concentrate on their work. Everyone seemed to be milling aimlessly, as if wondering if there really were an international criminal in their midst, and just what they were expected to do about it.

"Let's get back to the question of why he dumped Nicky —uh, the prototype —on our table," Shraga said, tearing his eyes away from the clumps of humanity passing restlessly to and fro across the lawns.

"I can think of two reasons," Pinny said promptly. "One, he was afraid of getting caught with it. My father had raised the alarm the minute he discovered the theft, remember? Say the guy has the black box under his arm, and the F.B.I. starts searching for it! The safest thing to do would be to put it down somewhere, fast."

"Abba did find it earlier than the crook expected," Ari agreed thoughtfully. "The crook must have expected him to at least finish his dinner first. In fact, there was no reason why he'd even go back to the lab at all that night, was there?"

"Sure there was!" Shraga said, sitting up with a light in his eye. "The presentation! Remember, Ari, our fathers were supposed to be giving a talk to the other scientists last night, telling them about the device and how it works. The talk was scheduled for seven o'clock."

"I don't think they were planning to actually let the other scientists *see* Little Nicky," Pinny objected. "They were going to just talk about it. It *is* still classified, you know. Top secret."

"True," said Shraga. "And in that case, our fathers might not have visited the lab until next morning. Which would have given the thief plenty of time to hide the thing — or to get it out of the hotel before the alarm was raised."

"Not likely." These two words seemed to be Pinny's refrain this morning. "I mean, wouldn't they need to get some notes or stuff from their lab before the talk? And I have another question," he continued in rising excitement. "Why would any intelligent crook pick last night to steal it anyway? With the talk coming up, it would be bound to be a close shave."

"When else?" Shraga asked reasonably. "This morning, some men from M.C.B. were supposed to be coming up in an armored car to take the weapon back to the city. Last night was the only chance he'd get."

"Why not after the talk, then?" Pinny argued. "That way, he'd have all night."

Ari was watching the two of them, fascinated. After all these years, his brother and his neighbor had finally begun to put their two super-bright heads together, and the results were like watching fireworks. "Yeah, Shraga," he urged. "Why not after?"

"I'm not sure," Shraga said slowly. "There must be some reason...some reason why the fellow couldn't get away without rousing suspicion later. Maybe during dinner was the only time he could slip away unnoticed."

"How do we know it's a 'he'?" Pinny demanded suddenly. "It could be anyone. A woman, even. Even a chambermaid!"

Shraga shook his head. "I don't think so. Everything points to the guy — okay, the *person* — knowing exactly what he was taking, and why. A chambermaid wouldn't have that kind of knowledge. Besides, how would she pick an electronic lock?"

"She didn't have to understand it," Pinny objected. "Just follow orders. But you're right," he abruptly reversed himself. "It doesn't ring true, somehow. The person who did this had brains... resources...quick wits. Also, he or she must have known about the talk last night and the fact that the weapon was to be picked up this morning."

"It has to be one of the scientists," Ari said forcefully. "It *has* to be!"

"Which one?" asked Shraga. A silence descended.

The bluebird that had woken him that morning was singing again, as if it hadn't a care in the world. Shraga looked up, shading his eyes with his hand, but he couldn't see the bird. Pinny heard it, too.

The clear notes floated back to him, as though urging him to good cheer. That's easy for you to say, he thought irritably.

Then he remembered his father's words earlier: *Cheer up, Pinny. All is not yet lost.*

I'm trying, I'm trying, he thought, stifling a sigh.

He took a small notepad from his pocket. In another pocket he located a pencil stub, all of three inches long. He started writing.

"What's the second reason?" Ari asked suddenly.

Pinny looked up. "Huh?"

"You said you could think of two reasons why the guy — uh, the thief — might have dumped the weapon at our table. What's the second reason?"

"Oh, that." Pinny shrugged. "Why, to direct suspicion at our fathers, of course."

"Well, that part worked beautifully," Shraga said gloomily.

"Sure did," said Pinny. He went back to his writing.

"Whatcha doing?" Ari asked.

"Making a list. I'm putting down all the scientists who have labs near Abba's and Dr. Morgenstern's."

Ari had something to say to that. "Why only them? There are dozens of physicists here this week."

"Those are the ones Tom Morrison interviewed last night," Pinny explained. "Anyway, we have to start somewhere, and they seem the most likely suspects. The other labs are on the other side of the hotel, so any of the other scientists caught wandering around near our father's lab would look out of place and raise suspicion."

"All right," Ari conceded, not so much because he agreed as because he felt anxious to begin somewhere. "Who do you have on your list?"

"Richard Fowley, from England," read Pinny. "Magda Brenner, Hungary. Manfred Isingard, Norway. Ilya Pim, Russia."

"Don't forget Natasha Gorodnik," reminded Shraga. "Niki's mother."

"That's right." Pinny wrote it down.

"What about Dr. Drucker?" Ari asked.

His fellow detectives looked surprised. The Israeli sat at their table, ate with them, and davened with them. How could they suspect him of making off with the weapon?

"Still," Pinny said thoughtfully, writing down the name, "you never know. His lab *is* in the right place..."

"I don't believe it's him," Shraga said. "He wouldn't let our fathers take the rap for something he did."

"I agree," Ari said staunchly.

"So do I," Pinny said. Grinning sheepishly, he started to rub out the name.

"No, leave it," Shraga said suddenly. "We may as well be thorough. It won't hurt to interview him along with the others. Even if he didn't actually have anything to do with this mess, he might know something that could help."

"You got it," Pinny said, reversing his pencil again. "So here's the plan."

"A plan —great!" Ari flexed his muscles, brightening at the prospect of a concrete course of action.

"We interview these people," continued Pinny. "One by one — subtle-like, you know? To try and see whether they had any motive to commit the crime."

"Good idea!" exclaimed Shraga. "And I think we should also try, discreetly, to find out whether anyone left the dining room during dinner last night — even for just a few minutes."

"Good." Pinny wrote down both ideas. He glanced at his brother. "Ari? Anything?"

"You're the idea men," Ari replied, sitting back on his palms. "Any plan you guys think up, I'll help carry out. So what should I do?"

It was a nice feeling to have his big brother turning to him for instructions. Pinny tapped his pencil importantly against the page.

"Let's divide up the suspects," he decided. "Ari, you tackle Isingard and Pim. I'll talk to Fowley and Brenner. Shraga, how about taking Gorodnik and Drucker?"

Shraga nodded. "Okay." Then he added, "How about making another list, Pinny? A list of questions that need to be answered if we're to get anywhere with this puzzle."

"Such as?" Pinny held the pencil poised over his notepad, waiting.

"Such as... One: Who might have managed to get a key to the lab where the weapon was? Two: Assuming the thief had to get rid of the stuff he'd stolen — fast — where'd he dump the diskette? Three: Who was missing from the dining room during dinner? And four, the biggie: Is he working alone or is some organization paying him to do it, and why?"

"The first three," said Pinny, still writing busily, "are technical questions. The fourth is more a matter of background. Once we know the answer to that, we know everything. I vote that question stays off the list."

"Lists, lists, lists! What's the difference?" Ari snapped in an access of impatience. "They're all questions that have no answers."

"I just want to classify all the material properly," Pinny said in an injured tone. "It makes things clearer if you do that."

"Not for me, it doesn't." Ari softened. "But you go ahead and classify all you want to. As long as there's some action involved somewhere. Something more than just all these lists!"

"There will be," Shraga promised.

At that moment, as if on cue, a muted roar came to their ears. Craning their necks to catch a glimpse of the place where the drive met the road, they saw three black cars turning into the hotel grounds. As they neared the front entrance, the cars slowed and finally stopped, one behind the other. Seconds later, Tom Morrison and his agents came bustling out to meet them. Car doors opened and shut with brisk, efficient thuds. Dark-suited figures emerged into the sunshine.

"More Special Agents," whispered Ari.

Then, as the agents congregated in a small, tight group, talking in low voices, another car — this one sleek, long, and navy blue — came speeding up the road. It executed the turn into the drive without slowing down much, so that there was a loud squeal of brakes as it pulled up to the hotel. The boys watched, curious to see who had arrived now.

This time, it was their own fathers who came hurrying out of the hotel to greet the newcomers.

"It must be Abba's boss," Pinny said, punching his brother's arm in excitement. "I wonder what he'll say about Little Nicky being gone?"

Shraga only shook his head. Whatever the president of M.C.B. might have to say, he was sure of one thing. It wouldn't be anything very pleasant.

3
Erev Shabbos Blues

Mr. Benson, president of M.C.B., remained closeted with Dr. Katz and Dr. Morgenstern for a long time. After that, he met with Tom Morrison, head of the F.B.I. security team detailed to the Lake View Hotel for the week-long international physicists' convention. The hotel manager — as anxious as any of them to solve this mystery once and for all, before it harmed his business — had set aside a small room for their use. In the corridor nearby hovered Shraga, Pinny, and Ari, trying to look inconspicuous and to gather from the expressions of the people going in and out of the meeting room what was happening inside.

Chaim, Shraga's younger brother, came upon them as they stood in a tight huddle just outside the door.

"Hey, what's going on?" he demanded. "Everybody's acting crazy today. Mommy won't talk to me, Daddy won't talk to me, and Mindy doesn't know any more than I do. What gives?"

"Sssh. Not so loud!" Ari admonished.

"Shraga," Chaim persisted, lowering his voice a fraction, "what's going on?"

Shraga wore the intent air of someone who is listening for all he's worth and not hearing much. "Don't you know?" he asked.

"If I knew," Chaim said patiently, "would I be asking you? Does it have something to do with the black box that was stolen?"

"It sure does have something to do with the black box," Ari put in, finally giving up trying to hear anything through the thick oak door. "Our fathers' bosses are in there."

"What for? What are they talking about?"

That was exactly what Shraga was dying to know. He said impatiently, "Look, it's complicated. Why don't you ask me later? I promise I'll explain then."

"Why not now?"

"I'm busy." Shraga turned back towards the door, every nerve tingling. Any minute now, someone was liable to come out with some news. What was happening in there?

"Busy?" Chaim folded his arms skeptically. "Doing what? Propping up a wall?"

"Chaim, just leave me alone, okay?" Shraga employed the age-old method for getting rid of pesky kid brothers. After an indignant glare that got him exactly nowhere, Chaim stalked away. Shraga resumed his suspenseful wait. Ari paced tensely back and forth. Another minute passed, then two.

"Shraga?" It was Pinny.

"Hm?"

"Do you know what time Shabbos starts?"

These seven simple words had the effect on Shraga of a brick wall toppling onto his head. Shabbos! Was it really coming — tonight? Shabbos was sane, Shabbos was beautiful, Shabbos spelled normal life. Where did Shabbos fit into the nightmare scheme of things they were living through today?

He was about to answer "I don't know," when the door to the meeting room opened and his father nearly stepped on Shraga's toes. Dr. Katz and their boss, Mr. Benson, followed. Blushing furiously, Shraga tried to stammer some sort of apology, but none of the men seemed to be paying him, or the other children, much attention. The door closed again behind them.

The boys looked at each other. In each of their eyes was the same question: What was going on? What had happened inside that little room? Silently, with one accord, they hurried after their fathers to try and find out.

They did find out. And Shraga also learned, quite soon, exactly where Shabbos fit in.

"All right, kids, gather round. We've got some serious talking to do." Dr. Morgenstern, together with Pinny's father, had seen Mr. Benson off in his long blue car and returned to the lobby, where both families had gathered as if by some instinct to hear what the two men had to say.

"About the secret weapon, Daddy?" Chaim asked eagerly.

"No. About Shabbos."

He led the way to a set of couches in a corner of the lobby. Remembering the get-together upstairs in her parents' room the day before, little Ruchie piped up, "Mommy, are we gonna talk about Little Nicky again today?"

Wincing, Mrs. Morgenstern reached out a distracted hand to pat the youngster's head. She wished with all her might that she'd never heard of that horrible "Little Nicky." To think that her husband and Dr. Katz had described to the children in vivid scientific detail only yesterday afternoon — little knowing of the disaster the evening would bring! "No, honey. Daddy just wants to say something to us. Sit quietly for a minute, okay?"

Obediently, Ruchie settled herself on her mother's lap and gazed expectantly at her father. Dr. Morgenstern took an extra second to smile at her — how precious his children seemed today, with the rest of his world suddenly so upside-down! — before turning to face the others.

"Shabbos starts tonight, and it's going to be different than any Shabbos we've ever spent before.

I want all of you to be prepared. We've got to keep the day special, no matter how hard it might be."

He glanced at Dr. Katz, who picked up from his friend.

"Originally, we'd intended to spend Shabbos at the kosher hotel where we davened yesterday. Unfortunately, due to circumstances beyond our control —" he threw a wry look at the F.B.I. man posted conspicuously at the lobby doors "— we can't do that anymore. We've been confined to this place until things clear up. It'll be comfortable, and we'll have the usual kosher food to eat." Here he tried, and failed, to inject a hearty note. "But I'm afraid it won't be very *Shabbosdik*."

"We'll do our best, Abba," Ari said quietly. At fourteen, he was the oldest of the kids, and he seemed to feel his responsibility to set the tone for the rest. The other children nodded solemnly, though the younger ones weren't quite sure what exactly was expected of them. It was Zevy who asked, "What will be different?"

His father answered him. "For one thing, we won't have a minyan to daven with on Shabbos, or a *sefer Torah* to *lain* from. We'll just have to do the best we can on our own." He spread his hands in a curiously helpless gesture. "I hope all of this will blow over quickly, kids. But until it does, please bear with us. We're going to need your coopera-tion... and your support."

"You've got it, Daddy!" Shraga cried. The others turned to look at him. He was a boy who usually kept his feelings well hidden inside. Under the curious scrutiny of his own family and the Katzes he blushed, deepening the emotional pink of his cheeks to a dull brick red. Hanging his head, he mumbled, "I mean, you can count on us."

"That's right," Pinny said robustly. "Every one of us. Right, you guys?" Under his fierce eye, the younger kids bobbed their heads up and down. The two scientists exchanged thin, sad smiles with their wives. The strain was beginning to tell on all of them.

It was a quiet group that went in to lunch presently. Shraga could never see their table without recalling, with a shudder, the moment when Zevy had raised his voice in the hushed dining room to announce, "Abba, is this the black box they're all looking for?" It was a quiet meal, with little conversation and none of the usual banter about the awfulness of the food. Only the littlest Katzes and Morgensterns appeared oblivious to the tension.

Shai Gilboa, seated between his foster parents, glanced from one face to the other around the table and read the same message in each one. Thoughtfully he fingered the scrap of paper in his pocket.

After lunch there was a movement to their various rooms, where they would rest, shower, and get ready for Shabbos. Pinny was glum as he laid out his white shirt.

"It won't seem like Shabbos in this place," he groused. "Why won't Tom let us leave just for a night and a day? We could promise to come back."

Ari only shook his head. He was feeling low, too, and not much like talking.

Pinny listened to his brother not talk for a while, until he grew bored. He left the room to search for some company. The upstairs corridor was empty. For a moment he considered knocking on Shraga's door, but something — some lingering shyness — held him back. "Maybe he's resting," he thought. It still felt strange to consider Shraga as a friend instead of someone to be studiously avoided. "Might as well see what's happening down in the lobby," he decided. As he was standing at the elevator, moodily punching the down button, Chaim came out of the room he shared with Shraga. Sighting Pinny, he waved.

"Hi, Pinny," he called, hurrying down the hall as fast as his legs could carry him. "Where're you going?"

"Downstairs."

"Guess I'll come, too." Chaim took up his position opposite Pinny and punched the already-lit button.

"Where's Shraga?" Pinny asked.

"In our room. He won't talk."

Pinny sighed. "I know the feeling. Well, here comes the elevator." Chaim would do as well as anyone to help pass an hour or so, until it was time to start changing his clothes for Shabbos. The ride down was smooth and fast. Stepping out of the elevator in the ornate lobby, Pinny was struck again by the miles of glass and glitter. Somehow, the place failed to charm him as it had the day he'd arrived. How far away that day seemed now!

"Look, there's Tom!" Chaim tugged at Pinny's sleeve. "Let's go talk to him."

Pinny saw the tall figure near the front entrance, speaking into his walkie-talkie. Maybe the senior F.B.I. man at the hotel would tell him a little about new developments on the case — if there were any. Just because Pinny and his own fellow investigators had had to put off their detecting until after Shabbos didn't mean the F.B.I. hadn't been making some progress. He hurried after Chaim.

Tom flipped the walkie-talkie into the closed position and returned it to its place on his belt. "Hi, kids," he said, greeting them with his easy smile. "What's up?"

Pinny relaxed. Though his father was under suspicion for the theft of the valuable device, the Special Agent didn't seem to harbor any grudge against the kids. Pinny looked up trustingly at the representative of law and order.

"Hi, Tom. Er, nothing much."

Tom peered at Pinny. "You kids are pretty shook up by all of this, aren't you?"

"Well, now that you mention it..." Pinny sighed. "I guess you could say we are."

"Nobody's talking to anybody, hardly," Chaim volunteered.

"That's bad," Tom said sympathetically. "Real bad. Listen." He beckoned them closer. "I know it doesn't look good right now, but I'm doing my best to try and clear both your dads. My higher-ups at the Bureau..." He broke off.

"Yes?" Pinny prompted eagerly. "What do they think?"

Tom looked sober. "To be honest, they don't like the way things are shaping up — in terms of your fathers, I mean. But I'm trying to get them to look into other possibilities. So cheer up, kids. The show's not over till it's over."

Despite the grim news Tom had given, Pinny felt his spirits lighten a little. Whatever his superiors might think of the two Jewish scientists, this big, tough, Special Agent was on their side.

"Thanks, Tom," Pinny said in a low voice. Then, just to show that he wasn't ungrateful, he added, "Don't think we're just sitting on our hands. Me 'n my brother and Shraga Morgenstern have a plan of our own. Come Sunday, we're going to start some real detecting."

Tom grinned. "Oh, yeah? Well, good luck. Investigating crimes is no easy work, y'know."

"Pinny and Shraga can do it if anyone can," Chaim declared with confidence. "You wouldn't believe what kind of I.Q.s they've got. They're the smartest kids in their schools!"

"Is that so?" Tom eyed Pinny with a certain respect. "Well, listen, genius. Anything you find that might help — anything at all — you bring it to ol' Tom, all right? I'll do what I can."

"Thanks a lot, Tom." Pinny's heart swelled with gratitude. "I mean that."

"I know you do." With an absent pat on Chaim's shoulder, the Special Agent half-turned away. He had his work to do.

"Well, bye," said Pinny.

"See ya later," Chaim chimed in. Tom nodded, gave them another flash of his white teeth, and strode away.

Chaim beamed at Pinny. "Boy, did you hear that? He's gonna help us! That Tom sure is okay!"

"Yes." Pinny felt buoyant as he fell into step beside Chaim. Sinking into one of the comfortable couches by the lobby window, he replayed in his mind the conversation with Tom Morrison. As he did, his determination to discover the culprit grew even stronger. His first motive, of course, was to help clear his father and Dr. Morgenstern. But beyond that, he couldn't help imagining the thrill of bringing the answer to Tom — an answer that shone with the light of truth and justice. It would be the thrill of a lifetime. He could see the headlines: "Jewish Boys Aid F.B.I. in Tracking Down Deadly-Weapon Thief!"

He was still lost in a dream of glory when a small hand tugged at his shirt sleeve.

"Pinny!" said Zevy. "Are you asleep or something? Ima sent me to find you. She wants to know if you've showered yet." Zevy himself was glowing with soap and virtue in his white shirt and navy Shabbos pants. Pinny shook his head. "Tell her — oh, never mind. I'll go up myself."

"Guess I'd better go, too," Chaim said, rousing himself from his fascinated study, through the broad window, of the F.B.I. men patrolling the grounds. The guard had trebled since the start of the convention — and all because of that little black box!

As the three made their way back to the elevators, Pinny remarked, "Well, I for one won't mind a break from all this over Shabbos — even if we do have to spend it in this place. A little peace and quiet will do all of us good." He was thinking of the strained smiles he had seen his father and mother exchange before.

He was right. A little peace and quiet was just what his parents, and the Morgensterns, and all of them, could use this Shabbos. Unfortunately, they were not to have it.

4

A Hundred Questions

Shai Gilboa wore a white shirt. On his black hair sat a white knitted *kippah*, and on his face was an expression of near-contentment as he watched his foster mother circle her hands before the Shabbat flames.

After murmuring the blessing over the candles, Mrs. Drucker watched him through her fingers. It was the first time since the day she and her husband had brought Shai home, months before, that he had looked like this — actually happy. She was almost afraid to breathe, for fear of breaking the spell.

Mr. Drucker, too, felt reluctant to say a word. Even the soft "*Shabbat Shalom*" with which he greeted his wife and foster son was spoken scarcely above a whisper. He was also watching Shai. What thoughts were flitting through the boy's mind, to make him almost smile like that? It wasn't much —

but after three months of scowls, even an almost-smile was something.

What Shai was thinking about would have surprised the Druckers, had they known. Shai had just become a bona-fide member of a very exclusive club. At least, that was the way it felt to him.

It was a detective club, and he felt honored to belong.

Yesterday, when the hotel had still been reeling from the theft of the secret weapon, he had coaxed the Russian kids, Nikolai Gorodnik and Alexei Pim, to be his partners in investigating the crime. It had been an impulsive move, designed to take his mind off his own, more personal troubles. Nikolai — or Niki, as the Americans had nicknamed him — had seemed eager enough, though Alexei needed some persuading. But today both of them seemed to have lost all interest in the enterprise. Alexei was moody and withdrawn, and Niki had been walking around with a crease of worry between his eyes. When Shai had tried to get them to talk about the case, they'd looked uneasy. Every time he pressed them, all they would say was, "Later." Only later never seemed to come. He wondered why.

The problem was the note. If not for that, the crime might have passed right over him — except for the fact that the F.B.I. kept calling Dr. Drucker in for more questioning. Though what they expected to learn from the Israeli, who'd been six thousand miles away when the secret weapon was developed, and was working his way through one of the "deluxe" kosher meals with the rest of the people at his table when it was stolen, was more than Shai could figure out.

As he'd done a hundred times that day, he felt in his pocket for the note he'd discovered on the floor of the woods, buried under the pine needles where the man had kicked it. Through the leaves of the tree where he'd been hiding, Shai had caught only a glimpse of the figure passing below. It had been a bird's-eye view of a bowed head and a navy-blue jacket, gone nearly as suddenly as it had appeared, so that Shai would have been hard put to describe the man, or even to say whether he'd been tall or short, thin or heavyset.

But the figure had left behind the note. And the note had been burning a hole in Shai's pocket ever since. Part of him wanted to hand it over to Shraga and Pinny, sons of the accused men. But he was reluctant to give away his only clue in the whole affair. Owning the note and being able to finger it where it lay hidden in his pocket made him feel important. "I know something you don't know" might have summed up his attitude, as he watched the F.B.I. scan the hotel and its grounds for clues. All day he'd been watching Shraga and Pinny, walking around so downcast and quiet. How different from the merry, careless, *pushy* kids they'd been only yesterday!

When they'd come after him then, he'd rejected their friendly overtures. Today, he realized with some surprise, he felt differently. It was as though seeing the way the American boys were suffering made him feel closer to them. They had something in common now.

All day he'd watched them, and all day his thoughts had been bouncing back and forth like the balls flying through the air at the hotel's tennis court: to share the note or not?

At last, he'd made up his mind. He would share it — for a price.

"I know something about the theft of the black box," he whispered to Shraga that afternoon, as the American boy came downstairs in his Shabbos clothes, the normally springy brown hair lying damply down for once. "Want to know what it is?"

"Sure," Shraga had answered — though not before a skeptical expression crossed his face. "What is it?"

"First I want you to agree to something."

A wary look from Shraga. "What?"

"I want you and Pinny to let me help you find the criminal."

Shraga had hesitated. "Anyone can try to find him. It's a free country."

"You know what I mean. I want to be a detective — like you and Pinny."

"How do you know about that?" Shraga demanded.

Shai didn't tell him that he'd eavesdropped on their strategy session that morning. Instead, he shrugged. "It doesn't take too much brains to figure that out."

Shraga shifted uneasily from one foot to the other. "Pinny's brother, Ari, is in this, too. We'd have to ask him."

"Okay. So ask."

"I will."

"And if they both agree?" Shai persisted. "Is it okay?"

"If they agree — fine." Shraga fixed him with a suspicious eye. "Are you sure you really have something for us?"

"Yes." Shai was clearly eager, and just as clearly telling the truth. "Something important." *At least, I hope it is.*

"All right, then."

And now, just five minutes ago, Shraga had come over to say, "It's a deal." The Americans would let Shai join their efforts to track down the thief. In return, Shai would show them his treasure.

"Starting after Shabbos, though," Shraga cautioned. "We don't do any detecting till then."

This was a disappointment to Shai. He'd been looking forward to starting right away. "Why not? We don't have to do anything you're not allowed to do. Why can't we just talk about it?"

But Shraga shook his head firmly. "No way. It's just not *Shabbosdik.*" And with that, Shai had to be content.

Still, the day would pass, this Shabbat that his foster parents took so seriously and that these American kids apparently did, too. How, he wondered, would the boys manage to pass a whole night and a day without continuing their search for the man who'd caused their own fathers so much grief, and — if the rumors he'd heard were true — the American government so much concern?

Pinny had come over just before candlelighting, also dressed in his best. "I hear you've joined us. Do you really have something that might help?"

"I think so," Shai answered cautiously. His fingers itched to reach into his pocket.

Pinny smiled and thrust out his own hand. After only the slightest hesitation, Shai took the outstretched hand and shook it briefly.

"Welcome to the team," said Pinny warmly.

No wonder Shai was smiling — almost.

Niki Gorodnik watched, with wondering eyes, the way the Jewish families at the next table celebrated their Shabbos. From time to time his glance traveled to his mother, talking her usual scientific talk with the other scientists at their own table. If his mother was Jewish, and if that meant that he, too, were a Jew, then why weren't they Jews like the ones he saw seated in their finery beside him? Why the blessings over the wine in its silver goblet, for which everyone from the youngest baby to the adults stood up? Why the braided bread, the sprinkle of salt, the softly chanted tunes sung in such heartfelt harmony? What did it really mean to be a Jew? And if he wasn't the real thing, what was he?

All these and a hundred other questions danced and circled in his mind as he plodded through his own, un-festive, Friday night fare. And behind it all, like the persistent humming of a pesky mosquito, buzzed the other question. Should he tell those American boys, the Jewish ones, what he knew? It might help their fathers in their moment of trouble. On the other hand — here he kept his gaze studiously fixed on his own hands, twisted together in his lap — it might get someone else in trouble. What was loyalty, and to whom did he owe his?

The boy with the hundred questions smiled dutifully as the waiter set a luscious-looking dessert before him. He even lifted his spoon and ate some, but he didn't taste a thing.

Not only Shraga and Pinny, but their parents as well, were determined not to let the trouble cloud their enjoyment of the holy Shabbos.

"Isn't it nice out here?" murmured Mrs. Katz. The two families were seated on the hotel's terrace after davening and a full, if unexciting, meal. It had been the strangest Shabbos meal Shraga had ever eaten, with each course coming to him encased in its silver-foil wrapping and tasting almost exactly the same as the course before.

"Amazing," Ari had muttered, peering at a piece of squash on his fork. "How do they manage to get rid of every single bit of flavor like that?"

"Practice," Pinny sighed. He poked listlessly at a piece of rubbery chicken. "If this were round, I'd say we could have a good game of catch with it."

As usual, one of their parents had admonished them to stop speaking ill of the food. None of the adults, however, went so far as to praise it.

But now, seated beneath the soft night sky, with summer breezes ruffling his hair and a trillion low-hanging stars seeming to wink at him from every side, a feeling of peace stole over Pinny. Glancing at the others, he saw that they felt the same. It was good to sit like this beside his family and friends, with the peace of Shabbos around them and their worries banished — at least for the moment.

"Regards and 'Good Shabbos' from Gitty, everyone," Mrs. Morgenstern said. Shraga's oldest sister, an eighth-grader, had elected to remain behind in New York for this, the final week of her final year at school. "I spoke to her just before candlelighting. She's having the time of her life, and practicing for graduation with her classmates every day."

"Did you tell her about...you know?" Chaim asked. It was the closest any of them had come to referring to the crime that had rocked their lives.

"No. Why give her something to worry about?" Mrs. Morgenstern settled a sleepy Vivi more comfortably on her lap. Ruchie, dressed in a frilly pink Shabbos dress with matching pink ribbons in her curly hair, was playing at her mother's feet on the terrace stones, still warm from the sun that had long since set.

No one argued with Mrs. Morgenstern. Why, indeed, give Gitty something to worry about, when they were all worrying quite enough already? It made Pinny feel good to know that at least one person thought they were having a high old time up here, without a care in the world. It made his own burden somehow a little easier to bear.

Shraga was also glad — but at the same time, in a way he wished his sister did know. More, he wished she were here with them, breathing the air with its hint of flowers and feeling the peace of Shabbos banish weekday cares. He looked up at the stars, forming their familiar patterns in the night sky. Was Gitty looking at the very same stars right now? Though he didn't usually spend much time thinking about his big sister —which kid did? — he found that he missed her now. A family should be together when the going got rough.

He glanced at his father. In the yellow terrace lights, Dr. Morgenstern looked years younger than he had that afternoon. *Baruch Hashem* for Shabbos, Shraga thought suddenly. He'd never appreciated the day as much as he did at this moment. But then, maybe he'd never needed it quite as much before...

Shraga's father stirred in his comfortable chair. "Well, Shmulie?" he asked Dr. Katz, smiling. "What do you say we go inside and learn a little?" He turned to his wife and Mrs. Katz, adding, "That is, if the ladies don't mind."

"Mind?" Mrs. Morgenstern echoed. "Just the opposite! Go, by all means. Learn good. After what's happened, we can all use the *zechusim*..."

Mrs. Katz nodded her agreement.

In the shadows where he stood listening, Shai Gilboa frowned in perplexity. What had she meant by that? Why should it make a difference to them in their time of trouble whether the men learned or not? On the contrary, he'd have expected the women to demand that the men stay with them and the children at such a time. It was another question in the slowly growing chain of them in his mind... He shook his head in the darkness. It just didn't make any sense.

He wasn't even sure why he was standing here, watching these two families and listening to their talk. If he were in the mood for family talk, why didn't he just sit with the Druckers, who would have been so eager to have him with them? Maybe it was *because* they were so eager to love him that he kept running away...

Again, he shook his head.

Shai wasn't given time to puzzle over his questions. As he watched from his hiding place, the two scientists rose to their feet and began taking their leave. Shai shrank further into the shadows. Dr. Katz and Dr. Morgenstern said "Good night" and "Good Shabbos" to the younger children, who'd be sound asleep by the time the men finished learning and came upstairs to their rooms.

"Good night, Ruchie. Sleep well," Dr. Morgenstern said.

"Kiss, Daddy!" cried Ruchie, reaching up her arms. With a smile, her father bent over and scooped the little girl into his arms. As he did, there came a curious scraping sound from high above.

Before any of them could look up, or even wonder where the noise was coming from, something big, dark, and very solid came hurtling down at them — to smash onto the terrace stones in the very spot where, seconds earlier, Ruchie had been sitting!

5

The Accident

For an endless moment, shock held everybody motionless. Then Ruchie opened her mouth into a round, perfect "O" and let out a piercing wail.

Immediately, every other voice was raised, too — in excitement, in fear, in outrage.

"What was *that*?" shrieked Mindy, clutching at Daniella.

"Ruchie, are you okay?" Shraga gasped.

"My baby! Oh, my baby!" Mrs. Morgenstern cried, drawing near the little girl as, still screaming, Ruchie wound her arms more tightly about her father's neck. "Ruchie, honey, it didn't hit you, did it?" She sounded very nearly hysterical.

"It didn't touch her," Mr. Morgenstern said, sounding not far from hysteria himself. "Right, Ruchie?"

Ruchie buried her head deeper into his shoulder and continued wailing.

"What was it? What fell?" Chaim wanted to know.

"Pinny, move away from there!" Mrs. Katz squealed. "Something else might fall down!"

"What was it?" Chaim repeated doggedly, inching closer to where Pinny was inspecting the shattered object on the patio stones. "And where did it come from?"

"From the second floor. I saw it fall!" cried Shai Gilboa, appearing out of the shadows.

So perturbed were the people on the terrace that none of them thought to wonder why the Israeli boy was suddenly in their midst. "What? What did you say?" Dr. Katz asked sharply.

"I — er, happened to be nearby, and I saw it fall. It came tumbling down from a window on the second floor. Or maybe it was the third." Shai pointed upward.

Dr. Morgenstern, having finally managed to unloose Ruchie's stranglehold on his neck, relinquished her to his wife. Ruchie stopped crying and starting hiccoughing softly in her mother's arms. Dr. Morgenstern went to crouch by the pieces lying on the stones. "Whatever it was, it appears to have been quite heavy." He had fully mastered his voice by now.

"It's one of those cement things — flowerboxes. They have them on all the window sills," Pinny announced excitedly.

"That's right," agreed Shraga. He touched one of the fragments with the toe of his Shabbos shoe, pursing his lips thoughtfully. "It would take a mighty big shove to move one of those things."

"What are you saying?" Mrs. Katz gasped. "That somebody *pushed* it down on us?" Even in the pale yellow terrace lights, her face was noticeably whiter.

"Let's not jump to conclusions," Dr. Katz said, trying hard to inject a calm note into the proceedings. He bent to look more closely at the shattered remains. "But I agree, it does look like one of the windowboxes."

"It is! I tell you, I saw the whole thing. It came tumbling right down from that window! With my own eyes I saw it." Again, Shai pointed upward. Automatically, every head went back. It was impossible, in the dark, to tell whether a windowbox was indeed missing from one of the upper floors.

Their screams had penetrated the lobby. Two receptionists, a bellboy, and a crew of assorted guests straggled out, peering into the gloom as their eyes tried to adjust to the dark. In the crowd Shraga could spot Dr. Manfred Isingard, the tall Norwegian, by his height and his head of silver hair, gleaming in the moonlight. The distinctive Hungarian accent of Magda Brenner was there somewhere, too. A stream of questions was met by an answering babble from the group on the terrace, impossible to untangle at first. Frightened by the noisy crowd, Ruchie started howling again. Her high-pitched screams punctuated the scene like some bizarre musical accompaniment.

Only with the appearance of the hotel manager, Mr. Stewart, did some semblance of order return to the group. As Mrs. Morgenstern led Ruchie away into the light and safety of the hotel, the manager listened to their story.

Mr. Stewart was a thin, balding man with huge horn-rimmed glasses and a habit of clearing his throat loudly when he was feeling agitated. He cleared it now.

"Hrmph! Strange goings-on," he said fretfully. "Never had such a thing happen in my hotel in all my twenty years here." He glared almost accusingly at the Katzes and Morgensterns. "*Very* strange goings-on indeed."

"I would suggest you look into this immediately, Mr. Stewart," Dr. Katz said crisply. "We were the victims here — or, rather, thank G-d, the near-victims. We'd like to know just how this...*accident*... occurred."

"Oh, we'll certainly check it out," Mr. Stewart assured him. He peered upward through his over-sized glasses. "I find it hard to believe that one of those windowboxes came loose by itself. Such a thing has never happened — not in all my twenty years here. *Hurrumph!* They're encased in concrete and weigh a ton — er, figuratively speaking, that is."

"And the alternative?" Dr. Morgenstern spoke quietly, so as not to frighten the women and children any more than they were already.

"Hm! Hurrumph! What do you mean? Preposterous!"

Shraga found it hard to believe, too. Who would have pushed one of those things onto the unsuspecting heads — almost — of the Katzes and the Morgensterns, relaxing for a brief hour before bedtime? Who had the strength to do it? And, even more important, who had the motive? Surely, whoever had something against the Jewish scientists had already done his evil work in stealing their invention. What was the point in harming or frightening them now?

He watched his father's face for a clue to his thoughts. Was it possible that it had actually been no accident? And if so, who was responsible?

Pinny's eyes met Shraga's. He saw the same questions reflected there. Who? Who?

The sound of running footsteps brought Shraga out of his reverie with a snap. A figure came sprinting onto the terrace, moving easily and scarcely breathing hard. It was Tom Morrison, senior F.B.I. man at the hotel. "I just heard." The words emerged clipped, almost angry. "What's this all about?"

Dr. Katz quickly filled him on the incident. Tom whipped out his walkie-talkie and murmured a few words into it. Then, replacing it in his belt, he frowned at the thickening crowd. "All right folks, we've got things under control here. There's been a little accident, that's all. Luckily, no one's been hurt. But if you keep standing around here in the dark, someone could be." He grinned. "Like, someone might step on your toe, young man," he told a wide-eyed bellboy who stood gawking nearby.

The bellboy giggled nervously. Some of the tension left the scene. Slowly, in ones and twos, the crowd began to drift back toward the lighted lobby, shivering a little in the night breeze.

Before long the terrace was deserted again, except for the Katzes, the Morgensterns, Tom Morrison, and Mr. Stewart.

The F.B.I. man stepped over to the smashed flowerbox and inspected it briefly. Rising, he turned to the hotel manager.

"How likely is it that that thing could have fallen on its own?"

Mr. Stewart sputtered indignantly. "*Hurrumph*! Impossible! Those things are made of reinforced concrete. I tell you, never in all my twenty years —"

"Okay, okay. I get the picture." Surprisingly, Tom winked at Pinny, who stood at his elbow. "Did any of you see or hear anything suspicious before the thing fell?"

"No, I —"

"*I* saw it! With my own eyes I saw the whole thing," Shai cried, pushing forward to stand importantly before the Special Agent. "Straight down from the third floor it fell, or maybe the second.

Such a heavy thing, you should have heard the crash when it fell — *tra-a-ach!*— on those stones."

Shraga, remembering the sound, shuddered. Daniella Katz moaned softly and clung more tightly to Mindy. Her father patted her shoulder absently. Chaim said, "What I want to know is, if it couldn't have fallen by itself, how *did* it fall?"

"That," said his father soberly, "is what we'd all like to know." He looked inquiringly at Tom.

The F.B.I. man shrugged. "The matter will be thoroughly investigated, you can bet your boots on that." To the hotel manager he said, "Who has the rooms on this side of the hotel? Do you know offhand?"

"Why, *hurrumph*, well, of course I do. Conference people, mostly — scientists, security. There are one or two empty rooms up there too, I believe. We'd have to check the register to be sure."

"Let's do that now." Tom eyed the group on the terrace. "Now, I want you folks to go upstairs and get yourselves a good night's sleep. This has been a shock. We'll get to the bottom of it, believe me. Good night."

A ragged chorus of "Good night"s came back to him. Shraga watched Tom lead a still *hurrumph*ing Mr. Stewart off. He felt very cold suddenly, and exhausted. His head ached from all the excitement and he wanted desperately to lay it down somewhere, anywhere, and sleep. Walking beside the others toward the lobby entrance, he could tell by their shuffling gait that they felt the same. Their walk reflected the way they felt: shocked, frightened, and very, very tired.

"As soon as we can get to a minyan," Dr. Morgenstern said quietly to Dr. Katz, "I think we should all *bentch gomel.*"

"I agree," said Dr. Katz. The two moved closer together and conferred in very low voices after that, too low for Shraga to overhear. His eyelids were beginning to droop, when a light hand touched his shoulder.

"Shraga?" asked Shai. "What did your father mean? What is '*bentch gomel*'?"

Shraga felt almost too weary to speak. This new, interested-in-everything Shai was almost harder to take than the old, reclusive one had been. Shraga tried to smile. "Tomorrow I'll explain, okay? I'm a little tired now."

Shai looked disappointed. After a moment, he went over to Pinny to try his luck there. Ari had Zevy by the hand and was half-leading, half-dragging him towards the stairs, and bed.

Many pairs of interested eyes followed their progress to the staircase. The elevators would have been quicker and more convenient for the weary families, but it was Shabbos. Shai found his foster parents seated in a corner of the lobby and ran over to tell them about his eye-witness encounter with real danger.

Stumbling, yawning, the two families climbed the long flights of stairs and bid each other a hurried good night before separating to seek refuge in their own rooms. Ruchie Morgenstern was already snoring softly in her mother's bed. Down the hall, Shraga undressed in the dark, almost too tired to think. After the shock, sleep was the only thing he wanted right then.

All the other things that needed to be thought about — vital, urgent things — would keep until tomorrow.

6

A Strange Day

By morning, most of the hotel guests had forgotten about the incident on the terrace the night before. Even young Ruchie seemed to have put it out of her mind. She was her old merry self next day, playing with her dolls and uttering her usual nonsense to them. Shraga watched his little sister with a smile, which turned into a frown when he remembered just how close she'd come to being terribly injured, *chas v'shalom.* His heart thudded as he recalled the hurtling flowerbox, and the crash on impact. Silently he murmured a heartfelt "Thank you" to Hashem for keeping them safe.

It was a sleepy sort of day. Because it was Shabbos, the Katzes and Morgensterns could not join the scientists in the special tours that had been planned for this day in place of their usual work in the labs. Only one modest seminar was held that afternoon, in place of the customary three or four. The older Katzes spent most of the afternoon in their room, talking quietly, as did the adult Morgensterns.

As for the children, they were very busy trying *not* to talk about the mystery which had taken over their lives and which was growing steadily more frightening. The most Pinny, Shraga, and Ari did was exchange significant glances when Tom came over to their parents at lunch and told them that the windowbox had, indeed, toppled from a window above their heads.

"It's hard to see how anyone could have pushed it, though," he said, shaking his head in frustration. "I checked some of the others; they're mighty heavy, those things."

"In that case," Dr. Morgenstern said slowly, "it's even harder to see how it could have fallen all by itself, isn't it?"

Tom nodded. "We're still investigating. That — *and* the other matter. You just enjoy your day. We'll keep you posted on new information as it comes in."

Tom's veiled reference to the theft of the black box, and the plans for the deadly weapon, was like an uncomfortable breath of cold in the warm room. Pinny dug his fork into the soggy mess that was labeled "home-style *cholent*" on his package. Brooding, he didn't even notice what he was eating. As the others watched in amazement, he shoveled in one mouthful after another until the whole thing was gone.

"You're gonna regret that move, boy," Ari said, shaking his head.

Pinny looked up. "What?"

"That." Ari pointed.

Pinny noticed, for the first time, his clean plate. He turned slightly green. "Did I really eat all that?"

"That's what I'd call a heroic act," Shraga grinned admiringly. "Something that calls for true-blue courage."

"And warped taste buds," giggled Chaim.

"*And* a cast-iron stomach," Ari added.

"That's enough, boys," Dr. Morgenstern said wearily. "Let's *bentch* and go learn something before our naps."

But the boys had no intention of napping. After their parents and the little kids had gone upstairs, Ari, Pinny, and Shraga found seats in a corner of the lobby — nearly empty on this sunny Saturday — and sat talking. Hard as it was, all three were determined not to make any plans on Shabbos. The most they allowed themselves were a few indirect references to the events of the last couple of days. However, they were soon joined by Shai, and it was clear that the Israeli boy had no compunction about discussing the very topic the others were trying to avoid.

"So how do you think the thief got into your fathers' lab? Where do you suppose that missing diskette is right now? Do you think the bad guys have it? I wonder what they're plans are. It's a little scary, isn't it? I mean, at least in Israel we know who our enemies are. I wonder what'll happen next?"

"Um. That's nice, Shai," Shraga said vaguely.

"Wonder if it's going to rain again?" Pinny murmured. "Look how cloudy it's becoming."

"Nah, those aren't rain clouds," Ari said. "Bet you it'll be clear tonight."

Shai stared from one to the other.

"What's the matter with you guys?" he demanded. The old Shai peeked angrily through his eyes, ready to be rejected. He shifted in his seat as if about to spring to his feet. "If you don't want me around, just say so."

Pinny sighed. "Look, Shai," he said. "It's not that we don't want you. Like we told you, we'll be happy to have your help — after Shabbos. Right now, we want to avoid discussing the whole thing, and especially making plans. Okay?"

"But why? This is important!"

"True," conceded Ari. "But keeping true to *Yiddishkeit* is even more important."

Shai looked baffled. "Yiddish-what?"

"You know," said Shraga. "In Hebrew you'd call it — uh, *Yahadut.*"

Shai thought about that. "But what does any of that have to do with our detective work?" He sounded outraged. "Don't you *want* to help your fathers?"

"Of course we do!" Pinny said.

"But it's Shabbos," Shraga explained patiently. "So?"

"So — it's a day that's different from all the others in the week. We dress different, eat different foods, say different *tefillos*, and think different thoughts. Get it?"

Shai didn't answer. Shabbat, back home in his previous foster families, had meant no more or less than a day off from work and school. It was a day to take a trip, to the beach perhaps, or to the park. Thinking different thoughts? It was a novel idea. Did the Druckers do that, too? For the first time, he found himself actually a tiny bit interested in what his foster parents thought about the lives they led. Was their *Yahadut* the same as these Americans' *Yiddishkeit*? On the outside they sure looked the same. And if he thought about it, it probably *was* the same. Were religious Jews the same everywhere?

Unconsciously, he reached up to touch the *kippah* on his head — the *kippah* he'd promised the Druckers he'd wear. In a way, it felt like a badge of some kind, to show that he belonged to these people, to their customs and *mitzvot* and observances. But inside, he knew that he really didn't belong. Not yet. He wasn't even sure if he was interested in belonging. Right now, he didn't know enough to decide.

"Right after Havdalah, we'll begin," Shraga promised. Shai's doubts fell away in a thrill of anticipation.

For the rest of the afternoon he sat with the American boys, talking idly of this and that, comparing Haifa to New York, telling them about his school and the games he played there, and listening to them tell about theirs. So the hours passed, until it was time for Havdalah.

As Pinny held up the braided candle with its flickering flame and listened to his father recite the familiar blessings to mark the start of a new week, his pulse quickened. Now they'd be able to get to work at last.

Shraga and Ari were feeling the same way. In their excitement, none of them noticed the shadows beneath their fathers' eyes, or the grim looks on their mothers' faces. As soon as Havdalah was over, Dr. Morgenstern and Dr. Katz announced that they were going to spend some time in their lab. Just before the onset of Shabbos, they'd received the call they'd been waiting for from the M.C.B. computer division. It was necessary, they said, to change the passwords for the powerful computer program that held the secrets of "Little Nicky."

"Good night, boys," Dr. Katz said quietly to his older sons. "Help your mother. Be good."

"Sure, Abba," Ari said, puzzled by his father's solemn tone.

"We always help," Pinny put in. His mind was far away, with all the suspects the detectives were going to begin interviewing this evening.

"Good," said Dr. Katz. "Ready, David?"

Dr. Morgenstern had been having a similar word with Shraga. "Your mother was very shaken up by what happened last night," he finished quickly, in a low voice. "Help her with the little kids, okay?"

"Sure, Daddy." Shraga hesitated, trying to formulate a question. His father's manner seemed very odd. But already Dr. Morgenstern was turning away. Together with Dr. Katz, he made for the labs at the back of the hotel. Shraga found Pinny and Ari on either side of him.

"Boy, all this must really be weighing on them," Ari said. "I've never seen Abba so — so serious. Have you, Pinny?"

"Not since the time Zevy swallowed that bottle of window polish and had to be rushed to hospital," his brother replied.

"My father was acting weird, too," Shraga told them. "Wonder what's going on?"

"Need you ask?" Ari said. "Robberies, accidents... It's enough to freeze anyone's blood."

"The best thing we can do is to solve it for them," Pinny declared. "Come on, guys, let's get started!"

"Let's find Shai first," Shraga suggested, hurrying after the others. "We promised."

"All right," said Pinny. "But he'd better keep his word about that 'something' he has to show us."

"He will," Shraga said, hoping his words would prove true. "Shai won't let us down."

Shai was glaring angrily at this foster parents, up in their hotel room. "What? Leave tomorrow? But why?"

"We think it's safest," Dr. Drucker explained patiently. "There have been strange and dangerous things going on these past few days. Your mother and I don't want you in the middle of it. We want to get you away, somewhere safe."

"She's not my mother," Shai said automatically. "And I don't want to be safe!" He waved his arms wildly, hardly knowing what he was saying. "I want to be here, to help solve the mystery. Besides, how can you leave? The convention's not over till Wednesday. And didn't the F.B.I. say you scientists have to stay till they finish with the case?"

"They did," Dr. Drucker spoke heavily. "And I intend to stay. But your — uh, Mrs. Drucker can take you on to Disneyland herself. I'll try to join you there as soon as possible."

Disneyland? Shai could dimly remember a time, only a couple of weeks ago, when a visit to Disneyland had seemed the height of happiness — a dream come true. Now, he shook his head stubbornly. Sure, he'd visit Disneyland — *after* all this was over. For the first time in his life he felt important. He was needed. Not only for the note nestling in his pocket, but for the help he could give to the two scientists and their families, including the boys he was beginning to think of as his friends. Leave? No chance!

The Druckers tried to persuade him to change his mind, but their words fell onto deaf ears. At last, they gave up. Mrs. Drucker was secretly a little relieved. She didn't want to leave her husband behind. In times of trouble, a family should stick together. She watched, resigned, as Shai ran off to find the American boys.

Shai hoped the others had waited for him before beginning the investigation. To his joy, he found them pacing the lobby impatiently. Their faces lit up at his arrival.

"Finally!" Pinny exclaimed. "Listen, Shai. If you want to be part of this, you'll have to be on time. We've been waiting fifteen minutes already!"

"Sorry," Shai said breathlessly. "My, um, parents needed to talk to me." He looked from one boy to the other eagerly. "So where do we begin?"

Pinny pulled the notepad from his pocket. "We've already divided up the list of suspects. Give me a second, Shai. I'll shuffle things around so you can get someone, too."

They were standing in a respectful circle around Pinny, when a diffident cough drew their attention. Turning, they found Niki Gorodnik standing there.

"Excuse me. Can I talk to you a minute?"

Shraga struggled with a surge of impatience. Stifling a sigh, he smiled and said, "Sure, Niki. What's up?"

Until he'd actually spoken the words, Niki had not been sure what they were going to be. They came out now in a rush — eager, excited, and a little anxious.

"If you're trying to solve the mystery of the black box, I want to help. Can I? Please?"

7

The Investigation Begins

Surprisingly, it was Shai who objected.

"Do you have any information we don't know about?" he demanded. "Otherwise, why should we let you in?"

Niki looked bewildered. "I just want to help." He gazed appealingly from Ari to Pinny to Shraga. "I won't be in the way, I promise. I — I thought maybe you could use an extra pair of hands." He waited.

"Sure we can," Pinny agreed, impulsive as usual. "We don't mind. Do we, guys?"

"It's fine with me," Ari said. Shraga slowly nodded, but inside he was wondering, a little resentfully, when Pinny was going to learn to think before he spoke. It wasn't that he minded Niki as a fellow detective. In fact, now that the Russian boy had turned out to be Jewish, Shraga thought it might be interesting to get to know him better. Why, Niki knew absolutely nothing about *Yiddishkeit*! Under normal circumstances, Shraga would have loved introducing him to some of the basics. Maybe when this was all over...

No, Shraga had no objection to Niki himself. He was just worried that the more people were involved in the investigation, the more cumbersome and time-consuming it was apt to be. And Ari's next words confirmed this fear.

"Well, if we've got another kid on board, we'd better fill him in on our plans," Ari said. "Let's sit down in that corner for a minute."

Obediently, the others followed Ari to an arrangement of small couches in a corner of the vast lobby. The wall beside them was mirrored. In a spy novel, Shraga thought as he took his seat, we'd make sure to be careful to turn away from the mirror before we said a word, in case an enemy spy was sitting across the room, watching the mirror and reading our lips! The picture made him smile and dispelled some of his frustration — but not all of it. "Ari, time's passing and the night's not getting any younger. Let's make this snappy, okay?"

"Sure." Ari glanced at his brother. "Well, Pinny? You've got the notebook. Shoot."

Embarrassed but pleased, Pinny pulled his little notebook from his hip pocket where he'd absently returned it when Niki came. He opened it to the page that contained their list of suspects. "These are the people, the suspects, we want to try to talk to tonight," he began. "Basically, it's the list of all the scientists who have labs near our fathers'. The way I figure it, if the F.B.I. thought it worth their while to question them, so should we."

"Question them about what?" Shai wanted to know. "Where they were when the crime happened?"

"That, too," Pinny nodded. "But Tom Morrison's probably gotten everything he could from them in that area. What we might do is try to find out a little more about the suspects, to see if there's anything in their background that might have given them a motive to steal the weapon."

Shai nodded. "Okay. So who's on the list?"

Pinny consulted his pad and began to read. "Manfred Isingard, Magda Brenner, Richard Fowley, Ilya Pim, Natasha Gorodnik —"

"Hey, that is my mother!" Niki protested, growing red in the face. "Why is my mother on the list?"

Pinny looked nonplussed. "Well, she's one of the scientists, isn't she? Her lab's right down the hall from our fathers'. It's not that we actually *suspect* her," he added, tripping over his own words in his haste to reassure Niki. "It's just that... Well..." His words trailed off lamely.

Shraga tried to help. "It's not just your mother. We have to question everyone, don't you see that?"

Niki stared back at him mulishly, making it clear that he most certainly did *not* see.

"Look," Shraga tried again, pointing to another name on the list in Pinny's hand. "Shai's father's in here, too."

"What?" Now it was Shai's turn to sit up. "I don't believe this! I'm trying to help you find the thief, and you're treating my own father — uh, foster father — like that?" He made as if to get to his feet. "And I trusted you guys!"

Shraga, Pinny, and Ari looked at each other helplessly. Then, before Shai could stomp off in anger, as he was about to do, Shraga said, very gently, "Please sit down, Shai. I want to explain something."

"Please?" he said again, as Shai hesitated.

Shai stood undecided. The old, truculent look was back in his dark eyes. Again he'd trusted someone, and again they'd let him down! He didn't stop to ask himself why he felt such a fierce loyalty to the man he refused to call "Abba." All he knew was the all-too-familiar pain of betrayal.

"Come on, Shai," Ari urged. "Sit down and listen. You've got it all wrong."

Glowering at them from under his eyebrows, Shai reseated himself with a plop. "So talk. Let's hear what you have to say."

"First of all," Shraga began quickly, "I think it was wrong of us to refer to anyone on the list as a 'suspect.' A Jew is always supposed to be *dan lekaf zechus*." For Niki's benefit, he translated the Hebrew words into English. "That means, to judge other people in a favorable way. Not to presume that they're guilty even if signs seem to point that way. And we definitely shouldn't presume guilt when we have absolutely no signs at all." He peered anxiously at Shai and at Niki, hoping to find a glimmer of understanding in their closed faces. Neither boy responded, though Niki gave a grudging nod. Heartened, Shraga took a breath and continued.

"We have to start somewhere, see? And we figured that speaking to those scientists — all of them — was as good a place to begin as any. Even if none of them knows the first thing about the crime, he or she may have noticed something that might help us."

"Like who left the dining room during dinner that night, maybe," Pinny put in.

Niki looked very thoughtful. It was Shai who spoke.

"So you're saying that you don't actually suspect Dr. Drucker of doing it? You just want to ask him if he saw anything that night?"

"That's right," Shraga assured him.

"Then why didn't you say so in the first place!" Shai burst out. But there was a gleam of something that might almost have been amusement in the depths of his dark eyes.

"Niki? Okay?" Pinny asked the Russian. Niki nodded — a little reluctantly, Shraga thought. "As long as you don't think my mother had anything to do with it."

"Look, we'd question the president of the United States if we thought he could shed any light on this mess," Ari told him. "*Dan lekaf zechus*, remember? No suspicion at this point, just lots of questions, for the sake of finding out everything we can about — well, about everything. Okay?"

"Okay," said Niki.

"Okay," said Shai.

"Okay," said Shraga, suddenly consumed with impatience. "Pinny have you revised the list? There are two more of us now."

Pinny nodded and proceeded to divide up the scientists among his fellow detectives.

He himself would question the English physicist, Richard Fowley. Shraga would seek out the Hungarian, Magda Brenner. Ari was assigned to Manfred Isingard, the tall Norwegian, and Shai would speak to his foster father, Dr. Drucker. As for Niki, the newest detective in their small band had ended up with not one, but two assignments. He'd speak with his own mother, Natasha Gorodnik, as well as to Ilya Pim, Alexei's father. The boys figured that Niki could converse with Pim in his native tongue, which none of the others could do. Niki didn't seem thrilled about the double assignment, but he accepted it with good grace.

The five stood up and shook hands solemnly.

"This is it," Ari said.

"Yeah," said Pinny. He suddenly looked very young and scared. It was as if he had remembered how much was at stake here.

"We've just *got* to find out the truth!" Shraga said, clenching his fists and jamming them into his pants pockets. Though he spoke softly, the words had the impact of a cry.

Shai, who up till now had regarded this detective stuff as not much more than a different sort of game, grew sober. Though his fellow detectives might not think of Dr. Drucker as a suspect, he knew that the F.B.I. men had spent quite a lot of time questioning him about the work he did in Israel. Uncovering the truth was something he also suddenly wanted, badly.

As for Niki, he gnawed his lip as he went off in search of his mother and Dr. Pim. He still hadn't made up his mind whether or not to share with his fellow detectives the tiny piece of information he had. Would it make any difference to their investigations? He hoped not. He hoped very much that what he knew was totally unconnected to the theft of the device.

But in his heart, he wondered...

Ari wasn't used to feeling nervous or shy, but he found himself feeling both of those things as he knocked on the door of the lab marked M. ISINGARD, NORWAY. There was no sound of footsteps from within, yet the door was flung open abruptly, almost dramatically, startling Ari. He gaped up at the silver-haired scientist.

"Yes?" The Norwegian towered over Ari, himself rather tall for a fourteen-year-old. "Can I help you, young man?" The accent was precise and patrician. Ari recovered his wits and gave the scientist an ingratiating smile.

"Uh, my name is Ari Katz. My father was one of the men who put together the, uh, device that was stolen from the lab the other night. My brother and I and a few of our friends are trying to see what we can find out about the crime. May I ask you a few questions, please?"

Isingard seemed to hover between annoyance and amusement. Thankfully, Ari saw the amusement win out. The thin, aristocratic lips twitched. "I've already answered a host of terribly tedious questions for the security men — your own F.B.I. However, I believe I might spare five minutes more of my time."

He held the door open. Ari went in.

Magda Brenner was not in her lab, but sipping coffee with Natasha Gorodnik in a corner of the lounge. That was where Shraga finally tracked her down. He stood diffidently near her table, first on one leg and then on the other, until she glanced up.

"You seem to be waiting for something," she said in her brisk way, black eyes snapping. "Is it me?"

Actually, it's both of you, Shraga thought, glancing from the elderly Hungarian to Niki's Russian mom. Aloud, he said, "Uh, yes, ma'am. I was wondering if I could talk to you for a few minutes — when you can spare the time."

Dr. Gorodnik looked inquiringly at Magda. "Shall I leave?"

"Nonsense, you've just begun your coffee," Magda declared.

"That's okay," Shraga said hurriedly. "I'd actually prefer if you were here, too, ma'am," he added, addressing Niki's mother. "I — I just want to ask you both a few questions about the night my father's lab was broken into."

The two women looked surprised. It was the Hungarian who said, "What, playing at detectives?" An unexpected smile took away the sting of her words. "All right, you may as well sit down." When Shraga had taken his seat at the extreme edge of the couch facing that of the two women, Magda took a sip of coffee and then set down her cup with a businesslike *click*. "Very well, Mr. Detective — ask away. What's the first question?"

Pinny was finding Richard Fowley, the wiry redhaired Englishman, more than willing to talk to him. In fact, he enjoyed the sound of his own voice so much that it was hard for Pinny to insert a question from time to time. He, too, had been sitting in the lounge when Pinny came upon him. Graciously, he invited Pinny with the wave of an arm to join him.

"What'll you drink, my boy?" he asked heartily.

"Um, I'm not thirsty," Pinny stammered.

"Well, I was just about to order something for myself. Sure you won't change your mind?"

"No, sir. Thanks, anyway."

A waiter approached. Fowley ordered a black coffee. Curiously, Pinny said, "I thought Englishmen always drink tea?"

Dr. Fowley gave him a slow smile. "Then I guess I must not be a genuine Englishman, eh?"

Pinny was at a loss to answer that one. They sat in silence until Fowley's coffee arrived. Fowley tasted it, emitted a sigh of satisfaction — "Good and hot, just the way I like it" — and leaned back against the cushions. "Well, go to it. Just what exactly do you want to know?"

Niki could not interview his mother, for the simple reason that Shraga was already doing that. Reluctantly, he went off in search of Dr. Ilya Pim. He fervently hoped he would not run into Alexei on the way. It might be embarrassing to explain that he was on his way to question Alexei's father about the theft of the little black box. To his relief, Alexei was nowhere near Dr. Pim's lab.

"Come in!" called a voice in response to his knock. Timidly, Niki entered. The scientist was sitting at the counter of his lab in his shirtsleeves, stirring something in a beaker. He seemed to welcome Niki's interruption. "No, you're not disturbing me," he said, assuming a cheerful note. "How can I help you?"

Niki told him.

As for Shai, he found his foster father in his hotel room, reading an Israeli newspaper by the light of his bedside lamp. Mrs. Drucker was sitting in a comfortable armchair, deep in a novel. Both looked surprised — and pleased — to see Shai. The pleasure faded somewhat when they learned the reason for the visit.

"Of course I'll talk to you," Dr. Drucker sighed. "Not that I think I can help. I've already gone over everything in my mind a hundred times, and with the F.B.I. even more than that. Poor Katz and Morgenstern, they're having a hard time..." He stopped himself and gave his foster son a faint grin. "Well, Shai? I suppose you want to hear my alibi. Do you want to ask questions or shall I just tell you what I was doing that night?"

Shai flushed. "No one's asking for an alibi. We don't suspect you. It's just that — well, the more clues we have, the better." His fingers were toying with the note in his pocket. Everyone was trying so hard to solve the mystery, while he held the single concrete clue in the whole affair.

Soon, very soon, he'd have to share his secret with the others.

8

The Detectives Report

Well, let's have it. The reports!" Ari plopped himself down on a couch in a corner of the lobby and motioned for his fellow detectives to do the same.

Shraga and Pinny sat beside him, while Niki and Shai took the couch facing theirs across a low table. Instinctively, the five hunched forward and lowered their voices.

"Who starts?" whispered Shai.

"The rain just did," Shraga pointed out. A light patter outside the large windows told the others, even before they looked, that he was right. It was hardly more than a drizzle, catching the lights outside the lobby and falling softly to the ground in a shower of silver.

"That's nothing compared to the storm we had the other night," Ari said impatiently. "Anyway, it wasn't exactly a *weather* report I was asking for! Come on, Pinny, you go first."

Grinning, Pinny flipped a salute. "Detective First-Class Pinny Katz reporting, *sir!*"

Shai snickered. Niki giggled nervously. "Knock off the wisecracks already," Ari ordered. He seemed to have decided that, as the oldest of the band, it was up to him to lead the troops tonight. "On second thought, I think I'll start with my own report first."

The others leaned forward again, interested.

"Shoot," said Pinny. He paused, then winked at Shraga and added solemnly, "*Sir.*"

Shraga was about to laugh, when he noticed the look on Ari's face and changed his mind. "Yes, Ari?" he said instead, encouragingly. "We're all ears."

Ari glanced at Shai and Niki to make sure they were with him, then began.

"Well, for one thing," he said slowly, "this Isingard seems to be some sort of big shot in his country — in Norway. I mean, not just as a scientist. From what he says, he's got clout."

"That makes sense," said Shai. "He's rich, isn't he?"

The others gaped at him. "How do you know that?" Shraga asked.

Now it was Shai's turn to stare back. "How do I know? I have eyes, don't I? Anyone can see that he's rich. Look at his clothes! Look at his hair — his shoes — his watch!"

"I guess I never noticed," Pinny admitted. Ari and Shraga confessed that neither had they. Shai looked incredulous. The first thing he noticed about people was whether or not they were rich-looking. *Maybe that comes from growing up poor,* he thought now, with a twinge of bitterness. That was something these Americans knew nothing about.

Niki was another story. The Russian boy was nodding his head vigorously. "That's right, it's easy to tell that he is rich. But that's not important, is it? What else did you learn about him?"

Ari reached into his pocket and took out a set of smooth, gold-colored cubes, the *kugelach* all the boys liked to play with. With his inborn grace and athlete's build, Ari was a natural at sports. Not only that, he *needed* movement, action, and lots of it. Deprived of these, he soon began to feel restless and irritable. At such times, he'd reach for his *kugelach* and start a lively game against himself. It kept his fingers busy and calmed him down. Niki watched in fascination as the little gold cubes rose and fell in Ari's capable hands, making a constant clickety-clack on the low table between their two couches, a quiet backdrop to their talk.

"There's more," Ari continued, finishing his first round and entering the second. "It's all tied in with the fact that he's so wealthy. He's got influence high up, I gathered — in government circles. He was even involved somehow, behind the scenes, in the Oslo accords between Israel and the P.L.O. this year. He mentioned that, like Yitzchak Rabin, he also once shook Arafat's hand."

Shraga grew excited. "Do you think he has terrorist connections? That would give him a motive for stealing the device and the plans."

"I don't know." Ari was clearly worried. The rhythm of the one-man *kugelach* match picked up speed. *Rat-a-tat-tat* went the cubes. Niki's eyes grew rounder as he watched.

"Is that all, Ari?" Pinny asked, when his brother didn't seem inclined to continue.

"I guess so. If I remember something else later, I'll speak up." Ari lifted his eyes from his game and swept them over the others. "Shraga, why don't you tell us how it went with that Hungarian woman — uh, Brenner, right?"

"Right." Shraga was silent a moment, gathering his thoughts. His mind was organizing the facts and impressions he'd picked up in his chat with Magda Brenner. It was easy to conjure up the white-haired old woman with the snapping black eyes that gazed at you so directly. What was harder to do was unravel her pleasant reminiscences of her childhood in Hungary from the cold, hard facts that might have a bearing on their case. At last he said, "Basically, Dr. Brenner didn't have anything to tell me about the night the black box was stolen — anything that we didn't already know, that is. She ate dinner, sat in the lounge having a cup of coffee with one or two of the other scientists, and then went upstairs. She says she likes to go to sleep quite early, and is usually up at the crack of dawn to begin her work. She's got an amazing record of accomplishment in her own country, actually."

"So you didn't learn anything suspicious?" Shai was disappointed.

"No-o-o..."

"That was the most wishy-washy 'no' I've heard in a long time," Pinny said. "What is it, Shraga?"

"Well, it may not be anything. But up until a few years ago, Dr. Brenner and her husband — she's a widow now — were members of the Communist Party in Hungary."

"Communists! That's suspicious!" Shai exclaimed in delight. Niki, who'd grown up under the Communists, looked less certain. Ari shook his head firmly.

"So what? Up until a few years ago, practically everybody in Eastern Europe and Russia were members of the Communist Party. It was the only way to get ahead. Wasn't it, Niki?"

Niki agreed with Ari. "I don't think that's so suspicious by itself."

"You never know," Pinny argued. "She could belong to a fringe group who'd like to see the Communists come back to power and glory. What wouldn't such a group do for a weapon like that!"

"She could also be Mother Goose in disguise," his big brother said disgustedly. He swept the *kugelach* into the palm of his hand. "Pinny, do me a favor and save the fairy tales for bedtime. We're talking reality here!"

Pinny looked chastened. Shraga hurried to defend him. "Oh, I don't know, Ari. We have to explore all sorts of possibilities before we hit on the truth."

"Okay, okay, let's move on." Ari flipped all five cubes up into the air and caught them with a flourish. The maneuver seemed to improve his temper. He replaced the *kugelach* in his pocket and said, "Shai, what about you?"

"My — er — Dr. Drucker knows nothing," the Israeli boy stated. "Just like he told the F.B.I. He is worried, though..."

"Worried?" prompted Shraga. "Why?"

Shai's eyes darkened. "Do you think he wants to be suspected of spying for Israel — or worse, stealing an American secret weapon? Do you think he wants to spend the next twenty years in prison?"

"I'm sure no one suspects him of that!" Pinny exclaimed.

"Oh, no? What about the F.B.I.? Tom Morrison was nice enough to warn my — to warn him that the...what did he call them? Oh, yes, the '*higher-ups*' at the F.B.I. are looking very seriously into his background. Very seriously indeed."

Despite his worry, Pinny had to suppress a smile at Shai's words, which unconsciously mimicked Tom's inflections so accurately. But he wasn't smiling a moment later when Shraga said, "Tom said pretty much the same thing about our fathers, Shai. The F.B.I. is nice enough not to suspect our fathers of doing it for money or power, but rather for Israel."

"Nice of them," Ari said dryly.

"Yeah. Shai, anything else?"

Shai shook his head despondently. Into the cheerless silence that followed, Niki spoke up hesitantly.

"It's interesting that you say that. Because my mother, and Alexei's father, Dr. Pim, are worried, too. They're afraid *they* might be suspected of stealing the plans for Russia... Or, even if that doesn't happen, that the whole incident could touch off an international problem. I know my mother is worried, and Alexei says his father is also very anxious." Niki waited for their reactions.

"It looks more like the work of a terrorist organization," Pinny objected. "Pretty unsophisticated stuff, if you ask me. I mean, look at the timing! A few minutes earlier, and my father would have stumbled right on the crook in the lab. And the way the black box was found right after it was stolen —"

"To direct suspicion at our fathers, of course," Shraga said impatiently.

"Maybe. Or maybe not. It could have been an act of desperation," Pinny insisted. "Because he was about to be caught with the thing under his arm."

"Maybe it was *meant* to look unsophisticated," Niki suggested. "To make us think it was a small band of terrorists, when really it was someone... much bigger."

"You mean," asked Ari, "like Russia?"

Niki looked unhappy. "Yes."

"Listen, guys. All this speculation is getting us nowhere," Shraga said. "Let's stick to the facts. Pinny, you haven't told us about your interview with Richard Fowley."

There was a frown between Pinny's eyes. Shraga's remark about speculation had poked a raw nerve in him. He thought that this kind of free-for-all discussion, where ideas were batted around like baseballs on a sunny day in the park, was the best way to get at the truth. "The facts" that Shraga was insisting on were, in his opinion, both less available and more boring. Though he had to admit that getting at them *was* a useful first step...

"First," he said, "let's finish with Niki. So your mom and Dr. Pim both know nothing that might help us? Apart from their worries, that is."

Niki hesitated only the slightest fraction of a second. "Nothing," he answered.

"Okay. Then here goes with Richard Fowley, the so-called Englishman."

"So-called?" Ari demanded. "Why do you say that?"

"He sure sounds English," Shai snickered. "Have you heard him talk?" He himself assumed a very British accent while asking the question. The others laughed.

"He may sound as English as the Queen," Pinny said stubbornly, "but let me ask you this. What sort of Englishman doesn't drink tea?"

"What?" Shraga was startled out of his laughter.

"Exactly that. He invited me to sit down with him in the lounge, and he was drinking coffee!"

"Big deal," Ari said scornfully. "So the guy likes coffee better than tea. That makes him suspicious?" The others smiled broadly.

"I still think —" Pinny began.

"The I.R.A.," Shraga said suddenly. "Maybe he's got that connection."

Ari fixed Shraga with an astonished eye. "And you were the one warning us about 'speculation'! What's the I.R.A. got to do with a normal, law-abiding Englishman, even if he *is* a coffee-drinking one?"

Shraga looked deflated. Heartened by his support, though, Pinny said, "He's a real smooth talker — you know the type I'm talking about? He would have made a super salesman, or maybe an actor. He sure doesn't look or act like any scientist *I've* ever met!"

"*And* he doesn't drink tea," Ari said, only half-joking now.

"Look," said Shraga. "We don't have an awful lot to go on. The way I read it, we haven't got a thing to stick on any of the people on our list. In fact, there are no facts. Nothing." His shoulders slumped.

"Not exactly," Shai said slowly.

Shraga looked up at him. "What?"

"Remember when I told you I had something to show you?"

"That's right!" Pinny sat up straight, eyes sparkling. "That's why we agreed to let you in on the detective stuff. I mean — uh —" he stammered, looking confused.

"I know what you mean," Shai said. "Those were the terms of our agreement. You let me in, and I show you...this."

Very slowly, he pulled a small, wadded piece of paper from his pocket.

"The note," he said.

9

Sinister Messages

L et's see that," Ari exclaimed, making as if to snatch the note from Shai's hand.

Shai pulled back. "I'll read it to you first." He was reluctant to let the treasure pass from his grasp. "It says," he read carefully, " *'Meet south entrance midnight. Bring our little friend.'* And it is signed, *Mr. B.*"

"Mr. B.?" Pinny repeated. "What kind of name is that?"

"I don't know," said Shai. And from the expressions on their faces, none of his fellow detectives were any wiser.

There was a silence, filled with unspoken questions and the muted noises of other hotel guests enjoying their drinks and snacks at adjoining tables. It was Shraga who broke the spell that seemed to hold the band of detectives in thrall.

"Where did you find that note?"

"In the woods," answered Shai. "Remember that day when you came to find me, Pinny? I had just found it then."

Pinny nodded. He remembered running off to find the other boy, at Dr. Drucker's request. Shai had been huddled in the branches of a tall tree like some sort of angry monkey. Earlier, when Pinny and Shraga had tried to befriend him, Shai had made his answer very clear: Nothing doing. Who would have believed, then, that that same boy would be sitting in a huddle with them now? Pinny shook his head. Life sure was strange.

"Who's the 'little friend'?" asked Ari suddenly.

Pinny turned to his brother in surprise. "Why, the little black box, of course!"

"Of course," echoed Shraga.

Ari looked at both of them, then rolled his eyes. "Geniuses," he muttered. "I'm surrounded by geniuses."

"It's obvious," Pinny said, almost apologetically.

Ari leaned back and folded his arms across his chest. "Shai, let's set this straight. You mean you were just walking along and happened to find that piece of paper?"

"Of course not! I was up in a tree, and I saw the man read it and throw it away."

"You *what?*" Ari, Shraga, and Pinny leaned forward in intense excitement.

"You mean you actually *saw* the guy?" Pinny yelped. Shraga made a shushing motion with his hand, while his eyes remained riveted on Shai.

"Yes," Shai whispered. "He was walking through the woods below where I was. He didn't see me." He paused thoughtfully. "And I didn't really see him, either."

"What do you mean?" asked Niki.

"I only saw the top of his head. I was looking down at him through the leaves, you know."

"Was he tall or short? Fat or thin? Come on, Shai, you've gotta give us more!" Ari pleaded.

"I'm sorry." Shai looked chagrined. "I didn't know he was going to be an important person to remember, or I would have tried to notice more. Besides, have you ever tried seeing what someone looks like from higher up? It's hard to tell anything."

Shraga nodded in doleful agreement. "Everything would be foreshortened from that angle. But Shai, *try*. Think back. Was there anything — anything at all — that stood out about him? Some little detail that would make you recognize him if you met him again."

Shai thought. And thought some more. He had a nagging feeling that there *had* been something... But in the end, sadly, he shook his head. "I don't remember anything."

Ari slammed a fist into the palm of his other hand. "It's so frustrating! Here you actually had a look at the guy, and he just walks out of your life!"

"I know," Shai said miserably. "I wish I could help more."

"You've helped a lot," Pinny told him. He stuck out his hand. "May I?"

Shai gave him the note. Pinny read it, turned it over to look at the back, scrutinized the front again, and then passed it on to Ari, who repeated the same moves before passing it to Shraga. Niki, for whom reading English was a chore, merely gave the note a cursory glance, nodded, and returned it to Shai, who stuck it in his pocket.

Pinny sat back against the sofa cushions as if suddenly exhausted. "So where does that leave us?"

"For one thing," Shraga said eagerly, "it gives us *two* men, not just one. Two people were working on this together!"

"I don't know," Pinny said slowly. "There was something about the way the note was worded... Almost like one person giving orders to another. Not as if they were equals. Like a boss and a subordinate."

"Yes!" Shraga exclaimed.

"A boss?" Niki asked.

"That means an employer," Pinny explained. When Niki still looked blank, he added, "Uh — someone who employs others to work for him."

"Like the way Mr. Manicotti employs the waiters," Ari said helpfully. "Or Mr. Stewart. He's the boss of the whole hotel staff."

"Mr. Stewart?" Shai objected. "I can't exactly see him sneaking into the lab at night."

"I was only using him as an example."

"Still, it *could* be him," Shai said, abruptly reversing himself.

Ari sighed. "It could be anybody."

"I'm going off my head," Pinny said, clutching it in both hands. He rolled his eyes at the others from between his fists. "We keep ending up at the same place where we started!" Abruptly, he let go of his hair and stood up. "Listen, I don't know about you guys, but I need some time to try and sort all this out. I feel like we're starting to go in circles here."

"Starting?" muttered Ari.

"He's got a point," Shraga said, standing too. "Let's all get some sleep and continue in the morning. At least we have one solid clue now," he added, with a warm smile for Shai. "A genuine fact."

Shai flushed with pleasure. Tenderly he patted his pocket. He, Ari, and Pinny got to their feet, all yawning at once. It was getting late.

Some hours later, in another part of the hotel, another person was listening to the silence and blessing it.

The hotel was asleep beneath the silver moon, and those inside it seemed to be slumbering just as soundly. He tiptoed down the all-too-familiar corridor toward what he persisted in thinking of as the "Jewish lab." How fervently he had hoped, on that fateful night, to have seen the last of both the lab and the weapon he'd stolen from it! But things had gone wrong. Dr. Katz had discovered the theft much too soon, before he, the intruder, had had the chance to hide it properly. The weapon was back in the hands of its owners, and the diskette with the plans had vanished, seemingly into the thin air.

And this afternoon, he'd received another message on his e-mail board from the sinister Mr. Big.

Find that diskette, the message had ordered, *or else*.

Remembering the shiver of terror that ran through him upon reading those words, he shuddered again now. He'd already searched, discreetly, wherever he could — but no red diskette had come to light. The F.B.I., he knew, had conducted a much more thorough search. No, he'd have to regard the diskette as gone forever.

The only other way to get to those secret plans was through the lab computer. What other choice did he have? Though "Mr. Big" had not spelled out the dire consequences of his failing to find the missing plans, he could well imagine what they would be. It must be done.

Mustering his courage, he walked quietly and stealthily through the dark halls until he reached the door he wanted.

It was the work of seconds to unlock the door with the electronic card in his hand. Looking down at it, he remembered how it had come into his possession. "Mr. Big" had somehow contrived to get the card to him in the most natural way possible.

"Oh, excuse me, sir," the young woman at the front desk had called after him that day. "This envelope was left for you. See, it has your name on it."

Surprised, he'd taken it and, as soon as he reached a quiet corner, ripped it open. Inside was the electronic card — the key to the lab before which he stood now.

Closing the door behind him, he strode over to the computer on the lab counter. He flicked it on and sat down in front of the screen. His job was to try and crack the codes that would lead him to the secret password he needed... The password that would give him access to the plans of the weapon he'd stolen.

The hours slipped past. Gradually the sky became streaked with the first faint roses and oranges of a new day. At the computer, a man tore at his hair and blinked to force his weary eyes to stay open. As the first *cheep!* greeted his ears from the birds that nested in the trees outside on the lawn, he rose in the clumsy slow motion of the very tired, and switched off the computer. His hours in front of the screen had been fruitless. He had no password, no plans — nothing at all to show Mr. Big for this night's work.

He shivered. Somehow, he must persuade Mr. Big — whoever and wherever he was — to give him a little more time.

Upstairs, at that crack of dawn, two other people were also wide awake. One of them was Dr. Katz. The other was Dr. Morgenstern. Though the pale gray light had hardly begun to filter into the hotel windows, both men were fully dressed. They tiptoed along the corridor and quietly opened the doors to their children's rooms. For a moment each listened to the soft breathing of soundly sleeping kids. Then, still in silence, they met in the corridor again.

Dr. Katz didn't need to look at his friend's face to know what the other man was thinking. The same memory was etched in both their minds. Dr. Katz marveled: Had it only been last night that he'd turned on the computer in their lab — and found the sinister e-mail message waiting for them? He felt as if he'd aged ten years since then.

He knew the message by heart. The unknown sender had talked about the heavy flowerbox that came tumbling down into their midst as they sat on the terrace Friday night — narrowly missing Ruchie.

That, said the message, *was just the first demonstration. I want the plans for the secret weapon, and I want them now. You will be notified tomorrow about how to get them to me.*

In the meantime, do not alert the authorities — or your children will suffer.

The message had been signed simply, "*Mr. B.*"

"It's time," Dr. Morgenstern said very quietly. Dr. Katz nodded. They started silently for the elevators. They knew what they had to do now.

10
"They're Gone!"

Shai Gilboa paced the ornate lobby impatiently. Here he was, all ready to go on with their adventure, and not a single one of his detective partners anywhere in sight! Where was everybody?

Shai was used to starting his day early. Back home in Israel, school started at eight, and he couldn't seem to drop the habit of early waking. This morning was no exception. He'd forced himself to stay in his room for a full hour after he'd first opened his eyes at the crack of dawn. But by now, he felt, there was no reason for anyone to be lingering in bed — and especially not his fellow detectives. They *couldn't* still be sleeping, not with this mystery hanging over their heads. Frowning, Shai continued to prowl the space in front of the elevators, checking his watch every few seconds.

Unlike Shai, most of the guests in the hotel were still wrapped in dreams on this Sunday morning. Shraga, Ari, Pinny, and Niki, however, were not among them. The first three were standing in the corridor outside their rooms — Ari with his tefillin bag under his arm — waiting for their fathers to appear for *shacharis*. As for Niki, he was in bed, but not asleep. He hadn't slept at all since a nightmare had woken him abruptly in the wee hours of the morning. From then till now, as the sky had lightened by degrees from black to gray to rosy pink, he had twisted and tossed in indecision. To tell or not to tell? The question troubled him and would not let him rest.

"Where can they be already?" Shai grumbled under his breath. Every time the elevator doors opened, he looked up expectantly. But it was only a chambermaid wheeling her trolley of fresh towels ahead of her, or a yawning bootboy with his collection of newly polished shoes.

The third time, however, proved the luckiest. Once again the elevators doors slid open, and out skipped a couple of kids he knew — Chaim and Mindy Morgenstern. He hurried over.

"Hey, aren't you Shraga's brother and sister?"

Chaim turned. "Oh, hi, Shai. Yes, we are. What're you doing up so early on a Sunday morning?"

"It's not so early. In Israel I'd be on my way to school by now — Sunday or no Sunday." Shai waved this away as unimportant. "Do you know where your brother is? And Pinny and Ari?"

Mindy was ever glad to be helpful. "Sure," she said. "They're waiting for our fathers so they can all daven together."

Shai's eyes narrowed in disappointment. "Daven!"

"Yes. *Shacharis.*"

"You could join us if you want," Chaim invited.

"No, thanks," he rejoined stiffly. "I don't bother with all that stuff."

"You don't? Ever? Doesn't your father mind?"

"He's not my father. And yes, he does mind. And *you* mind your own business!"

He felt a stab of contrition when he saw the hurt expression in the other boy's face — the face that had been so full of friendliness a moment before. "Sorry," he mumbled.

Chaim forced a smile. "That's okay."

"I just wish everyone would leave me alone about all that religious stuff. It's old stuff, from the past. Why should I waste my time with all that?"

Chaim and Mindy exchanged a glance. They could have told him why, but they felt they'd already said enough. It needed someone older and wiser than they were to explain to Shai why "all that stuff" was not only *not* a waste of time, but the most worthwhile way he could spend his days on this earth!

Instead, Chaim said simply, "You're wrong, Shai. One day, you'll see how wrong."

"Well, have a nice day," Mindy added. Brother and sister began walking away.

"Wait a second."

They turned. "Yes?"

What Shai really wanted was to continue the conversation. Those two quiet little words, "You're wrong," had been said with such absolute sureness that Shai found himself shaken. How could such young kids — a ten-year-old boy and a little girl with pigtails, no less! — be so positive about anything? But, under their steady gaze, he found himself faltering. "Uh, where are *you* two going so early on a Sunday morning?"

The words mimicked Chaim's, so that the question sounded nasty even though he hadn't intended it to.

Chaim flushed. "Out. I couldn't sleep."

"And I want to look for more stuff for my — my newest art project," Mindy put in. "Goodbye." This time she almost ran away, through the nearly empty lobby and out the big glass doors to the dewy lawn. Chaim was right behind her.

Shai stared at the doors through which they'd disappeared, then down at the expensive rug on the floor. He felt more desolate than he remembered feeling in a long time. "You're wrong," the rug seemed to echo. And the thump of the elevator door repeated, "*You're — wrong.*"

"Hello, Shai."

"Oh, hi, Niki." Shai was still feeling glum.

Niki didn't look much happier. He was pale and drawn, with big black rings beneath his eyes. "Where are the others?"

"Upstairs." Shai paused. "Praying."

"Oh."

An uncomfortable silence fell between the two boys. Without speaking, they walked over to the set of couches they'd occupied the night before and sat down to wait.

The wait was much longer than they'd expected. Outside, the shadows shortened imperceptibly across the sparkling lawn. The lobby started slowly to fill. People drifted from the elevators, some still stretching and yawning, in search of their breakfasts. A foursome went out to the tennis courts for an early game, swinging their rackets. Chaim and Mindy Morgenstern returned from their outing and disappeared into the elevator without even noticing Shai and Niki in their corner. The dining room began to hum. And still no sign of their friends.

"How long does it take to pray?" Niki asked finally.

"I'm not sure," Shai answered. Surely not this long, he thought. They must have finished davening long ago. What could be keeping them? To amuse himself while he waited, Shai began to try to devise reasons for the delay. Pinny had broken a shoelace and couldn't find a new one. Ari had come down with a dramatic case of chicken pox. Shraga, in one dazzling burst of intuition, had come up with the solution to their mystery and was now working out the final details...

But not even his wildest guess came anywhere near the truth.

"Knock," Pinny urged in a whisper.

"Why don't *you* knock?" Ari countered.

"I still don't think it's right to wake up our parents," Shraga said. He glanced uneasily at the door to his own parents' room. "But this is really weird. My father should have been out a long time ago."

"Ours, too." Ari shifted his tefillin bag from arm to arm, trying to make up his mind. "Maybe just a teeny little tap on the door. If they're up, they'll hear it, but if they're still asleep, it shouldn't wake them..."

Just then, the solution to the problem appeared, in the form of little Zevy Katz. He was still wearing his pajamas. Spotting the bigger boys, he rubbed his eyes. "What're you guys doing here?"

"Waiting for Abba," Pinny told him.

"Why? Is he still sleeping?"

"We're not sure —" began Pinny.

With a shrug, Zevy twisted the knob and walked into the room.

"Hey, wait," hissed Ari. "You're not supposed to —"

"Hi, Ima," they heard him say inside the room. "Where's Abba?"

The boys stared at each other. "Where's — What's going on?" Pinny exclaimed, half to himself. He followed his little brother inside.

His mother sat in an armchair by the window. In the opposite chair, holding Vivi, sat Mrs. Morgenstern. The boys gaped.

"Ma!" exclaimed Shraga. "What are you doing in this room? And where's Daddy, and Dr. Katz?"

Mrs. Katz looked at Mrs. Morgenstern. Then she looked at the boys. "Come in and close the door."

With the door closed behind them, the boys stepped tentatively forward. Something in the room seemed not right, somehow. *Danger*, Shraga thought suddenly. He smelled danger.

"Where's Abba?" Ari asked, setting down his tefillin bag. "We're ready to daven."

"You'll have to daven yourselves this morning," Mrs. Katz said quietly. "Abba and Dr. Morgenstern had to go away."

Shraga's mother raised a hand to stave off the torrent of questions she knew was about to come. "I'll tell you exactly what they told us. Late last night, the men woke us to say that they had to leave the hotel for a while."

"But — but how'd they get past the F.B.I men?" Shraga asked.

"They said there was only one man on duty outside at that hour. They were going to create some sort of a diversion." Mrs. Katz sighed worriedly. "Obviously, they succeeded."

"*Why* did they go?" Pinny spoke up, asking the question on all of their minds.

The women exchanged a glance. "It has something to do with the stolen device." Mrs. Morgenstern replied. "They're searching for some kind of information, I think."

"So that's why Abba sounded so strange last night!" Ari blurted. "They must have been planning this even then."

"They didn't want to tell us where they were going," Mrs. Katz continued. "In case anyone asks us where, we won't be able to tell them because we genuinely won't know."

"We're supposed to make believe we don't know anything about anything," Mrs. Morgenstern finished. She sighed. "Which won't be far from the truth."

"B-but — I don't get it!" Pinny sputtered. "What kind of information could they find outside the hotel? It was stolen from here! And we've got the F.B.I. on the spot and everything."

His mother made a helpless gesture with her hands. "That's all we know, Pinny. Abba said he knew it'd be hard for us, being in the dark like this, but he said —" she stopped and swallowed "— he said we'd be... safer this way."

"Safer," Shraga repeated woodenly. All at once, safety seemed very far away. He hadn't realized how much he depended on his father to make him feel secure. A tiny shiver ran along his arms, raising goosebumps.

"Tom Morrison," Pinny predicted, "is not going to like this."

Pinny was right. They were halfway through breakfast some three-quarters of an hour later — a gloomy and tension-filled breakfast, in which little Vivi's laughter seemed the only light and happy thing — when the chief security man sauntered over.

"Morning, folks," Tom greeted them pleasantly. "Sleep okay?"

"Fine," Ari answered for all of them. Shai jiggled excitedly in his seat, until Dr. Drucker gave him a warning glance. Mrs. Katz and Mrs. Morgenstern had given the Druckers — including an intensely curious Shai — the rundown as they were sitting down to the morning meal. Mrs. Morgenstern turned away to pick up a crust of bread that Vivi had been using for target practice. Tom glanced at the two empty chairs at the table.

"So where're the menfolks?" he asked Mrs. Katz casually. "Not working already, I hope? And on a Sunday, too."

"I — I'm not sure," Mrs. Katz said vaguely. "I haven't seen them this morning."

Tom looked surprised. "Have you had a look in the lab?"

Mrs. Katz shook her head without speaking.

Tom whirled away and walked with a rapid stride toward the dining room doors. It wasn't more than three minutes later that he was striding back to their table.

"I checked the lab — it's locked. Are both your cars parked outside?"

"I really have no idea," Mrs. Morgenstern said coldly. "Why don't you go see for yourself?"

That was exactly what Tom did. When he returned, his face was sober and flushed a deep pink. "The van is there, but the car is gone. It looks like they left the hotel grounds — against my explicit orders." He stopped, as if struck by a new thought. "Could they have gone to that other hotel, the kosher one, to pray? Like they did the other day?"

"No, we davened here today," Zevy piped up in his clear, high voice.

Tom frowned mightily. "Then *where are they?*"

No one answered.

His gaze swept them all. It was all Shraga could do not to drop his own eyes before that level stare.

"This is going to make them look bad," Tom said soberly. "Real bad." He caught Shraga's eye, then Pinny's. "I'll admit it, boys, I'm disappointed. Here I am, trying my level best to help your dads out of a very sticky situation, and now they go and do a disappearing act." He shook his head sadly. "It's not gonna look too good, back at headquarters."

With sinking hearts, Shraga and Pinny watched the Special Agent leave. It seemed to Pinny as if his last hope were walking away. He felt bad, as if he'd somehow let Tom down.

Shraga struggled to regain his composure. He hated this helpless feeling. What did it help to have a good mind, if he couldn't see past the fog of questions that stood in front of him? The questions seemed to mount higher and higher, until they formed a crazy mountain that threatened to topple down on them all.

He thought of his father. Where, Shraga wondered, was he was right now, this minute? Why had he and Dr. Katz run away?

And how could they, a bunch of kids, help their fathers out of the morass of trouble that seemed to be growing deeper every day?

11

What Happened to Mindy

As soon as breakfast was over, the boys headed for the sun-drenched hill where they'd sat together on the morning after the theft to form their plans. It was time for another huddle. There were only four of them this time: Niki had gone off somewhere right after the meal, together with Alexei Pim.

It wasn't a very merry procession that wended its way past the flowerbeds and tennis courts. Shraga and Pinny walked with bowed heads, as if the weight of their thoughts were too heavy for them. Ari tossed a ball methodically up into the air as he went, catching it neatly every time. Judging, however, from the expression he wore, he didn't appear to be getting much pleasure from his little game. Shai, on the other hand, seemed to be enjoying himself immensely. He chattered continually to his three unresponsive partners.

"Things are really getting exciting now! We have to make a plan. Where you do suppose your father went, Shraga? How about you, Pinny? Ari, can you guess what made them go? What do you think?"

"I think," Ari said, moodily swiping the ball out of the air with a neat jab of the wrist, "that we've done enough talking. It's time for some action."

"Yeah," Pinny said, flopping to the ground in "their" spot. "But what?"

"Our fathers took action," Shraga pointed out gloomily. "And look where it's got them."

"In deep water," Pinny sighed.

"In hot water," Ari corrected. "And lots of it." He looked intensely unhappy. "Wonder why they did it?"

Shai listened in growing dismay. Deep water? Hot water? Were they talking about taking a bath or solving this thrilling mystery? Impatience rose up in him like a geyser. "Why don't you all stop sighing and complaining, and decide what to do!"

Shraga's answer was to heave another sigh. "It's kind of hard to know what the right thing *is*, Shai. Any suggestions?"

"We could —" Shai stopped. "Or maybe —" He shook his head. Frustrated, he glared at Shraga. "You and Pinny are supposed to be the geniuses. *You* think of something!"

"Hah," Pinny said bitterly. "Fat lot of good we've done so far."

"Don't worry, kiddo," Ari said kindly. "Sooner or later, we'll lick this thing, *b'ezras Hashem.*"

"Yeah," sighed Pinny. He lay back on the prickly grass, closing his eyes against the sun. Defeat was written all over his face. "Wake me when it's all over."

Shraga looked over at the deflated lump that was Pinny Katz. Suddenly, Shraga sat up. "This is wrong!" he declared.

"I'll say," Ari grumbled.

"No, no. I mean, we're going about this the wrong way."

Pinny cracked open one weary eye. "I wasn't aware that we were going about it any way at all. Seems to me we've reached a dead end."

"No! True, our fathers have disappeared, but they did it of their own free will. Obviously, they've got something up their sleeve. Let's hope it works. Meanwhile, we've got work of our own to do."

"Detective work?" Shai asked eagerly. "Now you're talking!"

"That, too," Shraga said. "But I think there's something important we have to do first. To sort of get us in the right frame of mind."

Ari looked at him. Pinny, sitting up, did the same. A reluctant smile crept across his face. "You mean what I think you mean?"

Shraga nodded. "Yep. Let's do what we always do after breakfast — fathers or no fathers. Let's get out our Gemaras and do some learning." He glanced sideways at Shai. "*Then* we start detecting."

Shai made no effort to hide his dismay.

"I don't believe it! Learn — at a time like this? Ari said it's time for action, and I agree with him."

"I still want to see some action," Ari said calmly. "After we learn."

"But what's the use of learning all that old stuff anyway? That's for old men in long white beards."

"That's where you're wrong," Pinny told him. Gone were the defeatist slump of his shoulders and the melancholy droop of his head. The sun raised golden sparks on his curly blond hair, to match the sparkle in his eye. "Don't you see, Shai? This is what it's all about!"

"What what's all about?" Shai sounded disgusted.

"When we learn Torah, we reconnect to Hashem and to our fathers from long ago. It gives us hope —"

"and strength —" Shraga put in.

"— to carry on with what we have to do." Pinny punched the *sabra* in the arm. "*Bitachon*'s the name of the name, Shai. You gotta have faith."

Bitachon? Faith? When had Shai ever had faith in anyone or anything? He was a loner, standing up by himself against the world and the worst that it could hurl at him... Or rather, he *had* been a loner. Right now, he was sitting with three boys on a sunny hilltop — boys who were fast beginning to feel like friends. Slowly the scowl left his face, to be replaced by a look of uncertainty. "Well, I don't know about that," he said, to cover his confusion.

"Why don't you join us?" Ari invited. "You'll see how great it is. Learning sort of calms you down and energizes you at the same time." He grinned. "And afterwards, we'll try to work up some sort of plan. That's a promise."

Shai hesitated. Somehow, even with the three pairs of eyes fixed so expectantly on his, he couldn't say the words they wanted to hear. He looked away. "Maybe tomorrow," he mumbled.

Shraga was disappointed but tried not to show it. "Tomorrow's okay by me," he assured Shai. "Right, guys?"

"Sure!" Pinny said.

"A-OK!" Ari seconded. He stood up, brushing the grass and dried leaves from his pants. "Let's go."

Shai walked back to the hotel with the others. In the lobby they separated. Ari, Pinny, and Shraga went upstairs for their Gemaras, while Shai wandered off alone. He made sure to be well away from lobby by the time the boys returned there to learn — not so much because he was afraid they'd see him, but because he was afraid he'd be tempted to give in and join them right now instead of tomorrow.

After all, a kid had his pride.

The rest of the morning and early afternoon passed uneventfully. The sky grew briefly overcast before a light wind sprang up to dispel the clouds. A steady *thwack-thwack* of tennis balls came from the playing courts, along with the *bzzzz* of a diesel-engine lawn mower driven by one of the gardening staff. A feeling of peace seemed to wrap around the hotel and its guests — a peace that the Katzes and Morgensterns could not share.

There was still no sign or word from Dr. Katz or Dr. Morgenstern, though Tom Morrison questioned their wives more than once as to whether they'd heard anything. Shraga and Pinny's mothers walked around with rings under their eyes and haunted expressions. The boys looked hardly less haunted. This wasn't easy on any of them.

To relieve the tension a little, Mrs. Katz suggested that they all meet in the dining room at four o'clock for a quaint Lake View Hotel custom called "afternoon tea." This centuries-old English practice had become thoroughly Americanized by the addition of coffee and donuts, and was enjoyed by most of the hotel's guests on any given afternoon.

On this balmy day, there were only a dozen or two people milling around the mammoth hot water urn and pastry-filled platters. A smattering of scientists and F.B.I. men were among them. Mrs. Morgenstern accepted a styrofoam cup of steaming tea from a waiter and produced a bag of homemade cookies to distribute to her children and the Katzes.

"Only two each, kids. We don't want to ruin our appetites for dinner."

"Aw, Ma, that's nearly three hours away," Mindy protested. "And besides, who says we had any appetite for *those* dinners to begin with?"

"Mindy," her mother said firmly, though with a weary note. "That's enough. I've about had it with all of your *kvetching* about the food. There's nothing we can do about it, so let's just make the best of what we have."

Mindy was contrite. "Sorry, Ma." She and Shraga exchanged a glance. With their mother clearly so anxious about their father, this was no time to gripe about trivialities. Mindy took a thoughtful bite of cookie. *Poor Ma, this is so hard for her,* she thought. *And Mrs. Katz, too.* She was just wishing that there was something she could do to help, when her eye fell on Mrs. Katz's empty teacup.

"Can I get you some more tea, Mrs. Katz?" she asked eagerly. Without waiting for a reply, Mindy practically snatched the cup from the woman's hand and began elbowing her way through the milling crowd toward the urn. Shraga, watching idly, saw the steam rise up from a newly filled cup in the waiter's hand. He saw Mindy approach the table and hold out her own cup. His glance moved on...

A heartrending shriek pierced the air and cut through the babble of voices. Shraga's blood turned to ice as the shriek sounded again. Mindy!

He was at his sister's side at exactly the same moment as their mother. He didn't have to ask what had happened. Somehow, the urn had tipped over, sending scalding water splashing everywhere. And Mindy had been standing in the direct line of fire!

"Mindy! Oh, my baby, are you okay? Are you burned? Mindy, speak to me!" pleaded Mrs. Morgenstern, as the girl screamed and screamed.

"My — my — my arm," Mindy gasped as the tears ran down her face in a flood nearly as mighty as the one puddling on the floor at her feet, still giving off smoke. "My arm's b-burned, Ma. It hurts so much..."

"Cold water!" Mrs. Morgenstern called urgently. "We need some cold running water."

They could all see the ugly red welts rising all along her forearm. Just looking at them made Shraga feel hot. As he followed Mindy and their mother to the hotel kitchen, pity for his sister overwhelmed him. He found himself blinking back tears of his own. If only Daddy were here!

"Ma," he asked in a voice that shook despite his efforts, "is there anything I can do? Should I call an ambulance?"

Sandy, the towhaired Special Agent stepped forward. "Let me drive her to the nearest hospital, ma'am. It'll be faster than calling for an ambulance."

"Good idea," Tom Morrison said, pushing through the crowd. "Here, take my car. It's faster." He passed over his car keys.

"I go on duty at five," Sandy reminded him, taking the keys.

"I'll get someone to cover for you. Go quickly."

Sandy turned and started for the hotel door. Mrs. Morgenstern was about to enter the kitchen with Mindy, when the doors burst open to reveal Mr. Stewart, breathless and panting. The manager was waving something above his head.

"Wait, don't go yet! I have something for you. Here, please, take this; it's good for burns!" Mr. Stewart thrust a dish at Mrs. Morgenstern. "Ice cubes — for the little girl."

Mindy, crying softly in the circle of her mother's arm, shrank away. "No-o-o-o," she sobbed. "I don't want it. It hurts..."

"Cold water is much better," Mrs. Katz said firmly. She led Mindy, still in her mother's embrace, to a gigantic stainless-steel sink.

"Vitamin E!" called Magda Brenner, the diminutive Hungarian. "It's the best thing in the world. I know."

Mrs. Morgenstern held Mindy's arm under the running water, grinding her teeth together to keep them from chattering. It was up to her to be strong. Her husband had disappeared and her daughter had been burned — how badly, no one could tell yet. She couldn't fall apart now.

"Thank you," she said distractedly to Mr. Stewart, who was still hovering nearby with his ice cubes. "Shraga, I want you to take care of Ruchie and the baby while we're gone. Make sure Vivi has her bottle, and help Ruchie get into her pajamas."

"Okay, Ma," Shraga said quickly. "Don't worry about a thing."

"Yes, the boys will see to everything," Mrs. Katz told her. "I'm coming along with you." Mrs. Morgenstern shot her friend a grateful look and didn't protest.

Shraga bent closer to his sobbing sister. "You're going to be fine, Mindy. Don't be scared."

Mindy kept crying, her arm at an odd angle as she held it away from her body. Daniella Katz timidly stepped a little closer.

"I'll make sure no one touches your collage, Mindy," she said in a tiny voice. Mindy tried to smile at her young neighbor, but failed abysmally.

A chorus of goodbyes and *refuah sheleimahs* followed Mindy and the two women out the doors and through the lobby. Sandy was waiting in Tom's car, the motor already running. In no time at all the car had passed down the drive to the road, bearing its load of worried adults and a softly crying girl whose arm was growing more painful by the minute.

Shraga watched them go with a fearful heart. Would his sister be all right? And how had that urn managed to tip over, anyway? It had looked sturdy enough — no, more than sturdy: solid as a rock. What had happened?

"What next?" a voice asked querulously from behind him. Without turning, Shraga recognized the high-pitched tones of Mr. Stewart. "First that falling flowerbox, and now this. *Hurrumph!*"

The manager walked away, still grumbling out loud to no one in particular. Shraga stared after him. *First that falling flowerbox, and now this.* Was there really a connection?

He thought about it some more as he began walking back inside. It hadn't occurred to him to link the two incidents. And yet, both had happened within a couple of days of each other, and both had happened to members of the Morgenstern family. A shiver of cold apprehension ran up his spine, like the scurrying of a hundred tiny centipedes.

Were those two facts mere coincidence? Or had those "accidents" actually been...*planned*?

12

Shai's Turn

It was some four hours later when Mrs. Katz returned from the hospital, alone. She had left Mrs. Morgenstern with Mindy, who was ensconced in a hospital bed with her arm in bandages. The children surrounded her the moment she entered the hotel lobby, bursting with questions and the built-up suspense of those interminable hours.

"The doctors say she'll be all right in a few days, *baruch Hashem*," Mrs. Katz said, sinking gratefully onto the nearest couch. "The burn is serious, but treatable. They gave Mindy some painkillers to relieve the worst of the soreness. Hopefully she'll sleep tonight and feel much better by morning."

Pinny shook his head sadly. Poor kid, laid up like that with a burnt arm. And it had all happened so suddenly. He and Shraga had talked it over while waiting for word from the hospital. Shraga was convinced that there was something behind the two seemingly unrelated incidents: Friday night's falling flowerbox and today's tipped-over urn. Pinny wasn't so sure. The question wasn't so much *who* would want to cause them harm — the sinister thief still lurked behind the scenes somewhere — but rather, *why?* How could it possibly help that crook to injure a couple of innocent kids? What on earth did he hope to gain?

"Poor Mindy," Shraga said quietly.

"I wish Abba was here," Daniella said, her lower lip quivering.

Instantly, Mrs. Katz sat up and tried to look cheerful. "Me, too, sweetie," she said. "I'm sure he'll be back, and Mindy's father too, before long. Meanwhile —" she glanced at her wristwatch "— I do believe it's time for bed." She turned to the older kids as she remembered something. "Goodness, I hope you kids have had your dinners?"

"Oh, sure, hours ago," Ari said. He was about to add, "That is, if you could call that warmed-over aluminum-wrapped mess 'dinner'...," when he caught sight of the look in his mother's eye. He bit back the words.

"Ima," he said instead, "why don't you go see if you can get something to eat? We'll put the kids to bed. Won't we, guys?"

"I'll put myself to bed!" Zevy announced, with an overtired glint in his eye.

"Fine," Pinny said quickly. And Shraga added, "Hey, Zevy, How about lending me a hand with Ruchie and Vivi?"

"Sure!" Zevy said happily.

In a tight clump, as if they were afraid to be separated for a minute, the Katz-Morgenstern group made their way to the elevator. Mrs. Katz went tiredly to the dining room to see if they'd saved one of the kosher "airline dinners" for her. She thought of Mrs. Morgenstern, dining tonight on a chocolate bar and an apple off her daughter's hospital tray. Then she pictured Mindy, not crying anymore by the time Mrs. Katz had left, drowsy from the painkillers but still too fretful to sleep. With a sad smile, she bid them both a silent goodnight.

The children were restless next morning. Their fathers had not returned. With the new worry about Mindy hanging over their heads, no one could seem to settle down to anything. There were fewer comments than usual about the breakfast food, and afterwards the bigger kids allowed the littler ones to hang around with them for a change. This gave Mrs. Katz — in sole charge of the whole bunch — a welcome respite. Vivi Morgenstern, the baby, had been up at the crack of dawn and had just laid down for her morning nap. Mrs. Katz looked like she could use one, too.

"Let's take the kids for a walk or something," Ari whispered to Pinny and Shraga. "Ima looks exhausted."

"What about learning?" Pinny whispered back.

"We can do that later."

Shraga added, "And Shai said he might join us this time, remember?"

Pinny remembered. Shai chose that moment to appear, trotting up to them with a broad grin. Pinny was still startled by that grin; it contrasted so dramatically with the sullen face he had worn at the start of the week.

"So what are we doing today?" Shai asked eagerly. "Any plans?"

"We thought we'd take the kids on a walk down the road," Shraga told him.

"A walk? I thought we were detectives!"

"Just for a little while," said Pinny. "With Mindy in the hospital and my mother taking care of everyone, we thought it'd be nice to give her a break."

Shai thought about that. Though he would never have admitted it, he felt moved. Those boys really cared about their mother. It was nice when people took care of each other. Not that he'd experienced much of that in his own life...

The familiar chains of self-pity began to wind themselves around him. But Ari was already leading them toward the drive that led to the road. "Well, if we're goin', let's go!"

"Okay!" Shai cried, his mood changing again, swift as lightning. They'd only walked a few steps when Ari stopped short. "I just remembered — we'd better get permission first. Meet you back here in five minutes. Pinny, Shraga, keep an eye on the gang. C'mon, Shai." He went back inside to find his mother.

Shai, more reluctantly, did the same. Mrs. Drucker was up in her room, relaxing with a book in Hebrew. Shai poked his head through the doorway. "Can I go for a walk with the other kids?"

Mrs. Drucker looked up from her book. "Where are you going? Any place special?"

"No, just for a walk. Mrs. Katz lets." Shai hoped that was true. "It won't be for long. Okay?"

His foster mother was pleased to see Shai enjoying himself at last. She gave him a fond smile. "All right," she said. "But let me see you when you get back. Otherwise, I'll worry."

"Okay." Shai promptly withdrew from the door and disappeared. Carefree, he ran down the hall toward the elevator. As for Mrs. Drucker, she returned to her book, still wearing the smile.

She most certainly *would* see Shai on his return. Only the sight would not be anything like what she expected.

"Where're you off to, kids?" Tom Morrison asked. He and Sandy were standing beside the cars parked in the drive.

"Oh, hi, Tom," Pinny smiled. "For a walk."

"Where to?"

"No place special," Pinny answered. "Just walking."

Shraga studied the Special Agent's face to see if there was a particular meaning behind his questions. Were the kids to be confined to the hotel grounds as their fathers had been?

But Tom was all affability. "Sandy, didn't we pass some sort of dairy farm just up the road? You kids like cows?"

"Yeah!" shouted Zevy Katz, closely echoed by little Ruchie Morgenstern. "We wanna see cows!"

Sandy grinned at them and pointed up the road. "You just walk thataway, about — oh, half a mile, I'd say. You can't miss it."

Shraga looked doubtful. "Will the farmer let us in?"

"I don't see why not," Tom said. "Tell him the F.B.I. sent you." He and Sandy laughed heartily at that. Pinny laughed, too. Shraga just smiled politely, eager to be off.

The road was pleasantly shaded from the sun by tall leafy trees. "It's a nice day for walking," Pinny remarked.

"It's nice to see that there's a world outside that hotel," said Shraga.

"That's for sure," Ari agreed fervently. "Boy, I can't wait to put this place behind me."

"Like Abba did," Pinny said in a low voice. The others fell silent. They were all thinking of their fathers, wondering where they were, what they were doing, and if they were safe. Some of the light seemed to go out of the pleasant morning.

They walked on. The sun grew stronger, but there was still no sign of the farm they were looking for. Ruchie began to complain that her feet hurt. Ari was thinking about suggesting that they give it up and turn back, when Zevy let out a triumphant shout.

"Look! A cow!" He scampered up to a fence that enclosed a big, grassy field at the side of the road. "I saw it first!"

Before anyone could stop him, he had clambered over the fence and was running in the direction of the cow.

Only it wasn't a cow. To Shraga's horror, he saw sharp horns glinting in the sun, and the mean look in the creature's eye as it turned its head to glare balefully at the intruder.

"It's not a cow, it's a bull!" he shouted, running to the fence. "Zevy, watch out!"

The next few minutes happened in superfast motion. Ari reached the fence first, closely followed by the others. But there was someone there ahead of him. Shai had vaulted the fence a little further back and was already running at full tilt toward the spot where Zevy stood frozen in fright. The bull just glared.

Suddenly, a sharp noise rang out. It sounded like the backfire of a car. With an angry bellow the bull tossed its mighty head and began pawing the ground, sending clumps of grass — roots and all

— flying into the air. Zevy watched, petrified. The bull gave a last furious snort and began running right at the little boy.

As Ari began climbing desperately over the fence, Shai, still some distance from Zevy, thought quickly. He needed to distract that monster's attention, away from Zevy. What to use? He groped in his pocket and came up with his handkerchief.

A red handkerchief would have been best, but a white one was all he had. Bellowing at the top of his lungs, he waved his arms like a windmill above his head, with the handkerchief fluttering from one of his hands. The bull swerved sharply and began thundering across the field, in Shai's direction now.

Zevy awoke from his trance. Tears streaming down his dirty cheeks, he raced for Ari and the fence. But the bull paid him no mind. His fury was aimed at Shai, and only Shai. Zevy scrambled to safety and then turned, secure in Ari's arms, to see what was happening.

The others watched, too. Horrified, helpless, they stood by as the valiant young Israeli whirled around and began to run for all he was worth back to the fence.

He nearly made it. He had one leg over the top rail when the bull caught up with him. As the raging animal lowered his head to strike, Shai gave an agonized leap. One pointy horn caught his shirt at the shoulder. With a ripping sound, Shai tore free and was over the fence.

Gasping for breath, he felt the arms of the other boys go around him. "Shai, are you okay?"

"That was some move!"

"You saved Zevy. You're a hero!"

He didn't feel like a hero. He felt like a very small boy, trying hard not to cry. "M-my shoulder," he gasped. "I think it's hurt."

Gently, Shraga pulled away his shirt. His eyes widened. The tip of the bull's horn had dug deep into the shoulder and then, as Shai pulled free, etched a deep scratch that traveled halfway down the boy's arm. Blood was welling up in the gash.

"Shai, can you walk?" Ari asked urgently.

"I — I think so."

"You can lean on me if you have to. We've got to get you back to the hotel — now," Ari said. "You need a doctor."

The walk back was not nearly as pleasant as the way there had been. Each step made the throbbing in Shai's shoulder grow more intense. Soon the throbs turned into real pain. Pinny wadded up the handkerchief — it had still been clutched in Shai's hand — and pushed it against the injured place to try and staunch the blood. It helped, but only a little. After trudging what felt like miles and miles under a sun that felt increasingly hot, they reached the turnoff into the hotel drive.

Grimly, the small band moved up the drive to the hotel. They needed to find the Druckers and a doctor — in that order.

13

"You Gotta Have Faith!"

Shraga paced the terrace with his head down, deep in thought. He was back at the old "Who?" game. With each disturbing incident, the question grew more pressing.

Who stole Little Nicky?

Who dropped the flowerbox onto the terrace Friday night?

Who tipped over the hot-water urn?

And now, the newest question: Whose car had backfired near that field and startled the bull into charging?

Shraga had no doubt in the world that the answer to all these questions was the same. The noise of that unseen car *might* have been pure coincidence, but Shraga was beginning to believe otherwise. The thief who'd made away with the secret weapon was also the force behind the three mysterious "accidents" that had injured, or tried to injure, three of their group. *Who was it?*

Back and forth he paced under the fierce noonday sun. And, as Shraga perspired in the growing heat, his temperature began to rise in another way. He was boiling mad! If only he had that bad guy in front of him for just five minutes — just five minutes, that's all he asked — he'd... He'd...

What *would* he do?

Just as suddenly as his anger had ballooned, it collapsed. He felt young and powerless. He was just a kid. Dangerous things kept happening to his family and friends, and there wasn't a thing he could do to stop them. He stopped his pacing and stood still with his hands hanging helpless at his sides. If only Daddy were here, he thought dismally. If only...

"Shraga, there you are!" Pinny ran out onto the terrace. "What're you doing out here in the heat?"

"Just getting away from it all," Shraga said shortly.

"I don't blame you... But here's some *good* news for a change. The doctor fixed up Shai just fine! He doesn't even need stitches. The doctor just put some stuff on the wound that's supposed to knit the skin together in time."

"How much time?"

Some of Pinny's elation left his face. "Well, a couple of weeks. Shai's left arm's not going to be much use to him for a while."

Shraga transferred his self-pity to the Israeli boy. What a thing to happen on his first visit abroad!

"How are his spirits?" he asked.

"Oh, not bad." Pinny brightened. "Not bad at all. In fact, I heard him boasting to Niki just now — telling him all about how he outran that old bull."

Shraga smiled. "That's good." He hesitated. "Pinny, I'm not so sure that was really an accident."

"You mean, the backfire?"

"I mean the backfire."

"You know what *I* think?" Pinny asked slowly.

"No, what?"

Now it was Pinny's turn to hesitate. "You're going to think I'm nuts."

"Try me," Shraga urged.

"I think it wasn't a car at all. I think it was a gunshot!"

Shraga stopped dead in his tracks. He heard again the sharp, ringing sound, and saw the way the bull had tossed its head suddenly as if something had whizzed by, disturbing it...

"Maybe," he said in a near-whisper. "You just may be right."

"Should we tell the F.B.I.?" Pinny whispered back.

"No. We have no proof. A couple of kids with wild ideas..."

Pinny nodded. "Let's wait and see how things develop."

They resumed their walk to the door. "I'm starting to feel a little spooked," Pinny admitted. "What's going to happen next?" His usually peaceful blue eyes were troubled.

"I don't know," Shraga said heavily. "But I'm not so eager to find out." After a second, he added, "Pinny? Let's keep our suspicions to ourselves for now, okay? I mean, there's no need to make Shai more scared than he already is."

Pinny nodded in silent agreement. Shraga quickened his pace. "Well, time to go in, I guess. We've got something to do, remember?"

"Oh, right. We've got to plot some more strategy. That bad guy is around here somewhere, and we've got to find him!"

Shraga pulled open the door to the lobby. "I couldn't agree more, Pinny. Strategy — yes. But first, let's learn."

The two boys left the baking terrace for the air-conditioned comfort of the lobby. "Where is Shai now?" Shraga asked.

"With his parents, in their room," Pinny answered. "They wanted to hear how the accident happened."

Which brought Shraga right back to his original question. How *had* it happened?

Shai's spirits might have been good while he was bragging to Niki just now, but it was a different story as he stood before the Druckers in their hotel room.

Dr. Drucker seemed to have aged years in the short time they'd been at the Lake View Hotel. His face was gaunt, with lines of strain etched on his high forehead. His wife was in little better shape, tired and edgy and certain of one thing. "We're leaving this hotel. Right now, today!"

"What? Leaving?" Shai stared. "But we can't!"

"Oh, no?" His foster mother already had a suitcase out on the bed. She began opening drawers and taking out piles of clothes. Shai turned to his foster father and demanded, "Why?"

Mrs. Drucker snorted under her breath. "*Why*, he asks!"

"Shai, this place is dangerous," Dr. Drucker said patiently. "First the weapon gets stolen. Then there's a series of accidents that lands Mindy in the hospital and you — with that!" He motioned at the heavy bandage on Shai's arm. "Do you need more reasons?"

"It doesn't matter." Shai set his chin mulishly. "I'm not scared."

"Maybe you're not, Shai, but we are." Dr. Drucker was trying hard to keep the atmosphere calm, but there was a sense of growing tension in the small room. "We'll just cut our stay here short by a couple of days and go on to Disneyworld. You'd like that, wouldn't you?"

"I'm not a baby, and you don't have to talk to me like one! Disneyworld can wait. We have a mystery to solve!"

"It's not yours to solve, Shai. Leave that for the F.B.I."

Shai stalked over to the window and then whirled back around to face them. "Anyway," he said triumphantly, "the F.B.I. probably won't even let us leave. Aren't you a suspect in the crime, just like all the other scientists near that lab?"

"Maybe I am," admitted Dr. Drucker. "But I haven't been arrested. I'm sure it will be enough to leave an itinerary with the authorities, and maybe to call in now and then. After all, the conference is due to end in just two days."

"Then let's wait the two days. Please!" Shai begged.

His foster parents were startled by the unfamiliar note in the boy's voice. Shai saw them softening, and rushed on. "Look, I'm all right. This is only a scratch; it'll heal soon. I'll be extra careful from now on. Only don't make me go!"

"I don't know...," Mrs. Drucker said uncertainly, still holding an armful of clothes. "I don't like what's been happening in this place."

"It's going to be all right. Really," Shai said quickly. "We just have to have — to have *bitachon.*" Remembering Pinny's words, he added with a shaky grin, "You gotta have faith!"

Dumbfounded, the Druckers just stood and stared at their foster son. At that moment, there came a knock at their door.

"C-come in," Mrs. Drucker called faintly.

Pinny's tousled blond head poked through the doorway. "Excuse me, but can Shai come down now? We're ready to learn."

"Sure," Shai said eagerly. He glanced at his foster parents. "Um, is it okay?" They knew what he was asking about.

"Learn?" Dr. Drucker repeated in a daze. "Shai, you're going to learn?"

For the first time, Shai looked embarrassed. "Yeah, I agreed to try it. Why not?"

"Why not? No reason in the world." Dr. Drucker began smiling. "Go ahead, son. Go right ahead."

The last thing Shai saw before leaving the room was Mrs. Drucker, removing piles of clothes from the suitcase as if in a dream.

"Shai? Can I talk to you for a minute?"

It was Niki Gorodnik, sounding oddly unsure of himself. Shai looked up from the Hebrew book he'd been reading in a corner of the lobby. The Gemara session had ended an hour ago — and a strangely satisfying session it had been. The others had run outside for a quick game of ball ("To clear our heads," Ari had said), promising to return for a strategy session soon. Shai himself was under doctor's orders to take it easy for the next two weeks.

"Sure, Niki," he said now, laying aside the book. "What is it?"

The Russian boy sat down beside him. He cleared his throat. He plumped up one of the sofa cushions. He squirmed and fidgeted and cleared his throat again. Shai watched this performance in growing curiosity. At last he asked, "What?"

"Shai, there's something I have to tell. I — I wasn't sure I should..." There it was again: the question of loyalty. To whom did Niki owe his?

"Sure you should," Shai said promptly. "Tell me."

Niki faced him squarely. He'd come to a decision. "I'm going to tell you what I know, without telling you who it's about."

"What good is that?"

Niki just shrugged. The shrug said, as clearly as any words could, "Take it or leave it." Shai decided to take it.

"Okay, okay. Just tell me already."

Slowly, in his careful English, Niki asked, "Do you remember that night when the weapon was stolen?"

Shai made a face. "How could anyone forget?"

"Well, we were talking about whether anyone left the dining room that night, during dinner."

"Yes?" Shai sat up excitedly. "Did you see someone leave?"

"N-not exactly. But I did notice, towards the end of the meal, that he was gone."

"*Who*, Niki?"

But that was something Niki would not divulge. All of Shai's pressing and wheedling — and there was a lot — was about as useful as trying to break down a wall by throwing sand at it. Finally, he gave up.

"Just promise me one thing, will you?"

"What's that, Shai?"

"If you do decide to tell who it was...tell me first, okay?" Shai had an irresistible image of himself as the hero, parading the name of the culprit in front of the others. Today, over their Gemaras, the other boys had been the teachers while he'd been the ignorant one. It would be nice to know something they didn't.

Of course, he'd share it with them. They were partners, weren't they? But it would be he who'd have the precious information first. He just hoped it *was* really precious information, and not mere coincidence. After all, there could have been any number of reasons why someone would leave the dining room during dinner...

It has to be true, he thought. *It just has to be!*

"Okay Niki? Is it a deal?"

Now that he'd shared his secret — or part of it, anyway — Niki seemed relieved. "All right. A deal."

The two boys sat quietly for a few minutes, Shai still painting rosy pictures in his mind and Niki thinking about the remaining half of his secret. His bit of information wasn't going to be of much help, he knew, unless he gave away the name, too. But that he wasn't prepared to do yet.

"Niki?"

"Yes?"

"Why haven't you told anyone until now?"

Niki looked unhappy. "I don't know," he said. "Or maybe I do know. It's complicated."

"Try me."

"You see, it's a question of loyalty. Of — of who I belong to."

Shai nodded slowly. This was something he could understand.

Presently, Niki went off to the game room. He invited Shai to join him, but Shai declined. He found that he didn't feel much like company. Before, he'd been thinking longingly of the ball game the others were playing outside, and wishing he could join them. Now he was glad to be alone. Niki's question had brought back all his old feelings of loneliness.

It's a question of... who I belong to, Niki had said. Who did *he*, Shai Gilboa, belong to?

Just a little while before he'd spoken about having faith in Hashem. He was starting to believe that such faith was especially necessary for someone like him. After all, who else did he have to depend on?

A tiny voice whispered, "The Druckers. They really care about you, Shai."

He pushed the voice away and wandered out onto the terrace. That was one thought he sure wasn't ready to face yet.

Maybe it was the strong sun that melted the depressing thoughts from his mind, or the sight of the bright flowerbeds that chased them away. Whatever the reason, Shai found himself calming down. Things didn't look as bleak here, under the sun, as they had inside. He thought of Niki's piece of news. What exactly had he meant by "a question of loyalty?" Who had left the table during that fateful dinner? And how did Niki know about it?

Idly revolving these questions in his mind, Shai propped his elbows on the terrace railing and looked over. Just below him, the drive swept away toward the road. Someone was strolling up the drive, away from the hotel, his head and shoulders passing under the terrace rail where Shai stood lost in thought. Shai glanced down — and froze.

That head! That thick, near-black hair, with the bald spot in the center, up near the crown, where you wouldn't see it except from above! Where had he seen that head before?

Even as he posed the question, its answer came to him in a blinding flash. In the woods! He'd been up in the tree, looking down through the leaves at the person standing below him with that mysterious note. *The top of that head and the one below him now were one and the same!*

In his agitation, Shai must have made some movement. The move, or the sound it made, attracted the attention of the man below. He glanced up, then smiled pleasantly.

"Good afternoon. I hope you've recovered from your encounter with that bull this morning?" The entire hotel had heard the story of Shai's escapade.

Shai gulped. Smiling back was one of the hardest things he had ever done.

"Y-yes," he stammered. "Yes, I have... Dr. Pim."

14

The Detectives Confer

Shai was back inside the lobby almost before he realized he'd moved. Niki was nowhere to be seen. Shai wrinkled his brow... The game room! That's where Niki had been heading. Shai started for the same place at a run, then slowed down as he realized he was attracting curious stares. His feet were moving sedately by the time he reached the game room door, but his mind still raced.

"Niki!" he called, waving frantically to the boy at the computer. "Niki, over here, quick!"

Niki looked up from the monitor. Beside him, Alexei Pim glanced up, too. Both seemed to be wondering the same thing: What could be important enough to tear Niki away from the most exciting stage of the game they were playing?

Then, seeing the growing urgency in Shai's eyes, Niki suddenly knew. Slowly he got to his feet.

"You'd better take over here, Alexei. I'll go see what he wants." With even, deliberate steps he approached the doorway. "Shai, what is it?"

Shai grabbed Niki's arm. "Not here. We have to talk. Come on, let's go to our place."

"Our place" was the arrangement of couches on which the boys had plotted their strategy on *motza'ei Shabbos*. So much had happened since then, Shai reflected as they neared the spot. Including — Shai touched his injured arm with a wince — two more frightening accidents. He hurried ahead to their corner of the lobby, with Niki following more slowly. As soon as they were seated, Shai turned sparkling eyes on the other boy.

"It's Dr. Pim, right?"

Niki blanched. With an effort, he found his voice. "What — what do you mean?"

"The man who left the table during dinner, the night the weapon was stolen. It was Dr. Pim — Alexei's father! *He* left the dining room. *He* stole the weapon!"

"Sssh!" Niki implored.

"Well?"

"Well, since you know anyway..." Niki's head shot up. "But how *do* you know? Did you just guess?"

"It was no guess." Shai's laugh was short and dry. "Remember the note I found in the woods? The one that man threw away — a man I only got to see from above? Well, I just saw him from above again. And I remembered that the head I'd seen then, in the woods, had a bald spot right in the middle, on top of his head, where no one would normally see it. The man looked up — and it was him. Pim."

Niki nodded in a resigned sort of way. "I suppose it was only a matter of time before it came out."

"Why didn't you want to tell me his name?"

"He's Russian," Niki said simply. "And so am I."

"But you're also Jewish."

"Yes." Niki looked troubled. "The problem is, I'm not sure what that means, or how it fits into the rest of my life."

"Listen, Niki," Shai said. "I'm just as confused as you are about some things. But one thing is for sure. Now that you know you're a Jew, things are never going to be the same for you again. They can't be. Understand?"

Niki sighed. "I'm beginning to."

"Well, don't look so miserable about it. Just think how happy Shraga and Pinny and the others are going to be when they hear the news." Shai shook his dark head wonderingly. "Dr. Ilya Pim. Who would have thought it?"

Niki was uneasy. "Shai, what are you going to do?"

"What am *I* going to do?" Shai met his eyes. "It's not what I'm going to do, Niki — it's what *you're* going to do. You're going to come with me to find the others, and tell them what we've just discovered."

"I wish I'd never noticed him gone," Niki whispered. He looked unhappier than ever. "Why me?"

"That," Shai said in a burst of wisdom beyond his years, "is a question that has never had any answer — at least not that we can figure out." He stood up and motioned impatiently for Niki to do the same. "Come on. We've got a lot of figuring out to do."

They found Ari, Pinny, and Shraga resting on the grass after their game. Chaim and Zevy were still tossing a ball nearby. Seeing the bigger boys form a huddle, the younger ones came over.

"What's up? What's going on?" Chaim asked. When he got no answer, he tapped Shraga's back. "Hey, Shraga, what's happening?"

Shraga glanced at him distractedly over his shoulder. "Go 'way, Chaim. We're busy."

"But I want to —"

"*Go away,* I said!"

Chaim stared at his brother's back, his amazement even stronger than his outrage. He couldn't remember Shraga speaking to him in just that tone of voice before. Shraga must have something on his mind — something big. It figures that he doesn't want to let *me* in on it, he thought bitterly. He turned, to find Zevy at his elbow.

"C'mon, Zevy," Chaim growled. "We can have fun without them."

Zevy tossed the ball into the air, tried to catch it, and failed. Stooping to retrieve it, he said brightly, "Wanna play some more catch?"

"Nah," Chaim said dispiritedly. "Let's go to the game room."

The older boys, whispering earnestly together, didn't even hear them go.

At last, the huddle broke up. The boys flung themselves onto the grass. They stared at each other, still finding it hard to believe.

"So it was him," Pinny said musingly. "Alexei's going to be so upset... And Dr. Pim seemed like such a decent guy."

"Lost of crooks seem decent, till you get to know what they really are," Ari said. "Well, what do we do now? Go to our fathers — or straight to the F.B.I.?"

"Abba and Dr. Morgenstern first," Pinny said. "They deserve to know before anyone."

"Anyway, we've got an airtight case," Ari said complacently.

Suddenly Shraga, who'd been sprawled on the grass with the rest of them, sat up very straight. "Wait a second! Who says we have?"

"Have what?" Shai asked, bewildered.

"What did he say?" Niki asked anxiously.

"What're you talking about, Shraga?" Pinny demanded.

"Our case. What do we really have, anyway?"

All around Shraga, in an incredulous circle, his fellow detectives gaped at him.

"Shraga," Pinny asked without ceremony, "have you gone off your rocker?"

"No, no. Just listen. Pretend you're Tom Morrison, or his higher-ups at the F.B.I. A bunch of kids come running up to you, babbling something about finding the thief. You ask for evidence. And what do they give you?"

"They give you," Ari answered, "a guy who was reading a note in the woods, telling him to meet someone at midnight, and to bring their 'little friend.' And the same guy was missing from his place at the dinner table at the very moment that Little Nicky was being stolen!" Ari sat back, resting his case.

But Shraga wasn't impressed. "So? This is Morrison speaking now." He deepened his voice. "'Circumstantial evidence, kids. That's all it amounts to, sorry to say. So a guy throws away a scrap of paper asking him to meet someone somewhere, and to bring along some friend or other. So a guy has to get up to go to the bathroom during dinner. You call that evidence?'"

"But — but it's the same guy!" sputtered Shai.

"So?" Shraga leaned forward. "Listen, I'm not any happier about this than the rest of you are. I'm just trying to be realistic. And realism says, the F.B.I. is not going to arrest Dr. Pim or anyone else just on our say-so. We need *real* evidence."

"And how do you propose to get that?" Disappointment had sharpened Pinny's voice.

"The only thing I can think of," Shraga said quietly, "is to shadow Dr. Pim and see what he does next."

"Hm," Ari said. "Now that's an idea."

Niki was distressed. "Next? He already tried to steal the weapon. That's safe in New York now. What else do you expect him to do?"

It was Pinny who answered him.

"First of all, Niki, there's another person in the picture somewhere, remember? Pim's partner — the elusive 'Mr. B.' They may try to set up another meeting or something, and we've got to be there to hear it. And also..."

"Also what?" Niki asked impatiently, when Pinny stopped.

"Also," Ari finished for his brother, "there have been three so-called 'accidents' in the past few days. Either Pim, or this Mr. B., or both, must be behind them. I'm not sure what their motive is, but if they wanted to scare us off the trail —" he threw a menacing look in the direction of the hotel "— then all I can say is, they chose the wrong people to mess around with."

"Are we agreed then?" Shraga asked his fellow conspirators. "We shadow Pim until we find proof that our suspicions are right?"

"Or wrong," Niki said quickly. "Don't forget that."

"Let's do it! Let's follow him!" Shai exclaimed. "We'll catch him...what's the expression?"

"Red-handed," Pinny said grimly.

"Right," Shai said happily.

He would have to try again tonight.

He had hoped, when he'd reported failure the other time, that 'Mr. Big' would let him off the hook. Eagerly he'd scanned his e-mail screen at intervals throughout the day, hoping against hope that he'd find welcome instructions to drop the whole matter and just lie low.

Instead, the opposite had happened. Mr. Big had ordered him to spare no effort to crack the Jewish scientists' computer codes — the first step in unraveling the program that held the weapon's secret plans. *Better make it quick*, the message had read, *before they come back.*

He had to admit that there was a certain logic in this. Once the two Jewish scientists returned to the hotel — and they *would* return, if only to be with their families again — it would be much more difficult to enter the lab at night.

And so, once again, he would creep tonight through the deserted halls toward that dreaded lab. Again he would spend long hours staring at the computer screen, punching desperately at the keyboard with chilled fingers, waiting for something that never happened. Those passwords and codes were securely off-limits to trespassers, that much was becoming crystal clear. If only that infernal *Mr. Big* could see it, too!

He walked through the pleasant green woods, looking straight ahead and not seeing anything of the summer beauty around him. He was picturing to himself the night that lay ahead. He had a feeling it was going to be a long one.

15

Faithful Shadows

While their sons were plotting their strategy back at the Lake View Hotel, where were Dr. Katz and Dr. Morgenstern? Where, in fact, had they been since their abrupt disappearance in the early hours of Sunday morning?

Their anxious wives longed to know. Their children were itching to know, too. As for the F.B.I. agents stationed at the hotel, they were still grinding their teeth at the continued absence of the two scientists. In all the world, only the two men themselves knew where they'd gone — plus one other.

"Well, Jake? Will you help us?"

Jake Pfeiffer looked long and steadily at Dr. Katz and Dr. Morgenstern. He was taller than either of them, a long, skinny beanpole of a man with a yarmulka perched atop his wavy brown hair and an engaging smile that was not in sight at the moment. He looked unusually solemn as he slowly nodded his head.

"Whatever it is you two are up to, I know I can trust you. You wouldn't be involved in anything illegal."

"Certainly not," Dr. Katz said roundly. "In fact, what we're trying to do is catch a criminal."

"But we need your help, Jake," Dr. Morgenstern added. "Without the powerful computer you have here, our hands are tied."

Yaakov ("Jake") Pfeiffer ran the computer department of a small university, about an hour's drive from the Lake View Hotel. It had been Pinny's father who'd suggested that they ask Pfeiffer to meet them there. "We want to get away from the hotel in any case," he'd said to Dr. Morgenstern. "We have to, in order to keep the kids safe... As long as we're around, accidents can happen. If we're not there, this 'Mr. Big,' whoever he is, has no hold over us — or our kids. So why not go out to Jake Pfeiffer's place and try to trace this Mr. Big's message?"

And Shraga's father had to admit that the idea was sound. If they could discover where Mr. Big was transmitting his menacing messages from, they'd be one giant step closer to uncovering the true identity of the master crook himself!

Jake relaxed and gave each of the worried scientists a big grin. "Hey, cheer up! The question is not *will* I help you — but *can* I? Or rather, can my computer." He shrugged. "Well, only one way to find out." He motioned for them to follow him.

As they started down the empty gray corridors toward the computer department, Dr. Katz said soberly, "You don't know what this means to us, Jake. We're very grateful."

"Hey, it's the least I can do for a couple of former fellow yeshiva *bachurim*..." And the rest of the walk had been a stroll down memory lane. Their yeshiva days had been happy ones, and they seemed even happier now, looked back upon in this time of trouble.

That had been early Sunday morning.

Now, on Monday evening, both the physicists and their computer-expert friend were about ready to concede defeat.

"It's no use, guys," Jake sighed. He ran the fingers of one hand through his hair, making it stand up wildly on either side of his yarmulka. "I've tried every trick I know. Your man routed that message through Scandinavia. The e-mail service he used is extremely strict about guarding the identity of its senders. There's no way we can worm the name out of them." His glance was troubled. "Sorry. Really."

"That's all right," Dr. Katz replied. He sounded surprisingly cheerful. "We know you tried your best. And so have we. We tried, and it didn't work. We'll have to keep davening for another brainstorm, that's all."

"I'm for returning to the hotel," Dr. Morgenstern said. "I've never been happy about leaving the women and kids alone there. There's funny stuff going on at the Lake View this week."

"You're telling me," Dr. Katz mock-groaned.

Reluctantly, his friend cracked a small smile. "Seriously, though, what do you say we go back first thing in the morning?"

Dr. Katz smiled back. "Sounds wonderful to me."

"In that case," Jake Pfeiffer said, "let me take you two illustrious gentlemen out to dinner. There's no telling when we'll be able to get together again like this."

"You've talked us into it," Dr. Katz laughed, and Dr. Morgenstern laughed along with him. The mere thought of seeing their loved ones again was enough to banish all their cares. It was with lighter footsteps that they followed their old friend to his car.

"We don't *all* have to stay up tonight, you know," Ari Katz pointed out. "We could split up and take shifts. That way, we'll each get at least a few hours of sleep."

"Sleep?" Shai said scornfully. "Who needs sleep?" He sounded eager and happy. Again, Shraga marveled at the change in the Israeli boy. Something was happening to him here at the Lake View, and it was something good. He might have a long, ugly gash on his arm to show for his stay, but inside — where it didn't show — other, deeper wounds were healing.

He brought his attention back to the others. It was just before dinner, and they'd decided to finalize their plans now. Once darkness fell, they were determined to keep Pim under their eye every single minute.

"That's right, Ari." Pinny agreed with Shai. "I, for one, will be too wired up to sleep, wondering what was happening. I say we all shadow Pim tonight. If nothing happens then, we can always revise our plans tomorrow."

"Fine with me." Ari spread his palms. "I was going to volunteer for the midnight shift, but I guess I'll have company."

"I'll say you will." Pinny's eyes were agleam with excitement.

"We may just stare at Pim's door all night," Shraga, ever the realist, reminded them. "He may just sleep through it, you know."

"I know," Pinny said. "But we have no choice, do we? We have to be there, in case he makes a move."

"What about Alexei?" Niki asked suddenly. "The two of us usually hang around together in the game room after dinner. He'll get suspicious if I disappear with all of you — especially if he sees us trailing around after his father."

"I hope we'll be more discreet than that," Pinny argued.

"So do I." Niki regarded him fixedly. "But what *about* Alexei?"

It was decided that, to allay suspicion, Niki would be assigned to Alexei instead of shadowing Alexei's father with the rest of them. Privately, Shraga was relieved. The less people they had on Pim's trail, the less noticeable they would be. As for Shai, he was secretly even more relieved. He was the only one who knew about Niki's problem — the question of loyalty. True, he had *almost* decided to cast his lot with his Jewish friends rather than with his Russian compatriots — until Shai decided for him, by recognizing Pim himself. Better for Niki to keep Alexei company as usual tonight. Maybe he'd feel a little less guilty that way for helping to bring about Alexei's father's undoing.

The best that could be said for that night's dinner was that the kids swallowed it largely un-tasted. They were too excited about the night's plans to make more than token faces at the quality — or lack thereof — of the stuff on their plates. As soon as they could, they escaped back out to the lobby.

"Shai, you stand near the dining room door to see when Pim comes out," Ari ordered. "The rest of us will stay out of sight here in the lobby, waiting for your signal."

"Will do!" Shai scampered away.

Pinny and Shraga both turned at the same moment. Their eyes met.

"It's starting," Pinny said in a low voice.

Shraga could only nod.

The dinner had been delicious. The three old friends had travelled miles to find a good kosher restaurant, but the trip had been worth it. Now, much more relaxed than when they'd started out, they settled back in Jake's car.

"Where to?" he asked, starting the engine. "You're more than welcome to sleep in comfort at my house tonight. I could drive you back to the campus to pick up your own car in the morning."

It was a tempting thought. The night before, the physicists had camped out on a couple of rather lumpy couches in the university's student union building. Regretfully, Dr. Morgenstern shook his head.

"That's kind of you, Jake, but we don't want to put you or your family at risk. Whoever's behind the theft of our device — not to mention that falling flowerbox — would not scruple to hurt other innocent people. It's bad enough that we had to get you involved." He shook his head. "No, we won't set foot in your home — not till this is all over."

"Let's hope that's soon," Jake said, suddenly deadly serious.

"Amen," said Dr. Katz.

They drove back to the campus, to its lumpy couches and deserted corridors — and its powerful computer. As they pulled into the darkened parking lot, Dr. Katz glanced at his watch. "It's only just past eleven, David. I can't say those student union couches seem very appealing right now. What do you say we give the computer one last try?"

Dr. Morgenstern looked doubtful. "We don't want to keep Jake so late. He's done enough for us already — more than enough."

But Jake said quickly, "I don't mind one more try before I leave you guys. Who wants to end such a pleasant evening, anyhow?" He was whistling as he parked his car and used his key to reenter the computer building.

A short time later, the three men were bending over the computer screen. They tapped into the scientists' computer back at the lab, to check whether there'd been any further message from the sinister Mr. Big.

There was no message. But what they did find made their eyes open very wide.

"Did you see what I just saw, Shmulie?" Dr. Morgenstern asked.

"I sure did," Dr. Katz replied, still staring at the monitor.

Jake Pfeiffer looked from one to the other, then back at the screen.

"Somebody," he said, though by now it was obvious to all of them, "has broken into your computer, guys. And I don't think it's anyone you want poking around in there, is it?"

His two physicist friends shook their heads, grimly and in unison.

Dr. Pim's evening routine had not been wildly exciting. In fact, his young shadowers found it downright boring. After dinner, he'd enjoyed a leisurely cup of tea in the lobby. Then he went out on the terrace for a solitary ramble beneath the stars. Up and down he strolled, while the boys chafed and fidgeted in their hiding places all around him. They were beginning to feel slightly ridiculous. Was Pim, or wasn't he, the master criminal they were after? Right now, his actions couldn't have been more innocent.

The boys quickly realized that they would attract Mrs. Katz's attention if they all disappeared for hours, so they took turns making casual appearances wherever their families were. Chaim Morgenstern persisted in trying to latch onto the bigger kids, but they managed to shake him off. They all breathed a sigh of relief when Mrs. Katz swept the younger kids up to bed. Mrs. Morgenstern was still at the hospital with Mindy.

"Don't stay up too late now," Mrs. Katz called back just before the elevator doors closed on her.

"We'll actually be staying up *early*," Pinny murmured to his friends. "Till early morning, that is."

"I feel bad," Shraga said.

"Me, too," Pinny admitted.

"We're doing it for Abba," Ari reminded his brother fiercely. "And for your father, Shraga. Remember?"

They remembered. Quickly, they hurried back to the terrace to relieve Shai.

"Hey, where were you so long?" Shai hissed from the shadows. "I was scared he'd leave and I'd have to follow him myself."

"We're here now," Pinny soothed. "Maybe you should go show your face to your — to the Druckers now."

They watched Shai trot off, then settled down to observe Pim again. At about ten o'clock, Pim, together with his son Alexei, retired to their room. Niki let out a big yawn. "Maybe we should do the same thing."

"What? This is when the real action starts," Ari exclaimed. "If he's going to make any sort of move, it's bound to be at night, after everyone's in bed."

Niki thought longingly of his own bed, but said nothing. A detective's life is not an easy one.

Ari was right. It was nearing midnight when Pinny, who'd been manning the lookout post on Pim's floor, dashed down the service stairs to report excitedly that their suspect had just left his room.

"He'll be down any second now! Quick — hide!"

16
Caught Red-Handed!

By the time Pinny came down with his news, the other boys had been prowling the grounds around the hotel for a miserable few hours. It was chilly out there, despite the windbreakers they wore, and the damp grass had soaked through their sneakers. But they wanted to raise no curious eyebrows, which would assuredly happen if they were seen hanging around the deserted lobby at that time of night.

Now they pounded quietly around a corner of the hotel to the side entrance near the labs. They chose that door because it was not in the line of sight of the clerk at the night desk. Shai slipped inside and tiptoed as far as the game room door, which gave him a clear view of the elevator.

"Though he'll probably use the stairs, just like I did," Pinny whispered. "Otherwise he stands a chance of being seen in the lobby."

"How'd you manage to get down before him?" Shraga asked curiously.

"I was hiding at the head of the stairs. It has a good view of Pim's door. The minute I saw his door open, I —"

"Sssh," Niki shushed them. "Somebody is coming!"

It was Shai, almost incoherent with excitement. "He came down the steps. He's sneaking back this way."

Shivering with apprehension and the cool mountain wind, the five boys crouched at the door. Ari, the tallest, held it open a fraction of an inch and put his eye to the crack to see. After hours in the darkness, his night sight was nearly perfect. Five, six, seven, ten endless seconds passed. Then, "It's him," breathed Ari. His voice was hardly louder than the sigh of the wind. The others caught their own breaths and found that their hearts were pounding uncomfortably and their jackets felt suddenly too tight. Shraga's palms prickled. He wiped them on his pants legs, thinking, "So it's really true. It was Pim all along." Somehow, even until this minute, it had felt like a game.

But it was no game. There was Ilya Pim, large as life, dressed in black pants and a dark sweater.

"He's stopping at the door of the lab," Ari reported in the softest of undertones. No one had to ask him which lab he meant. "Now he's taking something out of his pocket. It must be an electronic card... Yes. He's unlocking the door... He's inside."

Pinny, at Ari's back, distinctly heard the click of the lab door closing. Very quietly, Ari closed the door where they stood and turned to face the others.

"Well." He stopped, took a deep breath, and said again, "*Well.* He's in there, all right."

"What now?" Niki asked nervously.

"Good question." This from Pinny.

"What do you suppose he's doing in there?" Shai wondered.

"The computer, of course," Shraga told him. "He must be trying to get to the plans for Little Nicky."

"He can't do that," Pinny objected. "Didn't our fathers say there are passwords and things."

"Exactly," said Shraga, softly. "But Pim may not know that."

"The question is." Ari reminded them all, "what's our next move?"

That stumped them. Up until now, they'd been so busy faithfully shadowing Pim that they hadn't thought ahead to the moment — if it would ever come, which they'd each secretly found a little hard to believe — when they'd actually catch the Russian scientist in the act. Well, the moment had come. Pim had broken into their fathers' lab. They'd caught him red-handed.

Now what?

"Should we wake Tom up?" Pinny whispered. "Or get one of the other guards from outside?"

"Let's wait a little," Niki suggested.

That seemed like a good suggestion, if only to postpone the need to make any other decision. Ari manned his post at the crack in the door, and they settled down to wait. Conversing in whispers, they tried to reconstruct the crime. Pim's stealthy visit to the lab during dinner last Thursday night... Dr. Katz's unexpected raising of the alarm, which forced Pim to abandon the weapon he'd just stolen — right at their very own table... The flowerbox that had "accidentally" fallen into their midst on Friday night... The hot-water urn spilled on Mindy... The bull, enraged by an unseen pistol shot, charging directly at Shai and nearly succeeding in his terrifying purpose...

"It's hard to picture Pim as the person behind all those nasty accidents, though," Shraga said thoughtfully. "He seems like a gentle sort of guy."

"He is." Niki sounded sad. "You should hear Alexei speak about him." He sighed deeply. "It's going to be very hard on him if they arrest his father..."

"Well, it'll be hard on us if they arrest *ours*!" Pinny said vehemently. "Guys, I say we move now, before he leaves the lab."

"I'm with you," Ari said immediately. "I'm sick and tired of all this waiting."

"So that's it?" Shraga asked as a lump of nervous tension filled his stomach. "We just walk in there and say, 'You're under arrest'?"

"What if he has a gun?" Shai said.

That brought them up cold. Each could very clearly recall the sound of the pistol shot yesterday, ringing out in the clear summer air. In the close quarters of the lab, Shraga thought vaguely, it would make a much louder noise...

"I've got it!" Ari said. "Gather round and listen to the plan. The rest of you go in first and confront him. Then, when he's busy dealing with you, I slip in and disarm him. He'll be taken completely by surprise. It's a cinch to work!"

"I'm not so sure," Niki objected, sounding more than a little nervous now.

"If only Tom were here," Pinny moaned.

"Forget that kind of talk," Shraga rejoined firmly. "We've got to figure out what *we* can do, *now*."

"We could go call Tom," Shai suggested.

Shraga opened his mouth to speak, but what he intended to say would never be known. Because at that precise instant in time, a car pulled rapidly — almost wildly — into the hotel drive. One car door closed quietly, and then another. There was a noise of light running footsteps, and then a pair of figures appeared in front of them. They were making for this very door!

"Who —?" began Ari.

"Daddy!" Shraga cried. Even in his astonishment he remembered to keep his voice low.

"Abba!" Ari and Pinny ran forward to surround their father. "You're back!"

"Out of the way, boys," Dr. Katz whispered forcefully. "Someone's been tampering with our computer. He may be in the lab yet. Stay back, please." He and Dr. Morgenstern flung open the side door and plunged into the dimly lit corridor.

"But Daddy, that's just what we —"

"Sssh!" There was no mistaking Dr. Morgenstern's meaning. The five boys fell into a ragged line behind the men and followed them to the lab door.

Dr. Katz stopped. "Ready?" he asked Dr. Morgenstern.

A curt nod and an echoing "Ready" came back at him.

"All right. One, two, three — here goes!" Dr. Katz produced his own electronic card, rapidly unlocked the door, and was through it, all inside three seconds. Dr. Morgenstern was right behind him and the five junior detectives crowded close behind *him*.

"Stop what you're doing!" Dr. Katz shouted. "We've got you covered!"

Ilya Pim turned very slowly in his swivel chair to face them.

"So you're the one who stole our device," Dr. Morgenstern said with something that was almost satisfaction. "The truth at last." It was a few minutes later. Dr. Katz had insisted that Dr. Pim turn out his pockets, claiming that his colleague had Dr. Pim "covered." In actuality, Dr. Morgenstern had nothing more in his hand than a thick fountain pen, but the dim light from the computer screen and Dr. Katz's obscuring figure made sure that Pim couldn't know that. The Russian scientist obediently emptied his pockets, moving very slowly, almost as if in a trance. He had no gun.

"Yes," he said now, hoarsely. "I took the weapon. I —"

"We knew it!" crowed Pinny. "You left your seat during dinner, and then —"

"Pinny," said his father. "This is not the time. Dr. Pim will have plenty of opportunity to tell his story to the authorities." His eyes sought his eldest son's. "Ari, can you track down one of the F.B.I. people and bring him in here?"

"No!" Pim's agonized cry startled them all. They turned to face him again. His face had gone white and drawn. "No, please. Don't call them. They will arrest me. My poor Alexei..."

"I'm sorry, Pim," Dr. Katz said. "We have no choice. You've committed a grave crime, and placed Dr. Morgenstern and me under suspicion. I don't know which government or what sort of organization you're working for, or whether you're playing a lone hand. That's not really our business. We just hand you over to the authorities. They'll do the rest."

"Please," Pim whispered, covering his face with his hands. "You don't understand. It's not the way you think." He lifted his head suddenly, and in the eerie light of the computer monitor Shraga saw, to his amazement, that the man's cheeks were wet. "If you'll only let me explain..."

"I'm sorry," Dr. Morgenstern began again. "We really have no choice in the matter."

"Please, Abba," Pinny whispered. "Look, he's crying." The boy sounded close to tears himself.

"Can't we at least hear him out?" Shraga pleaded with his own father. "He hasn't tried to hurt us or anything. Let's give him a chance to explain."

"Oh, hasn't he?" Dr. Morgenstern half-turned to address his son. "Who do you suppose threw down the windowbox that nearly landed on Ruchie?"

"You don't even know about the other accidents," Shai informed him.

"What? What accidents? What are you talking about?" Alarmed, Dr. Katz turned too.

"Mindy got burned," said Ari. "She's in the hospital."

"*My Mindy?*" Dr. Morgenstern looked as though he were about to fly right out of the lab. "In the *hospital?*"

"She'll be okay, Daddy," Shraga said hastily. "Really. Mommy said so. Don't worry."

"And I got scratched by a bull this morning," Shai said, not without a touch of pride. "See?" He showed off his bandaged arm.

"This is worse than I thought," Dr. Katz muttered. "Let's go, Pim. You'll get your chance to explain — to the F.B.I."

"But I had nothing to do with any of those things!" Pim cried. He seemed bewildered. "You must believe me!"

Pinny took a deep breath and stepped closer to his father. "Abba," he said softly, "Let's do it. Let's listen to him. Please?"

"Please?" echoed the other four boys. Four pairs of eyes were raised to the two Jewish scientists, waiting for their answer. Dr. Katz looked at Dr. Morgenstern. Dr. Morgenstern hesitated, took a deep, calming breath — and then nodded his head.

"Very well," he said. "We'll listen. But after that, we call in the F.B.I."

"Thank you." Pim slumped abruptly back in his chair as if the relief were too great to be borne. "For myself, and my son, I thank you from the bottom of my heart."

"Don't thank us yet," Dr. Katz said grimly. "Let's hear what you have to say first."

"Very well," said Dr. Pim. "You shall hear everything. From the beginning."

There in the darkened lab, as the hour crept past one o'clock and the Lake View Hotel slept, he faced his small audience and began his story.

Coming Soon...
THE LITTLE BLACK BOX
Part 3:
The Secret Revealed

Shraga, Pinny, and their friends have finally tracked down the man who stole the deadly weapon their fathers brought up to the Lake View Hotel — but their triumph is a short-lived one. Just when they think they've solved the mystery of the Little Black Box, up crops a second, deeper mystery: the identity of the man who's the brains behind the whole sinister operation.

Dr. Morgenstern placed a hand on his son's shoulder. "It's part of galus, Shraga. You've seen that yourself, haven't you?"
Shraga nodded silently.

"To goyim, *Jews often make the perfect scape-goat.*"

"Do you really think that's going to happen here?" Pinny asked, eyes wide. Would their fathers continue to be suspected of a crime they had never committed?

Dr. Morgenstern shook his head firmly. "Don't worry, Pinny. The F.B.I. will find the right culprit."

He sounded confident, but deep inside he couldn't help feeling uneasy. Would the F.B.I. find the true criminal — the mysterious Mr. Big?

Their fathers might tell them not to worry, but Shraga and Pinny are finding it more and more difficult to obey.

"I'm worried," Pinny said. "We're right back where we started from...**and** this crook is busy arranging accidents."

"We have to be very careful," Shraga agreed. "But how can we be careful all the time?"

"We'll just have to be, that's all." Pinny slouched further against the van. "Shraga, we have to find out what's happening. We **must** find out who Mr. Big is. We've just **got** to!"

"I know," Shraga said. "And we will, Pinny. I know we will. Hashem will help us. We'll do everything we can, and we'll find out exactly who is trying to destroy our fathers' reputations by putting all the blame on them." His eyes flashed. "We'll capture Mr. Big and clear our fathers' names!"

As if there weren't already enough to worry about, there's Niki Gorodnik's strange behavior to account for.

"Niki," Pinny said after a few moments. "What's bothering you? Did we do something to upset you?"

"Oh, no. Nothing like that."

"Then what's wrong?"

Niki stared fixedly at the computer screen. "Nothing is wrong."

"But —"

Niki suddenly whirled around. "I said that nothing is wrong!" He pushed back his chair with an angry scrape and stood up. "Leave me alone!" He rushed out of the game room.

Shraga and Pinny eyed each other unhappily.

"Something **is** wrong," Shraga said finally. "I wish I knew what."

Chaim Morgenstern, Shraga's younger brother, is none too happy either. Here he is, rarin' to help solve the mystery — but the bigger kids won't even let him in on their planning sessions!

"Hi, guys," Chaim said. "What're you up to?"

"Nothing," Shraga said quickly. "Uh...are you planning on staying here?"

Chaim folded his arms. "And why shouldn't I? This is just as much my room as it is yours."

"We just have something we want to talk about, that's all."

"Something to do with detective work?" Chaim's scowl grew blacker. "That's fine. I'll just stay right here and listen."

"But Chaim...," Shraga began.

Chaim interrupted him. "Why can't you tell me what's going on? I'm not a baby!"

The door slammed shut behind the four older boys. Chaim clenched his fists, feeling furiously angry. Why wouldn't they tell him what they were doing? Why did they have to treat him like a little kid?

No one knows it — least of all Chaim himself — but he's going to be the one to save the day when the bigger kids find themselves in more trouble than they can handle alone. Stick around for the spine-tingling conclusion to THE LITTLE BLACK BOX mini-series, as all questions find their answers at last, in... **The Secret Revealed!**

A SHRAGA MORGENSTERN/PINNY KATZ
MYSTERY TRILOGY

THE LITTLE BLACK BOX

PART 3

THE SECRET REVEALED

Created by Libby Lazewnik
Written by Perel Schreiber

TARGUM/FELDHEIM

First published 1995

Phototypeset at Targum Press

Printing plates by Frank, Jerusalem

Published by:
Targum Press Inc.
22700 W. Eleven Mile Rd.
Southfield, Mich. 48034

Distributed by:
Feldheim Publishers
200 Airport Executive Park
Nanuet, N.Y. 10954

Distributed in Israel by:
Targum Press Ltd.
POB 43170
Jerusalem 91430

Printed in Israel

Contents

The Little Black Box
Our Story So Far...

Shraga Morgenstern and Pinny Katz have a mystery to solve.

Someone has made off with the prototype for a super-secret device that their fathers created and brought up to the Lake View Hotel for the week-long international physicists convention. Though the prototype itself is soon found, the diskette containing the plans is still missing. In the wrong hands, the device can act as a lethal weapon — one that threatens the lives of innocent people everywhere!

The F.B.I. is busy investigating the theft of the Little Black Box, but that isn't much of a consolation to our heroes. It seems that their own fathers are under suspicion of the crime! If the boys don't succeed in finding the real culprit, their fathers could lose their jobs — or even end up in jail.

Tom Morrison, chief Special Agent in charge of

security at the convention, has issued strict instructions to Dr. Morgenstern and Dr. Katz to stay on the hotel grounds until the investigation is complete. But sometime in the dark reaches of the night, the two scientists slip away without a word to anyone. And to make matters worse, the children suddenly become the target of a series of frightening incidents — designed to look like simple accidents — that leave two of them hurt and all of them badly shaken. Where will it all end?

But our band of young detectives won't give up. Niki Gorodnik, the Jewish boy from Russia, knows something no one else does... until Shai Gilboa, the Israeli, figures it out for himself. The trail of clues leads our friends on a midnight chase after a sinister, shadowy figure. Could they have found the real Mr. Big at last?

The boys are about to learn that one secret only leads to another. Before the triumphant conclusion, they'll find themselves in more danger than they ever dreamed possible!

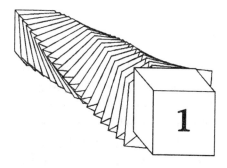

Pim's Story

The time before dawn is the coldest, darkest part of night. At such an hour, all the scientific labs at the Lake View Hotel should have been locked and silent. But strangely enough, one laboratory at the end of a hallway held no less than eight people, all frozen in place. Five boys and three men. Waiting.

The bright fluorescent lights set into the ceiling were turned off. In the dim lab, the eerie blue glow of the computer screen turned Dr. Ilya Pim's face into a mysterious mask. His eyes were in shadow, his cheekbones thrown into harsh relief. His expression was haunted.

Dr. Pim sat with his hands dangling loosely at his sides. Although he was desperately ashamed, he felt an unexpected surge of relief that he'd been caught trying to break into the computer codes that would unlock the key to "Little Nicky." Its inventors, Dr. Katz and Dr. Morgenstern, had promised to listen to his story before deciding whether or not to have him arrested, but even if these Jewish men and boys decided to turn him in to the F.B.I., the worst was over. There would be no more lying. No more gnawing remorse. No more dishonor. At long last, he'd be through with Little Nicky — a device designed for peaceful purposes that had the potential to become the newest, most frightening weapon known to mankind.

He looked at each one of the boys in turn: Shraga Morgenstern. Pinny and Ari Katz. Shai Drucker. His gaze lingered on Niki Gorodnik for a long moment, then turned to the two scientists, who returned his stare sternly.

"I was the one who stole your prototype," Dr. Pim began, his voice strained but clear. "I took both the device and the red diskette."

"The red diskette — where is it?" Dr. Morgenstern's face showed a kind of desperate hope. "Where did you hide it?"

Dr. Pim shook his head despairingly. "It is no longer where I hid it. I put it in the children's game room, but it is now gone."

"You put it in the *game room*?" Dr. Katz looked horrified. "But one of the children might have played with it, activated the computer codes..."

"No. No, that could not have happened! Your codes could not be broken." Dr. Pim smiled bitterly. "I know that. I have tried, these past two nights, to break them myself."

"But what happened to it?" Dr. Morgenstern demanded.

Dr. Pim's shoulders slumped. "I saw my own son try to use it. When the computer demanded that he type in a password, he assumed it was a defective game and threw it away." He looked intensely unhappy. "I returned the following morning to take it from the wastebasket. It was no longer there."

There was an appalled silence.

"So someone has the diskette," Pinny whispered. The diskette with the plans, the code words, the designs for Little Nicky were in somebody's hands. "Someone..."

Dr. Pim shook his head. "No. I do not think so. Perhaps it was thrown away. I believe it no longer exists."

"Never mind what you believe. I want to know how you stole Little — uh, the device — to begin with," Dr. Katz said coldly. "And why."

Dr. Pim met his eyes. "I left the table in the dining room that evening. I had deliberately stained my tie, to have an excuse to leave the room. I took the box and the diskette only a few minutes before you, Dr. Katz, discovered the theft."

The Russian scientist looked so miserable that Shraga felt a sudden rush of unexpected pity for him. Despite his admission of guilt, despite the suspicion that had fallen on his own father and on Dr. Katz because of this man's actions, the Russian seemed to be under some kind of terrible pressure.

Dr. Pim continued tiredly. "I was ordered to deliver the device at midnight. I knew your presentation would take hours. I could not afford to delay until later and risk missing my deadline."

"Meet south entrance midnight. Bring our little friend," Shai quoted. "Signed, *Mr. B.*"

Dr. Pim's jaw dropped. "How —?" he gasped.

Triumphantly, Shai pulled the well-creased and smudged note out of his pocket, wincing a little as the sudden movement jarred his sore shoulder. "I saw you drop this," he explained, unable to keep a note of pleased importance out of his voice. "I found it under the leaves. So who is this 'Mr. B.' that you were supposed to meet?"

"Let me see that," exclaimed Dr. Morgenstern, reaching out for the note. Shai surrendered it reluctantly. Shraga's father scanned the slip of paper, then passed it on to Dr. Katz. "So you're working together with someone," Dr. Morgenstern said grimly. "Who? Who else is involved?"

Dr. Pim shook his head helplessly. "I do not know."

"Oh, c'mon!" Ari burst out. "Do you really expect us to believe that?"

"It is the truth." Dr. Pim insisted. "I have never met this Mr. Big."

"Mr. Big?" Dr. Katz repeated sharply, looking up from the grubby note. "Is that the 'Mr. B.' of the note?"

"Mr. Big." Dr. Morgenstern gave Dr. Katz a

quick look, thinking of the threatening e-mail message he and his partner had received. "Is that what your accomplice calls himself?"

Dr. Pim's eyes flashed. "He is not my accomplice!" he snapped. "I would never do this willingly. He forced me to steal your prototype, and now that the diskette is lost, he insists that I break your computer passwords. Mr. Big is not my partner. He just — *orders* me..."

"But — but why?" Niki breathed. "Why do you obey him, if you do not wish to?"

"That's right. How do we know you're not doing this for the money?" Dr. Katz spoke as if the words had a bad taste. "How do we know you aren't simply a thief for hire?"

"No! I'm not —" Dr. Pim stopped. His gaze wavered from Dr. Katz to Niki. He seemed to find it easier to speak to the Russian boy. "I'm being blackmailed."

"Blackmailed?" Dr. Katz stared.

"What is blackmail?" Shai demanded.

"It means being forced to do something you don't want to do, or else someone will give away your secrets," Shraga said mechanically. "But — blackmailed?"

"Blackmailed!" Dr. Morgenstern sat down abruptly. "How could this — this — this Mr. Big of yours blackmail you?"

"That's right," Pinny said, thinking aloud as his mind leapt ahead. "Anyone who calls himself *Mr. Big* must be American. Or at least, someone with access to American culture. How could someone like that come up with enough guilty secrets to blackmail a professor from Russia?"

"Well, Dr. Pim?" Ari challenged. "Your story doesn't seem to make much sense."

The Russian scientist flushed, then drew himself up. "Believe me, I wish it didn't make sense. But it does." He sighed. "The secret is not mine, but my family's. I am sure you know that the Kremlin has opened up many files that were kept hidden for decades. Mr. Big must have discovered the secret in one of those opened files."

"But what is the secret, Dr. Pim?" Shraga's father asked gently. Now he seemed to be sad, rather than angry.

"The — the secret..." Dr. Pim half-turned his head away. Pinny was horrified to see tears standing in the older man's eyes. The others stared down at their feet, embarrassed.

Then Dr. Pim turned back, his emotions under control. "The secret," he said in a steady voice, "involves my father."

"The famous war hero?" Shraga asked, remembering the pride with which Alexei had spoken about his grandfather. "The one who held a mountain pass against the Nazis?"

"Yes. You see, it is that very story that Mr. Big threatens to expose."

"I don't understand," Shai said, bewildered.

Dr. Pim spread his hands. "It seems that Mr. Big has seen copies of files about that battle, where my father — who was a captain in the Russian army — held the pass against the Nazis and prevented them from penetrating deeper into Russia. It seems that... Well, according to Mr. Big, the official story and the story my father told me as a child are...different." He stopped.

"Different?" Dr. Morgenstern prompted.

"Yes. Different." Dr. Pim swallowed again. "My father had always said that the Germans were threatening to surround his army base, and he had devised a strategy to prevent disaster." He rubbed tiredly at his eyes. "His plan involved sending scouts into territory under German occupation to discover enemy movements. It was a — a suicide mission."

"Suicide mission?" repeated Shai. "What does that mean?"

"That means the scouts knew they would probably be killed," Shraga explained in a low tone.

"Yes." Dr. Pim nodded miserably. "It was necessary, my father always told me, to do this. Enough scouts managed to return to give him the information he needed to lay an ambush. But...the files Mr. Big has...make out a different case. They say that my father sent out scouts when he might have chosen to go himself. He sent them to their deaths...while he stayed behind. I do not know if these files tell the truth. But...they might." He fell silent.

"Even if it is," asked Ari, "why is that so terrible?"

Dr. Pim's head came up suddenly. His eyes flashed. "You do not understand. Captain Pim was given a medal for his heroic actions. My father died in peace, known as a war hero. My mother still lives. My father's memory is her greatest pride. How could I let her vision of my father's courage be destroyed? Mr. Big threatened to publish the files, to prove to the world that my father may have been nothing but a coward, who let others go to their death while he remained safely behind! Even if it is not true, enough people will believe it."

"But...," Ari began again, but Dr. Pim overrode him.

"Perhaps you think this is mere foolishness. You think me sentimental. But this is my family's honor. Not just my father, but all of us: myself, my son, all our relatives. I could not allow this to happen. Mr. Big's information might not even be true, but how could I take this chance? I could not. And so...I did what he demanded. I stole your device." Dr. Pim lowered his head. "I have not had a moment's rest ever since the day he first made contact with me..."

"I don't understand something," Shraga said slowly. "You say he gives you orders. But you've never met him?"

Dr. Pim shook his head. "No. I have not. Except for that message," he nodded at the note in Dr. Katz's hand, "one phone conversation, and the delivery of the key to this lab, I have had no direct contact with him. All the other messages were left on my computer."

"But Dr. Pim, surely you realize that a blackmailer never leaves his victims alone?"

"That's right." Dr. Morgenstern's face looked sober in the dim light from the computer screen. "This Mr. Big would have haunted you for the rest of your life, forcing you to commit other crimes, or possibly demanding money in return for silence."

"I know," Dr. Pim whispered. "I have been dreading that ever since I arrived here in America. He kept promising that once I delivered the weapon, it would all be over. But I never really believed it."

"Don't you have *any* clue?" Pinny said despairingly. "Any idea at all who Mr. Big might be?"

Dr. Pim lifted his arms. "I wish I could help. I, too, want to see him arrested." He gave a sad smile. "I don't think I've had a moment's peace of mind since I agreed to Mr. Big's demands. I see the consequences of what I did. I know I must make up for it — whatever the price. But..." He shrugged again. "I have no clue. Nothing. His messages are brief and to the point. When I failed to secure the weapon, he simply ordered me to find the diskette."

"You said you spoke to Mr. Big once on the phone," Shraga said intently. "Couldn't you get any clue to his identity at all?"

Dr. Pim shook his head. "No. His voice was disguised. Muffled."

"But you know it's a man."

"Yes," Dr. Pim stopped and frowned. "No. I am

not sure. It sounded like Mr. Big was talking through a handkerchief into the phone." He paused again, thinking. "It might have been a woman with a deep voice. There was no way to tell."

"A *Mrs.* Big?" Pinny said doubtfully.

"It could be Magda Brenner, then," Shraga murmured, thinking of the Hungarian physicist.

Dr. Pim looked at him sharply. "Why do you say that? Do you think that Mr. Big is one of the scientists in the hotel?"

Shraga flushed under the scientist's scrutiny. "Well — yes. I do. We all do. It *has* to be someone on the spot, someone who knows what's happening."

"You may be right," Dr. Pim said slowly. "The order to find the diskette came even before I reported my failure to steal the prototype weapon. Surely it is someone on the spot... Someone in this hotel!" He stopped, his eyes darting from side to side. "Someone is watching us — someone who may know that I have told you all this..."

Then he lifted his head higher. "But that does not matter. Not anymore. Whatever you decide, gentlemen," and here Dr. Pim nodded to Drs. Katz and Morgenstern, "I leave myself in your hands. If you choose to report me, so be it. But if I may, I beg that you believe me when I say I never wanted to be a part of this. I was forced to do what I did. If you release me, I promise to do all I can to help bring this criminal to justice."

Dr. Pim took a deep breath. "Perhaps you think

I do not deserve mercy. Perhaps you are right. But I ask it anyway...for Alexei. For my son."

He stopped speaking, and waited.

"I believe you!" Niki blurted in Russian, breaking the strained silence. They all turned to look at him, but Niki had eyes only for his countryman. "I believe you," he repeated, this time in English. "I believe you were forced. I believe that you want to help us."

"I believe you, too," Shraga said quietly.

Pinny, then Ari, nodded their assent. Shai glanced at the note in Dr. Katz's hand. "I also believe you," he said, a little grudgingly. "I say, let's not tell anything to the F.B.I. — for now."

"And you?" Dr. Pim asked, looking steadily at the two Jewish scientists. "Will you report me?"

Dr. Katz rubbed at his eyes. "Allow us a moment, please, to discuss this. David?" The two men retired to the far corner of the room and conversed in low, hurried tones. The others watched them nervously — all except Ilya Pim, whose eyes seem focused on something nobody else could see.

After several endless minutes, the men returned to the waiting group.

"All right, Dr. Pim," said Dr. Katz. "We're willing to give you the benefit of the doubt. We agree that you're probably telling the truth when you say that you've been blackmailed into this crime. If you promise to cooperate and help us try to find the *real* criminal — Mr. Big — we will not deliver you to the authorities tonight."

Dr. Pim inclined his head, his eyes bright with unshed tears.

"There is one qualification, though," Dr. Morgenstern added gravely. "Dr. Pim, we might find ourselves with no choice but to report you later on. Circumstances may force our hand. If that happens, we give you our word to tell you before going to the F.B.I. with this information."

"Of course," Dr. Pim said. "I understand."

Ari glanced at the window. The sky was lightening with the first pink flush of dawn. "It's morning already," he pointed out, yawning.

"Yes," Niki said. "Maybe we should get some sleep?"

"Sleep!" Pinny exclaimed. "We can't sleep now! Abba, there's so much to tell you..."

"There is?" Dr. Katz looked at his son. "We were only gone for two days. What's been happening?"

"Plenty, Abba," Pinny said, exchanging a significant glance with Shraga. "Believe me, plenty!"

"If I may suggest something," Dr. Morgenstern said mildly, "this may not be the best place for a long discussion. We don't want to be found here, do we? Let's get the computer shut off and the lab locked... Oh, that reminds me!" He turned sharply to Dr. Pim. "Doctor, how did you get into the lab?"

"You said a key was left for you. But these are electronic locks." Dr. Katz gestured towards the door. "So how did you get in?"

Dr. Pim slipped a hand into his pocket and held out a card. "Mr. Big left me this. An electronic key."

"I know what it is," Dr. Katz said impatiently. "But how did he leave it for you?"

"He left it at the desk, in an envelope with my name on it."

"*Who* left it there?" Pinny asked eagerly.

"I don't know," Dr. Pim replied. "The receptionist simply gave it to me. She said the manager had found it lying on the desk."

"Maybe the manager is Mr. Big!" Shai exclaimed.

Ari snorted. "*That* guy? Mr. Stewart? No way."

"What did the manager say, Dr. Pim?" Pinny asked again. "Didn't he explain?"

Dr. Pim shook his head. "There was nothing to explain. The envelope had been left there when nobody was around."

"A likely story," scoffed Shai. "I tell you, I'll bet it's the manager!"

"Wouldn't that be pretty obvious?" Shraga argued.

Shai folded his arms stubbornly. "Maybe he thought we would think that."

"What about the envelope?" Ari interrupted. "How was your name written on the envelope? Was it handwritten? Could that be a clue?"

"Maybe we could dust it for fingerprints," Pinny said excitedly.

Ari rolled his eyes. "Yeah, right. Where are you going to get a fingerprint kit from? Tom Morrison?"

"Why not?" Pinny demanded. "He's the top F.B.I. Special Agent here! We could — oh, yeah. I forgot." He looked sheepish. "We can't show the envelope to Tom. It would implicate Dr. Pim."

"Getting back to the subject," Dr. Katz said. "Dr. Pim, *was* there any hint on that envelope?"

"I don't think so," Dr. Pim replied. "My name was not handwritten, but stamped onto the envelope with a stamp kit." He pulled the envelope out of his pocket. "You see? There can be no clue in this."

Pinny reached out a hand. "Can we see that?"

Ari gave him an amused look. "Fingerprints, remember?"

"But we just said we can't show the envelope to the F.B.I.!"

"We might have to in the future, though," Shraga said quietly.

"All right, all right." Dr. Katz held up a hand for silence. "Let's lock up the lab and get out of here, okay? Dr. Pim, I think we should take that electronic card." He stretched out his hand, but stopped when Dr. Morgenstern touched his sleeve.

"Just a minute, Shmulie." Shraga's father pulled Dr. Katz to one side and whispered urgently in his ear. A look of dismay settled over Dr. Katz's face.

"I suppose you're right," he said heavily. He turned back to Dr. Pim. "You'd better hold on to that card for now. Better not to let Mr. Big have a chance to suspect that we've learned the truth — or at least part of it. There's nothing left to steal, anyway," he added a little bitterly. "No prototype, and no diskette, either. It can't do any harm for you to keep it."

Dr. Pim nodded and slipped the card back into his pocket.

"Let's go, boys." Dr. Morgenstern herded the children out the lab door. They filed obediently into the corridor and waited as Dr. Katz locked the door behind them with own his electronic card. Quietly they walked down the hallway, looking everywhere but at each other — at the pale yellow lighting, at the thin strip of carpet under their feet, at the unadorned metal walls. Nobody looked at Dr. Pim as he hurried ahead of the rest of the group, walking quickly until he disappeared around the curve of the corridor.

One part of the mystery may have been solved, but a greater mystery remained: *Who was Mr. Big?*

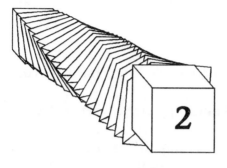

Recap

A bba?"

"Yes, Pinny?" Dr. Katz glanced at his genius son, walking down the corridor at his side.

"What — what was it that Dr. Morgenstern said to you? That made you decide not to take the card from Dr. Pim, I mean?"

Dr. Katz grimaced, then glanced at Shraga, who had drawn nearer to hear the reply. "It may not be pleasant to think about, but we're still under suspicion. You both know that."

Pinny nodded soberly. Shraga merely scowled.

"You also realize that we might end up having no choice but to report Dr. Pim's part in all this to the F.B.I." Dr. Katz paused. "If that happens — and I hope it doesn't — we don't want to have to find ourselves trying to prove that *we* aren't the ones blackmailing Dr. Pim."

"Huh?" Pinny blinked.

Shraga caught his breath. "You mean, if you handled that card, the F.B.I. might accuse *you* of having given it to Dr. Pim in the first place? Because it would have your fingerprints on it?"

"Exactly." Dr. Katz jammed his hands into his pockets. "Your father's right, Shraga. We have to be as careful as we can with this. We can't afford to take any risks."

"It's not right," Shraga said angrily. "Dr. Katz, they might twist anything into looking suspicious!"

"Yeah," Pinny chimed in. "Isn't there *anything* we can do to stop them? It's just not right!"

"I know, Pinny. I know how you feel." Dr. Katz glanced from one boy to the other. Depressed as he felt over the entire situation, his heart lifted at the sight of the two boys working together, talking together, more at ease than he'd ever seen them together in all their lives.

Dr. Morgenstern placed a hand on his son's shoulder. "It's part of *galus*, Shraga. You've seen that yourself, haven't you?"

Shraga nodded silently, remembering how Niki had angrily shouted, *"Who needs you — a couple of stupid Jews!"* before the Russian boy had discovered that he, too, was Jewish.

"For goyim, Jews often make the perfect scapegoat."

"Do you really think that's going to happen this time?" Pinny asked, suddenly fearful.

Dr. Morgenstern shook his head firmly. "Don't

worry, Pinny. The F.B.I. will find the right culprit." He sounded confident, but deep inside, he couldn't help feeling uneasy. *Would* the F.B.I. find the true criminal — the mysterious Mr. Big who had blackmailed Ilya Pim into committing this crime? Would their decision to protect the hapless Russian scientist lead to further trouble, or even prevent the solving of the case?

"Abba," Pinny said after a moment, "where *were* you?"

"We were really worried," Shraga added earnestly. "All of us."

"Including Tom Morrison," Pinny said unhappily. "Except I think he was more upset than worried."

"Yes, I would imagine so," Dr. Morgenstern said drily. "Well, don't worry, boys. We'll take care of it. As for where we were..." He exchanged glances with Dr. Katz. "We wanted to take care of something, and we felt it would be...safer...for you children if we weren't here."

"Safer?" Pinny's eyes were wide. "But —"

"But Daddy," Shraga broke in, "things haven't been safe at all! We have to tell you what's been happening!"

"Oh? What?" Dr. Morgenstern looked at him sharply.

Shraga gulped a little, suddenly realizing exactly what he was going to have to tell his father. "Well, uh, first of all, like we said before — Mindy's in the hospital."

Dr. Morgenstern stopped short, appalled. In the

whirlwind of events and revelations, the few words Shraga had blurted out about Mindy's situation had flown entirely out of his head. "Mindy! You said she was burned. What —"

"It's okay," Shraga added hastily. "She has second-degree burns, but she's all right."

"Take a deep breath, David," Dr. Katz urged, holding his friend by the arm. "Shraga says she's all right."

"Fine. Okay." Dr. Morgenstern pushed his yarmulke back and forth on his head, picturing his precious daughter on a hospital bed. "How did it happen, Shraga?"

Quickly Shraga explained about the falling hot-water urn.

Dr. Katz looked thoughtfully at the boy. "Shraga, how did the urn fall in the first place?"

Shraga frowned. "Well, I don't know how, really. It all happened so fast. It looked like it was just —"

"An accident," finished Pinny darkly. "Uh-huh. Sure it was an accident! Like the bull that chased Shai was an accident! Like the flowerbox falling was an accident!"

"What was that?" Dr. Katz turned and looked at Shai. "Shai, *what* happened to you?"

"We went to a farm," Shai began slowly.

"Shai was great," Shraga interrupted. "Zevy went into a field where there was a bull, and Shai distracted it from Zevy so Ari could rescue him."

Shai blushed. "It was all just because of the loud noise —"

"What kind of noise?" Dr. Morgenstern demanded.

"Like a car backfiring, I'd say," Ari told him. He wrinkled his nose in perplexity. "Only, there were no cars around..."

Pinny and Shraga looked at each other. Shraga gave a tiny nod. Pinny took a deep breath and turned to his father.

"Abba, Shraga and I think it might have been something else. We think...we think it was a gunshot that frightened the bull into charging at Shai."

Shai looked startled.

"A gunshot!" Ari burst out. "That's ridiculous! How could —" His voice trailed off, and an uneasy look crossed his face. "I guess it *did* sound sort of like the caps some kids set off on Purim, but —"

"It *was* a gunshot," Shai stated. "I didn't want to scare anyone by saying so before." He turned to the scientists. "Pinny and Shraga are right. I'm sure of it!"

Dr. Katz chewed his lip worriedly. "Okay, there was some kind of shot. What happened after that?"

"Well, the bull started chasing Shai." Pinny gulped and looked at his Israeli friend. "Boy, it's a good thing you can run so fast. You made it back to the fence just in time. I was scared stiff!"

"So was I," Shai admitted frankly. "But I wasn't hurt too much." He touched his bandaged left shoulder, wincing again.

"*Baruch Hashem,*" Dr. Katz said fervently.

Shai opened his mouth, closed it, then opened

it again. "Yes," he said slowly. "*Baruch Hashem.*"

"By the way," Shraga said, "they traced that falling flowerbox to an empty room on the third floor."

"So we're no closer to knowing who was behind it," Pinny added despondently.

Dr. Morgenstern stopped walking. He turned to Dr. Katz. "Shmulie," he said softly, "It looks like the kids are more vulnerable without us around. We were wrong to leave."

"You may be right." Dr. Katz's eyes hardened. "I'm not going to let this go on any longer, David. Let's go find Morrison and tell him what's been happening. He's got to realize that these 'accidents' are all deliberate."

"Planned by Mr. Big," Dr. Morgenstern agreed.

"Do you really think so, Daddy?" Shraga asked.

"Yes."

"But why would he?"

The two fathers exchanged glances over their sons' heads. "Let's just say," Dr. Katz said finally, "that we've found a reason to think that way." There seemed to be no point in frightening the children and letting them know that Mr. Big had personally threatened to harm their families.

They entered the lobby. The scientists made a beeline for the row of house phones at the back of the lobby.

"Who are you calling, Daddy?" Shraga called, trotting after them.

"Your mother." Dr. Morgenstern hurriedly dialed his hotel room number. "I want to let her know that — Miriam?... Yes. Yes, we're fine... No. Downstairs... Yes. I'll be up soon. Is Mindy all right? *Baruch Hashem!*... No... That's all right. We can —"

"*Dr. Morgenstern! Dr. Katz!*"

The two men whirled around, the phone still held to Dr. Morgenstern's ears. Tom Morrison, senior agent of the F.B.I., came striding across the lobby towards them. His usual smile was nowhere in sight.

"I'll talk to you later, Miriam," Dr. Morgenstern said quietly. He hung up the phone and turned, unmoved by Tom's apparent annoyance. Dr. Katz gave the children an encouraging smile before turning to face the angry agent.

"Where have the two of you been?" Tom demanded without preamble. "Can you give me a good reason why I shouldn't arrest you both right now?"

"Good morning, Morrison," Dr. Katz said coolly. "It's nice to know you were concerned about us."

Tom scowled. "Of course I was concerned. I told you that you were confined to the hotel until this mess is cleared up, and then you both go and disappear without a word!"

"What did you think?" Dr. Morgenstern asked, raising his eyebrows. "That we skipped the country, leaving our families behind?"

Tom glanced down at the boys. Pinny smiled at him hopefully. Tom smiled reluctantly back. "No, I didn't," he said with a sigh, turning back to the two men. "But I'm telling you right now, my superiors weren't very happy about it at all. Where did you go?"

Dr. Morgenstern rubbed his chin. "We went to a university in upstate New York. A friend of ours there has a very powerful, very sophisticated computer system. We hoped that we could use that system to determine exactly who sent us a threatening message and see if anyone is trying to tamper with our computer codes." And they *had* discovered somebody tampering with their codes, and rushed back to the hotel — just in time to confront Ilya Pim in their laboratory. But Dr. Morgenstern couldn't reveal that to Tom.

"Threatening message?" Shraga stared at his father.

"What was that?" Tom exclaimed. "A threatening message? When did this happen? And why didn't you tell me?"

"It was sent to us," Dr. Katz replied, "the day after that *accident* happened with the flowerbox." His tone was sarcastic. "And as for why we didn't tell you — well, the sender threatened to arrange for more such 'accidents' to happen if we reported it to the authorities. But since the incidents are apparently happening anyway, I don't see that it can hurt to tell you about it."

Tom nodded grimly. "You're right. Believe me, I've been more and more concerned about what's been going on. Did you keep the message? Can I see it? I'd like to have it checked for fingerprints."

Pinny nudged Ari triumphantly. Ari nudged him impatiently back.

"It wasn't a written message," Dr. Katz said. "It was e-mail."

"E-mail?" Tom repeated thoughtfully. "Hmm, that won't be so easy to trace..."

"E-mail!" Shai blurted. "That's what —" He stopped short, chagrined.

"What was that?" Tom glanced at the boys.

"Nothing," Shai mumbled, embarrassed with his near-slip. He'd almost mentioned Dr. Pim.

"Look here, Mr. Morrison," Dr. Katz said. "The point is, our children have been exposed to dangerous accidents and a criminal is claiming responsibility for it. So what are you going to do about it?"

Tom tapped absentmindedly at the walkie-talkie hooked to his belt. "First of all, as I said, I *have* been concerned. This news about the e-mail message makes things more serious, though. I hope you saved a copy of the message. I'll take a look at it and send a copy back to my superiors, who can check the style for any known criminals. As for tracing it back to its source..." He shook his head. "I'm sure you're both aware that it's incredibly easy to send e-mail anonymously."

"What do you mean?" Niki asked.

Tom glanced at the boys. "The electronic network is enormous," he explained. "Our criminal could have sent it through half-a-dozen relays. Many people accept a message and simply pass it on. Believe me, it's very easy to make such a message impossible to trace."

"We know," Dr. Morgenstern said. "As far as we can tell, the message was routed through Scandinavia. I don't see how it can ever be tracked down."

"Well, we'll do our best. I'll personally get to work on it right away."

"You know an awful lot about it, Mr. Morrison." Niki's voice was respectful.

Tom grinned at him. "A good F.B.I. agent has to be aware of what's going on in the world. Besides, I've done my share of investigating computer fraud."

"But who would agree to pass on such a threatening message?" Pinny protested, eyes wide.

Tom shrugged. "People play games over the network, too. Maybe the sender thought it was some kind of mystery game — kids playing at Sherlock Holmes, stuff like that. But in the meantime," he added, looking stern again, "the two of you are staying *right here*. I don't want you trying to pull something like that again. I'm having enough trouble convincing my superiors you're innocent in the first place, without having to try and explain why you disappeared without explanation. No more leaving the hotel. Is that understood?"

"But my daughter!" Dr. Morgenstern protested. "Mindy's in the hospital. Surely you'll let me go and visit —"

"Absolutely not. I'm sorry, professor." Tom was

sympathetic but firm. "After this stunt of yours, the two of you are going to have to show your good faith by staying put."

"But —"

"I'm sorry, Dr. Morgenstern, but that's the way it's going to be." Tom shook his head, almost in wonderment. "Running off in the middle of the night to check things out in a university... Which university, by the way? Who's your friend?"

Dr. Morgenstern shook his own head. "We're not going to tell you," he said evenly. "As far as we can tell, anything we do or say is being construed as potential proof of our guilt. We're not going to implicate someone who was merely trying to help us get at the truth."

Dr. Katz jammed his hands into his pockets. "We'll give you the message from Mr. Big —"

"That's what the criminal called himself?"

"Yes."

"One last thing, Mr. Morrison," Dr. Katz added. "About...Little Nicky."

"Yes?"

Dr. Katz glanced uncomfortably at Dr. Morgenstern, who gave him a small, sad smile of assent. "Under the circumstances," Dr. Katz continued, "we've decided that it might be too risky to keep the blueprints of the prototype listed in our computer here. After all, someone who is capable of breaking into a locked room and stealing the prototype and diskette might also be capable of breaking our computer codes and getting all the necessary details."

"That's true," Tom said, his expression grim. "I'd hate to see it happen, but it's certainly a possibility."

"We know." Dr. Katz wasn't enjoying this. "So we've decided that it might be best to find some other way of protecting Little Nicky. Our lab doesn't seem to be safe anymore."

"Yes?" Tom prompted. "What are you getting at, Doctor?"

"With the red diskette missing —" Dr. Katz stopped. "Unless you found it in the last two days?"

Tom grimaced. "Believe me, I would have let you know if we had!"

"All right, then. With the red diskette still missing, the only remaining copy of the plans for Little Nicky are back in M.C.B. in New York, where we can access them through the network with our computer here. Dr. Morgenstern and I have decided that it would be safer to make a new copy of the plans, delete the file from our computer so there's no more possibility of contact, and give our copy to you." Dr. Katz gave the F.B.I. agent a wry smile. "That way, nobody can suspect us of trying to make off with Little Nicky. And it will certainly be safer in your hands."

Tom nodded in approval. "I'll be glad to accept the responsibility. Excellent idea," he said. "If you recall, I suggested this at the beginning, when you first arrived at the hotel. It's probably the safest way."

The safest way. Pinny sighed. Why did it feel like nothing would ever be safe again?

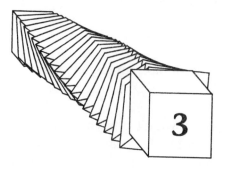

Determined Decisions

The sun rose over the horizon. The lobby, deserted only an hour earlier, was now the scene of bustling activity. The daytime receptionist had already taken her place behind the front desk; F.B.I. agents converged on the entrances and conferred with their walkie-talkies. Several scientists and other hotel guests, passing through the lobby on their way to the dining room for an early breakfast, looked curiously at the crowd of Jewish boys and men standing together, all clearly distinguishable by their proud badges of yarmulkes and tzitzis. Tom Morrison stood in the center of the group, dominating the scene with his easy smile and his air of competence.

Pinny stifled a yawn and watched Shraga and Niki do the same. They were all tired from being up overnight, tense at the strain of avoiding any mention of Ilya Pim to Tom, and nervous about a situation that seemed to have no solution.

"We're not getting anywhere by discussing this," Dr. Katz finally said wearily. "Let's go upstairs and say hello to the rest of the family."

"Isn't it...isn't it time to pray?" Shai ventured shyly.

Shraga threw him a warm look. "It certainly is," he said. "It's full daylight now."

"Full daylight." Ari rolled his eyes and groaned. "I haven't stayed up all night like this since Shavuos!"

Dr. Morgenstern started and looked at his watch. "So it is. I guess time flies when you're having fun, eh, Shmulie?"

"I'm not exactly sure that's what I'd call it," Dr. Katz said dryly, looking sidelong at Tom Morrison. "But the boys are right. It's time for minyan."

"What minyan?" Pinny said under his breath. "We're stuck here, remember?"

Dr. Katz looked at the boys and then suddenly turned to fix Tom with a steely gaze. "I've had it," he said abruptly. "We've all had it. This has got to stop!"

"I beg your pardon?" Tom raised his eyebrows. "What are you talking about?"

"This — nonsense!" Dr. Katz's arm swept in a broad circle, encompassing the entire hotel. "Confining us to virtual house arrest, refusing to allow us to go down the road to the kosher hotel to pray for half an hour in the mornings —"

"Denying me the right to visit my daughter in the hospital," Dr. Morgenstern added with quiet vehemence. "No, Morrison. We're not going to put up with it any longer."

"It's for your own good," Tom explained. "I just want to make sure —"

Dr. Katz slowly straightened to his full height. "*We — have — had it*," he repeated. "Enough is enough. If you want to keep us here on the hotel grounds, serve a warrant. Arrest us. Then we can post bail and have a little freedom."

"You've told us often enough that you believe we're innocent," Dr. Morgenstern pointed out. "You say that it's your superiors who are suspicious of us. If that's the case, why can't you trust us enough to give us permission to leave the hotel grounds temporarily?"

Shraga watched, wide-eyed, as the boys' fathers faced down the F.B.I.'s chief agent at the Lake View Hotel.

"Now, just a minute," Tom began, but Dr. Morgenstern interrupted him.

"Surely this message from Mr. Big proves that we're innocent. Or do you think that we would deliberately endanger our children's lives to try and clear our names?"

"No, I don't think that," Tom answered. He had regained his composure. "I *do* believe you. The problem is that I'm not the final authority here. My higher-ups in the F.B.I. are still operating under the theory that the two of you could be implicated, and that includes the possibility that the accidents were nothing more than that — accidents — and the message from this Mr. Big of yours could be nothing but a decoy."

"Do you believe that?" Dr. Katz challenged.

"No, I don't. I'm going to do everything I can to trace that message, believe me. But as I said, it's incredibly easy to arrange for e-mail to be sent without leaving a trace."

"Well, you'd better make up your mind," Dr. Morgenstern said coldly. "If I march out the hotel door, what will you do? Arrest me? Fine. I'll post bail and go visit my daughter anyway."

"There's no way out of it, Morrison," Dr. Katz said. "You might as well give in."

Tom glared at them. "I don't *give in*, Dr. Katz. However, as for allowing you to leave the hotel..."

Shraga and Pinny held their breaths.

Tom shrugged. "All right. But I'm going to insist that you tell us exactly where you're going, and you're going to have to agree to have one of my agents accompany you at all times."

"That's reasonable enough," Dr. Morgenstern said, smiling his relief. "Your agent will be probably be a little confused, though, watching us pray."

"You'd better tell him that we're praying, not talking in secret code," Dr. Katz added testily.

"You just relax, Doctor. I said I'd let you leave, didn't I? Why don't you go take care of making that copy of your plans for me, and then you're free to go. I'll detail one of my men to come with you." Tom lifted his walkie-talkie and issued several crisp orders before turning back to the two Jewish scientists. "Does that suit you, gentlemen?"

"Yes, it does. But if you don't mind, we'll hold off on getting the plans for Little Nicky until after we get back."

"Why?" Tom frowned at them. "Don't you trust me?"

"It's not a matter of trust, Mr. Morrison. A religious Jew doesn't do *anything* before praying, that's all."

"I see," Tom said. "All right, then. Let me know when you're ready to give it to me. You can watch me put it away for safekeeping."

"Thank you, Mr. Morrison." Dr. Katz turned away from the F.B.I. agent and bent towards the children. "The van is parked out front," he told them in a low tone. "Go wash up a little, then wait for us in the car. We're just going upstairs for a minute."

"To say hello to Ima?" Pinny asked.

"To say hello to Ima."

"And I want to get Chaim, too," Dr. Morgenstern added. "We'll be downstairs soon." The two fathers hurried away.

Pinny hesitated. "Um...Shai, do you want to come with us?"

Shai hesitated for a minute. "I don't know."

"Come on. It's worth trying," Shraga urged. "Will you?"

Shai looked from one to the other. A slow, shy

smile transformed his face. "All right," he said. "I'll come."

"Great!" Pinny clapped him delightedly on the back. Pleased with his success, he turned to Niki. "How 'bout you, Niki? Do you want to come, too?"

But Niki, who had been downcast ever since leaving the laboratory, backed away. "No, I cannot. I cannot..." He turned and almost ran away from them, hurrying towards the bank of elevators across the lobby. The four boys stared after him, puzzled.

"I wonder what that's all about," Ari said.

"I dunno," Pinny answered with a shrug. "But let's go wash up and get out to the car."

The boys retired to the palatial washroom just off the lobby and washed their hands and faces. Feeling slightly revived after their long night, they recrossed the lobby and went out into the cool morning air. Shraga took a deep breath and felt his lungs expand. On such a beautiful morning, it seemed certain that everything would work out.

"Whoops!" Ari snapped his fingers. "My tefillin are upstairs. I'll be right back, okay?" He headed back into the hotel. Shai started to follow him, then turned and strolled over to the other side of the parking lot. Pinny and Shraga, deciding that he would rather be alone, made their way over to the Katzes' big van.

"I'm worried," Pinny said as the two of them leaned against the side of the van. "We're right back where we started from."

"No," Shraga corrected, feeling his spirits sink again. "It's even worse. We've solved one mystery, only to find out that there's somebody else — Mr. Big — behind the whole thing. Dr. Pim has no idea who he is; neither do we —"

"And this crook is busy arranging accidents," Pinny added miserably. "So far, only Mindy's really gotten hurt, and she's, *baruch Hashem*, doing okay. Shai's shoulder is painful, but it didn't even need stitches. That's all very fine, but who's to say that nothing else is going to happen?"

"We have to be very careful," Shraga agreed. "But how can we be careful all the time?"

"We'll just have to be, that's all." Pinny slouched further against the van. "Shraga, we have to find out who Mr. Big is! We've just *got* to!"

"I know," Shraga said. "And we *will*, Pinny. Hashem will help us. We'll find out exactly who is trying to destroy our fathers' reputations by putting all the blame on them." His eyes flashed. "We'll capture Mr. Big and clear our fathers' names!"

Pinny grinned at him, catching his enthusiasm. "We sure will!"

"How, though?" Shai asked from behind them. Pinny and Shraga jumped. They hadn't heard him come up.

"I keep forgetting how fast you are on your feet, Shai," Shraga gasped. "Boy, did you scare me!"

"Sorry. But I heard what you said. How *do* you plan to find Mr. Big?"

"We'll do the best we can, that's all," Pinny said

with determination. "We interviewed some of the scientists before. We'll keep shadowing them —"

"Shadowing?" Shai repeated.

"We'll follow them very closely, just like we were their shadows."

"Oh." Shai nodded. "I understand."

"Pinny's right," Shraga said. "We can cross out Dr. Pim now, but we still have several possibilities: Richard Fowley, Manfred Isingard, even Magda Brenner." He grinned at Shai. "I don't think we have to worry about your — I mean, Dr. Drucker, and I can't see Niki's mother being involved either, can you?"

Shai shook his head. "No, of course not!"

Shraga looked thoughtful. Dr. Drucker, as a religious Jew, was obviously innocent; and Dr. Gorodnik, Niki's mother, seemed equally ridiculous as a suspect. But at the same time, Shraga felt that there had to be more suspects than just the three scientists whose labs were closest to their fathers'. Mr. Big might be someone who would look out of place near the labs and needed Dr. Pim to do his dirty work for him.

"Shraga?"

"Huh?" Shraga blinked.

"Wake up. Here they come." Pinny nodded at the entrance of the hotel, where Drs. Katz, Drucker, and Morgenstern could be seen making their way through the revolving doors. Ari followed close behind, with a sleepy-eyed Chaim Morgenstern bringing up the rear. Sandy, Tom's second-in-command, walked discreetly behind Chaim.

"Here they come," Pinny repeated. "I guess we're ready to go."

"Yes," Shraga said, looking Pinny in the eye. "We're ready to go."

Pinny caught the underlying meaning and nodded. Yes, the two of them were ready to do everything — anything — to solve this mystery and clear their fathers' names.

The kosher hotel welcomed the newcomers warmly. After davening, the Lake View Hotel contingent went with the rest of the minyan to the dining room for a hot, hearty, kosher breakfast, a welcome change from the dreary packaged meals they'd been served for the last several days. Shraga considerately put together a small bundle of cake for his younger brothers and sisters. Pinny and Ari did the same.

"Bring back a piece for Niki, too," Dr. Morgenstern suggested.

Shraga gave his father a quick smile. "Good idea, Daddy. Thanks."

Dr. Katz drove them back to the hotel. Mrs. Morgenstern was waiting for them in the lobby. As soon as the boys arrived, she gave them a hasty hello, then hurried outside. She and her husband were going straight to the hospital to check on Mindy. Chaim watched from the window, frowning as he saw his parents drive off, followed by an unmarked car with an F.B.I. agent inside.

"What's going on, Shraga?" Chaim demanded, turning to face his older brother. "Where did you find Daddy?"

Shraga looked at him, amused. "What do you mean?"

"You know exactly what I mean. You were down here before I was. In fact, I don't even think you went to sleep at all last night! Your bed was still all made up this morning. What's going on?"

"Nothing much," Shraga said evasively.

Chaim scowled even harder. "This is detective work, isn't it? You're trying to solve this mystery! I'll bet you two are working on figuring out who broke into Daddy's lab!"

"No, we're not," Shraga said, truthfully enough. They *already* knew who had broken into Dr. Morgenstern's lab: Dr. Pim. Now, they were trying to figure out the identity of the mysterious Mr. Big.

"Well, you're doing *something*." Chaim glared at Shraga and Pinny. "Why won't you tell me?"

"You're too young, Chaim," Shraga said, not realizing how patronizing he sounded.

"I am *not*! Tell me what you're doing!"

Shraga sighed. "Let's just say it has to do with Daddy's black box."

"But the black box was found!"

"The diskette wasn't," Shraga pointed out. "How a bright red diskette could disappear is beyond me, but —"

Pinny cut in impatiently. "Oh, forget it. You're

just too little, Chaim. Sorry, but you'll only get in our way."

"Get in your way!" Chaim sputtered. "For your information..."

Ari, already halfway to the elevators, turned and called across the lobby, "*Nu*, Pinny? Come on!"

Glad to escape Chaim, Pinny trotted after his older brother, leaving the two Morgenstern boys to face each other.

"C'mon, Chaim," Shraga said quickly. "Let's go give the others that cake we brought from the hotel."

Still muttering under his breath, Chaim followed Shraga to the elevator. "When will Daddy learn with us?" he demanded. "If he's gone to the hospital now, I mean?"

Shraga shrugged. "Later, I guess." He suddenly remembered that his father and Dr. Katz intended to give Tom Morrison their copy of the plans for Little Nicky. Would Dr. Katz take care of it on his own, or would he wait for Dr. Morgenstern to come back? And would this gesture finally prove to Tom that the two Jewish scientists were honest and sincere?

Perhaps the gesture *would* have proven their sincerity. But at that very moment, Dr. Katz was discovering, to his dismay, that they wouldn't be able to give the prototype plans to Tom at all.

After entering the lab and automatically locking it behind him, he flipped on the computer, waited patiently for the machine to run through all its checks, and tapped in his personal code for gaining entry into M.C.B.'s network. Automatically, he began to set things in motion for copying the plans. Only when the computer began beeping insistently did he jerk his head up and stare at the screen in shock.

Instead of the familiar bright blue logo of M.C.B., red letters glared on the computer screen: ACCESS DENIED.

Access denied! How could it be? The code had worked fine only a few days before...

Thinking that he might have made an error, Dr. Katz typed in his code more carefully. The same signal flashed on the screen. He tried Dr. Morgenstern's. The same thing happened.

ACCESS DENIED.

Dr. Katz sat back in his chair, suddenly overcome by a wave of depression. He and his friend had been up the entire night, working desperately to discover the culprit. For what purpose, if not to prove their innocence? And now? ACCESS DENIED.

M.C.B. might be standing behind them in the crisis — his boss had come down to the hotel to promise his support — but the top executives of the company had evidently decided that the two Jewish physicists could not be completely trusted. They were no longer permitted access to Little Nicky, the device they themselves had worked so long to develop.

ACCESS DENIED. Would their careers survive this fresh disaster?

Staring bleakly at the flashing red message on his screen, Dr. Katz was afraid to even think of the answer.

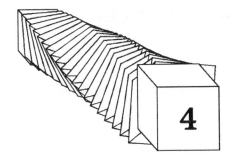

4

The Missing Link

Unaware of the newest twist of misfortune, the boys gathered together in the lobby after a fruitful learning session.

"Where's Niki?" asked Pinny, looking around.

"Yeah." Ari glanced around the lobby, too. "I haven't seen him since we went to *shacharis*."

Shraga frowned. "Do you think he's avoiding us?"

"I get that impression," Ari said. "He really looked upset this morning, you know."

"I'll call his room," Shai offered, getting up from his comfortable seat on the couch. "Maybe he doesn't know we want to — shadow? — this morning."

"Thanks, Shai." Ari sprawled deeper into his armchair and pulled his set of *kugelach* out of his pocket, turning the little metal cubes over in his palm. Shai spoke on one of the house phones for a moment, then came back, his face looking baffled.

"He said we should work without him."

"That's weird," Shraga said. "He was so interested in joining us."

Ari shrugged. "Well, no use sitting and worrying about it." He flipped the five *kugelach* into the air, caught them on the back of his hand, then flipped them up again and snatched them out of the air. "What do we do next?"

"Well," Shraga said hesitantly, "Pinny and I were talking about it this morning."

Ari suppressed a smile. Only last week, wild horses couldn't have dragged those two into speaking distance of each other, and now... "Were you, now. And what did our two resident geniuses decide?" His tone was mild. Pinny grinned, a little sheepishly.

"Well, Shraga and I think that we should check out some of the other scientists."

"Sounds fine. Isn't that what Shai was saying before? 'Shadowing' people?"

"Uh-huh." Pinny looked at Shai and tossed the Israeli boy a wink. "Shai's new word for the day. So who should we start with?"

"How about him?" Shai suggested, pointing across the lobby. Richard Fowley leaned against the front desk, looking about him with a bored air. Even as the boys watched, the Englishman tipped his hat politely to the receptionist and strolled out of the hotel.

"Talking to him won't help," Pinny muttered,

remembering the long-winded interview he'd had with Fowley a few days earlier. "All he likes to discuss is himself. B-o-o-ring!"

"Well, we have to start somewhere." Ari heaved himself to his feet. "Okay, here's how we'll work it. If he stays out in the open, we're having a game of ball or something. If he starts moving away, whoever has the ball should pretend to aim badly and throw it in Fowley's direction. That'll give us a good excuse to stop the game and move towards him. One of us can continue to shadow him. If you lose sight of him, come back here. We'll meet afterwards and discuss what we've got."

"That's a great plan," Pinny said. "I thought you said that you don't have any brains?"

Ari laughed as he headed for the front doors of the hotel. "Kid, you may be a genius at mathematics and science and everything else under the sun, but when it comes to plain old action, I'm your man!"

Out in the bright sunshine, they spotted Fowley strolling down a footpath near the lake. Ari shoved Pinny ahead of him. "Go!" he bellowed. Pinny looked back at him, startled, then caught on. Shai raced ahead, screeching, "Catch me! Catch me!" Shraga pounded on behind. Busy with their mock game of tag, they ran back and forth across the green grass, always keeping within earshot of Fowley. The Englishman only gave them a fleeting glance as he continued his stroll along the lakeside.

The boys yelled and dodged among the trees for

a while, keeping a covert eye on Fowley. Finally, after several exhausting minutes, they saw the scientist disappear back into the hotel.

"That was a great waste of time," panted Shraga.

"Good workout, though," Ari said cheerfully. "C'mon, let's go back inside and see what he's doing."

"It's silly to expect a criminal to do anything out in the open," Pinny argued as he followed his older brother back to the hotel lobby. "He's got a private room, after all. A private lab, too. Why should he do anything suspicious out here?"

"But we can't see what he's doing in his room," Shai said. "We might as well watch what we can."

"Exactly." Ari stepped through the revolving door and entered the lobby. "So keep your eyes open, guys. Let's go."

Shraga, a little more stocky than the others, was still badly out of breath. He trailed behind his friends, panting heavily. Ari might enjoy all that exercise, but Shraga would much rather exercise his brain.

As Fowley headed for the elevators, Shai distinctly heard a faint *clink*. He nudged Pinny excitedly and pointed to a small object lying on the floor just behind Fowley. "A secret message!" he whispered.

"Think so?" Pinny eyed the tiny, glinting object with interest. "Microfilm, maybe?"

Shraga, coming up behind them, snorted. "It's

probably a button off his jacket. Why don't we just look and see?"

It wasn't a button, though; it was a cuff link.

"Real gold, I think," Ari said, balancing it on his palm. "Real fancy, too. Initials and all."

"Typical," Pinny agreed. "He probably had it made to order or something."

"Yeah...GF. Here, take a look." Ari was just handing the chunky cuff link to Shai when Pinny, with a cry, snatched it out of his hand.

"What's your problem?" Ari demanded.

"GF! The initials are GF?"

"I said so, didn't I?"

"You don't get it." Pinny peered at the cuff link himself, then looked up, flushed with excitement. "Dr. Fowley's first name is Richard. So why should he have cuff links with the initials GF? It should be RF!"

"Hey, you're right." Ari took the cuff link back from his brother, examined it again, then handed it over to Shai to look at. Shai gave it only a cursory glance before passing it to Shraga.

"And not only that," Pinny continued breathlessly. "He doesn't like tea, remember? He drank coffee during my interview with him. What kind of Englishman doesn't like tea? I'll bet he's an imposter. And now he's made a *real* mistake!"

The four boys looked up from their huddle around the little gold cuff link to see Fowley, apparently oblivious to his loss, enter an elevator. The doors closed smoothly behind him.

"Third floor," Shai murmured, watching the blinking display above the elevator doors. "He's on the third floor."

"Hey, that's our floor."

"I know. Almost all the scientists are on either the third floor or the fourth, I think."

"Look, I'm telling you, it makes sense. He *must* be an imposter!"

"Okay, Pinny," Ari said. "Let's say you're right. What do we do now?"

Pinny clenched his fists. "If that guy is Mr. Big..."

"Yes, but we have to prove it first," Shraga interrupted. "We've discussed that before. You know we need proof. How about this? One of us — no, better if two of us went — two of us can go up to his room on the third floor and give him back his cuff link. Whoever goes can look around his room, maybe get a few clues that way, and ask him to explain why his cuff links have the initials GF when his first name starts with an R, not a G."

"Good thinking," Pinny said approvingly. "Do you want to go?"

"I guess so. Will you come with me?"

Trembling with excitement, Shraga and Pinny headed for the elevators, ready to confront Richard Fowley with his cuff link and try to answer the question: was this British scientist really an imposter named Mr. Big?

The elevator rose with agonizing slowness. It seemed forever before the doors opened on the third floor.

"Which room is his?" Pinny whispered.

Shraga nodded to his right. "Room 314. I saw him go in yesterday."

"Good work," Pinny murmured again as they walked four doors down. "Stay sharp, now. We have to be careful."

They knocked at Room 314. After a minute, the door swung open to reveal Dr. Fowley.

"Yes? What can I do for you?" He gave Pinny a second look. "Ah, the young Sherlock Holmes! Well, what are you investigating today?"

Pinny started to bristle at Fowley's condescending tone, but controlled himself and held up the gold cuff link. "Is this yours? We saw you drop it downstairs in the lobby."

Fowley blinked at the cuff link, then inspected his arms. "I say, I *have* lost a cuff link. Thank you. Jolly good of you boys to bring it back to me."

He reached out for it. Pinny pulled his hand back.

"Excuse me, Dr. Fowley," he said firmly. "But we're not so sure it's yours."

"I beg your pardon?" Fowley crossed his arms, looking amused again. "Do you think I stole it? Is that your new mystery?"

Shraga had been trying to crane his neck to see beyond Fowley into the hotel room. Giving this up as a lost cause, he focused his attention on the Englishman. "Well, Dr. Fowley, since the initials aren't yours, we're not sure the cuff link belongs to you."

"The — initials?" Fowley stared at the cuff link on his right wrist. "Ah. The initials." With a sudden, abrupt movement, he reached out and snatched the cuff link out of Pinny's hand, stuffing it hastily into his pocket. "I, er, can explain." He cleared his throat. "You see..."

Five minutes later, Shraga and Pinny returned to the lobby. They looked elated. Ari and Shai, quivering with impatience, pounced on them as soon as they came out of the elevator.

"*Nu?*" Ari hissed. "What did you find out? What did he say? What excuse did he give you? What does his room look like?"

"Let's sit down," Pinny whispered back. "Come on."

The boys settled down on one of the many couches dotting the lobby.

"Well, first of all," Pinny began, "he was really casual when we first showed him the cuff link. He looked surprised to see it was missing from his sleeve, and thanked us for finding it. But when he reached out to take it, I pulled my hand back and Shraga asked him why the initials didn't match his name."

"He got real flustered," Shraga continued. "He snatched the cuff link back and started stammering. Then he said that he had *two* first names: Geoffrey and Richard. He doesn't like the Geoffrey much, so he's called Richard, but Geoffrey is really his first name, so that's what his cuff links say."

"Ridiculous," Avi said flatly. "Nobody has cuff links with initials they don't even use!"

"That's what I thought, too," Pinny agreed. "We tried to push a little, but he just said a quick 'thank you' again and practically slammed the door in our faces."

"So you never got to see his room?" Shai asked.

Shraga shook his head. "Nope. He stood right in the doorway all the time. Just like he had something to hide."

For a moment, the foursome sat silently, savoring the implications of Fowley's behavior. Then Pinny burst out, "He *must* be an imposter! What else could possibly make sense?"

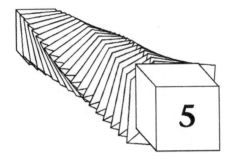

Fowley Unmasked

"O kay, then," said Ari. "Now that we know that, what do we do next?"

"How about if we follow him a little bit more and see if we can dig up some more evidence?" Shraga suggested. "I'd like to have a little more proof before we go to the authorities."

"Why don't we go to the authorities now?" Pinny said eagerly. "Tom! Let's go talk to Tom. He'll be glad to help us if we tell him we think we've found Mr. Big."

"Maybe we should," Shai said dubiously, but Shraga interrupted him.

"No, not yet," he insisted. "We'll sound ridiculous if we go to anyone with a story about cuff links and wrong first names. Let's get a little more proof first."

Pinny frowned. "Oh, all right. So what will we do this afternoon? Shadow him again?"

"I'll shadow him," Ari volunteered. "You guys would be too obvious, after the cuff link incident."

"Okay, but take Shai with you."

Shai flushed a little, but seemed pleased. "How about Niki?" he asked. He knew what was bothering the Russian boy, but he didn't want to tell the others. He wasn't sure they'd understand.

Shraga bit his lip. "Yeah, what about Niki? Did you notice him at lunch today?"

"Something's bothering him," Pinny agreed. "Shraga, how about if we go talk to him this afternoon while our fellow detectives go after Mr. Big?"

"If he *is* Mr. Big," Shraga amended. "We still don't have real proof."

Ari shrugged. "Hey, whatever you guys want. *I'm* convinced that Fowley's Mr. Big, but I'm willing to go along for a little longer."

"Not *too* much longer," promised Shraga. "If Fowley *is* Mr. Big, believe me, I want to see him behind bars as soon as possible!"

So Ari and Shai went off to shadow Dr. Fowley while Shraga and Pinny searched for Niki. They finally tracked the Russian boy down in the game room, playing listlessly with a computer game.

"Hi, Niki." Shraga slipped into the seat next to him. "How ya doing?"

Niki put the game on pause and turned to eye Shraga warily. "I am fine."

"Imagine," Pinny said in a low voice. "Alexei Pim was probably sitting right where you are now, and he tried to use the red diskette."

Niki gave an involuntarily shudder and glanced at the wastebasket.

"Incredible," Shraga said softly. "He held it in his hand. If he'd realized what it was, this whole mess would be over by now. And he just threw it away..."

Niki shrugged and turned back to the computer game.

"Niki," Pinny said after a few moments. "What's bothering you? Did we do something to upset you?"

"Oh, no. Nothing like that."

"Then what's wrong?"

Niki stared fixedly at the computer screen. "Nothing is wrong."

"But —"

Niki suddenly whirled around. "I said that nothing is wrong!" He pushed back his chair with an angry scrape and stood up. "Leave me alone!" He rushed out of the game room.

Shraga and Pinny eyed each other unhappily. "Something *is* wrong," Shraga said finally. "I wish I knew what."

Pinny nodded and sighed. "I just hope Ari and Shai are having more luck than we are."

"Why don't we go and find out?"

Shai and Ari endured a long, boring wait outside the closed door of Fowley's lab. When the Englishman finally emerged, the boys hurried after him, picking up the rest of their small band of detectives on the way.

"What do we do now?" Shai whispered.

Shraga looked at the Israeli boy's eager face, marveling. Six short days ago, this kid had been a sullen, miserable twelve-year-old who refused to look at the *frum* boys, much less talk to them. And now? Shai's face lit up often with that smile so like the sun coming out from behind a cloud. Ironic that his transformation had come about through such miserable circumstances...

His train of thought was broken when Fowley suddenly turned and strode down the corridor in their direction.

"Scatter!" Ari hissed. Shraga, Ari, and Shai dodged back into the lobby, while Pinny walked boldly towards the scientist. Ari remained near the door to the corridor, eager to see what their subject would do.

"Hello, Sherlock," he heard Fowley greet Pinny. "How's the detective business?"

"Fine," Pinny said stiffly. Fowley smiled and nodded and walked on.

Ari quickly backpedaled and hurried over to the row of house phones. When Fowley entered the lobby, Shraga and Shai were nowhere in sight. Ari had his back turned, holding an animated conversation with the dial tone. Out of the corner of his eye, he saw Fowley cross the lobby and enter another door.

Suddenly, a voice spoke at his elbow. "What do we do now?"

Ari jumped and turned to face Pinny. "Don't do

that! You scared me."

"Sorry." Pinny looked anxiously across the lobby. "Shouldn't we follow him? Where're Shraga and Shai?"

"Right here," said a quiet voice. Shraga peeked cautiously out from behind a blue plush sofa. "C'mon, we'd better catch up with him."

They followed the British scientist to a large room with bright lights and comfortable chairs. Several technical magazines and journals lay scattered across a glass-topped coffee table. Fowley picked up a magazine and made himself comfortable in a large armchair.

Pinny and Shraga hesitated just outside the door to the reading lounge. Shai and Ari stood further back.

"What next?" Shai hissed.

Pinny held up a warning hand. "Come on," he muttered to Shraga. The two boys strode into the room. Fowley looked up inquiringly.

"We seem to keep running into each other, don't we?" he remarked.

Shraga flushed and snatched up a science journal. He sat down on a couch and concentrated on turning the pages with absorption. Pinny quickly sat down next to him.

Fowley, amused, watched them. "*Tomorrow's Science*? I wouldn't expect that to be reading material for lads your age," he chuckled.

Pinny looked up hotly. "I'll have you know —" he started, but Shraga interrupted him.

"Dr. Fowley, look! There's an article here that you wrote. How interesting!"

Pinny, remembering how much Fowley loved to talk about himself, quickly picked up on this new topic of conversation. "You didn't tell us that you were published, Dr. Fowley."

To the boys' surprise, Dr. Fowley turned pale and dropped his magazine. "P-published?" he stammered. "Oh, yes. Yes. Of course." He quickly stood up and hurried out of the room.

Shraga and Pinny stared at each other. "Why?" Shraga finally said. "Why should he run out like that?"

"I don't know. Let's try and see if that article has any clue."

They struggled to read the abstruse essay. "*Quantum physics has taken a monumental leap forward,*" Shraga read laboriously. "*With our further understanding underlying the...*" He read a little further, then made a sound of frustration. "Quarks? This is deep stuff."

"I can't make head or tails of it, either," Pinny confessed. "Fowley must be a lot more brilliant than I thought he was, to write a paper like this."

"Hey, you two, what's going on?" Ari poked his head through the door. "Fowley left the room five minutes ago. What are you doing in here?"

Pinny held up the journal. "We found an article he wrote in this magazine. When we mentioned it, he got real flustered and practically ran away! We're trying to figure out what got him so nervous."

"Any luck?" Ari asked, coming further into the room with Shai trailing behind him.

"Not really," Shraga admitted. "It's real advanced stuff. We can't figure it out."

"Here, let me try." Ari held out his hand.

Pinny looked skeptical. "C'mon, Ari. Quantum physics isn't really your thing." If Pinny and Shraga couldn't understand the complex scientific paper, how could Ari?

"Couldn't hurt, though." Ari pulled the magazine out of Shraga's unresisting hands. "Let's see, now... *Dr. Richard Fowley is a frequent contributor to* Tomorrow's Science. *His last paper,* 'A Study of Erratic Isotopes,' *was published in January 1992. A graduate of* —"

"What are you reading?" Pinny demanded, grabbing the journal.

Ari snatched it back, then pointed to the small boxed text on the bottom of the page. "See? There's a sort of biography about Fowley here."

"But —" Pinny stopped short, feeling caught out and foolish. It hadn't even occurred to him or Shraga to check Fowley's biographical blurb for anything suspicious.

Ari raised his eyebrows and grinned at him. "You were hunting for clues in his article? What did you think — he's going to sneak in some secret message in a paper on physics?"

Shraga smiled despite himself. "I guess not," he said. "What else does it say about him?"

"Well, let's see. *A graduate of Oxford, Dr. Fowley*

has pursued a career in —"

"Hey!" Pinny shouted. He yanked the journal out of Ari's hands.

"Look, kid," Ari began, annoyed, but Pinny was already babbling excitedly.

"You don't get it! It says he graduated from Oxford!"

"Yeah?" Ari folded his arms. "So what?"

"But he told me he graduated from Cambridge!"

The four boys stared at each other.

"But — that means —" Shai stammered.

"It means he was lying," Ari finished softly.

"It means he's an imposter," Shraga added.

"It means," came a British voice from the doorway, "that we'd best have a little talk."

The boys whirled around to find themselves face-to-face with Dr. Fowley.

"Sit down, lads," Dr. Fowley said quietly.

Ari moved nervously to stand in front of the younger boys. "Don't try anything," he warned.

"Try anything?" Dr. Fowley looked blank.

"Yes." Ari clenched his fists. "I won't let you hurt anyone."

"*Hurt* anyone?" The Englishman shook his head, astonished. "Young man, what are you talking about?"

Pinny suddenly realized that Fowley wasn't acting. He really didn't understand what Ari meant.

"Dr. Fowley," he said from his position behind Ari's shoulder, "you must realize that we've discovered many discrepancies between what you've told us and what's actually the truth. Your name isn't Richard, but Geoffrey; you told us you went to Cambridge, when the real Richard Fowley went to Oxford; and you don't do any work in your laboratory. If you're not Richard Fowley, then *who are you*?"

The question hung in the air.

"I'm Geoffrey Fowley," the scientist said at last. Ari opened his mouth to protest, but Fowley added, "Richard Fowley's brother."

It was the boys' turn to look astonished. Geoffrey Fowley smiled faintly and moved into the room, sitting down in the same comfortable armchair he'd occupied earlier. "Permit me to explain," he said.

"You see, my brother, who is a professor at Oxford University, was invited back in midwinter to participate in this convention. You must understand that such an invitation gives a scientist a great deal of prestige. Richard felt sure that being here would be very good for his career."

Fowley paused for a moment, then gave a wry shrug. "Unfortunately, things didn't work out quite as Richard planned. Two days before he was ready to fly to America, Richard came down with an illness that confined him to his bed. There was no way he could attend this gathering. I can't begin to tell you how upset he felt at the thought of losing such an opportunity to advance up the collegiate ladder."

"What ladder?" Shai looked bewildered.

"I'll explain later," Shraga hissed.

"At any rate," Fowley continued, "Richard came to me and begged me to take his place at the convention. I had no objection to a free trip to America and a week-long vacation in a four-star hotel, so I readily agreed."

"What do you do really?" Shraga asked curiously.

"My own field is computer systems, actually. My brother briefed me about his own work — enough to allow me to get by without anyone suspecting the truth." He shook his head ruefully. "Except for you boys."

After a moment, Shraga spoke up hesitantly. "But Dr. Fowley, how do we know that what you're saying is true?"

Fowley sighed. "Yes, I suppose I deserve that. If you'll come up to my room this evening, I'll be glad to show you my passport — with my *real* name — and we can even call Richard, if you'd like." He paused. "I *am* telling the truth, young man. And I would ask you all to keep my secret for me. After all —" here he smiled "— I'm not harming anyone. I'm helping my brother, that's all, and the convention will be over in another few days." He spread his hands engagingly. "Well, lads, what do you say?"

"Can we tell you later, sir?" Ari said. "We'll think it over and let you know."

"Certainly. I quite understand." Fowley got to

his feet. "Discuss the matter among yourselves, and give me your answer at dinnertime." He smiled at them again. "I do hope you'll agree to keep my secret. If you do reveal the truth, I shan't suffer for it, but my brother certainly will. Think it over, hmmm?"

Ari watched the Englishman leave. His face was sour. "Emotional blackmail," he growled. "That's almost as bad as what's happening to Dr. Pim."

"You don't really plan on telling on him, do you?" Pinny asked.

Ari shrugged. "Nah. I guess he's right that he's not doing any harm. But one thing *did* occur to me."

"What's that?"

"He's a computer man, he says," Ari said slowly. "He may be telling the truth about being Geoffrey Fowley...but he could *also* be Mr. Big."

"Ohhh," Shraga said softly. "The e-mail messages."

"Exactly."

The four boys exchanged dismayed glances.

"Everything we've found out about him so far is just evidence of his being Geoffrey instead of Richard," Shraga added. "He *may* be after Little Nicky, but how can we tell?"

"We're right back where we started from," Pinny said gloomily. "We've uncovered a blackmail victim and a fraud, but we're no closer to identifying Mr. Big."

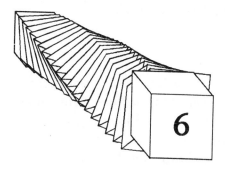

Or Isingard?

The four detectives took the elevator up to their floor in a disconsolate mood. Even the chime as the elevator doors opened seemed more gloomy than usual.

"Come into my room," Shraga suggested. "We'll have more privacy there."

"Good idea," said Pinny. "We could use a little privacy to talk things out."

But when they got to the room, Chaim was already there.

"Hi, guys," the younger boy said, looking from his brother to the Katzes and finally at Shai Drucker. "What're you all up to?"

"Nothing," Shraga said quickly. "Uh...are you planning on staying here?"

Chaim folded his arms. "And why shouldn't I? This is just as much my room as it is yours."

We just have something that we want to talk

about, that's all."

"Yeah? Well, go ahead. I'm not stopping you."

Pinny cleared his throat. "Well, Chaim, it's sort of something private."

Chaim's scowl grew blacker. "That's fine. I'll just stay right here and listen."

"But Chaim...," Shraga began.

Chaim interrupted him. "Why can't I be a detective too? Why can't you tell me what's going on? I'm not a baby!"

Shraga glared back at him. "You're not all that much of an adult, either!"

"I'm not leaving." Chaim sat down on his bed with an air of finality.

"Fine! Don't leave!" Shraga whirled and stomped to the door. "We'll go somewhere else!"

"Good!" Chaim shouted after him.

The door slammed shut behind the four older boys. Chaim clenched his fists, furious. Why wouldn't they tell him what they were doing? Why did they have to treat him like a little kid?

Meanwhile, in the hallway, Pinny said, "Let's go check out our room. I doubt Zevy's there now."

Sure enough, the Katz boys' hotel room was empty.

"Finally," Shraga sighed, sinking onto Zevy's bed with an air of relief. "Let's talk *tachlis*."

"Yes," Shai agreed. "Like, what do we do now?"

"I think we have to agree that we're at a standstill with Fowley," Pinny began. "One of us should still keep tabs on him to make sure he doesn't do anything more suspicious than pretend to be his brother, but there's not much more we can do."

"Uh-huh." Shraga lay back on Zevy's bed and stared moodily at the ceiling. "I think we should take him up on his offer to show us his passport, though."

"That's all very fine," Ari said impatiently, "but who are we going to concentrate on now?"

"Isingard, I think," Shraga said reflectively, sitting up again. "After all, he said himself that he's involved with the peace process in the Middle East."

"Yeah," Pinny said, remembering. He made a face "Isingard shook hands with Arafat — and he didn't even have to!"

Shai made a face. "It's not something I'd choose to do, but it doesn't necessarily make him a criminal."

"He may be a terrorist sympathizer," Shraga insisted. "We all know there are plenty of goyim out there who are always ready to take sides against the Jews. Isn't it possible that Isingard is one?"

"And if that's the case," Pinny added soberly, "there's every possibility that he plans to sell Little Nicky to some terrorist organization."

The warm hotel room seemed to grow suddenly chilly.

"Well, whoever Mr. Big is, he hasn't succeeded yet," Shraga said with resolution. "Even if he *does* have the red diskette already, he obviously hasn't been able to break the codes to get at the plans."

"Yeah," Ari said with little conviction.

"Well, let's see what we can do about checking out Dr. Isingard." Shraga stood up. "I'll stick to Fowley, if you'd like."

"I think it would be better if Pinny did," Shai said. "Dr. Fowley has spoken with him before."

"Yeah, Shai's right," Pinny said, making a face. "He thinks I'm just a kid, but at least he talks to me."

"Fine. Pinny will talk to Fowley while we watch Isingard." Shraga rubbed at his eyes, yawning. They'd been up all night and had a long, frustrating day. "We've got a couple of hours 'till suppertime. Let's meet back here fifteen minutes before that and see what we've got."

Shraga lounged on a plush sofa in the lobby, strategically positioned near the row of house phones. Shai loitered nearby, ostensibly absorbed in watching the vast fountain sending feathered sprays of water in all directions. Ari, standing in the first-floor foyer overlooking the lobby, leaned precariously over the ledge, straining his ears to catch the phone conversation going on directly below him.

Manfred Isingard, tall and imperious, sat in a straight-backed chair, talking on the last phone in the row. The boys had followed the Norwegian scientist from his laboratory to the lobby, where Shai had overheard Isingard ask the concierge to put him through to a reputable travel agent.

Shraga, too impatient to wait for an elevator, had bolted up the steps to the first floor to let Ari know what was happening. Then he hurried back downstairs and made himself comfortable on a sofa, eager to overhear what travel plans Isingard had in mind.

Now, the boys held their breaths and listened as the silver-haired professor spoke on the phone in stiff, cultured English.

"Yes, that is correct. First Egypt, then Israel... Oh? I see. Yes, I understand... No, five days in Egypt should be long enough. Three days in Israel... For the day after tomorrow; I cannot leave before that. First class, of course. An evening flight... No, do not call me back. I'll wait... That is confirmed? Excellent. Thank you."

Isingard hung up the phone and sat in his chair for another moment. A smile of anticipation flickered across his patrician features. Then he picked up the receiver once more and requested an outside line. After a moment, he dialled a number. Shai couldn't tell what the numbers were, but it seemed obvious that it was long-distance, possibly even out of the country.

"Sergei, my friend! Wonderful news. Do you remember our discussion before my arrival here in the States?... Yes. Exactly... Yes! Twice so far. After five days of stalking, I think I have our target pinpointed... Yes, tomorrow morning will be my best chance... Of course I will take one along! No, no..."

Shraga and Shai looked at each other in mounting excitement. What was Isingard planning?

"Of course," Isingard said finally. "Before six o'clock in the morning... Certainly, Sergei. I will call you when I have news — and we will meet in Egypt in three days. Goodbye, my friend."

Isingard put the phone back in its cradle and stood up. Shai shrank back into the shadows as the scientist passed him on his way to the elevators. Even as the elevator doors closed, the door to the stairwell burst open, and Ari came zooming over to the younger boys.

"How much could you hear?" he panted.

Shraga's eyes were round. "He's going to Egypt! *And* to Israel! Straight from here!"

"Not that." Ari shook his head impatiently. "The second phone call! He said something about tomorrow morning, didn't he?"

"Oh, yes!" Shai sat down next to Shraga. "Six o'clock tomorrow morning. And he will take something with him. The plans! He must have the red diskette!"

"That first phone call," added Shraga. "It can't possibly be a coincidence that he's going to Egypt straight from here. Why should he, unless he has something to do with Little Nicky's disappearance?"

"Maybe he has something to do with terrorists," Shai said darkly. "A man who's friendly with Arafat..."

"No one said they're friends," Pinny objected.

"They just shook hands."

Ari sat down next to the other boys. He mused, "We know he's rich. We know he's got political influence. And now he's going off to Egypt and Israel."

"*And* he said he's been stalking something," Shraga put in. "For five days, he said. It's been five days since Little Nicky and the red diskette first disappeared. What else could it possibly mean?"

"It means," Ari said slowly, "that we'd better forget about Fowley for a while and concentrate on Professor Manfred Isingard. Come on. Let's go find Pinny and Niki and figure out what we're going to do next."

At 5:40 the following morning, Pinny and Ari Katz tiptoed out of their room to tap at Shraga's door. Pinny, remembering the incident of the switched shoes — how long ago it seemed! — thought about the way things had changed in the last few days. Shraga was a friend now. At least that much had come out of this mess.

Even as Ari raised his hand to give a soft tap, the door opened. Shraga, blinking sleepily but dressed in shirt and pants, slid quietly through the half-open doorway and carefully closed the door behind him.

"I see you woke up on your own," Pinny whispered.

"Yeah," Shraga breathed. "Ready?"

Ari and Pinny nodded silently. The threesome

made their way to the elevators.

Shraga quickly pushed the button for the first floor. "We can't take the elevator down to the lobby!" he whispered urgently. "There's a night clerk, remember? It would be way too obvious!"

The doors opened on the first floor.

"We'd better take the stairs from here," Shraga continued, stepping forward.

"Okay," Pinny whispered. "But be real quiet, okay? We don't want anyone to notice us."

They tiptoed down the stairs. At the door to the lobby, they found Shai, frozen stiff in fear.

"Hey, it's just us," Ari whispered. "Relax."

Shai's shoulders slumped with relief. "Why didn't you take the elevator!" he hissed. "I thought you were Isingard!"

"Change of plans," Shraga explained in a low voice. "C'mon. Let's go outside and see what Isingard's up to."

The four boys made it outdoors with little incident. With the sun not quite up yet, the mountain air was chilly. They shivered as they made their way around the hotel to the woodland beyond.

"Okay," Ari muttered out of the side of his mouth. "What do we do now?"

Pinny shrugged. "We wait, I guess." His voice was little more than a whisper. He turned to Shai. "Hey, Shai, what happened with Niki? I thought you said you would tell him what's happening and get him to come with us."

Shai jammed his hands deep into his jacket

pockets. "He didn't want to come. He didn't even want to listen. He just said he was too tired from two nights ago to wake up early."

Shraga drew closer. "Did you tell him about Fowley? About what we found out?"

"Yes. He just shrugged his shoulders and walked away."

Shraga sighed and didn't ask anything more. It would probably be best if they didn't talk now, anyway. Isingard would be showing up any second, and voices can carry a long way in the early morning silence.

They waited. It seemed to get colder. Faint rustlings sounded in the grass, and birds began to twitter. The dew soaked through their sneakers. Pinny shifted uncomfortably. If this was the country, he'd be more than happy to stick to Brooklyn.

Then Shraga jabbed him excitedly in the ribs. Pinny's heart suddenly began hammering overtime. Manfred Isingard had just stepped out of the hotel and was headed their way.

The boys sank deeper into the wet grass, holding their breaths as the tall, aristocratic scientist entered the wooded area. The Norwegian was only a dozen yards away. What if he saw them?

As Isingard went deeper into the woods, Pinny pointed wordlessly at the binoculars hanging around the scientist's neck. Ari nodded, then grabbed Pinny's arm and gestured wildly. Pinny, unable to ask Ari what in the world he was trying to say, made a face at his older brother. Ari poked

Pinny's belt, then pointed at Isingard again. Pinny turned, looked again, and caught his breath.

Two small, oblong boxes were strapped to Isingard's waist.

Pinny's mind raced wildly. A radio and a remote-control device? A walkie-talkie? A bomb with a timer and detonator? Together with the binoculars, those little boxes seemed to offer ample proof that Isingard was something other than a scientist. Maybe he was on his way to a rendezvous with a fellow criminal, or even a terrorist! They'd tracked down Mr. Big at last!

Shraga tugged at his arm. When Pinny turned to look at him, Shraga jerked his head in Isingard's direction.

"Let's follow," he mouthed.

Pinny nodded. One by one, the four boys crawled through the dew-soaked grass, trying to make as little noise as possible. Ari, instinctively protecting the younger boys, was in the lead. They'd gone about fifty feet when Ari came to an abrupt halt. Looking over his shoulder, he motioned for the others to come alongside him, laying an unnecessary finger over his lips to keep them quiet.

Pinny eased over to the right and crawled forward until he was next to Ari. Shraga was right behind him. Shai remained in the rear, lifting his head cautiously out of the grass to see what was happening.

Only two dozen feet away, Isingard stood motionless and silent, staring into the distance. Abruptly, the tall scientist raised his binoculars and peered through them; then, without lowering the binoculars, he reached for one of the boxes strapped to his belt.

Ari wasted no time. With the smoothness of an athlete, he rolled to his feet and lunged forward. Pinny and Shraga were right behind him with Shai at their heels, desperate to reach the scientist before he could activate whatever terrible devices he was carrying.

Unfortunately, even an athlete can't always avoid the hazards of uneven and slippery ground. Six feet away from the unsuspecting Isingard, Ari slipped on the wet grass and landed flat on his face with an *oomph!* Pinny and Shraga, moving too fast to avoid his sprawled form, crashed right into Ari, tumbling into a tangled heap. Shai skidded to a horrified halt just in time.

At the sudden loud noises, Isingard whirled around, his eyes flashing with fury. The woodland had suddenly gone silent.

"You boys!" he roared. His voice was still aristocratic, but it sounded terrifying. "What are you doing here? Do you realize what you've *done*?"

"Dr. Isingard," Shraga gasped from his position on top of the Katzes. He struggled to his feet and began to back away, bumping into a frozen Shai. "We —"

Isingard bent over and shook his finger at Ari and Pinny, still a tangled heap of arms and legs on the ground. "*Five days* I've been stalking them!" he thundered. "Five days! And I finally have them in sight, I am finally ready to take a shot of them, and you have to come make all this noise and scare them away!" His arms swept in a wide circle. "Why must a group of noisy boys be outside at six o'clock in the morning?"

Ari, pinned to the damp earth by his brother, squinted up at the enraged scientist. He stared at the two devices strapped to Isingard's belt unbelievingly.

The two menacing devices were perfectly ordinary and commonplace.

One was a tape recorder. The other was a camera.

"Dr. Isingard," Ari croaked, finally squirming out from under Pinny and getting to his feet. "What — what were you looking for?" He reached down and hauled Pinny to a standing position. Pinny, his eyes fixed on the little camera and tape recorder strapped to Isingard's belt, prudently slipped behind Ari.

Isingard glared at all four of them. "For five days, I have been stalking a pair of *calorinus glarimus*. They are native to North America and have never been seen anywhere else. I finally had them pinned down. I was going to record their song, to take their picture — and you boys had to blunder in with your infernal noise!" He was stoking himself into a fury again. "Now they have flown away, and I have only one morning left until the conference ends. Who knows if I will be successful tomorrow?"

Shraga's mind raced, putting together Isingard's remarks with the binoculars, the camera, and the tape recorder. "Dr. Isingard," he said feebly, "are you a *bird* watcher? An ornithologist?"

Isingard snorted. "I most certainly am, young man. I see you know the correct term. Yes, I am an ornithologist. Who else would be outdoors at six o'clock in the morning? One must be out in the woods this early to record birdsong. Any later, and sounds of civilization can intrude — motors and the like." He seemed to have regained his temper, although he still looked annoyed. "May I ask why you boys chose this moment to fall at my feet?"

"We were shadowing you," Shai blurted before any of the other boys could say anything.

Isingard stared. "Indeed?"

Pinny gulped. "We — we're trying to catch the criminal who stole our fathers' prototype, and we — well..." Words failed him. How could he tell the aristocratic scientist that they'd thought his binoculars and tape recorder were proof of criminal activities?

Isingard, however, apparently didn't need to have things spelled out. He looked from one boy to another with narrowed eyes. "Do you mean — do I understand —" He stared for another moment, then threw back his head and laughed. "Marvelous," he chuckled. "You were following me to see if *I* was the culprit, is that it?"

Pinny and Shraga nodded, exchanging relieved

glances as the scientist laughed again. At least Isingard wasn't furious with them anymore.

"My dear young men," Isingard said when he'd finally finished laughing. "May I ask why you centered your suspicions on me?"

"We overheard your telephone calls yesterday," Shraga admitted. "When you called a travel agent about flying to Egypt and Israel from here, and when you called a friend to say you were tracking something. I'm sorry, sir, but we're all so tense that we automatically assumed it had something to do with the stolen device."

"I see." Isingard shook his head, still amused. "Well, my young friends, I do intend to travel to Egypt when this conference is over. I have never seen the great annual migration of birds over Egypt and Israel before, and my friend Sergei and I have been planning this trip for over a year. Is there any other incriminating evidence you would like me to explain?"

"No, sir," Pinny said unhappily. "And we're really sorry that we disturbed your bird watching. I hope you get another chance at your *carolinus* —"

"*Calorinus glarimus*," Isingard corrected. He sighed. "Well, if you boys would be so kind as to go back to the hotel, perhaps I can still spot them this morning."

"Thank you, sir. And we're sorry, really," Shraga mumbled as he and the other boys made a hasty retreat.

Silently, the foursome trudged through the wet

grass and out of the woods. They said nothing to each other as they crossed the hotel grounds and entered the lobby. In the last three days, they'd smoked out three red-hot leads and seen all three of them fizzle into nothing. Exhausted by their lack of sleep and lack of success, they made their way across the huge lobby to the elevators, each one feeling that they were back to square one. Would they ever find the real Mr. Big?

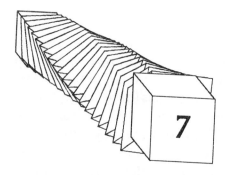

Loyalties

All Tuesday long, Niki Gorodnik made it his business to keep away from the Jewish boys who had been his fellow detectives for two days. He'd invented one lame excuse after another when they approached him about joining them. He'd seen the hurt in their faces, but the hurt in his own heart was much, much worse.

Ever since Ilya Pim's revelation the day before, he hadn't been able to look any of them in the face — not Pinny nor Shraga, not Ari nor Shai. And Alexei Pim! He'd been friendly with the Russian boy, but he couldn't help thinking what Alexei would say if he knew that Niki had betrayed Alexei's father.

But he hadn't betrayed him. Not really. All he'd done was tell Shai that he knew of someone who had left the dining room during that fateful dinner, nearly one week ago, when the prototype weapon had been stolen. It was Shai who had put things together and confronted Niki, insisting he confirm that it was Ilya Pim, Alexei's father, who had left the room that night.

And he *had* confirmed it. He'd had to. And he'd been there when they'd burst into the "Jewish lab" and caught Ilya Pim red-handed. He'd heard Dr. Pim's confession.

Niki couldn't help thinking that even if the others would be willing to go the authorities, he wouldn't be. He couldn't be. Ilya was his countryman. Ilya hadn't deliberately planned to steal Little Nicky; he'd been forced into it, blackmailed into doing all the dirty work for Mr. Big.

Oh, *why* had he given Shai the clue that led to Dr. Pim?

It was the right thing to do, a voice whispered inside him. *You did the right thing.*

But had he? Had he *really?* What right did he have to betray a fellow Russian to these American boys?

These *Jewish* boys?

Niki felt miserable. That was the crux of his whole problem. Was he a Russian first and foremost — or a Jew? Shai seemed to think that being a Jew came first. Niki wasn't so sure. Why should he cast his lot with the Katzes and Morgensterns, just because his mother happened to be Jewish? Was it right to choose to help the Jews at the cost of harming a fellow Russian? And what was being

Jewish all about, anyway?

The same guilty thoughts were chasing themselves around his brain when he felt a hand on his sleeve. He looked up, blinking, straight into the stunned white face of Ilya Pim.

Niki recoiled, then forced a smile to his face. "Good morning," he said faintly.

"Good morning, Nikolai." Pim lowered his voice. "Tell the boys that I received another e-mail message today from Mr. Big. Tell them to come to my lab to discuss it after breakfast."

Niki swallowed. "Yes, all right," he managed to say.

Ilya straightened. "Yes, a beautiful morning," he said loudly. "Perhaps you and Alexei could go for a walk today."

"Th-that would be nice," Niki stammered. He escaped into the dining room and hurried over to his table. His mother was already seated and sipping from a steaming cup of coffee.

"Good morning, my son," Natasha greeted him in Russian, setting down her coffee cup. "And what are your plans for today?"

"I don't know," Niki said unhappily as he slipped into the chair next to hers. "I — I haven't decided yet."

"Hmm, hmm." Natasha picked up her cup again and sipped, eyeing her son over the rim. "Well, Nikolai, if you have no plans, perhaps you wouldn't mind spending a few hours with your mother today?"

"What?"

"After lunch, I think," Natasha said casually. "There is a seminar here this morning that I must attend. Jorg Ronin of South Africa is presenting a very interesting theory."

"Oh." Niki looked at his mother, nonplussed. He knew how hard it was to fool her. Ever since his father died when he was a little boy, Natasha had been both mother and father to him, dealing out love and strictness in equal doses. What did she have in mind now?

Almost furtively, he turned his head to look at the "Jewish table." His former partners-in-detection all looked sleepy and downcast. The foray against Isingard early in the morning must not have worked out very well.

Even as Niki watched, Pinny leaned forward and said something to Shai that Niki couldn't catch. Shai's face blossomed with that shy smile, and he nodded, a little self-consciously. Niki sighed and turned away. What were they discussing now? Maybe that "learning" of theirs that they seemed to be so fascinated with. What could there be in a Hebrew book to make their eyes light up like that? Did it have —

"Hi, Niki!"

Niki jumped. Alexei plopped himself down in the next chair, grinning. "I enjoy calling you by your American nickname. What are your plans for today?"

Niki's wince did not go unnoticed by his mother.

"Hi, Alexei," he said, smiling feebly. "Would you like me to call you 'Alex'? Then you will have an American nickname, too."

"Oh, no." Alexei shook his head and laughed. "My name is too special for that."

"Too special?" Niki repeated blankly.

"Yes." Alexei buttered a piece of hot toast with a flourish. "I have the same name as my grandfather, you see. The famous war hero." He waved his knife in the air. "My father, he always says that it is a proud responsibility, to be named for a man who helped Mother Russia against the Nazis!"

Niki stared at his plate, thinking of Ilya Pim's story. What would happen if Alexei found out that his grandfather might not have been a hero at all? What if he found out that Niki knew? What if he discovered that it was Niki who betrayed his father to the Jewish boys?

Where did his loyalties lie?

With Russia: Alexei and Ilya?

With the Jews: Shai, Shraga, Pinny, and Ari?

And which list did his mother — and he himself — belong on?

The breakfast the waiter brought was delicious, but Niki ate it mechanically, wishing there were some way he could make his confusing questions disappear as easily as the food on his plate.

After breakfast that morning, the boys gathered together for their daily learning session. Today, despite their drowsiness and discouragement, the session was particularly satisfying. For Shraga, it took his mind off the furious argument he'd had with Chaim, who had awakened at six and discovered that Shraga had gone off detecting without him again. For Pinny and Ari, it was a welcome diversion from their embarrassing encounter with Isingard. For Drs. Katz and Morgenstern, learning with the boys was the one bright spot in a gloomy situation.

Shai, coming to join the boys for the third time, found himself somewhat taken aback when Shraga clapped him on the shoulder.

"This makes it a *chazakah*," Shraga declared, grinning. "This is it, Shai. There's no turning back."

"What was that?" Shai stared at him.

"A *chazakah*," Shraga repeated. "Three times in a row makes something permanent. Welcome to the club, Shai."

Shai's gaze dropped to the *gemara* in his hand. Was he really "part of the club"? The boy who had been passed from one set of foster parents to another before finally being placed with the Druckers had never been part of anything. He'd certainly never considered himself to be one with these religious boys who took their *Yahadut* — *Yiddishkeit* — so seriously. Was this really where he belonged?

"Well, c'mon," Shraga urged, not noticing, or pretending not to notice, Shai's hesitation. "Let's get started."

The hard, brittle defensiveness melted away.

Shai was part of a group now, part of something that warmed him from inside out. He belonged.

"Right," he said softly, opening his *gemara.* "Let's get started."

Nearly an hour later, they all closed their *sefarim* with a twinge of regret. Dr. Morgenstern was the first to notice Niki Gorodnik standing a few feet away, watching them.

"Did you want to talk to one of us?" he asked, getting to his feet.

Niki jumped. "Oh, yes. Um...Shai."

Shai looked at the other boys for a moment, then got up. He followed Niki away from the others.

"What is it, Niki?" Shai said quietly. "Do you want to hear about this morning? Isingard is not the criminal. We found out that he is only busy watching birds. But we could —"

"That is not why I wish to speak to you." Niki shifted his weight uncomfortably. "I — Dr. Pim spoke to me this morning. He wants us to come to his lab." His voice dropped to a whisper. "He got another message last night."

"He *did*?" Shai whistled under his breath. "When should we go talk to him?"

"This morning, he said." Niki twisted his fingers together. "Look, I — I can't go with you. I am meeting Alexei outside. I must go; he is waiting for me." And before Shai could say a word, Niki darted away.

"What is *wrong* with that kid?" Pinny said as he came up to Shai.

Shai sighed. "I think he's confused," he said slowly.

"Confused? About what?"

Shai just shook his head.

"He told me that Dr. Pim wants to talk to us," Shai said instead. "In his lab."

"Yeah?" Pinny lowered his voice instinctively. "About — Mr. Big?"

"Yes. He received another message."

Pinny rubbed his hands together. "Good! We can use another clue."

The four detectives hurried through the lobby and into the corridor that hosted the labs of Drs. Magda Brenner, Richard Fowley, Manfred Isingard, their fathers, and Ilya Pim.

"Looks like the only suspect we've got left is Magda Brenner," Pinny grumbled as they passed the white-haired scientist's door. "And I sure have a hard time imagining her as Mr. — excuse me, Mrs. — Big. *That* nice old lady? No way."

"I can't imagine it, either," Ari agreed. "But if we forget about her, who are we left with?"

"Just every other scientist at this convention," Shraga said moodily. "Don't forget, with Ilya Pim doing the dirty work, Mr. Big doesn't have to be someone with access to this corridor."

"Just someone with access to a copy of Abba's electronic card," Pinny said sourly. "How in the world did Mr. Big manage that one?"

"I don't know. I wish I did." Shraga stopped in front of the door to Ilya Pim's lab and knocked softly. They heard rapid footsteps, and then the door opened.

"Come in, boys," Dr. Pim whispered. "Quickly."

They filed inside. Dr. Pim locked the door behind them.

"I am glad you came," he said as he offered them chairs. "I wish to show you the latest message I have received from Mr. Big. If he really is watching my movements, it would be best if I do not have any contact with your parents. I will ask you boys to tell them what happened."

"Of course," Ari said.

"We'll tell them," Pinny chimed in, pleased to be entrusted with such important information.

"Good." Dr. Pim looked around at the four eager faces. "Where is Nikolai?"

The boys looked at each other. "He said he was going outside with Alexei," Shai said finally.

"Ah... Well, perhaps that is for the best. Come, boys, I will recall the message on-screen so you can see it."

Dr. Pim turned to his computer and logged into the Internet. The boys watched, fascinated, as he manipulated the mouse and brought a few words of text up on the screen.

"This is it," Dr. Pim said soberly. "Look."

They all leaned forward to read the latest message from the sinister Mr. Big.

Time is running out. The original plans are no longer available. Better find the red diskette — or else.

"The plans are no longer available," Shraga read aloud. He had a sinking feeling in his stomach. Did Mr. Big really know *everything* that was happening in the hotel?

"Yes, I wondered about that. I do not know what it means," Dr. Pim said, looking worried. "Of course, I do not intend to search for the red diskette — or rather, if I do look for it, it will not be for Mr. Big's sake. But I thought your fathers should know about this."

"Yes," Pinny said mechanically, staring at the screen, "they should. I — I guess we'd better go tell them right away."

Shraga stood up. The others followed his lead.

"Thanks a lot, Dr. Pim," Ari said. "We appreciate your help."

Dr. Pim smiled faintly. "Anything I can do, I shall. I want to see this man caught as much as you do."

"Shraga," Shai said in a low voice as they filed out of the lab, "what did Mr. Big mean when he wrote that *the original plans are no longer available?*"

Shraga put a finger to his lips and waited until they were out in the corridor. "Our parents deleted the plans from the computer," he explained in a whisper, "so nobody could get hold of Little Nicky that way. That message means that somehow, Mr. Big knows that they deleted the passwords and —"

"No, they didn't," Ari corrected gloomily.

"What?" Pinny, Shraga, and Shai all turned to stare at Ari.

"I guess Abba didn't tell you, Pinny. Maybe he didn't want to worry you."

"Worry me about *what*?"

Ari hunched his shoulders. "Abba and Dr. Morgenstern can't get into M.C.B.'s network."

"What do you mean?" Shraga demanded. "Why can't they use their own passwords?"

"That's just the point," Ari said bitterly. "The passwords have been changed."

"How?"

"How do you think? By M.C.B."

"You mean — their bosses won't let them into the network?" Pinny looked horrified. "Poor Abba!"

"Poor Daddy," Shraga whispered. How could their parents feel, knowing that even their employers didn't really trust them? He felt a renewed surge of determination. Even if everyone else suspected his father and Dr. Katz, *he* would prove to the world that Mr. Big, not the two Jewish scientists, was behind the theft of Little Nicky! He'd unmask the true crook and save his father's reputation.

Somehow, he'd do it.

After a subdued lunch, the Gorodniks left the dining room for their planned outing.

"Well, my son," Natasha said as they went out into the bright afternoon. "How did you spend your morning?"

"I was with Alexei." Niki stared across the large parking lot. "We went walking in the woods."

Natasha merely nodded. The taxi she had ordered pulled up alongside them.

"Come, Nikolai." She opened the door and gestured for him to enter. Niki clambered into the taxi and moved over so his mother could sit down next to him.

"To town, please," Natasha told the driver. The man nodded and moved off.

"Where are we going?" Niki asked after a few moments of silence.

Natasha smiled down at her son. "I thought I would take you for a very American pastime."

"Yes?" Niki felt interested despite himself. "Baseball?"

His mother laughed. "No, not baseball! Ice cream."

"Ice cream?"

"Yes, ice cream. It is a very American thing, to eat ice cream."

Niki gave his mother an uncertain smile and turned his attention to the scenery outside the car window.

After a ten-minute drive, they arrived at a small town. Natasha directed the driver to drop them off at an ice-cream parlor and return for them in an hour and a half. Niki followed his mother into the cheerful shop. They found an empty booth and ordered huge ice-cream sundaes.

"This is a treat for me, too," Natasha said conspiratorially. "I will enjoy this."

"So will I," Niki said, looking eagerly at the waiter returning with their orders.

For several minutes, the delicious ice cream commanded all of Niki's attention. Then his mother reached across the table and tapped his hand with the back of her spoon.

"Nikolai, I have been watching you these last few days."

Niki flushed and put his own spoon down. He didn't know where to look.

"You have been troubled. Unhappy." Natasha paused, then asked gently, "Nikolai, are you upset because you have discovered you are Jewish?"

"That's part of it, Mama." Niki still couldn't bring himself to look at her.

"And what else, my son?"

Niki glanced up. His mother's eyes were so understanding, so ready to listen to whatever he said, that he couldn't stop himself. Suddenly, everything spilled out in a rush: his tentative friendship with the Jewish boys he'd originally insulted, his partnership in their detective work, his discovery of Ilya Pim's absence at the dinner table on the night of the theft, and his subsequent betrayal of Pim to the other boys. Natasha said nothing as the words poured out of her son.

"I betrayed him, Mama," Niki said finally, feeling drained. "I couldn't decide if my loyalty belonged to a fellow Russian, or a fellow Jew — and in the end, I betrayed him and gave away his secret." Niki stopped and looked pleadingly at his mother. His shame over what he'd done to Ilya and Alexei was finally out in the open. "Mama, did I do right?"

Natasha was silent for several minutes. "That is a very hard question to answer, Nikolai," she said at last. "All of us go through life wondering if our choices were correct. But in this case, I believe you were right."

She paused for a moment, marshalling her thoughts. "Being Jewish is — inescapable. You and I are Jews, my son. That can never change. Russian, American, Israeli — if one is Jewish, it is all the same. And Jews — Jews have always done whatever they felt was right, even if others did not agree or approve." Natasha smiled at her son. "You did what was right. And I think that now, even Ilya is glad that you did."

Niki nodded hesitantly, but said, "Mama, maybe I *am* ready to be Jewish, but — I don't know what it means."

Natasha laughed a little. "I don't know either, Nikolai. I never really worried about it before. But now, I think it would be worthwhile to find out. For both of us." She looked thoughtful. "You see how these Jewish boys and men treated Ilya, even after all the suffering he caused them. If that's what it means to be Jewish, Nikolai, it must not be such a terrible thing, hmm?" She tapped her spoon on the tabletop. "I will promise you this, my son. When we return to Moscow, I will find someone who can tell us more about Judaism. You and I can learn about it together."

"And now, Mama? What should I do now? Should I still be friends with Alexei?"

"I don't see why not, Nikolai. But if, as you say, you have not spoken to the Jewish boys for two days, then I would also suggest that you become friends with them again." Natasha looked at her son with compassion. "A good decision is often a hard one. You have made a good, difficult decision, Nikolai. Now you can move on."

Niki looked down at his melting ice cream. "All right," he said slowly. "I will."

"Good."

It *was* good. Niki felt peaceful and comforted for the first time in two days. He looked up at his mother. "And will we really learn more about being Jewish when we go home?"

"We will, my son. I promise it."

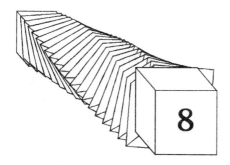

8

The Bunsen-Burner Barbecue

L ater that afternoon, Niki met Shraga, Shai, Pinny, and Ari coming out of the woods in back of the hotel, each carrying an armful of kindling. Chaim, Daniella, and little Zevy were there too, wandering among the trees and picking up twigs and thin sticks.

"What are you all doing?" Niki asked, puzzled.

Pinny grinned at him. "We're having a barbecue tonight!"

"A barbecue?" Niki repeated. The word was new to him.

"Yeah, a barbecue. You know, a cookout? A wienie roast?" Pinny saw that Niki still looked confused. He held out his armful of wood. "We're going to make a fire and roast hot dogs and potatoes for supper," he explained. "We've had enough of those lousy airplane meals, so we're making a meal of our own!"

"You have permission for this?" Niki was impressed.

"Oh, sure," Ari said easily. His armful of wood was much larger than anyone else's. "Mr. Stewart said we could make the bonfire on the edge of the parking lot. We just have to collect some stones from the lakeside and make a ring for the fire. The kitchen is giving us a bag of potatoes, and we got the concierge to order a couple of packages of kosher hot dogs from town. They should be bringing it here pretty soon."

"You'll join us, won't you?" Shraga asked a little anxiously.

Shai opened his mouth, ready to make excuses for Niki, but the Russian boy spoke first. "I would like that, yes. Thank you." He gave them all a shy smile.

Shai closed his mouth with a snap. He looked astonished.

"Great!" Shraga said happily. "Come on, let's go put this wood down. My arms are just about ready to give out."

The boys staggered along the grass until they reached the parking lot, where they dumped their armloads of kindling with relief. Ari busied himself with arranging the wood into a teepee form so it would burn efficiently.

"Here!" Zevy called, running up to his big

brother. "This will help!"

Ari smiled at the three twigs the small boy proudly held out. "Thanks, Zevy. We'll use those to start the fire." Zevy beamed as Ari carefully laid the flimsy twigs at the edge of the teepee.

"We should get more," Pinny said, eyeing the stack of wood critically.

"You're right," Ari agreed, rising to his feet and dusting off his hands. "Let's go."

Niki followed the others into the woods. Shai dropped back to talk to him privately.

"Niki, is everything all right?" he asked quietly.

"Yes." Niki smiled at him again. "You were right, Shai."

"I was?"

"Yes. You were." Without another word, Niki walked away, his head bent as he searched for fallen sticks and branches. Shai stared after him for a moment, then shrugged and followed.

By the time they'd collected enough wood for a really good fire, it was already five o'clock.

"Let's wait until after dark," Ari suggested. "It'll be more fun that way. Say, just about the time everyone goes in for dinner —"

"Which I, for one, will be more than happy to pass on," Shraga said, grinning.

"Yeah, so will I. So we'll all come out here then. I'll light the fire, and we'll get started on our barbecue."

"I can't wait," Pinny said, licking his lips with anticipation.

"Well, we'll have to," Shraga said reasonably. "They haven't come back with the hot dogs yet."

"Let's go inside while we wait," Pinny said. "It's cooler in there." The air seemed oppressive outside.

Inside, they found all four of their mothers seated together in the lobby. Mrs. Katz looked up as they trooped in, and waved for them to come over.

"You are doing something else American, I hear," Natasha Gorodnik said to her son, her eyes twinkling. "A barbecue! I hope you have a good time."

"You will be careful, won't you?" Mrs. Drucker asked.

"Oh, yes," Shai assured her, smiling happily. Mrs. Drucker blinked, then smiled uncertainly back.

"I must say, you all look excited," Mrs. Morgenstern remarked as she shifted Vivi from one arm to the other. "When are you going to start your barbecue?"

"We figure on having it right after they serve dinner," Shraga said with an impish grin. "We'll really appreciate the change!"

Mrs. Katz looked around at the circle of smiling faces. "At least we don't have to worry that you'll complain about the food tonight."

"Nope," Shraga said happily. "No need to worry about *that*."

"I should have worried," Shraga sighed, nose

pressed against the streaming dining room window.

Seemingly out of nowhere, storm clouds had come hurrying over Lake View Hotel. By the time it was dark, a summer downpour to rival that of last week was throwing sheets of water against the windows and filling the darkness with noise.

"There goes our barbecue," Pinny mourned.

"All that wood is going to be soaked, but good," Ari muttered.

Shai merely stood staring out at the rain. He'd really been looking forward to eating some good-tasting kosher food, but now their barbecue was literally a washout.

"It's not fair," Chaim groused. "I really wanted some hot dogs!"

"Maybe we could have the barbecue tomorrow," Niki said hopefully.

Ari shook his head. "The wood's soaked through now. It won't dry out by tomorrow night."

"Well, boys," Dr. Katz said with forced cheerfulness as he came over to the window where they stood, "I guess you'll be joining us for dinner, after all."

Pinny made a very eloquent face. "No, thanks," he mumbled.

"I'd rather eat a raw hot dog," Shraga muttered.

None of the older boys felt like forcing down another tasteless packaged meal, though Chaim, Daniella, and Zevy eventually gave up and went back to the table, where they unenthusiastically ate what was in front of them. The five detectives remained at the window, gazing glumly out at the rain. The downpour had slackened into a thin, sullen drizzle.

"Can't the cooks make the hot dogs for you?" Niki asked.

Pinny shook his head. "No, they can't."

"But they are kosher."

"Yeah, but we can't cook our food in a non-kosher pot." He sighed. "There are a lot of laws about kosher food, Niki. Maybe we can explain them to you sometime."

Niki gave him a shy smile and turned his attention back to the window. The rain had just about stopped, but there was no way to make a fire with soaking wet wood.

"What do we do now?" Ari said.

Pinny shrugged. "Go hungry, I guess." Only a few scientists remained at their tables; most had already finished eating and left the room. "Let's go to the lab and visit Abba and Dr. Morgenstern."

The others agreed to this plan. They hurried out of the dining room, through the lobby, and into the side corridor, where they passed Magda Brenner going into her lab. She smiled and nodded at them. They nodded back, then walked on to their fathers' door, where they knocked until Dr. Katz unlocked it and let them in.

"What's doing, boys?" he asked.

"Nothing," Pinny grumped.

Dr. Morgenstern, at the computer, turned to

smile sympathetically. "Well, I'm afraid there's not much doing here, either." His smile faded as he gestured at the blank screen. "We're still cut off from the M.C.B. network. All we can do are a few on-site experiments." He pointed to a small beaker bubbling over a gas flame.

Shraga nodded. "Ari told us about that, Daddy," he said quietly. "I'm sure they'll change their minds. The really scary thing is that Mr. Big knows about it somehow."

"I know." Dr. Morgenstern looked bleak. "When you told me about that message Ilya Pim received..." He sighed. "At least that terrible criminal hasn't tried to stage any more accidents."

"Baruch Hashem for that," Dr. Katz said quietly.

Pinny spoke up. "Abba, can't we try to figure out who Mr. Big might be?"

"What?" Dr. Katz rubbed the side of his nose. "Pinny, what exactly did you have in mind?"

"Well, we've investigated a few of the scientists." Pinny counted them off on his fingers. "Dr. Fowley and Dr. Isingard so far. Dr. Isingard seems to be in the clear; so does Dr. Fowley. And we all feel that there's no way Dr. Brenner could be Mr. Big."

Shraga lifted his hands. "So who's left?"

"Only all the other scientists," Ari said sourly. "Now we have thirty suspects instead of four or five."

"Plus Mr. Stewart," Shai said firmly.

Ari eyed him. "You keep bringing up the hotel manager, Shai. How come?"

Shai shrugged. "He always seems to be around when things happen. He was there when Mindy got burned —"

"But he brought her ice," Niki protested.

"Which is the worst possible thing for burns," Shai retorted. "Besides, maybe he just wanted to look good."

"How *is* Mindy doing, Daddy?" Shraga asked.

"She's much better, *baruch Hashem*, " Dr. Morgenstern replied. "I think they'll discharge her tomorrow. She'll come back to the hotel to sleep and then go home with us the following morning."

"The week's almost over," Pinny murmured, half to himself. "We don't have much time left to track down Mr. Big."

"I still say it was Mr. Stewart." Shai folded his arms stubbornly. "It took him a long time to appear after the flowerbox fell down. Maybe he was busy coming downstairs after pushing it himself!"

Dr. Katz shuddered at the memory.

"And *anyone* could have followed us to the farm," Shai continued, touching his sore shoulder. "I think it was Mr. Stewart."

"But how could Mr. Stewart know about Little Nicky to begin with?" Pinny demanded impatiently.

Shai shrugged. "Maybe he heard about it."

"Could be," Dr. Katz agreed, "but don't forget, Shai, Mr. Big is also someone in a position to get access to Kremlin files. Otherwise, how could he be blackmailing Dr. Pim?"

"That's true." Shraga thought for a moment,

then brightened. "Dr. Brenner used to be a member of the Communist Party. *She* could have access to files from the Kremlin!"

"I thought we decided Dr. Brenner wasn't our culprit," Dr. Morgenstern said mildly. "For that matter, why are you so sure it's a scientist?"

"Well, let's be logical about it." Shraga held up one finger. "Mr. Big knew about Little Nicky's existence. One of the scientists would be most likely to know about that. Point number two." He held up a second finger. "Mr. Big is someone in the hotel. He knows what's going on, and the 'accidents' had to be arranged by someone who was right here on the spot. And as for point number three —" Shraga gave a shrug. "Well, who else could it be?"

Pinny laughed. "I'm not so sure that last point of yours is all that logical, but I have another one for you." He held up four fingers. "Point number four. Mr. Big is someone who is clever enough to tamper with electronic locks. Don't forget, he managed to get a copy of the key to this lab. That can't be easy."

"It's *supposed* to be impossible," Dr. Katz muttered.

"Well, he managed it somehow. So it *must* be one of the scientists. Nobody else could figure something like that out."

"Not necessarily," Shai said. "I am sure Mr. Stewart could get hold of a key. After all, he is the manager."

Shraga suddenly looked very thoughtful. He

was about to speak, when his father glanced at his watch and jumped to his feet.

"Eight thirty!" he exclaimed. "I'm supposed to be outside already."

"Are you taking Ma to the hospital?" Shraga asked.

Dr. Morgenstern nodded hurriedly as he moved towards the door. "We want to discuss treatment with Mindy's doctor tonight. Shmulie, your wife wants to come along. I hate to leave you in charge of all the kids like this, but — oh, no." He made a face at the experiment still bubbling on the bunsen burner. "You can't leave that by itself." He bent over the beaker and frowned. "Twenty more minutes at least. I don't want you to have to wait that long, but you'll have to stay here and babysit this thing before babysitting the kids."

"No, Abba, you won't." Pinny had a sudden gleam in his eye that Ari recognized from long experience as the start of a new idea. "*We'll* watch it for you."

"You will?" Dr. Katz looked at his son.

"We *all* will," Pinny said eagerly.

"Well..."

"Oh, let them, Shmulie," Dr. Morgenstern said. "Here, Shraga. Take my electronic key so you can lock up when it's finished. Pinny, make sure to turn the flame off in twenty-five minutes. Leave the beaker to cool on the lab table, all right?" he smiled goodbye and vanished into the hallway.

Dr. Katz hesitated for another moment, then

relaxed and smiled. "Well, why not? Pinny, you boys can babysit for our experiment while I tend to the little ones. See you later, boys." He waved a hand and went out. The door clicked shut behind him, locking automatically.

"Pinny," Ari snapped as soon as Dr. Katz was gone, "are you totally out of your mind? Do you think I have nothing better to do besides sit around and watch some purple liquid boiling away on a —"

"You don't get it," Pinny interrupted, looking extremely pleased with himself. "This experiment of Abba's is cooking on a gas flame, right?"

"Yeah. So?"

"So, don't you see? It's a fire! A perfectly kosher flame!"

"A perfectly ko—" Ari looked at him with his mouth open. Shraga laughed out loud.

"Perfect, Pinny! You're a genius!" Shraga darted for the door. "I'll be right back with everything we need." He ran out and down the corridor towards the lobby.

"I don't understand," Niki said plaintively. "What is so kosher about the bunsen burner? And what is Shraga getting?"

Pinny grinned and clapped him on the shoulder. "Fire itself is always kosher, Niki. It's pots and surfaces that are a problem. But just plain fire? We can have our barbecue right here at the bunsen burners! Shraga went to get the hot dogs and a couple of sticks from outside so we can roast 'em."

"And the potatoes?" Shai asked eagerly. "Will he get potatoes, too?"

"If he can carry that much, he will!" Pinny turned to Ari with a mischievous light in his eye. "Still not interested in watching Abba's experiment for him?"

Ari chuckled. "I don't mind Abba's experiment that much, but yours is a whole lot better!"

They waited impatiently until Shraga returned, juggling three packages of frozen kosher hot dogs, half a bag of potatoes, and several damp sticks that he'd retrieved from the soaking woodpile in the parking lot.

"This should do it," he panted as eager hands relieved him of his burden. "We'd better wait until that experiment is finished, though."

"We don't have to. There are four bunsen burners," Pinny said. "We can use the other three. Come on, I'm starved! Let's get to it."

They tore off the plastic wrapper and carefully pierced the frozen hot dogs with their sticks. Ari turned the three remaining flames onto "high." Niki and Pinny started roasting their hot dogs immediately, while Shai and Shraga tried to hammer a stick into a raw potato. The first potato slid off the stick. The second one split in two. On the third try, they finally succeeded.

Laughing and talking, they held their hot dogs and potatoes over the blue gas flames. The delicious smells of sizzling hot dogs and roasting potatoes filled the laboratory.

"A whole lot easier than a bonfire," Shraga said approvingly.

"Why, thank you," Pinny grinned.

"Should we have a *kumzitz*?" Ari asked with a smirk.

"A what?" Niki looked from Ari to Pinny.

"A sing-in," Pinny explained. "Singing songs around the fire. You do that around a bonfire, but I can't imagine doing it around a bunsen burner!"

Ari made guitar-playing motions with his potato. "Nah, you're right. It doesn't work." Grinning, he put the potato back over the flame.

The delicious smells grew even stronger. The hot dogs began to curl and drip.

"This was the best idea ever," Niki sighed.

"I think they're almost ready," Shraga said, eyeing his hot dog critically.

"They should be," Pinny said. "The fire's certainly hot enough."

"And we're certainly making enough smoke," Ari added, waving his free hand in front of his face. "I hope that it won't do any harm to Abba's experiment."

"Nah, that beaker is sealed. It should be okay." Pinny took his eyes off his hot dog to glance at the clock on the wall. "It's been almost half an hour, though, so I guess we'd better get it off the flame."

"Good," said Shai. "Then we will have another flame to work with."

Pinny took a pair of tongs and lifted the beaker off the fire, placing it on the wooden table in the corner.

"There," he said. "That should do it." He came back to the bunsen burners. "Now we've got four flames, five or six roasted hot dogs, and three half-roasted potatoes. Shall we dig in?"

"Dig in?" Niki repeated.

"Start eating."

"Oh, yes!" Niki drew his hot dog away from the fire and sniffed it appreciatively. "It is ready, I think. Everybo —"

Suddenly, out of nowhere, a siren shrieked.

Niki stopped in mid-syllable.

Shai froze with a hot dog halfway to his mouth.

The siren sounded again, wailing urgently up and down the scale.

They all stared at each other. The wail sent shivers of fear down their backs. Where was it coming from?

What did it mean?

What was going on?

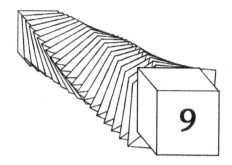

What's Wrong with Shraga?

For one heart-stopping moment, Shraga was convinced that the siren was some kind of alert, warning of imminent attack. He remained frozen in place, too scared to move. The same fear was mirrored in the other boys' eyes; Shai's face was especially white.

It's Little Nicky, Shraga thought wildly. Mr. Big found the red diskette and broke the passwords. He's going to destroy the hotel and bring it crashing down over our heads!

The siren continued to wail.

The sound of footsteps pounding in the corridor outside shook the boys out of their paralysis. Ari was the first to realize what was happening.

"The smoke alarm!" he gasped, pointing to the

small white disk affixed to the ceiling. "We set off the smoke alarm!"

With chagrin, the boys realized that Ari was right. Their makeshift barbecue had, indeed, generated a great deal of smoke — enough to set off the lab's alarm. What were they supposed to do now?

Shai dropped his hot dog on the floor and leaped for the bunsen burners to turn them off. Smoke from their roasted hot dogs continued to rise towards the ceiling. Niki waved his hands in the air, frantically trying to fan away the smoke. Pinny darted for the wall where two lab coats hung on hooks. He snatched one off and ran back into the middle of the room, swinging it vigorously in a desperate attempt to fan the smoke away from the alarm and stop that awful noise. Shraga followed his example, waving the second lab coat wildly in the air and entangling it with Pinny's.

The siren shrieked on.

Then a scream sounded above the babble of voices in the hallway, rivalling even the wail of the fire alarm.

"The children!" Magda Brenner cried. "The children are inside!"

The voices swelled into a crescendo.

"The children!" Dr. Brenner shouted again. "I saw the children go inside! Somebody help them!"

The boys were still frantically flapping at the smoke when the door burst open. In dashed Tom Morrison, followed by a wild-eyed, disheveled Magda Brenner, Dr. Fowley, Dr. Isingard, and Ilya Pim.

"What's going on here?" Tom boomed. "Where are your parents? What set off the alarm? Is everyone all right?"

"We —"

"Where is the fire?" Ilya came dashing forward, his face pale. "Are you children all right? Who did this to you?" He clearly thought that Mr. Big had arranged for another "accident."

"It's —"

"Little children in a laboratory alone!" Dr. Brenner's dark eyes flashed. "Where are your parents? How could they allow you to remain here by —"

"All right, ENOUGH!" Tom's shout silenced them all. Only the siren continued to wail. He glanced up disgustedly at the shrieking smoke alarm. "Turn that thing off."

Pinny and Shraga, beet-red with embarrassment, frantically waved the lab coats under the alarm again — to no vail. Finally, Ari climbed up onto the counter and manually switched off the siren. The ensuing silence seemed very loud.

"Thank you," Tom said icily. "Now, then, I would like an explanation."

Shraga looked at Tom, opened his mouth, then stopped. The color slowly drained from his face, leaving him pale.

"Are you all right?" Ilya Pim hurried forward and took his arm. "The smoke — did you —"

"No," Shraga shook his head mechanically. "I'm fine."

"What happened?" Tom insisted.

Pinny took a step towards the F.B.I. Agent. "It's all my fault, really," he said bravely. "You see, our fathers both had to leave the lab, and I volunteered to watch an experiment for them."

"And the experiment...?" Tom's gaze swept the laboratory, rested momentarily at the beaker on the lab table, the potatoes and sticks, then dropped to the hot dog on the floor. "What exactly did this experiment consist of?"

Pinny's face turned even redder. "Well, we sort of used the bunsen burners for an experiment of our own," he admitted. "It was my fault..."

"Oh, come on, Pinny." Ari stepped forward and put an arm around his younger brother's shoulders. "We were all responsible," he told Tom firmly. "We were supposed to have a barbecue tonight and it got rained out. We decided to roast our hot dogs in here instead. We're all equally to blame."

Pinny threw him a grateful look.

Tom turned to the scientists crowding in the doorway. "All right, folks," he said briskly. "The show's over. If I could just ask you to step aside...?"

Dr. Isingard, tall enough to see over Tom's shoulder, glanced into the room one last time and walked out. Dr. Fowley was right behind him. Ilya Pim hesitated a moment, looking at the boys to make sure they were all right, then departed. Only Magda Brenner remained.

"Dr. Brenner?" Tom said in a polite, stiff tone.

"These boys need to be spoken to," she said angrily. "Such silly doings! In my country, they —"

"Please, Doctor." Tom gave her a reassuring smile. "Believe me, I'll make sure they get *all* the talking-to they need."

Pinny gulped.

"Well..." Magda glared at them once more, then reluctantly turned. "Very well, then."

She walked out, leaving the boys facing a very angry-looking F.B.I. Agent.

"Now, then..." Tom began.

Ten long minutes later, Tom left, his scathing lecture still ringing in their ears. The five chastened boys sat down again, staring moodily at the cold, shriveled hot dogs lying on the lab table.

"Are we really going to eat these?" Niki said doubtfully, prodding his hot dog with a dubious finger.

Ari shrugged. "I guess. Unless you feel like going to bed hungry tonight."

Pinny picked up his hot dog, then set it down again. "I can't," he sighed. "I'm still way too embarrassed about what happened."

Shai, whose hot dog had fallen on the floor and subsequently been deposited in the garbage, nodded vehemently. "And how he yelled at us!"

"I guess he was right, though," Pinny said, looking at Shai. "I mean, it was pretty dumb of us. I'm sorry I thought of it, that's all. Boy, we sure looked dumb — in front of the F.B.I. and all."

"That's not the least of it," Shraga muttered.

"What?" Pinny was startled.

"Oh, nothing." Shraga lapsed back into brooding silence.

Pinny eyed him, frowning a little. He was about to speak when Niki's comment distracted him.

"I will tell you why I am disappointed," Niki said. "After all this talk, I wanted to taste good, kosher food."

Ari laughed despite himself. "Well, it's kosher, all right, but I doubt it's very good!"

Pinny nodded ruefully. "Sorry, Niki. I'd invite you to join us for our packaged meals tomorrow, but they're not very good either."

"Maybe you could come up to Brooklyn for a day or so," Ari suggested helpfully. "My mother's cooking is out of this world."

"Out of this world...?" Niki asked.

Ari grinned. "Delicious."

"Oh."

After a few more minutes of listless conversation, the boys began to eat their cold, burnt hot dogs. From the looks on their faces, it was clear that even the packaged meals tasted better than this.

"I guess we'd better turn in," Ari finally said. "Let's get this place cleaned up and go up to our rooms. We'll get together tomorrow morning and try to work something out."

"We don't have a lot of time left," Shai warned, looking a little worried. "Tomorrow is the last day of the conference. After that, everyone will leave. How can we be detectives then?"

Pinny shoved his chair back and stood. "I don't think you have to worry about *that*," he said bitterly. "If we don't solve the case, the F.B.I. is likely to solve it — their way."

"In that case, we'd better solve the case ourselves. Right, Shraga?" Ari nudged his younger neighbor.

"What? Oh. Yes." Shraga plastered a smile on his face, but it only remained there for a few seconds before he turned away to stare at the tabletop once more.

As the boys began to clear up the remains of their barbecue, Pinny edged over to Shraga. "Shraga, what's wrong with you?" he asked softly. "Are you upset about what happened? Do you think our parents are going to be really mad at us?"

"It's not that," Shraga mumbled. He stood up hurriedly. "Come on, let's go."

They finished cleaning up and filed out of the lab. Shraga was the last one out. He closed the door and heard it lock behind him, but instead of turning away and following the others down the corridor, he remained standing in place for a long moment, his face troubled and pale.

"Shraga?" Shai called. "Are you coming?"

With a sigh, Shraga hurried after the boys. But all the way through the lobby and up the elevator to the third floor, he remained silent. Thinking.

By eleven thirty the following morning, the sun had dried the wet grass and grounds. Except for the damp wood piled at the end of the parking lot, there was no sign of last night's downpour as the boys settled down on a sunny patch of lawn to discuss their options.

They'd had a difficult morning: first dragging themselves out of bed after two nights of little or no sleep, then going off to the kosher hotel for minyan and breakfast and receiving a very stern lecture from Drs. Katz and Morgenstern for their thoughtless escapade the night before. Even the learning session after breakfast fell somehow flat. Pinny blamed Shraga for that.

"What's wrong with you this morning, Shraga?" Dr. Morgenstern had asked. "You look like you're a million miles away."

Shraga had given his father a weak smile of apology and tried to concentrate, but he seemed to be staring at the page of his *gemara* instead of studying it. After a few more attempts to get his son more involved in learning, Dr. Morgenstern had given up and worked with Shai, who was determined to show that he was just as intelligent as the others. But Pinny had been distracted by Shraga's peculiar behavior. What was *wrong* with him? Why was he acting like this?

Now, as they sat down in a rough circle, Pinny decided to tackle Shraga head-on.

"What's on your mind?" he asked him pointedly. "You haven't said more than a dozen words since that mess in the lab last night."

Shraga stared at his shoes. "There's nothing to

say," he muttered.

Pinny scowled. "Why can't you tell us —"

"Look, Shai had a good point last night," Ari interrupted. "If we're going to track down Mr. Big, we have to do it *now*. Today."

"Yes, but how?" Niki gestured helplessly. "We have no clues. No suspects. How can we find him?"

Pinny propped his chin in his hands. "Our problem is that the trail is too cold," he said thoughtfully.

"It is very warm today," Niki said, bewildered.

"That's not what I mean, Niki. The *case* is too cold. Too old. Any clue we have stretches back way too far. I mean, Ilya Pim was blackmailed before he arrived in America. All those e-mail messages are impossible to track down. Even the 'accidents' can't help us; anyone in the hotel could have caused them. If we're supposed to find a criminal according to motive, means, and opportunity..."

"Say that again?" Shai asked.

"Motive." Pinny ticked off the points. "That's the reason why someone does something. In this case, that's easy: Mr. Big is after Little Nicky, either to sell to a terrorist organization or to give to some other country. Means is the ability to commit the crime. In this case, it had to be someone capable of getting a key to the lab — which is supposed to be impossible — and someone who's also capable of getting into the Kremlin files to blackmail Dr. Pim. That can't help us, because we don't know who can or can't do that. Opportunity is figuring out who had a chance to commit the crime, who was around when it happened. Who can we cross out? Nobody. Almost everyone was in the dining room when the water urn tipped over; half the hotel probably saw us leaving to go to the farm and could have followed us; and as for the flowerbox, it fell from an unused room. If someone managed to get inside, it'd be a cinch to push it over and then run downstairs so he would seem innocent. The E-mail messages? The whole world has access to a computer these days. So what are we left with?"

"Nothing," Ari said with a sigh.

"Nothing," Niki echoed.

"No," Shai said stubbornly. "There must be someone that is more suspicious than the others."

"Like Mr. Stewart?" Ari teased him. "Okay, let's take him. Motive, means, and opportunity, just like Pinny said. Motive? He qualifies. Opportunity? Okay, he qualifies for that too. Means? Who knows? But how can we pin anything on him?"

"I am more worried about Dr. Brenner," Niki said suddenly.

"*Her*? I can't imagine her hurting anybody."

"But she is always around," Niki insisted. "Even last night. She knew we were in the lab. Why should she pay attention to where a group of boys go?"

"You might have a point there," Pinny said. "But still..." He threw up his hands with exasperation. "We're just going in circles.

"We sure are." Ari looked at Shraga. "Well,

Shraga? Any ideas?"

"Huh?" Shraga seemed to wake from a reverie that had taken him far away.

"I *said*," Ari repeated with elaborate patience, "we're in the market for a good idea."

Shraga scrambled awkwardly to his feet. "Look, I'm sorry. I have to take care of something." He began to walk away, slowly at first, then breaking into a run.

They all stared after him.

"Something is on that kid's mind," Ari said aloud. "I wonder what?"

"Yeah, so do I." Pinny scowled. Until now, he and Shraga had been getting along just fine. He'd almost managed to forget the cold war that had existed between the two of them for the last eleven and a half years of their life. But now? Shraga was treating him so coolly that they seemed to be back where they'd started.

The meeting broke up soon after that. With nothing resolved and nothing else to do, Pinny set out to search for Shraga and try to figure out what was wrong. He found him sitting in a corner of the lobby, brooding as he stared unseeingly at the mirrored wall.

"All right, Shraga," Pinny said bluntly. "I want to know what's the matter with you."

Shraga jumped. "Pinny! I — I didn't see you."

"So I noticed." Pinny leaned over the back of the couch. "We want to have another meeting after lunch."

"A meeting?" Shraga gulped. "Uh, I don't know, Pinny. I don't think I can make it..."

"How come?" Pinny demanded.

"I just can't." Shraga pulled himself to his feet. "I have something to work on this afternoon. I'm sorry."

Pinny's fists clenched as he watched Shraga hurry away. That Morgenstern! So he had something to work on, huh? What was he planning? To solve the mystery himself and get all the credit? He'd thought that they'd agreed to solve the mystery in order to clear their fathers' name, but Shraga seemed to be more interested in glory-hunting. *Why* wouldn't he tell Pinny what was on his mind?

"I saw the whole thing," Ari said quietly, coming up to Pinny's side. "What did he say?"

"Nothing." Pinny's face was like a thundercloud. "Boy, was I wrong about that kid. I was starting to think that he might be a good guy after all, but look how he's acting! Forget it. I can live just fine without Shraga Morgenstern."

"Hey, come on," Ari protested. "Give him the benefit of the doubt, will you? So he's upset about something. He'll come around after a while."

"Forget it," Pinny said again coldly. "From here on in, Shraga Morgenstern and I are going our separate ways." And with that, he stalked away, leaving his older brother staring unhappily after him.

Shraga Morgenstern trudged up the stairs to the third floor, his brain whirling. He wasn't used to trusting his intuition; he preferred slow, logical thinking. But this time, he wasn't so sure. Everything seemed to fit in place with the sudden thought that had hit him like a ton of bricks the night before.

The only trouble was, the idea itself was so bizarre!

Shraga tried to think things through clearly. What did Mr. Big have to have? The knowledge of Little Nicky's existence. The ability to blackmail Ilya Pim. The opportunity to cause the three "accidents." And, most important of all, the ability to obtain the electronic key to his father's lab.

It all fitted together, like a puzzle whose missing piece had just fallen into place. But if he was right, then the ramifications were almost too frightening to think about. And how could he ever prove it?

None of the boys would believe him. He couldn't tell them about his suspicions without finding some kind of proof. No, much as he longed to tell the others about his fears, he didn't dare. He had to come up with some kind of plan and prove who was really Mr. Big, once and for all.

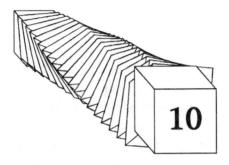

10

Detective vs. Detective

Chaim Morgenstern watched his older brother toy at his food at lunchtime, which was hardly surprising. But Shraga was obviously avoiding the eyes of the other boys at the table, and that wasn't usual at all.

"What's wrong with you?" Chaim asked.

"Me?" Shraga gave him a quick, sidelong glance, then turned away. "Oh, nothing."

"Something's bothering you," Chaim persisted. "Here you and Pinny were best friends for the last couple of days, and now all of a sudden you're not even talking to each other. What gives?"

"Nothing."

"Oh, sure. Nothing." Chaim felt himself getting hot under the collar again. "You've been treating me like a baby from day one, and I'm sick of it! Tell me what's happening."

"Chaim — *leave me alone.*"

Chaim recoiled as if slapped. He glared at his brother for another moment, then shoved back his chair. His mother looked at him with surprise.

"What's wrong, Chaim?" she asked.

"Nothing," Chaim mumbled. "I'd like to be excused. Please," he added from between clenched teeth.

"All right," Mrs. Morgenstern said quietly. "Don't forget a *berachah acharonah.*"

Chaim looked disgustedly at his plate, then transferred the glare to Shraga. "I didn't even eat a *kezayis,* Ma." Without another word, he strode away. If this was the way his older brother wanted to behave, he would just have to put a plan of his own into operation. Something he'd been thinking about for a long time now...

"Is everything all right, Shraga?" Mrs. Morgenstern asked, leaning across the table.

"Yes, Ma." Shraga avoided his mother's eye.

"Do you know what's bothering Chaim?"

"I don't think it's anything, really." Shraga still refused to look at his mother. "He's just a little upset."

Pinny, overhearing the conversation, glowered at his former fellow detective. I wish I knew what was bothering you, he thought angrily. I wish I knew what *you* have on your mind.

Right then and there, Pinny made up his own mind. Enough of this. If Shraga wanted to go solo, then all agreements were off. The Morgenstern kid was obviously on a hot lead of his own, and just as obviously, he wasn't interested in sharing it with anyone. Well, if that's the way he wanted it, it was fine with Pinny. He'd shadow Shraga himself and find out exactly what he was up to!

Richard Fowley, seated comfortably in an armchair in the reading lounge, raised an eyebrow as Shraga came in. "Yes, young man?" he drawled. "Did you come to look at another issue of *Tomorrow's Science*?"

"N-no, sir." Shraga stopped in the middle of the room and stood there, fidgeting. "I'd like to ask you something."

Fowley frowned. "I thought you had decided that I wasn't the guilty party you were looking for."

"We agreed not to tell anyone who you are," Shraga said as evenly as he could. He could feel drops of sweat breaking out on his forehead. "And really, Dr. Fowley, I think you owe us a little appreciation. We're keeping your secret for you. Why can't you just answer a few questions for me?"

Fowley laid down his copy of the *New York Times*. "I suppose I do owe you lads a favor," he conceded. "What would you like to know?"

As Shraga quizzed him about his hotel room and the rooms on either side, Pinny remained just outside the door to the reading lounge, listening hard. Why did Shraga want to know so much about people on the third floor? They were on the third floor themselves. So were Fowley, and Isingard, and half the other people involved in the convention. Why the sudden curiosity?

It didn't make sense.

Shraga seemed to be finished questioning Fowley. Pinny hurriedly ducked into a small, deserted room nearby, watching breathlessly as Shraga left the room and walked back down the corridor. Shraga's hands were jammed into his pockets and his head was down; there was little chance that he'd notice Pinny. Sure enough, he walked right past Pinny's hiding place, muttering something to himself as he headed back towards the lobby.

Pinny let Shraga walk another thirty paces before he stepped out of the little room to follow him. Something was bothering Shraga. Bothering him a lot. What was going on?

Pinny, preoccupied with his thoughts, didn't notice someone trailing behind him, observing everything he did.

"Dr. Isingard!"

The tall, silver-haired scientist, standing right next to the huge fountain in the middle of the lobby, turned inquiringly as Shraga hurried up to him.

"Good afternoon, young man," Isingard greeted him. "What exciting events do you boys have planned for today? More playing at spies? Bonfires in laboratories? Or merely a new suspect?"

Shraga smiled sheepishly at the Norwegian. "Nothing, sir. I was just wondering — were you able to find those birds you were looking for? The *caro — calo —*"

"*Calorinus glarimus.*" Isingard looked amused. "Yes, I did. I photographed them and recorded their birdsong this morning. Very kind of you to ask."

"Uh, thanks. I'm glad." Shraga shifted his weight from one foot to the other. "Well, sir, as long as you've already done that, I was wondering — could you possibly lend me your binoculars? For half an hour or so?"

"Indeed?" Isingard looked down his aristocratic nose at Shraga. "And may I ask why you wish to use my binoculars?"

Shraga shifted back to the other foot. "Actually, it — well, it has to do with detective work..." His voice trailed off.

"I see." Isingard shook his head, but he was still smiling. "Very well, young man. If you come to my laboratory at three o'clock, I will lend you my binoculars."

"Thank you very much, sir," Shraga babbled nervously. He turned and hurried away.

Isingard watched him go, a trace of amusement still on his lips. Then he turned and walked right past Pinny Katz, who was huddled on a couch nearby. He didn't notice a third figure standing in the corner, watching his every move.

Pinny stooped and pretended to tie his shoe at his bedroom door, while actually watching Shraga out of the corner of his eye. Shraga glanced at him briefly, then opened his own door and disappeared inside.

Pinny swung open the door to his room and hesitated in the doorway. Ari, sprawled comfortably in the armchair and playing idly with his *kugelach*, looked up at him.

"What's up, kid?" Ari flipped the *kugelach* into the air. "Are you interested in planning another meeting? Well, why don't you come in and close the door?"

"I —" Pinny looked back towards Shraga's room. Chaim Morgenstern was just going inside.

"Well?" Ari said impatiently. "Look, Pinny, either come in or come out."

Pinny glanced down the hall again. There was Shraga, coming out of his room and walking towards the elevator. Why had he gone in there for a total of ten seconds? It didn't make sense. "I'm going out," he told Ari hurriedly. "I'll see you later." He slammed the door shut behind him. Ari stared at the closed door for a moment, then shrugged and dismissed the entire incident.

Three doors down the hallway, Pinny raised his fist to knock on the Morgenstern boys' door just as Chaim opened it.

"Chaim," Pinny said quickly, "what did Shraga do while he was in here?"

"What?" Chaim looked at him strangely.

"Shraga was just here," Pinny repeated. "What did he do?"

Chaim slid out of the room and closed the door

behind him. "He pulled the curtains back and opened the balcony door. Why?"

"Just asking. Talk to you later." Pinny dashed over to the elevator and looked at the glowing number above the doors. Shraga had gone down to the lobby. Without another word, he ran to the stairwell, taking the steps two at a time in his hurry to stay on Shraga's trail.

He was too distracted to notice the soft echo to his footsteps on the stairs.

Three o'clock came and went. Pinny watched Shraga tap on the door to Isingard's lab, speak to the scientist for a moment, then come back down the hallway, carrying the binoculars in their expensive leather case. Pinny shrank into the corner as Shraga walked through the lobby, a troubled look on his face as he fiddled with the binoculars. Shraga was clearly on the trail of something here. And just as clearly, he was seriously worried.

For the first time, Pinny felt a twinge of alarm. Was Shraga only trying his hand at finding a solo solution to the mystery — or was something seriously wrong? Ari was right about judging Shraga favorably. But in that case, what explanation would there be for the other boy's strange behavior?

He watched Shraga train the binoculars on the hotel. What could he be looking for? Something on the third floor, probably; after all those questions he'd asked Fowley, the third floor definitely had a role to play in this mess. But *what?*

Pinny had no binoculars, but he peered up at the third floor himself. The fourth room from the left had open curtains fluttering out the partially open balcony door. What was he looking at? He glanced back and saw Shraga nod once, then sigh as he slipped the binoculars back into their case.

What had Shraga seen? Why the strange questions to Fowley about the residents of the third floor? And why, *why* did Shraga look so worried?

Shraga went back inside. Pinny waited a moment, then followed.

Silent as a shadow, someone followed Pinny, too.

"Well, this is our second-to-last airplane meal," Dr. Morgenstern said with forced cheerfulness. "This one, then breakfast tomorrow morning, and then we're home and back to Ma's great cooking."

"I think I'll wait till lunchtime tomorrow to eat, then," Chaim muttered, poking a leathery piece of meat with his fork.

Daniella tugged at Mrs. Morgenstern's sleeve. "Is Mindy coming back to the hotel tonight?" she asked anxiously.

Mrs. Morgenstern smiled down at her little neighbor. She knew how much Daniella revered Mindy. "Yes, she is," she said reassuringly. "Dr. Morgenstern and I are going to go pick her up right after dinner."

"I'll come along if you'd like, David," Dr. Katz volunteered.

"Thanks, Shmulie. I'd appreciate it."

Dr. Katz looked at his wife. "I think you should come along, too," he suggested. "You've been babysitting for two families practically nonstop this week. I think you could use the break."

Mrs. Katz smiled and shook her head. "Really, it's not a problem. I don't mind at all..."

"Go ahead, Ima," Ari offered. "Pinny and Shraga and I will watch the kids." He glanced across the table. "Right, guys?"

"Right," Pinny said automatically. Shraga nodded, distracted.

"Well..." Mrs. Katz hesitated, then smiled again. "All right. Thank you, boys. I appreciate it."

"We *all* appreciate it," Mrs. Morgenstern added. "But we'll put the kids to bed before we leave. We have an appointment to speak to Mindy's doctor before she's discharged, but it's not until eight thirty. There'll be plenty of time."

By eight fifteen, the younger children were settled in bed, although Daniella insisted that she wouldn't be able to sleep until Mindy was back. Ari volunteered to take be on duty first.

"First shift," he said. "Pinny, come get me at nine o'clock, okay?"

"Okay," Pinny said absently, his gaze following Shraga's back as the boy hurried down the hall towards the elevator. "I'll be back then."

He half-ran down the hall and caught up with Shraga just as the elevator doors opened. Shraga jumped nervously as Pinny followed him inside.

"Are you going to the lobby?" Shraga stammered.

Pinny pushed the button marked "L" and shrugged his shoulders. "I thought I might like one last crack at the game room," he said casually. It wasn't a lie, he told himself. He was only saying he *thought* he'd do it, not that he'd *actually* do it.

"Oh." Shraga's relief was obvious.

As soon as the elevator doors opened, Shraga hurried across the lobby, passing Chaim Morgenstern sitting on one of the couches and Tom Morrison by the front doors. The F.B.I. Agent spoke to Shraga for a moment. Shraga looked down at his feet and mumbled something. Tom nodded and waved him through.

Pinny started forward, then stopped. No, it would be better to go out the side entrance — it would be too obvious to go out the front doors.

He hurried across the lobby and out the smaller entrance, half-running around the corner of the building to find out where Shraga had gone. He *had* to find out what Shraga was up to!

Then he caught sight of Shraga. He was standing near the wall of the hotel, his hand on a large drainpipe and his head tilted back as he squinted at something high above him. Even as Pinny watched, Shraga took a deep breath, settled his glasses more firmly on his nose, and began to climb.

This was too much. Pinny dashed forward. "Shraga!" he hissed.

Startled, Shraga let go of the drainpipe and slid three feet down to the ground. He stumbled, regained his balance, then whirled around and raised his fists in a defensive stance.

"Shraga, it's only me. Relax."

"Pinny," Shraga gasped, fear and relief mingled in his voice. "What are you doing here?"

Pinny stalked forward until the two boys were practically nose-to-nose. "I might ask you the same thing," he said. "What exactly were you trying to do?"

Shraga swallowed. "Please, Pinny." He sounded almost desperate. "I — I can't tell you, but it's important. Really important. It's about the case."

"Fine," Pinny said. "I'll just join you. What exactly are you doing?"

"I can't tell you. I *can't.*" Shraga swallowed again. "Pinny, please just let me go."

"No." Pinny leaned forward. Now they *were* nose-to-nose. "Why — can't — you — tell me?"

Shraga turned away. "You'd never believe me," he whispered.

Pinny grabbed Shraga's chin and forced the other boy to face him. "Try me."

Shraga stared at him for a long second, then jerked his chin away.

"All right," he said in a low voice. "All right. You asked for it. Listen to this..."

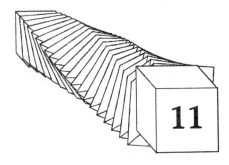

The Search

S hraga turned to face the wall, running one hand lightly along the length of the drainpipe. "I think I know the identity of Mr. Big."

"Really?" Pinny grabbed Shraga's shoulder and pulled him around again. "Who?"

Shraga leaned forward and whispered urgently in Pinny's ear. Pinny looked dumbfounded.

"What? Are you out of your mind? Why on earth..."

"Pinny, we don't have time," Shraga interrupted. His face looked desperate. "Believe me. I know he's not there right now, but I don't know how much time we have. His balcony is right under this drainpipe, so we can climb up and search his room. But we have to move fast." The urgency in his voice convinced Pinny.

"Okay, okay," Pinny surrendered. "We'll do it

your way. Let's get going." He still sounded dazed.

Cautiously they began to climb, their sneakered feet feeling for toeholds in the dark. As they passed the second story and started up towards the third, someone else put a hand on the drainpipe and began the climb.

The two boys clambered over the wall of the balcony and paused for a moment to get their breaths.

"Now what?" Pinny hissed. His shock had receded, leaving skepticism in its place.

Shraga set his jaw. "Now we go in. Let's work fast — he might come back any minute."

"What are we looking for anyway?" Pinny whispered as they carefully slid the glass door wide open and went inside.

Shraga spoke over his shoulder. "The red diskette."

Pinny sucked in his breath and looked around the room. It was a replica of his own, only much neater. "*Here*?" He was incredulous. Then, seeing the stubborn, almost desperate expression that settled on Shraga's face, he backed own. "Okay, okay. Where do we start?"

"Anywhere." Shraga bent over the little desk and started opening drawers. "Just hurry."

Pinny made the first find. "Take a look at this," he hissed as he drew a small attache case out from under the bed. "It's got combination locks."

Shraga came over and examined it. "Is it locked?"

Pinny tried it. "Yes."

"Shake it," Shraga suggested. "See if you can tell what's inside."

Pinny shook it cautiously. "Something heavy, I'd say. Maybe metallic."

"Keep looking." Shraga put the case aside.

"I've got something!" Pinny whispered presently. "If I'm not mistaken, it's a radio transmitter." He brought it over to Shraga. "Take a look. What do you think?"

Shraga examined the radio. "I think this is more than a transmitter," he said. "I think it's a short-wave radio. That means that he could talk to someone halfway around the world."

"Someone halfway around — you mean, terrorists?" Pinny sounded thunderstruck. Was there something to Shraga's mad accusation after all?

"Or Russians. Yes." With determination, Shraga turned his concentration back to his own search.

Pinny returned the portable phone and the shortwave radio to the suitcase. He searched among the shelves of the closet, running his hand along the top shelves where he couldn't see. He found plenty of dust, but no red diskette.

Shraga opened and closed bureau drawers in frantic haste. They'd been in the room for fifteen minutes already. It was close to nine o'clock. The whole thing was taking much too long.

Someone, crouched on the balcony outside and peeking into the room, thought so, too. As he strained to catch his breath after the climb, he tried to see what the others were doing. Searching for something, he decided, watching them. But what? And whose room was this?

Pinny checked in the suitcase once more. He slid his hand into the side pocket and pulled out a card case. His eyes widened as he flipped it open and saw the large variety of identification cards tucked inside.

"Shraga," he whispered. "There's a whole bunch of cards here... They're all I.D. cards or driver's licenses!" He stared at Shraga. "What's going on here? What kind of guy has four different names?"

"Someone working under an alias," Shraga answered grimly without looking up. He glanced again at his watch. Twenty minutes. It was taking too long. "We'd better give it up," he said unhappily. "Try to put everything back the way you found it. We don't want him to realize that anyone was here."

He closed a final drawer. Pinny put the suitcase back in the closet and arranged it as he'd found it, then came around the bed and hauled Shraga to his feet. "Come on," he said. "Let's get out of here."

"Yeah," Shraga said, feeling close to panic. Twenty-two minutes. "Is everything the way we found —"

He froze. Pinny froze. On the balcony, Chaim Morgenstern froze too.

Footsteps in the hallway had stopped at the door.

There was the sound of a lock sliding open.

There was no time to try to dodge out onto the balcony, and the closet was much to narrow to hide in. Without stopping to think, both boys bolted into the bathroom. Pinny clambered into the bathtub. Shraga stepped in beside him and drew the curtain shut.

Someone stepped into the room.

Pinny and Shraga exchanged frightened glances. Had they left any signs of their search? Would the owner of the room realize that someone had been there?

The footsteps came into the room, then stopped. There was a muffled exclamation, then the sound of drawers opening and closing, and items being rapidly shuffled around.

Pinny and Shraga looked at each other despairingly. They hadn't been careful enough. What would happen now?

The footsteps came closer. The door to the bathroom slammed open.

The two boys crouched behind the shower curtain, afraid to even breathe.

The curtain ripped away. A man stood there, tall and muscular, a look of fury in his blue eyes and a wicked-looking pistol in his hand.

It was Tom Morrison.

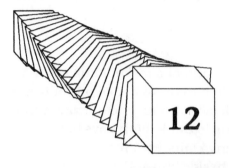

Mr. Big

What are you two doing here?" Tom demanded coldly.

Pinny wished he could turn into some kind of little bug and crawl away. Shraga, his face white and stiff, eased in front of Pinny. This was his fault. "I was looking for something," he said in a quivering voice.

"Were you, now," Tom said softly. It sounded even more chilling than the angry tones of a moment before. "And exactly what were you searching my room for?"

Shraga's gaze was fixed on Tom's face. "I was looking for the red diskette," he said, straining to keep his voice steady. "I'm sure you know what that is."

Even now, Pinny hoped against hope that this was all a mistake. He looked up at the F.B.I. Special Agent, waiting for him to give his easy smile and put away his gun.

But he didn't smile. And his gun still pointed at them.

Shraga kept talking, stalling for time as he frantically tried to think of some way of getting out of this predicament. "You're Mr. Big," he said. "I started to suspect you last night. When the smoke alarm went off, you were the first one into the lab to see what was happening. How did you manage to get in? You must have had a key."

"He has a master card," Pinny whispered from behind Shraga's shoulder. He couldn't believe this was happening. "He showed us, on the first day."

"I wasn't there." Shraga kept looking at Morrison. "That explains an awful lot, though. You had a master card, so you could give a copy of it to the thief. You knew about the secret weapon — after all, you were brought here to guard it. As an F.B.I. agent, *if* that's what you really are, you probably had access to Kremlin files." He licked his lips. "You're blackmailing Ilya Pim, aren't you?"

Tom said nothing, but his eyes were hard and furious.

"As for opportunity..." Shraga gulped again, remembering the flowerbox crashing down, Mindy's shriek of pain, Shai's desperate leap for the fence with a furious bull right behind him. "You were there when the water urn fell over..."

"So were a lot of other people," Tom said, his voice still dangerously soft.

"A lot of other people couldn't have gotten into

a locked room to push over a flowerbox," Shraga countered. "And it was you who suggested our walk to the farm," Shraga continued implacably — though his voice shook.

Pinny sagged against the wall and closed his eyes.

"And the bull," Shraga went on. "That bull was set off by a gunshot. It was probably that gun you're holding that frightened the bull into charging us."

"Circumstantial evidence, kid," Tom snorted. "Nobody's going to believe a story like that."

"Maybe not." Shraga tore his gaze away from that horrible-looking weapon in Tom's hands and looked up at Mr. Big's face. "But we're going to tell the authorities — the *real* authorities — about this. Our parents, too. We're not going to let you get away with blaming our fathers for something you did."

"Is that so?" Tom leaned forward. Shraga and Pinny shrank back. "Get moving," he ordered. "Both of you. Into the room."

The boys looked at each other. They looked at Tom — at Mr. Big. Then they looked at the gun in his hand.

Without a word, they walked out of the bathroom and stood in the middle of the hotel room. Tom had them to walk over to the floor lamp and sit down with their backs to each other and the lamp in between them. Then he tied their hands behind their backs, bound their ankles together, and cuffed their bound hands to the lamp pole for good measure.

"That'll hold you for a while," Tom said coolly.

He slipped the gun into his pocket and looked at Pinny. "You know, kid, you told me that the two of you were a pair of geniuses, but I didn't believe you. Too bad, I guess. I underestimated you. Well, now it's just a matter of getting rid of a mistake. It won't take me too long."

Tom leaned over and flicked on the radio. He turned the volume up. The radio announcer gave a loud discourse on the benefits of using Softi tissues.

"That'll keep anyone from hearing you yell for help," he said pleasantly. "I'll be back in a few minutes with some...special equipment. Then I can take care of you — permanently."

He flicked off the light and went out.

Chaim Morgenstern had seen Tom Morrison enter the room. He saw him yank his gun out of his pocket and enter the bathroom. He heard his brother talking and then saw Tom march both boys out at gunpoint into the middle of the room.

After that, Chaim didn't see anymore. Terrified that Tom would spot him and take him captive too, the boy dived recklessly over the balcony wall and climbed — or, more accurately, slid — down the drainpipe as fast as he could. He had to go for help — and fast!

Pinny and Shraga sat on the floor in the dark room. They'd managed to shuffle around until they were sitting side by side, but there was little else they could do. The knots in the ropes binding them were all too secure — Tom had made sure of that. And there were the metal cuffs connecting them to the lamp. They were well and truly trapped.

"I can't believe how stupid I was," Pinny said bitterly. "I trusted him. I believed in him, Shraga. I thought he was a genuine hero, a real good guy. Remember how he always said that 'he's on our side'?" Pinny didn't wait for an answer. "I was always ready to run to him and tell him what was happening," he continued miserably. "Anytime we came up with a clue, I was ready to run to him and tell him. You were the only one who realized that we had to keep our distance."

"That's not true, Pinny," Shraga said quietly. "I never suspected Tom. I just didn't want to go to the F.B.I. without proof. And I never would have suspected him at all if you hadn't kept saying that Mr. Big had to be someone with access to the key to the lab. If you hadn't made that point, I don't even know if I would have realized what was happening when he burst into the lab last night."

"That's nice of you to say, but I was still dumb. I —"

Shraga sighed. "Pinny, let's not worry about that now, okay? I was just as stupid, letting us get caught like this. We need to find a way out now, not blame each other."

"There *is* no way out," Pinny whispered. "We can't break through metal handcuffs. And he'll be back any minute." He shivered in the warm room.

"Shraga, I'm — I'm sorry that I thought you were trying to solve the case by yourself. I should've realized that you were really worried about something." He shivered again. "I'm glad you're here with me, Shraga. I wouldn't be able to face this alone."

"Let's say some *tehillim*," Shraga suggested softly. "We can't get ourselves out of this mess. Only Hashem can help us now."

And as the two boys davened together, they found comfort in something else as well. In fear and prayer, a friendship that had been waiting to happen for a dozen years was finally brought into being. If only they could find a way to escape...

But there was none. Only eight minutes had gone by when the key scraped in the lock and Tom returned.

"Well, now," Tom drawled, thumbs hooked into his belt as he eyed Shraga and Pinny. "Time to take care of you two permanently."

They stared back at him. There was nothing to say. With the radio still on maximum volume, nobody would hear any shouts or cries for help. They were bound hand and foot, completely helpless. There seemed to be no escape. If only somebody knew where they were!

"The first step is to get you out of the hotel. It's really a pity you stumbled onto this, boys. I was almost beginning to like you.

He leaned down to remove the handcuffs and tossed them onto the bed. Then he drew a tightly corked vial out of his pocket and poured a clear-colored liquid onto a towel, soaking it thoroughly.

"You first," he said, reaching down and dragging Shraga up into a half-standing position.
Shraga struggled as best as he could, but Tom held
him easily with one hand twisted in the front of his
shirt. "Can't let that great brain of yours have a
chance to come up with an escape, now, can I? It
never pays to be too smart, kid. Too bad you had
to learn it the hard way."

Still holding Shraga up with one hand, Tom
pressed the wet cloth firmly over his captive's nose
and mouth. Shraga stiffened at the sickly-sweet
smell that flooded his senses. Instinctively, he tried
to get away, but Tom held him fast.

The whole thing was so fantastic, so much like
a bizarre adventure story, that it was a moment
before Shraga realized what was happening. He
was being drugged! Chloroform, or something... He
felt himself grow dizzy as he involuntarily breathed
in the horribly sweet fumes. With his glasses askew
and the drug beginning to take effect, Tom's intent,
sinister face seemed to shimmer and waver before
his eyes. His bound ankles scuffled desperately on
the carpet. He had to escape!

Pinny watched, horrified, as Shraga's hands,
bound behind his back, twisted frantically in an
attempt to get away. Shraga tried to turn his head,
tried to fight the effects of the chloroform, but Pinny
could see that his friend was already weakening.
The silent struggle lasted a few more seconds; then
Shraga's eyelids sagged shut, his legs turned to

rubber, and he collapsed to the floor.

Tom let go of Shraga's shirt and watched the boy fall into an unconscious heap at his feet. He took a second towel and tied it across Shraga's mouth, gagging him against any possible outcry. He looked down at his prisoner for a brief moment, rubbing his hands with satisfaction, then stepped over Shraga's motionless body and reached out for Pinny.

"Now you, kid. Hey, don't look so scared! There's nothing to worry about." Tom's white teeth, which had always flashed at him before with such a pleasant smile, now showed in a merciless sneer. "Trust me. You won't feel a thing."

Pinny's agile mind raced frantically, wildly. There was no way to avoid the chloroform. Already Tom had pressed the wet towel to his face. Already Pinny felt the first insidious effects of the anesthetic drug. There was no way he could avoid breathing in the soporific fumes, but maybe...

Pinny held his breath, then closed his eyes and forced himself to go limp, allowing Tom to support all his weight. Tom would think that he'd already lost consciousness. Maybe he could remain just awake enough to do something later on, while Tom was off-guard.

The towel remained pressed against his nose and mouth. Pinny saw flashes of red and purple against his closed eyelids. Why didn't Tom take the towel away? A feeling of dizziness swept over him. *Stay awake*, he told himself desperately. *Don't give in. Don't breathe. Stay awake...*

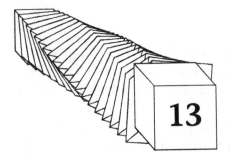

The Chase

Chaim Morgenstern dropped the last three feet to the ground and set off for the lobby at a dead run. He had to tell someone what was happening, but who? His parents weren't there. The Katzes weren't there. He couldn't exactly tell the F.B.I. agents that their leader was a crook. It would all take much too long, and who knew when Tom would do something horrible to Pinny and his brother?

Ari, Chaim thought desperately. Ari can help.

Chaim burst through the lobby and bolted across towards the stairwell. Just as he flung the door open, he came face-to-face with Ari Katz, coming down the stairs.

"Ten after nine," Ari muttered. "Pinny should've been back already. I wish —" He stopped short as a wild-eyed Chaim grabbed his arm.

"Ari!" Chaim gasped. "Pinny! Tom! Mr. Big! Shraga!"

"What?" Ari stared. "Kid, you're not making sense."

"But I *am*," Chaim said, panic rising in his voice. "I saw them go in his room and he has a gun and he's gonna do something awful and we have to get help and —"

"Whoa!" Ari ordered, grabbing Chaim by the shoulders and giving him a good shake. "Who's 'he'? Slow down and talk to me, Chaim. Are Shraga and Pinny in trouble?"

It took another precious minute before Chaim managed to give a coherent account of what was happening. Once Ari understood, though, he wasted no time.

"We can't tell anyone about this," he said grimly. "It'll take too long to explain. Go get Niki and Shai — I saw 'em sitting at the other end of the lobby."

Chaim whirled and dashed across the lobby, Ari following more slowly as he tried to come up with some kind of plan for rescuing Shraga and Pinny from Mr. Big. Four kids. What could four kids do against Tom Morrison?

Niki and Shai came hurrying to meet him with Chaim panting behind.

"Okay," Ari said in a low voice, all too aware that they were attracting curious looks from others in the lobby. "Niki, Shai — Tom Morrison is Mr. Big. There's no time to explain. He's got Pinny and Shraga."

Niki gasped. Shai turned pale.

"We'll have to stop him ourselves," Ari continued. He turned to Chaim. "Chaim, go back to the
third floor and find a safe place to watch Tom's
door. *Don't do anything to put yourself in danger.* If
you see him come out, take the stairs and let me
know."

Chaim nodded and ran to the elevator.

"Niki, Shai, I'm going to watch by the elevators
in case he comes that way. I want you two to stand
guard by the side doors, just in case I miss him."

"All right," Shai whispered. He felt faint. Terrified. Frozen stiff. Why weren't their parents here to
help them?

"Go to it," Ari said. "And *behatzlachah.* Good
luck!"

Just before the elevator doors opened on the
third floor, Chaim was seized with a sudden burst
of panic. What if Tom were waiting right there?

The doors opened. There were indeed people
waiting for the elevator, but not Tom. Magda Brenner and Manfred Isingard filed into the elevator,
eyeing Chaim as the boy slipped past them. A hotel
bellboy, dressed in his smart uniform and cap,
waited politely for the hotel guests to enter the
elevator before he followed them inside, pushing a
bulging laundry cart.

Chaim looked nervously down the hallway. His
own room was only six doors away. It would be so
easy just to go in there and hide...

But Ari was counting on him. Shraga and Pinny needed him. And Tom Morrison's door was just eight doors in the other direction.

Chaim settled into a crouch behind the potted plant near the elevator, keeping a careful watch on Tom's door.

A flash caught his eye. Chaim looked at the carpet just in front of Tom's door. Something was lying there.

He looked again. Then his eyes widened. He broke out of concealment and ran down the hall to pick up the pair of glasses lying pathetically on the carpet, one lens cracked in two where someone had stepped on it.

Shraga's glasses.

It took another moment for the implications of that to sink in. Then, with shocked understanding, Chaim took off for the stairs like an Olympic gold-medal runner.

The elevator doors opened in the lobby. The bellboy with his cap pulled down over his eyes exited first, with Dr. Brenner and Dr. Isingard right behind him. Ari glanced at the bellboy, then at the laundry cart, then looked away. He was waiting for Tom Morrison, not for some dirty laundry.

A sudden frown crossed his face. Dirty laundry. Since when did bellboys push carts of dirty laundry through the main lobby? Why didn't he go down to the service entrance?

He looked again at the laundry cart. The bellboy

was already heading for the side exit, walking fast with his head bent down. And the laundry cart —

Something was moving inside.

Not much. A sort of tiny twitch along one side. But it was definitely there.

Ari took two steps towards the bellboy. The man walked faster.

Then Chaim Morgenstern burst out of the stairwell. "Ari!" he shrieked. Heads snapped around to look at the young boy racing towards them.

Chaim's shout was all Ari needed to confirm his suspicions. He dashed forward, shoved the bellboy to one side, and grabbed the laundry cart. The man shouted and reached for Ari, but the fifteen-year-old was already running.

The laundry cart was heavy and cumbersome. Ari pushed it as fast as he could, but the "bellboy" caught up with him easily. He grabbed Ari by the arm and gave it a quick twist. Before he knew what was happening, Ari was flying through the air. He landed on the carpet with a crash.

Gasping for breath and trying to see past the stars whirling across his vision, he picked up his head in time to see the "bellboy" grab the cart and start running again — towards the main exit, this time.

"Stop him," Ari tried to shout, but the words came out as a croak. Besides, there was too much noise for anyone to hear. Magda was shouting furiously about the boys and their pranks, Chaim was shrieking for help, the receptionist had come from behind the front desk and was demanding an explanation, and everyone else in the lobby was abuzz with questions and exclamations.

Ari staggered painfully to his feet and started after the "bellboy." The cart in front of him rolled onward, faster, towards the exit —

And then Niki and Shai came flying out of their hiding place behind the side doors. Niki tackled the uniformed man around the ankles, sending him crashing to the floor, while Shai snatched the laundry cart away from him and bolted in the opposite direction. There was a flurry of arms and legs, and then Niki was rolling away as the man sprung up and dashed after Shai.

Gasping for breath, Shai ran for the side entrance. He was almost there when the doors opened — and in came Dr. and Mrs. Morgenstern, Dr. and Mrs. Katz, Mindy Morgenstern, and the Druckers.

"Take this," Shai gasped, giving the laundry cart one last shove in the Morgensterns' direction.

"Shai, what's wrong?" Dr. Drucker grabbed his foster son by the shoulder as Dr. Morgenstern seized the laundry cart.

"It's —" Shai's lip trembled. "Oh, Abba," he wailed, burying his face in Dr. Drucker's shirt. It was the first time he'd ever called him "Abba," but that didn't matter now.

"What —" Dr. Morgenstern stared down at the laundry cart.

Ari dashed up to them and ripped the lid of the cart open. "It's Pinny and Shraga," he panted in explanation. "Mr. Big did it!" He whirled around and pelted after the uniformed bellboy, who had given up on retrieving the laundry cart and was now pounding across the lobby towards the side corridor.

"You're not getting away now," Ari gritted as he drew closer to the fleeing Mr. Big. "I won't let you!"

"Shraga and Pinny? What is Ari —" Mrs. Morgenstern peered inside the laundry cart and jumped back with shock. "Shraga!" she choked, horrified at the sight of her son lying bound and gagged inside. "And Pinny, too! What happened?"

Mrs. Katz clawed at the laundry cart. "Pinny! Are they all right?" She ripped the gag off her son's mouth. "Pinny! Speak to me!"

Pinny's eyes were half-open but unseeing. Shraga's eyes were closed, but his breathing was regular.

"They'll be okay, I think," Dr. Morgenstern muttered, feeling Shraga's pulse. "They're just — asleep? Unconscious? We need a doctor here!" He whirled around to face Shai, who was still sobbing on Dr. Drucker's shoulder. "Shai, what's going on?"

"Mr. Big," Shai said, his voice muffled.

Dr. Katz smothered an exclamation and ran across the lobby after his older son.

Ari chased Tom Morrison out of the lobby and into the laboratory corridor. He was only a few feet away now. In just another second, he would tackle the false F.B.I. agent and —

Without warning, Tom stopped short, pivoted

around, and faced Ari. His face shone with perspiration from his desperate bid for freedom. There was a gun in his hand.

"Stay back," he snapped.

Ari skidded to a halt and froze.

"Right," Tom said with satisfaction. His labored breathing eased. "You'll do just fine as a hostage. Now we're going to walk, nice and slow, down the hall to the exit at the end. Nothing's going to go wrong this time."

Ari willed himself not to change expression as the door just behind Tom quietly opened.

"You heard me, kid." Tom gestured with the gun. "Get moving, I said." He started to turn.

With a yell, Ilya Pim launched himself at Tom's back, sending him crashing to the floor. Ari pounced on the struggling men and snatched at the gun, sending it skidding down the hallway out of harm's reach. By now, Dr. Katz and Dr. Morgenstern had come running from the lobby, and they joined Dr. Pim in wrestling Mr. Big into submission.

Lights and noise from the lobby spilled into the normally quiet corridor. Magda Brenner's shrill voice rose above the rest of the clamor.

"What are those boys doing! First they set off a fire alarm, now they disturb the whole hotel..."

Mr. Stewart, the hotel manager, came bustling to the front of the crowd. He gaped at the sight of the three men holding a struggling bellboy. "*Harrumph!* I would like to know why you've attacked a member of my hotel staff! This is a respectable hotel. Never, in all my years, has anything like —"

Ari leaned down and ripped the cap off the bellboy's head. A collective gasp arose from the watchers as Tom Morrison's infuriated face came into view.

"But that's —" Dr. Brenner began.

"Isn't that —" Dr. Isingard said at the same time.

"*Harrumph!* That can't be —" sputtered Mr. Stewart.

Ilya Pim got to his feet, his face pale but his eyes proud. "Mr. Stewart," he said almost politely, "I think you should call the police."

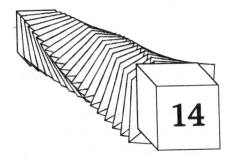

14

The Finer Points

Mrs. Katz carried another tray of cake to the dining room. "That should do it," she mused, eyeing the laden table. "Even our boys can't eat much more than that."

Mrs. Morgenstern laughed. "You can never tell, can you?"

Chaim opened another folding chair and set it down. "We've only been back home for a week, Ma," he said with a grin. "We're still making up for those packaged meals."

Shraga poked his head into the room. "The Druckers' car just turned into the driveway!" he announced.

"Oh, good." Mrs. Morgenstern wiped her hands on her apron. "Take them into the living room where the others are, Shraga. We'll sit down to supper in a few minutes."

"Hi, Shai!" Pinny greeted the Israeli, as the

Druckers followed Shraga into the living room. "Join the crowd!"

Shai looked around him and smiled. "Crowd" was putting it mildly. Dr. Katz and Dr. Morgenstern stood in one corner, arguing over something in an open *gemara,* while Mindy Morgenstern and Daniella Katz were giggling together in the opposite corner. Chaim Morgenstern valiantly tried to keep his little sister Ruchie from sitting on his baby sister Aviva. Zevy Katz played busily with a set of Lego in the middle of the room, while Ari Katz sprawled comfortably on the couch next to Pinny.

"How ya doing?" Pinny asked as Shraga and Shai sat down beside him.

"I am fine." Shai looked both of them up and down. "And you? How do you feel?"

Shraga rubbed his forehead. "All headaches and dizziness gone, *baruch Hashem!*"

"*And* he's got a new pair of glasses," Pinny added with a twinkle. "Don't worry about us, Shai. We're all right."

"But after what happened...," Shai persisted.

"No, really, we're fine. We both felt sick for a day or two, but that's all." Shraga leaned forward. "And you, Shai? Is everything okay?"

Shai studied his fingers for a moment, then looked up. "Yes," he said softly. "*All* of us are fine."

All of them. That was the best part: it was all of them. Finally, after so many years, he was part of a family. Calling the Druckers "Ima" and "Abba" came so easily now.

Mrs. Morgenstern poked her head into the room. "Dinner!" she called.

When all three families were comfortably seated and happily eating, the conversation turned once more to the events at the Lake View Hotel.

"There are an awful lot of things that I haven't figured out yet," Gitty said, frowning.

"Such as why you stayed behind and missed all the fun?" Shraga asked with a grin.

"I had graduation practice, for one thing," Gitty returned in a superior voice.

"Oh, have you graduated?" asked Mrs. Drucker.

Gitty beamed. "Three days ago!"

She smiled through the chorus of "mazel tovs" that greeted her words. Then she turned back to Shraga.

"Okay, first question. How did Ari and Chaim realize that the man with the laundry cart was really Tom Morrison?"

Shraga began, "I —"

"It was me!" Chaim exclaimed. "I saw Shraga's broken glasses on the floor," Chaim said. "That meant that he wasn't in the room anymore."

"But Ari didn't know that." Gitty swivelled to look at him. "Well?"

Ari swallowed a mouthful of chicken. "Two things, really. First of all, what was a bellboy doing pushing a laundry cart through the lobby? He should've gone down to the service entrance. But that only made me look at him a second time. I saw something moving. Even dirty laundry isn't alive, so I knew it had to be Pinny and Shraga."

"So who was moving? Shraga, was it you?"

"Nope," said Shraga, shaking his head ruefully. "I was out like a light. All credit for that goes to Pinny."

"Since he drugged Shraga first, I had time to realize what Tom was doing to us," Pinny explained. "I managed to hold my breath enough so I wasn't totally out. It was weird, really. I mean, I could feel myself being dumped into the cart and wheeled along, but I couldn't get myself to move. All I managed was to twitch my foot a little."

"Well, it was enough." Ari saluted Pinny with his fork. "That's all that counts."

"What counts," said Dr. Katz on a more serious note, "is that we're all here, together. Safe."

"*Baruch Hashem,*" Mrs. Katz added quietly.

"And we all lived happily ever after," giggled Mindy. "Mr. Big is safely behind bars..."

"Did anyone ever find out what Morrison planned to do with your device?" Dr. Drucker inquired.

Dr. Morgenstern nodded soberly. "He intended to sell it to the highest bidder."

Mrs. Drucker shuddered. "One little black box that can do so much harm."

"Any other questions?" Chaim asked Gitty with an air of importance.

"Well...one or two." Gitty looked at her father. "Daddy, that diskette never turned up?"

Dr. Morgenstern shook his head. "No. It must

have been thrown away, after all. No need to worry about it anymore; not only have we changed the passwords, but the diskette's probably been exposed to too much damage to work, anyway."

"Funny how a diskette could just disappear," Pinny said thoughtfully.

"Well, don't let it worry you. *Baruch Hashem,* M.C.B. is happy that the case is closed."

"They're happy with you, too, aren't they, Abba?" Chaim asked.

Dr. Morgenstern chuckled. "I think they're also embarrassed for suspecting us when we turned out to be the heroes." He looked around the table. "You *all* did."

"Shai and Niki figured out who stole the prototype," Pinny observed.

"And Pinny asked the crucial questions to help solve the mystery," Shraga added.

"Yeah, but *you* figured out that Tom was Mr. Big," Pinny countered.

"And Chaim saved our lives," Shraga said, looking at his little brother. "I guess we were wrong to leave you out of it, Chaim."

Chaim's chest swelled with pride.

"And Ari rescued Shraga and Pinny from Mr. Big," Shai said.

"Well, so did you and Niki. I couldn't have done it alone." Ari sobered for a moment, thinking of that horrifying second when Tom had confronted him in the corridor. "In fact, if not for Ilya Pim, Tom would have gotten away."

"Poor Dr. Pim," Mrs. Drucker said sympathetically. "I hope nobody plans to charge him for anything."

"Oh, no," Dr. Morgenstern assured her. "Nobody's pressing charges. Not only that, but he told me that the files Morrison showed him about his war-hero father were falsified. He's got nothing to be worried about."

"I'm glad," said Shraga. "He's a nice guy."

"Well, Morrison sure wasn't," Pinny declared. "What a creep! He was being so friendly to us all along, just so he could pick up some hints about Little Nicky."

"The scary part is that it wasn't the first time," Ari said. "Sandy told me they've discovered at least three other military secrets that he's sold to foreign powers."

"Well, he can't do us any harm now." Chaim sat back. "He can't get hold of Daddy's little black box."

The conversation turned to the Druckers and their future plans. Shai sat comfortably next to his foster father, feeling more at peace than he ever had in his whole life.

"And you're really thinking about changing to a religious school?" Shraga asked. "That's super, Shai. I'm really glad."

Shai smiled. "Well, Ima and Abba would like it. And I think that after spending time with you and seeing what *dati* boys are like, I will enjoy it also."

"You're going to be thirteen this year, aren't you?" Ari asked, leaning across the table. "We ought to rustle you up a pair of tefillin from somewhere."

"Don't worry," Dr. Drucker said with a smile. "We already ordered them — months ago."

Shai looked startled, and then very pleased.

"Tefillin," grinned Shraga. "The only little black boxes that *really* matter."

"Well said," his father applauded.

"When are you going back to Israel?" Mrs. Morgenstern asked the Druckers.

Mrs. Drucker glanced at her husband. "Next week, but — actually, my husband is due for a sabbatical."

"What's that?" Ruchie asked her mother, tugging on her sleeve.

"It's a year off from work at a university," Mrs. Morgenstern answered.

"We're thinking," Mrs. Drucker continued, "about spending it here in the States."

"Hey, great!" Pinny exclaimed. "You'll keep in touch, Shai, won't you? Let us know if you're really coming?"

"Oh, yes!" Shai promised.

"And we'll be keeping in touch with Niki, too," Shraga added. "He's a good kid. Now that he's interested in learning about being Jewish, it's important that we help him out."

"We both will," Pinny said stoutly. "That's what friends are for."

Dr. Morgenstern and Dr. Katz looked at each other and hid their smiles. Yes, their two sons had become good friends at last.

Gitty helped Mrs. Morgenstern clear the table and bring in dessert. Mindy and Daniella disappeared upstairs.

"The rest of the summer is going to be pretty boring," Shraga said reflectively.

"Think so?" Pinny gave him a sidelong grin. "Well, maybe we can come up with something to do."

"I'll bet," snickered Ari. "Why don't you two open a detective agency, now that you have all this experience?"

Pinny refused to get annoyed. "Who knows? Maybe we will."

The talk wound down as the younger children, comfortably full, wandered away from the table. At last, only Shraga, Pinny, Ari, and Shai remained sitting with the adults.

"You really will keep in touch, Shai, won't you?" Shraga asked, licking his spoon.

"Yes." Shai smiled at these, the first real friends he'd ever had. "I will write, but my English is not so good. Can I write in Ivrit?"

"Hey, it's fine with me," Ari said. "It'll be good practice for us."

"Well, if we —" Shraga broke off as Mindy and Daniella made a grand entrance into the dining room, holding something big and colorful behind their backs.

"What've you got there, Mindy?" Mrs. Morgenstern asked with a smile.

"Shraga's birthday present." Mindy beamed at her older brother.

Shraga, taken aback, blinked at her. "My birthday present?" he stammered.

"Yes." Mindy came forward. "I'm giving you my latest collage, because you're a nice enough brother not to make fun of me, and because —well, because I think you deserve it."

"Hey, how come no one's making collages for me?" Pinny complained with a twinkle.

"If Mindy will teach me, I'll make you one!" Daniella piped up.

"Now, this collage is very special," Mindy continued. "I call it a high-tech collage, because it combines the wonders of science with the wonders of Hashem's world."

"That's nice," said Mrs. Drucker.

"Thank you." Mindy presented it to Shraga. "And here it is!"

With a flourish, she whipped the collage from behind her back and presented it to Shraga.

"Uh, thanks," Shraga said, feeling awkward. He took the collage and laid it on the table. "That's really nice of you, Mindy. It's —"

He stopped and stared.

So did everyone else at the table.

Pinny was the first one to find his voice. "Mindy," he croaked. "That's it! That's the red diskette!"

Mindy beamed down at her collage. "Yes, isn't it a pretty color? Daniella found it for me in the garbage can in the game room. I think it adds the perfect —"

"You don't understand!" Ari grabbed at the collage. "Mindy, this is *the* diskette — the one from Little Nicky!"

"What?!" Mindy gaped at him in disbelief.

Dr. Katz shook off his paralysis and took the collage from Ari. "Yes, Mindy, this is the diskette we were all looking for." He looked at her. "You say Daniella found it in the garbage?"

"But...but..."

"Do you mean to tell me that we all ran around like crazy looking for this thing, and you had it all along?" Shraga demanded. "Why didn't you *say* so?"

"She was in the hospital during the last half of our stay," Dr. Morgenstern murmured.

"But *still!*" Shraga turned to his little sister. "Mindy, didn't you know we were looking for a diskette?"

Mindy sagged down in her chair. "Everyone said they were looking for a diskette," she said weakly. "Nobody said it was red."

Dr. Morgenstern stared at his daughter, then slumped back and let out a roar of laughter. "They combed the entire hotel," he gasped, "and my nine-year-old daughter had it stapled to a collage!"

Dr. Katz was laughing now, too. "All that worry for nothing..."

Soon the entire table was convulsed with laughter.

Mindy smiled sheepishly. "Daddy, you can have it back if you want," she said in a small voice.

"A *stapled* diskette?"

Mindy giggled despite herself. "I guess not."

"Besides," Shraga said, grinning as he reached out for the collage, "it's mine. Nobody's taking it back. I'm going to keep it as a souvenir of the wildest week in my life!"